A WOMAN CAN HAVE GREAT SEX, MARRIAGE, AND A CAREER—BUT CAN SHE HAVE THEM ALL AT THE SAME TIME?

JESS—She'd turned her back on love when she'd found her husband playing doctor after office hours. Now she was a lawyer, a senator's aide in Washington, learning that politics was a dirty game, but not nearly as dangerous as romance.

BEN—He was sexy, irresistible, working for the political opposition and proving to Jess that Italians deserved their reputation as lovers. But la dolce vita wouldn't keep their relationship from turning sour if he betrayed her.

ELIOT—He'd been D.O.A. in bed during their marriage, but now, ten years later, he was back in Jess's life, charming their daughter Susan, promising that love could be sweeter the second time around.

"MODERN ROMANCE IS FEATURED IN THIS COMIC TALE OF SEX AND POLITICS IN WASHINGTON."

—The Dallas Morning News

LIBERATED LADY

TRISH VRADENBURG

A DELL BOOK

Published by
Dell Publishing Co., Inc.
1 Dag Hammarskjold Plaza
New York, New York 10017

ISBN: 0-440-14833-2

Reprinted by arrangement with Macmillan Publishing Company

Printed in the United States of America

October 1987

10 9 8 7 6 5 4 3 2 1

KRI

To My Mother,
who showed me anything was possible . . .

and

To George,
my husband, my lover, my partner.

CONTENTS

PART ONE

Livingston, New Jersey

1973

1

When she thought about it three months later, Jess realized that that no good son of a bitch was probably gleefully humping Pamela at the same time she—his loving, wonderful wife—was putting the finishing touches on his birthday cake. Jess wondered then if it would have made any difference had she actually known.

She imagined a little fairy, somewhat on the order of Tinker Bell, flitting through the small hole in the screen over the kitchen window and whispering in her ear, "Guess what? Eliot is, at this very second, huffing and puffing and about to explode into the cavity of that little tart of a nurse in his office. How do you like them apples, sweetheart?"

Having imparted this bit of gut-wrenching news, Tinker Bell would sprinkle her fairy dust, do a perfect in-air flip, and gracefully make her exit.

That would have left Jess to consider the alternatives. She could: (a) take her sharpest Sabatier knife—the one she used to cut thighs from drumsticks in one swift motion—go down to Eliot's office, and plant it right between Eliot's shoulder blades; (b) cancel the party, explaining to everyone she had just come down with bubonic plague; (c) go ahead with the party and place the birthday cake smack in the middle of Eliot's smug face, thereby not only delivering a surprise party, but also an unforgettable scene about which people could reminisce for years to come; or (d) go ahead with the party as planned.

Even three months later, she knew she would have chosen "d," thereby sparing everyone she cared about at this party, as well as the majority about whom she didn't give a damn, any major anxiety or discomfort.

Such was the kind of goody-two-shoes Jessica Simon Kantor was. She didn't like to make waves. She wanted to be admired, to be thought well of, to be liked. In short, she wanted to excel at what she had been primed for ever since she had gotten her first Sparkle Plenty at the age of two and a half: the perfect mother and wife.

And up until the time she found out about Eliot's extra-curricular activities, she thought she had done one hell of a decent job. Then again, she had neglected to notice that she also had become one hell of a boring broad.

2

Three towns away—fifteen minutes by car, thirteen if you used the right zigs and zags to avoid the traffic lights—Eliot Kantor sat finishing up some paperwork under his Princeton undergrad and Harvard Medical School degrees.

They were more than respectable degrees, so he made sure Jessica had them handsomely embossed on pure mahogany wood—subtle understatement. There were other degrees on the wall as well—some honorary, some representing real achievements—but none as meaningful in the outright status department as these two. They were prominently displayed. If he thought he could get away with it, he would have flashed strobe lights on them, too.

Actually, there was very little in Eliot's office, waiting room included, that was not carefully chosen and placed. From the magazines with a wide enough range to accommodate anyone's taste (including some esoteric ones such as *Commentary* and *Mid-East Report,* which no one read but were updated monthly) to the handsome collection of wise owls in his office (some really quite valuable), everything was done to perfection. The motif, as Eliot liked to refer to the decorating, was decidedly eclectic.

As usual, he looked quite serious—not unattractive, mind you, because Eliot was really almost sexy in an Ivy League, studious sort of way. Six feet tall, lean, nice hazel eyes behind the 20–200 prescription tortoise-rimmed glasses, curly dark brown hair, good teeth, well tailored, never without a

designer tie. Good packaging, if you didn't mind that perennially stiff look he had.

Pamela didn't seem to mind one bit. Pamela. Pamela was
the kind of nurse that every doctor's wife (and indeed every
patient's wife) dreaded. Let's cut to the core here. She was
stacked, gorgeous, and totally willing. Worst of all, she knew
it. Here was a woman who was on top of all her assets and
liabilities (and every man she met wished he could be, too).

Pamela knew that what she had should not be wasted.
There was no question that Pamela was beautiful enough to
be a Hollywood starlet. Everyone said so. But for some un-
fathomable reason she desperately wanted to become a nurse
and have a doctor for a husband.

To her credit, she was smart enough to know that she
wasn't very smart. She was determined. She was a plugger.
She was streetwise. The gray matter didn't matter one bit.
She used what she did have and if that's what you had to do,
a face somewhere between Grace Kelly and Cybill Shepherd
and a figure that was 38–23–35 wasn't bad ammunition.
And most important, she knew none of it would last forever.

At face value, Eliot would have seemed an odd choice. He
was nothing unusually special and he was already married.
But he appealed to Pamela and she knew he had potential.

The married part couldn't have bothered her less. It was
inconvenient, true, but easily remedied. And he was Jewish.
Her half-Protestant, half-Catholic mother had told her Jewish men made the best husbands. They were pushovers for
anything their wives wanted.

Not that it was difficult to find a Jewish doctor in the
East, but for some reason she had honed in on Eliot. It
threw her a little. She knew she was far from Eliot's first, but
he wasn't acting like he intended her to be his last either.
The best Pamela could be sure of was that right now he was
only sleeping with her (unless you counted the few times he
had enough strength left for his wife).

It infuriated her. Eliot was one of the few men who was
unwilling to give up everything for the pleasure of having

her. Perhaps that quality was Eliot's main attraction. He was a challenge.

Jess was trying her utmost not to feel hassled.

Naturally she had decided to do the party herself. She prided herself on being an excellent cook. Although at the time she had gotten married, the most she had mastered in the kitchen was boiling an egg, she subsequently had taken tons of cooking courses at the Adult School: French Feasts; Italian Delicacies; Cooking Chinese (Mandarin and Szechuan); Desserts with a Flair; Epicurean Hors d'Oeuvres; Low-Cholesterol Masterpieces (Eliot had had a heart attack phobia for about two months); Tasty Diet Cooking (all the recipes came out tasting like cardboard); and, most recently, Indian Intricacies.

It was ingrained in her subconscious that a good hostess never had precisely the right amount of food for everyone. Therefore, she made sure to prepare more food than eighty ravenous people could possibly consume (much less the forty who were actually attending).

Leftovers showed you cared. ("Take some potato pancakes home, Aunt Erma. You just reheat them at 350 degrees. Honestly, there's no way we could eat them. They'll just be thrown out. It's a sin." That was a thoughtful niece.)

Perfect niece, perfect mother, perfect wife—she wore the titles well. The world was hers.

She looked around her reasonable-sized kitchen and smiled to herself, which was the right thing to do in this room. That's why she had decorated it in yellow. Yellow was a sunny, *up* color. So it made your personality sunny-side up. Everything was coordinated with the harvest gold refrigerator with its instant ice and matching self-cleaning oven. Even the canisters picked up the color scheme. Was this not truly a girl's dream?

"No, Mother, it's not too much of a strain. I love doing it," she said into the phone. It was her mother's fourth call of the day and Jess's answers were beginning to sound like a recording.

She knew the next question and she detested answering it. "I'm wearing the black, remember? Mother, I'm twenty-eight years old. Why do you still ask me what I'm going to wear?"

It was a useless question and Jess knew it. The only result it would produce was the one she most wanted to avoid: a concerned, selfless lecture. She mouthed the words as her mother spoke.

"Because I care, darling. Thank God I don't take the easy way out. I personally wouldn't have picked the black, but it's your party. Are you expecting a death?"

"No."

"If you need help zipping it up, I can come early."

"Thanks, Mother. That won't be necessary."

"Just letting you know I'm at your disposal, sweetheart. By the way, how are you keeping Eliot away until seven-thirty?"

"Bob Richardson's going to pick him up after work. He's pretending to take Eliot somewhere and then get lost."

The oven buzzer mercifully went off. She lifted the receiver so her mother could hear the buzzer clearly. "Gotta run. I'll see you tonight."

"You don't take care of yourself. You know, you could be pregnant."

"Not unless you know something I don't."

"You push yourself too hard."

"Stop worrying. I'm too young for a coronary. See you later."

She hung up in the middle of one of her mother's classic deep sighs and went to the oven, thinking.

Jess sure hoped Eliot would be surprised. He wasn't tuned in to noticing much at home—the good and the bad news. Well, for today's purposes, anyway, that little trait would come in handy. That only left 364 other days in the year to think about.

Take out the quiche. Look at how nicely the crust has come out. What a pretty yellow kitchen. Think happy thoughts. Don't focus. Repress. Jess had rather handily taught herself not to concentrate on the hard-to-deal-with. Today is a day of happiness. Focus on that.

Pamela walked up to Eliot's desk and waited. She was wearing, perhaps, the tightest, shortest, lowest-cut nurse's uniform that had ever been made. It didn't take him long to smell her presence. The seventy-five-dollar-a-half-ounce of Joy had been a good investment.

Eliot raised his eyes from his paper and slowly allowed them to make their way up Pamela's inviting body, lingering three extra seconds on those incredible breasts and then moving up to her sensuous lips. She smiled seductively and bent over him, ample cleavage showing, and pointed at a word on the paper.

"I think you misspelled the name," she said softly.

"Did I?" he asked, addressing her cleavage, practically salivating.

"Maybe not." Aware she had achieved her goal, she stood up straight.

"You smell delicious."

"Do I?" she asked innocently.

Eliot got up and pulled Pamela toward him. He could feel himself getting hard. So could Pamela. That feeling—that power—never ceased to please her.

"You fit perfectly," Eliot told her in what he imagined was his sexiest voice.

"I do a lot of things perfectly."

"You don't have to tell me."

She smiled coyly, planning her next move. She tried not to look annoyed when the phone rang. She shrugged her shoulders and went to answer it.

"Doctor Kantor's office," Pamela answered in her professional voice. "One moment, please, Mr. Richardson. I'll tell Dr. Kantor you're calling."

She handed Eliot the phone, never removing her eyes from his. Men like eye contact. She knew that. Eliot reluctantly took the phone, putting his hand over the mouthpiece.

"I've got that appointment with him today," Eliot reminded her apologetically.

"Well, then have a good time." Pamela slowly ran her tongue across her upper lip.

Eliot looked torn. Pamela adored that look. A minor challenge.

She came closer to him. She gently caressed his face and circled his ear with her finger. Her left hand slipped under his trousers, then his jockey shorts, right to the object at hand. It responded effortlessly.

A very minor challenge.

"Think of me," she whispered into Eliot's ear.

He wasn't torn anymore. "Make it an hour," he said into the phone. "Something just came up."

And indeed it had.

When Jess looked into her self-cleaning double oven to check on the marble fudge brownies, she noticed her reflection. She stopped as though she were observing a stranger. For that flash of a second she saw herself objectively. It wasn't bad either.

Okay, she was the first to admit that she wasn't drop dead material. But on the other hand, she knew that with her dirty blond hair, compliments of Mother Nature, and almond-shaped green eyes she was very attractive. She had worked hard to stay slim. Her breasts were their own masters, as though they could stand firm on their own independent judgment, which in a less kind way could be defined as small-breasted. Still, they were perky and fit well with the rest of her body. Eliot had always admired small breasts, which was fortunate. Her skin was perfectly smooth and her face seemed to radiate its own naive happiness with life. She was wearing her shoulder-length hair in a ponytail, and although, as her mother often reminded her when she was growing up, her face was a little too thin not to have hair cascading around it, she felt pretty—almost like a teenager.

But she wasn't a teenager. She was a full-fledged adult. There were times Jess felt she was just playing that role. She still felt so young. She couldn't believe she was actually twenty-eight, mother of a four-year-old girl, the wife of a doctor, the mistress of a perfectly decorated home, the owner of a Chevy Caprice station wagon and an Airedale puppy. Could this really be her or was she still playing house?

It wasn't clear to her until one day when she went out for lunch with three of her girlfriends. They had gone to one of those new cutesy restaurants. This one was called Monopoly. Each table was named after a different property in the game.

They had sat at Pacific Avenue. Everything was done in green, including the cranberry salad, which tasted only minimally more vile than it looked. Even the white wine spritzers had a touch of green food coloring in them. They giggled as they sipped. Afterward, they all feigned being a bit tipsy to prove they'd gotten their money's worth.

They dropped Barbara off first, making sure to wait until she was safely inside. This was their usual precaution just in case some deranged killer was waiting for them to pull away so he could jump out of the bushes and hack Barbara into little pieces, or, worse yet, rape her.

But this time Jess really *watched* Barbara as she walked down that path to her split-level, and in that moment she realized that Barbara, a little bit overweight, perhaps even a bit frumpy looking in her tweed suit and matching rayon blouse with bow, looked like every grown-up mother she had ever envisioned: Harriet Nelson and Margaret Anderson rolled into one.

And since Jess and Barbara had been best friends since third grade, if Barbara fit into the grown-up category, so did Jess. Well, so be it. It was a good life and, boy, was Eliot going to be surprised. Maybe it would even make him happy. She was willing to settle for satisfied.

Just let this ladder not fall, she thought as she put the last thumbtack into the banner. She carefully climbed down and backed up, looking proudly at the sign she had made. It was printed in crimson and white, Harvard's colors, each "i" dotted with a little Princeton Tiger. It read: Happy 30th Birthday, Eliot!

Jess looked around the room. Every piece of furniture in place. No dust. Silver shining. Glass Windexed within an inch of its life. Shag carpet vacuumed to attention. Throw pillows casually thrown at the exact same angle. It looked perfect. Next stop, *House Beautiful*. She was pleased. She only prayed Eliot would be, too.

Eliot certainly looked pleased at that moment, but not exactly for the reason Jess would have chosen.

His shoes and socks were still on. His designer tie was still in place, as was his shirt, which was half unbuttoned and sweaty. Other than that, he didn't have much of the Brooks Brothers look left at all. Everything else was limp. Eliot looked totally sated.

Pamela smiled, delighted, and although she had not seen the banner, the message was identical.

"Happy 30th birthday, Eliot," she cooed.

Luckily, Jess didn't know about Eliot's little indulgence at that time.

Well, at least she thought she didn't know. Any shrink worth his $75 per fifty minutes would have given her one of those patronizing, nonjudgmental smiles and told her that every cuckold partner knows about it on some level: It's merely a matter of facing life and dealing or avoiding the obvious—oops, time's up, mustn't run over.

Suffice to say, innocent little Jess hadn't focused on the obvious, so the party was a piece of cake for her to pull off.

3

Jess took a full fifteen-minute bubble bath that night. Bubble baths were something she reserved for proms and very special occasions, so she savored the sensation.

She pretended there were cameras zooming in on her and that she was the model in an ad for a new bubble bath product as she picked up some bubbles and sensuously blew them into the air.

As she took her hair out of the rollers she prayed it would fall into place. She hadn't remembered until that morning to make a beauty parlor appointment and by then they were all booked, so she did it herself. Not bad, she thought, as she combed the perfect flip one last time.

She was annoyed with herself when she had difficulty zipping up her black dress and fleetingly thought she should have taken her mother up on her offer.

Looking in the mirror, she nodded approvingly. It was hard to imagine that she was a woman who had worked all day.

It certainly felt like a successful party. Everyone was laughing merrily, stuffing themselves with food, bragging about their latest accomplishments. Nothing terribly serious. No one attacked anyone else for voting for Nixon, discussed the possible implications of the mysterious Watergate break-in, or analyzed the efficiency of the Environmental Protection

Agency. Everything was banter, gossip, and drivel—sure signs of a truly enjoyable event.

Jess floated from group to group with platters of symmetrically arranged hors d'oeuvres in hand, regrettably ending up at the foursome she least desired to be with, her parents and her in-laws.

They were handsome couples. Having made it through the Depression, penniless, working like mad, amassing relatively comfortable sums of money, they were survivors.

Jessica's father, Jack Simon, owned his own insurance business. He was extremely personable and easily could have charmed anybody into buying anything, including avalanche insurance in Palm Beach, had he tried.

But he was an honest man and therefore he made a comfortable rather than an enormous living. This was a quality his wife, Estelle, publicly admired and privately despised. After all, why shouldn't she have like everyone else? Everybody looked out only for themselves. Why shouldn't he? He didn't have a monopoly on goodness and honesty. Caveat emptor, etc., etc., etc.

Jessica's father would nod his head amiably and then do whatever was necessary in order to live with himself in dignity.

At a very young age Jess realized that Estelle nagged and Jack turned her off. He simply shook his head in agreement and didn't hear one word she was saying. Jess thought her father must have invented selective hearing.

What gnawed at Jess was that her father never bothered to fight back. That was particularly troublesome to Jess because she sensed that her mother wanted him to stand up to her, to thrash it out, to at least talk about their differences. But Jack never would. Perhaps that was his way. He never argued about anything.

So by the time she was ten, Jess hugged her father, laughed with him, loved him, but never thought of him as anything but a weak man. She determined that the man she married would be strong.

Eliot's father, Harry Kantor, was defeated in a different way. Harry had built his small jewelry business into one of the most successful jewelry concerns in the Northeast. He worked day and night to do it. There were articles written about him, chapters in books devoted to him, and testimonial dinners given in his honor.

Outside of his home, he was a king. Inside his home, he was the man who never became a doctor, which is what he promised his wife, Loretta, he was going to be when they got married. He took all the tests, sent in all the applications, and was turned down by every medical school. Loretta was relentless. She had married a future doctor. She pressured him to repeat exams, take courses, do everything conceivably possible to get him to carry that little black bag that would make her Mrs. Doctor. In the end, the best he could do was to make a few million in the jewelry business. But a doctor, he wasn't.

So Loretta went to work on her only child—a son, thank God—who fortunately had an acumen for science and, ultimately, medicine. The throne and the crown became Eliot's, which was fine with Harry. He had enough going for him in the outside world, and in an odd way he sort of liked being married to the one person who didn't treat him with infinite respect.

Although Harry considered his kid a bit of a wimp, he admired Eliot's academic achievements and was committed to his family.

Besides which, Harry screwed around like crazy. Loretta never seemed to notice. She spent her time immersed in Eliot's life. She was one of the lucky ones: It paid off for her. Her son depended on her. Eliot was forever seeking his mother's approval, and that hadn't stopped when he became a doctor—and certainly not when he got married.

"You should have had help, a nice caterer," Loretta told Jess as she munched on a stuffed mushroom, which could have used a little more onion powder.

Estelle looked proudly at her daughter. "Only you could get away with a surprise party."

"Maybe he won't even be surprised," replied Jess.

"Eliot doesn't suspect a thing," Loretta assured her daughter-in-law with one of her I-know-him-better-than-anyone half smiles Jess had grown to hate. "I talked to him today and, believe me, I'd know. My little boy keeps nothing from me, does he, Harry?"

"You're safe, Jess. She'd know."

"I doubt there's anything Eliot's ever kept from me," she continued smugly.

Harry shook his head in total agreement. "The Gestapo's methods look gentle compared to her interrogations."

Loretta gave her husband one of her sharper kill-'em-dead-in-their-tracks looks. "A joke. Always with those adorable jokes. The truth of the matter is we're just very close. My Eliot and I always had something . . . special."

Uncomfortable silence. People changing positions, clearing throats, finishing drinks. Who would pick up the ball? Estelle to the rescue.

"Jessica planned this party very carefully. I still don't know how you got away with it. What do you have here—maybe forty people—and still Eliot is in for the surprise of his life."

"Let's hope," Jess said, crossing her fingers for luck. "Every night that he came home this week I was making these huge casseroles that we didn't eat."

"Loretta's right. You should have had help."

"Mother, I love to cook."

Eliot's mother sighed. "This new generation for you. Finally when they can afford it, they want to do everything themselves."

Ignore the witch. Go on with the story. "Anyway, one night he found me frying mushrooms, maybe eight pounds' worth. He didn't say a thing and he *hates* mushrooms."

"Then he knows," snapped Loretta, not at all amused by the story. "My son's no idiot."

"I don't even think he focused on the mushrooms," replied Jess defensively. She knew thin ice when she saw it.

Too late. Loretta was outraged. "Why should he focus on mushrooms? He's a doctor. He's concerned with life and death. Thank God he can't be distracted by mushrooms. His power of concentration is a gift."

She's going to ruin my party, thought Jess. I want to kill her. No, she's my husband's mother. It would be rude to kill her. Maybe just maim her. . . .

In the midst of these gleeful thoughts, Susan tore excitedly into the room announcing she had just heard her daddy's car pull up. Jess clapped her hands to get the group's attention.

"Everyone quiet! Eliot and Bob are here."

Perhaps he should have gotten some advance notice after all, because when Eliot walked into the house he sounded like one incredibly spoiled brat complaining bitterly, yelling at Bob.

"What a wild goose chase. Next time find out exactly where you're going before we take a three-hour ride to oblivion. I have better things to do with my time, goddamn it."

"Will do," Bob replied pleasantly.

Jess realized that the look on Eliot's face when forty screaming people echoed *"Surprise"* as he turned on the living room lights would probably follow her to the grave.

And yet, when asked to describe that look in later years, she was hard pressed. It was a combination of shock, fear, amazement, and a tinge of disgust. Not even the remotest corner of his face held out any hope for "pleased."

Eliot's mouth remained open for the whole time it took the group to sing "Happy Birthday." It was both amusing and embarrassing, depending on one's relationship to the honoree. Quite a picture, especially with Susan hanging steadfastly to his leg, looking like an appendage.

At the end of the song everyone came to hug Eliot and, somewhere during that time, Eliot managed to close his mouth, though not into a happy, delighted smile. In fact, he looked rather dazed for the rest of the evening.

"Now that's the look of a surprised person," Estelle noted delightedly to Loretta. She won that round, anyway.

Loretta looked at Estelle with disdain. "Didn't I tell you? Eliot was in the acting club in high school." Split decision.

By the end of the evening it almost looked as if Eliot was enjoying himself. After all, these were his family and quasi-friends joining together to celebrate with him. Sometime during the party that thought must have occurred to him because by the time people started mentioning that they really ought to be leaving, Eliot had begun to smile. Once or twice he even laughed.

Jess figured the worst part had been when the cake was brought out. Eliot had to be dragged into the dining room and then looked pained through the second rendition of "Happy Birthday."

Jess was beginning to wish she had written a simple "Eat It, Eliot" on the lousy cake. Did he have any idea how long it took just to decorate that fluffy white cake with perfect fudge filling? Did he think a Harvard Pilgrim and a Princeton Tiger were easy to make out of frosting not from a can? That was one whole course alone.

Don't get hostile, she told herself. Different people react differently. And, as mentioned, by the end of the evening Eliot looked as if he was starting to have a good time.

Jess estimated it to have been about one-thirty when the last of the guests finally departed. They were standing at the door waving good-bye, Eliot's arm around Jess's waist. She was feeling good about the evening, half because everyone complimented her on what a success the party had been, half because it was finally over.

Jess heaved a sigh of relief and walked back into the living room, trying her best not to use her peripheral vision and take in the mess that still had to be attended to.

She plopped down on the couch, feeling she deserved it. Eliot followed her in, but just stood there, taking a somewhat regal pose, giving her one of his sphinxlike smiles.

She sighed, resigned. All right, Eliot. Let's have the zinger.

"Congratulations. Another success. Everyone was raving about what a phenomenal job you did—all by yourself."

Talk about surprises. So Eliot really had liked it. Could have fooled her. "It wasn't that much," she said with as much false modesty as she could muster.

"You could have had help, you know. People probably thought I couldn't afford it," he said half jokingly, but she knew it was no joke.

Kill him with sweetness, she thought. "I wanted it to be a personal gift from me to you."

Jess walked over to Eliot. They kissed. Nothing passionate, but a little more than a "hi-I'm-home-after-this-cruddy-day" kiss.

"Well, the whole thing was very thoughtful—as always." His delivery was a little off, but Jess was not about to pick up on it. Switch gears.

"You were surprised, weren't you?"

"I'll say."

"I knew it," Jess smiled triumphantly. "I pulled it off." Jess looked at his face. Not a hint of a smile. Then she asked the question she had rehearsed not asking all evening. Why didn't her mouth obey her resolve? "You didn't like it, did you?"

"I didn't say that," he said with a shrug and looked at himself in the mirror above the fireplace.

"But you didn't?"

He was fixing his hair, wondering if he needed that haircut Pamela had mentioned. "I could have lived without it," he responded. "You know I hate surprises."

She had him on that one. "No, you don't. You never want to know what present I'm getting for you."

Maybe just a trim. "Well, I hate surprise parties. You know that."

"How would I know that? You never mentioned it."

He turned toward her and stated flatly, "You could have asked."

"Asked?" she repeated incredulously. "Somehow I figured if I asked if you liked surprise thirtieth birthday parties, it might give it away."

"It's kid's stuff. We're not kids anymore, Jessica." He used her full name when he wanted her to realize he was talking to a grown-up. He liked grown-up names. He couldn't imagine calling Pamela "Pammy." Never. She was a woman, not a girl.

Jess wasn't buying. "I'm twenty-eight, you're thirty. What is that: old-age material?"

"I don't need it shoved down my throat that I'm thirty. And you're not twenty-eight. You won't be until next month."

Jess shrugged her shoulders. "Close enough."

"You're the only woman I know who makes herself older."

"Because it doesn't matter to me. I enjoy the concept of getting older. I'm happy, healthy. We're having a wonderful, carefree life together." She had purposely overemphasized the "carefree" bit.

Eliot hadn't noticed. He was in a funk now. "It's damn near the middle. I've lived almost half my life and look where I am."

"Where are you? You're a successful doctor, you have a lovely home, a family that loves you. . . ." What was the problem? It all sounded so good.

But it didn't sound good to Eliot. Should he tell her? Not the Pamela part—that much he knew would be counterproductive. But he could tell her what had been eating at him all day. Maybe she would understand if it had happened to her.

Eliot had been shaving at his mirror that morning when

he noticed it. His first gray hair. At first he froze in place. Then he quickly pulled the hair out and flushed it down the toilet, disposing of the evidence as rapidly as possible. Tangible proof that he was getting old. At least with Pamela he didn't feel it. She treated him like the stud he always wanted to be. None of this responsibility shit. He looked at Jess and knew she'd never understand. She'd probably have some lecture about accepting life and considering a gray hair distinguished. Well, she could forget it. He wasn't ready to be considered distinguished. Not before he had lived some.

"I'm going to bed. We can clean up in the morning."

It was a ploy. He knew Jess was psychologically incapable of leaving this mess until morning.

She surveyed the area. Two hours with help, minimum. "Can't you help me get a little of this done?"

Eliot was getting angry now. Some sense of injustice had hit him. *"No!* I work hard all week. I don't expect to have to do housework on top of it."

It wasn't worth a fight and, besides, it was still his birthday. "All right. I'll be up soon . . . maybe three or four hours."

Eliot looked at her, gave a businesslike nod, and started for the stairs.

"Eliot," Jess called after him. He turned as Jess picked up a party horn and blew it. "Happy Birthday."

"Thank you," he responded grudgingly.

"You're welcome." The hurt was unmistakable.

She watched him as he climbed the steps and she knew. It had to be her fault. Somewhere along the way she had failed. She just couldn't pinpoint exactly where.

4

Sex. Jess was beginning to think that that three-letter word caused more havoc, discord, and discontent than any other word in *Webster's Dictionary*.

Sex had not been a great subject in the Kantor household for a long time.

In the beginning, Eliot had been insatiable. That petered out quickly enough. Sensing this was crucial to her marriage, Jess desperately tried to reignite the flame (although she was willing to settle for even a flicker).

Jess read books, watched shows, attempted different approaches. Nothing did the trick for Eliot. He always found something wrong.

She tried oils (too greasy), feathers (too ticklish), new positions (too uncomfortable), baths (too slippery), forests (too public), backseats of cars (too juvenile), in the living room (what if the rug got discolored?), the kitchen (too kinky).

For a while they tried it in the shower, which wasn't too bad until the night Eliot got overenthusiastic and they fell right through the guaranteed unbreakable glass doors, leaving Jess to explain how it happened to the repair man the next day. She told him she had fainted from dieting. He smiled knowingly.

Whatever the solution was, Jess couldn't find it. She tried discussing it with Eliot, but that always made him uncomfortable. The best he could do was squirm in his seat and mumble "Don't worry about it."

Not that sex was the most vital thing in the world to Jess. She had never liked it much, but she expected that feeling to disappear once she got married. The fact that it hadn't annoyed her. After all, everyone else in America was not only doing it with frequent regularity, they were also talking about it, enjoying it, loving it, rhapsodizing about it. She figured there must be something to all this hoopla. At the very least, she wanted to know enough about sex to make a valid decision one way or another.

But whatever "they" were doing, it sure wasn't terrific at her house. Generally, the whole act from start to finish took eight minutes. She wasn't sure if that was *Guinness Book of Records* material, but she felt confident it wasn't far from it.

And as far as sexually satisfying her, Eliot hadn't even entered the ballpark. Eliot was adamant that Jess had orgasms; she simply hadn't recognized them when they came.

Well, what good was that? He felt her orgasms, but she didn't? Was that the next best thing to being there? Sorry, she would imagine herself saying, I'm busy this evening. Why don't you go ahead and have my orgasm for me?

In her frustrated, angry moments, Jess asserted that it was her birthright to experience her own orgasm, and she was damn well going to fight for that right. Well, she could fight all she wanted. It was a battle for one. Eliot wasn't playing.

And then there were the times that were okay, the times Eliot really got into it—when he caressed her, kissed her tenderly, and then went to it (eleven minutes—sheer heaven).

Jess got a little nervous a few days after the surprise party fiasco when she found herself being steered straight to the lingerie department by some overachieving saleswoman in a cute little boutique.

She wondered if her body language was shouting "This body needs help!" She half expected the saleswoman to yell out "Show this poor unfulfilled young lady something from our 'you, too, can have an orgasm' designer line."

Jess bought the slinky one made of baby blue silk with matching maribou. The gown had an uplifting effect that gave her a hint of cleavage. It was about the best she could hope for.

Actually, she looked damn sexy, almost irresistible (she prayed). When Jess glanced at the bill she hoped Eliot really was a successful doctor. As she left, she made a mental note that if she ever opened a boutique, that saleswoman would be first on her list to hire.

Tonight, Jess figured, would be perfect for the seduction. As she put on the finishing touches, she could hear Howard Cosell making an ass of himself on "Monday Night Football."

She had taken close to an hour to get ready. She looked approvingly at her reflection in the full-length bathroom mirror. She shook her head encouragingly: all systems go. This time she knew she would knock him dead.

"Is it almost over?" she yelled from the bathroom. No response. "Eliot, is it almost over?" No response. It didn't alarm her. Jess knew he'd never dare die during a football game. She opened the door and patiently tapped her bare foot. "Eliot . . ."

"Hmm, what? Did you say something?"

"I asked if it was almost over."

"Fourth quarter."

"Then it's almost over, right?"

"Five, maybe ten minutes more."

That's what she had estimated. "What's the score?"

"Oakland's killing them, forty-two zip. The Steelers don't have a prayer."

"Good."

That meant no chance for overtime. Jess knew Eliot wouldn't miss a second of "Monday Night Football." He loved to watch it, to know everything about the teams, to use the lingo. This was his chance to feel like one of the boys.

Eliot had been a lousy athlete in high school, not even

making junior anything. He quit the chess team after the jocks made fun of him. "Finally made the big team, huh Eliot, baby?" He hated the feeling. But now he could be like all the other guys, living the games vicariously. Age—the great leveler.

Jess figured she might just give Eliot a postgame preview as she did her best to slink her way over to the bed.

"I got something . . . sexy today. What do you think?" She struck her most alluring pose. No response. Eliot was totally engrossed in the tube. "Eliot," she repeated, annoyed.

"Hmm, what?"

"What d'ya think?"

"About what?" he asked absently.

Try that sexy tone again, she told herself. "The outfit. I changed since dinner."

"Uh, it's nice," he responded, disinterested.

Be patient, Jess. The game is still on. She forced a smile. "You're not getting your money's worth. At this price, it's supposed to be spectacular."

"It looks great, okay?" he responded, annoyed at being bothered during a crucial play.

"What about what's in it?" No response. She sighed. "I've lost you again." She came up behind him, put her arms around him and whispered in his ear, "Eliot, there's a live woman in your room."

"I'm watching the game. You're distracting me."

"That's the most encouraging thing you've said to me all night," Jess countered, watching the TV with new interest. "Boy, look at those guys. I love when they pat each other on the rump like that. Eliot, that halfback is getting more action than I am. Can't we turn off the TV and practice our own end plays?"

"Jess, I want to watch the end of this game," he snapped.

All right. She would try to talk reasonably with him. "I know it's not the teams, Eliot. You hate Oakland and Philadelphia. Is it the suspense, sweetheart? Because if it's that, I think it fair to tell you it's pretty improbable they'll score seven touchdowns in six minutes. You might have noticed there are only eight people left in the stands. That's telling, Eliot." She nuzzled his ear and put her arms around his neck.

"It's Pittsburgh," he hissed.

"What?"

"Pittsburgh. It's the Pittsburgh Steelers. Not the Philadelphia Steelers. At least keep your teams straight."

"Is this a capital offense, Eliot?" He gave her a narrow look. "I mean, I know it's serious getting Philadelphia and Pittsburgh mixed up like that, but is it punishable by death?"

"Jess, I want to watch this. Do you mind?"

Mind? Sure she minded. That wasn't a question. That was a command. She felt like knocking him in the head. Instead, she obediently removed her arms from around him.

She shouldn't have pushed him, she thought. She shouldn't have made fun of his teams. What the hell, it was only a few minutes more.

She sat down next to her night table and took out a bottle of half used apricot-colored nail polish. No, that would take too long to dry and, anyway, her polish looked just fine. She grabbed an emery board and started to file. She could feel her pent-up energy mounting.

That Howard Cosell sum-up. Sweet relief. The game was finally over. She watched as Eliot mechanically got up, turned off the TV, and went to the bathroom. She listened closely to hear if he was brushing his teeth. He was. Good sign. Not that he hadn't brushed his teeth every night since she'd known him, but it still felt like a good sign.

Jess hurriedly fluffed up her hair and draped herself on the bed, waiting. Not a minute too soon. Eliot opened the door and came out of the bathroom. Wearing pajamas. Not a great start but, she figured, not insurmountable.

She could feel herself tighten as Eliot picked up the latest edition of *Newsweek* and turned on the eleven o'clock news.

"Eliot, sweetheart." No response. "Honey . . ." No response. *"Eliot!"* she shouted.

"What? What's the matter?" he asked, shaken.

"I'm sorry. I didn't mean to yell." She calmed herself and smiled sweetly. "Honey, do we have to watch the news tonight?"

She could almost see him mount his high horse as he started his lecture. "Jessica, this country is falling apart. We're on the way to severe moral decay. Don't you care about that? Don't you want to know what's happening with Watergate? Don't you think it's your obligation to have full knowledge about the world around you?"

"If I can change it by watching the news tonight, I'm willing. Otherwise, I'll catch it in the morning paper and give Jaworski a call by noon."

He clearly was not amused. "That's a very parochial view, Jessica."

She knew he was trying to divert her. "Eliot, darling, you look so incredibly sexy." She slid closer to him.

"I'm exhausted, Jess," he said, clicking off the remote control.

Jess started to kiss his face very gently. "Relax . . ."

"Not tonight, Jess."

"C'mon, you'll enjoy it. Close your eyes."

Eliot shook his head. "I'm not in the mood."

"Let me put you in the mood," she cooed, stroking him gently.

She started to work on him using light, even strokes. It was still soft. Nothing. She worked harder. Still soft as fresh putty, not even a glimmer of hope in that organ. She looked at his impassive face.

"It's not going to work." He put down his book. "I've got an early day tomorrow. Good night, hon." He kissed her on the cheek, puffed both of his down feather pillows, and turned on his side—the left one, facing away from Jess.

That feeling of helplessness was coming over her again.

What was the best way to handle this? Whatever it was, she knew she wouldn't choose it.

She stared at the ceiling for as long as she could without speaking—maybe thirty seconds. She wanted to make sure that no tears were rolling down her face when she spoke. History had proven them to be no asset in this relationship.

"Do you realize it's been three weeks since we've made love?" she asked in her most controlled voice.

"You keep a record?" Good, that had caught him off balance.

"I have to do something with my nights. Eliot, you're a role reversal of that old joke, you know, how do you keep a Jewish girl from having sex? Marry her." No response. She felt her anger well up and instinctively knew that whatever came out of her mouth next would not be in a quiet decibel. *"Eliot!"*

"Stop yelling."

"I can't help it. I'm frustrated. I don't know what else to do."

"Just keep your voice down, will you?"

"When I talk in civilized tones, you don't answer."

Eliot was adamant. "You know I can't tolerate yelling. When I was growing up, no one was allowed to speak normally. You had to yell to be recognized. I vowed to have a quiet house when I grew up."

"When I was growing up I wasn't allowed to have sex. I vowed to have it after I got married. You grant my vow, I'll grant yours."

"Jessica, why do you want to fight?"

Did he really not understand? "I don't want to fight. I want to love. That's the point."

"I'm under a lot of pressure," Eliot whined, hassled. "I don't need this at home."

"What kind of pressure?" she questioned, concerned, immediately wanting to pat his head soothingly.

"I don't want to talk about it."

"Then how can I help?" she asked helplessly. "Look, I'm

sorry. I don't want to put pressure on you. It's just that we're married, you know. Making love is a legitimate, normal function."

"We'll do it soon," he assured her. "I promise."

"When?" she asked with a decided air of defeat.

"Soon. Trust me." He leaned over and kissed her forehead gently. "Now go to sleep. Sweet dreams."

Eliot puffed his pillows once more, turned over on his left side, and magically fell instantly asleep.

When Jess finally heard the confirmation of the rhythm of Eliot's snores, she realized she had been lying in the same position staring at the ceiling for close to half an hour. The tears she felt rolling down her face were no longer a novelty to her.

5

Jess often wondered how it was possible to survive as a loner. Had it not been for her girlfriends, Jess was convinced she would have gone stark raving mad.

It wasn't that she told them everything—far from it—but they were there if she needed them. They were a support system for each other. They had a bond. They weren't intrusive, they just cared. They got each other through life with sharing, candor, and, most important, laughter.

Her "group," as she tended to think of them, consisted of Miriam, Carmen, and Barbara.

Miriam was the most predictable. The joys of motherhood and marriage were how she defined herself. Anything which contradicted that sphere was not allowed to enter. Short in height, a little overweight, with sparkling blue eyes and carrot red hair, she was a smart, intuitive woman—very warm and loving.

Given that, it was odd how easily Miriam got on Barbara's nerves. Not that Barbara was such a tolerant lady. She was highly opinionated, certain of her blacks and whites. Barbara was a large-boned woman, nearly six feet tall, but because she stood straight-arrow erect, she seemed even taller. Her hair was a frizzy mud brown, which she never bothered to shape. Still, she was attractive with a style all her own. Her most striking feature was her jet-black eyes, which narrowed with each judgment she made. Most people, but women in particular, were intimidated by her, mainly because she had that rare ability to be deadly sarcastic at will. Knowing this, she tried not to be. Except when it came to Miriam. Miriam pushed buttons Barbara didn't even know she had.

There was nothing about them that meshed and yet, somehow, it was never an issue. They rubbed each other wrong. Both Miriam and Barbara had accepted that as a function of their relationship and, in a way Jess never quite understood, seemed to thrive on it.

Carmen was the novelty for the group. Puerto Rican and feisty as hell. No one told her what to do. No one even tried. At first glance, it would have been hard to guess that this petite, olive-skinned, unconventionally pretty woman with high cheekbones, delicate mouth, and soft sable brown eyes had so much spunk in her. She was able to laugh at life's ironies because she knew she couldn't escape them. And after all, she figured she had "made it." She had, at least physically, escaped the neighborhood she always professed to despise. Emotionally, she was still there.

The four women worked on many projects together. It was one way they could get together and still feel they accomplished something.

"I think that about covers it," Jess summed up efficiently. "If everyone pitches in, the P.T.A. should be able to raise enough money to buy the new tire equipment for the playground."

"Tires. . . ." Carmen smiled and shook her head. "In my old neighborhood we could have stripped ten cars for you in twenty minutes." She snapped her fingers. "Poof—a new playground."

"Yesterday's junk, today's antiques," noted Miriam philosophically as she looked through the chocolate candy Jess had put out, poking a hole in the bottoms, searching for a caramel.

Barbara smiled dryly. "Try to keep in mind you've entered a different echelon of society, Carmen dear."

Unlike Miriam, Carmen adored Barbara's sarcasm. It was one of the two things she thrived on. The other was handing her credit card to some snotty saleswoman, telling her to "charge it." "I've tried to upgrade my values, Barbara. It's a bit of an adjustment from tenement living on the Lower East Side. In those days I never knew rooms came with cross-ventilation."

"But your values aren't so different, are they?" questioned Miriam, disappointed she had chomped on a cream-filled chocolate.

"No. I just replace things. Instead of sitting on a fire escape, I lounge on a veranda. Beer is out. Gin and tonics are in. At least in those days I had a little energy."

"Sweetie, no one told you to have five children in six years," Barbara reminded her.

"Danny wanted to have six," countered Carmen, grabbing her heart. "He thinks I'm holding out on him. I'm looking into an operation to surgically tie my legs together. One thing tenement and suburban living have in common: I want to escape from both of them." But not enough to leave the security. Danny had been her ticket out, she wasn't about to throw that away.

"Rough week, huh?" Jess asked, knowing the answer.

"Four kids with chicken pox and one with colic. Life's a snap." She often wondered how her own mother had coped with eight kids and never complained. A different generation.

"But they'll never get chicken pox again," Jess pointed out helpfully.

"Not everyone's an optimist like you." Carmen smiled at Jess, thinking her friend was a cross between Snow White and Mary Sunshine. "It's a blessing. Don't you ever have any conflicting emotions?"

"Sure. So I volunteer and then I'm home with Susan and happy when Eliot comes home." Why did it sound like a prerecorded message?

"Right," Miriam wholeheartedly agreed. "Who needs this women's lib stuff? We've got the best of both worlds."

"You're in luck, Miriam," said Barbara charitably. "I don't feel like fighting today, even if that is one of the more asinine statements you've made."

"Hey, Jess," said Carmen, trying to divert the usual Miriam-Barbara confrontation, "that was some party you ran. Eliot seemed to love it."

Loved it? What party was she at? "He did," Jess concurred offhandedly. She could play "see no evil" as well as the next person. She imagined her mother nodding approvingly: Good girl, you didn't air your dirty linen in public. You're a lady.

"I saw this great article in the *Times* about how to keep your husband happy if he's working late," Barbara remarked. Barbara never missed reading the *New York Times* and she always reported anything even remotely interesting.

"Oh, yeah," remembered Miriam, who could also quote chapter and verse from the editorial page. "It was next to the one on preventing your pet fish from getting fleas."

"Right," said Carmen, who tried her best to keep up with both of them. "Across from the '60-Minute Gourmet' column on diet caviar au gratin—certainly a staple in our house."

Jessica's interest was piqued. She read the newspaper as faithfully as the rest of them, but the contest on who knew what never interested her as much. She didn't remember these articles. She assumed it was on one of those days she had devoted to nonstop cooking for wonderful Eliot's party. In retrospect, she should have read the paper. "What did it say, the husband one?"

"Surprise him at the office with a picnic supper. Candlelight, et cetera," answered Barbara sultrily.

"What a super idea," thought Jess aloud. Her wheels were spinning.

Susan rushed in excitedly. She couldn't wait to tell her mother about the important phone call she had just received. "Mommy, that was Hayden Rabinowitz from my nursery school. He wants to marry me and have twenty kids."

Carmen shook her head. "They're starting younger and younger."

"At least he's Jewish," Miriam noted with relief, having no trouble envisioning the four-year-old in a white dress and veil.

"Hayden and Susan. Susan Rabinowitz. Susan and Hayden Rabinowitz," sang Susan, her black patent leather shoes skipping back into her own little world.

"You'd better watch that one," joked Barbara.

"Start slipping the Pill into her orange juice," warned Carmen, only half jokingly, seeing shades of herself in the child.

But Jess wasn't paying much attention to any of it. She was too busy planning a temporary solution to her own problem. Her mind was rushing full speed ahead.

"You know, Eliot's working late again tonight. Maybe I'll just bring him that picnic supper. Little Red Riding Hood to the rescue."

6

In later years, when she was in a better position to dispassionately diagnose that fateful night, Jess realized that she was worse than a hopeless romantic, she was a hopeful one.

So sure was she that her adorable little gesture would do the trick, she had forgotten to look for any of the negative signs. Had she really taken at face value that Eliot had to work late so frequently? She supposed she didn't want to know. Why then had she set herself up as she had?

She didn't even realize how ludicrous she must have looked that night getting out of her gas guzzling, suburban station wagon. She wore a red skirt, white Peter Pan collar blouse, and red cape with a hood that didn't quite cover her head. Carrying her natural wood picnic basket on her swaying arm, she passed an elderly couple as she entered Eliot's office building.

"I'm on my way to Grandma's house," she told them sweetly.

She thought that this was one of the most unconventional things she had ever done. Well, why not? Maybe she was getting more of a sense of herself after all.

Stepping out of the elevator on the third floor, Jess mechanically turned right and walked to the end of the corridor to Eliot's office, making a mental note that he ought to have the landlord put a fresh coat of dismal grayish-white paint on the walls. It wasn't like Eliot to overlook such a thing. He was, after all, an attender to details.

Jess noted with pride her husband's name on the office door. "Hi, doc," she said proudly to the name as she opened the door.

Stepping into the well-decorated, perfectly coordinated reception area, she noted that everything was exactly in place. Sometimes she imagined Eliot coming out incognito after each patient departed, straightening up all the magazines, rearranging the chairs, and checking the carpet for telltale lint.

"Empty." Jess looked around, relieved. "Good timing, Jess."

She jauntily walked back to the examining offices and then stopped dead in her tracks. She heard heavy panting and gasping. There was no mistaking that was Eliot. Her first instinct was stark fear. She could feel her blood drain.

"Eliot," Jess cried, alarmed. "My God, he's having a heart attack."

She hurriedly ran to the room where the sounds were coming from. She was starting to panic. "Don't worry, I'm coming."

She remembered the instant shocked sensations she had felt when she had ice water thrown in her face at camp; when she had found out that her cat, Bootsie, had been run over by a fire engine; when she came home one summer to find her family had moved and she was living in a new house.

None of those even approached the shock that surged through her body when she opened the door and found her stark naked husband pumping like mad on top of his nurse.

Giving him the benefit of the doubt, she figured maybe this wasn't Eliot at all. She looked again—this time more closely. No, there was no mistaking that uptight rear end. That was definitely Eliot's. Jess's jaw dropped approximately three inches as Eliot raised his head and looked quizzically at her.

"Jess, I wasn't expecting you," Eliot said breathlessly.

Was that his excuse? I would have done this at a more

convenient time if I'd known you were in the neighborhood? Why don't you give me fifteen minutes to finish this up and then reenter. Would he break into a chorus of "If I Knew You Were Coming I'd a Baked a Cake"?

Was she supposed to apologize for not phoning ahead? She was trying to put the whole thing in perspective, but all she could feel was paralyzed.

To his credit, Eliot did seem momentarily uncomfortable. "Uh, Jess . . . you remember Pamela."

Jess nodded woodenly.

"Pamela, you remember my wife."

"Hello, Mrs. Kantor," said Pamela cordially.

Was this a social event? If so, Jess was clearly overdressed.

Eliot got up from on top of Pamela, revealing the perfection of Pamela's body: not a stretch mark in sight and the biggest boobs she had ever seen outside of the *Playboy* centerfold she had once glanced at—all right, stared at.

Wait a minute, hadn't Eliot always said he didn't like big breasts? How tolerant of him to make an exception in this case. An equal opportunity screwer.

Jess watched as Eliot grabbed a towel and put it around himself. An odd time to get modest. Was he embarrassed? Clearly the two women in this room had already seen his wares. Was there a line outside? Take a number, ladies.

Pamela didn't move a muscle. No towel for her. No, sir. Pamela was perfectly comfortable as is. Jess almost admired her. Here was a woman who could feel at home in any given situation.

Eliot cleared his throat. That at least took the suspense out of who was going to speak first.

"Well, this has got to be one of those moments in life that is really awkward for everyone involved," he noted half self-consciously, half jokingly. "I mean, here we are, three mature, grown-up people experiencing a totally awkward moment. I mean, I know it is for me. We're all feeling a little bit embarrassed right now, which is perfectly natural."

Jess looked at him disbelievingly. Did he really think he

was going to get out of this with some of his Psych 101 jargon?

"I'm not embarrassed," smiled Pamela with her big doe eyes.

"Well, you," Eliot said with a laugh. "Nothing embarrasses you."

A joke? They were going to have an intimate little joke while she was standing there? Hello! Perhaps you didn't notice there's another person in the room?

Jess was surprised when she heard her reasonably steady voice say, "Why don't I wait in your office?"

"Great idea. I'll be right there."

How sporting of him. "It might help if you were fully clothed," she advised him icily.

"Oh, that'll only take a minute," he replied cheerfully. Gee, he was taking this well.

Jess turned to leave, amazed that her feet were actually taking orders from her head. Walking toward the door, she spotted Pamela's crisp white nurse's cap on the floor. She bent down and picked it up; dusting it off, she carefully handed it to Pamela.

"Isn't there some code that says you have to wear this at all times?" she asked dryly.

"You're allowed to remove it on special occasions," Pamela replied sweetly.

Jess nodded. She was in no condition to take both of them on. That much she knew.

Pamela turned over, revealing a perfect flip side. What an ass. Cute, perky, gorgeous. Bitch.

Jess turned, opened the door, and then quietly closed it as she exited. Damn it. Why hadn't she slammed it? Could she go back and say she'd forgotten to do something and then slam it? No. Too late. The drama, at least of that moment, was over.

Standing in Eliot's office, she found herself looking aimlessly into space. This was no time to black out. She shook her head back to consciousness. She had to think, quickly.

What did all this mean? Well, she knew what it meant, but what did it really *mean?* Suppose she gave him the benefit of the doubt? A one-night fling. A mistake. Overcome by momentary passion. Seduced by an irresistible temptress. She thought of those incredible breasts, of that phenomenal behind—hell, it was possible. It would have almost been inhuman to ignore what Pamela offered.

Still . . .

Jess stared at all the items in Eliot's office. She knew each one of them. Her eyes zeroed in on the degrees first. What a smart person he was. Brilliant. Ask anyone.

She focused on the elaborate collection of owls on Eliot's desk. The owl wearing the doctor's garb, looking very wise, distinctly stood out from the rest. Too blatant to even be considered symbolic.

Her eyes moved to the shelf behind Eliot's desk. The mandatory allotment of family pictures, professionally framed, rested there. Her attention was caught by a photo of herself and Eliot. His arm was around her. They both were smiling broadly. The perfect couple. This was the only picture surrounded by a needlepoint frame. Jess hated doing needlepoint, but the result made it worth the tedium. On the frame in red, white, and blue lettering was the message, "Our love will keep us together. . . ."

Jess very deliberately walked over to the picture, took it in her right hand, and hurled it against the wall, glass shattering into smithereens. It felt good.

The door opened and Eliot, fully, even neatly, dressed, walked in. Seeing the picture, he quickly decided to say nothing. Wise decision, thought Jess.

"So . . . what brings you here?" Eliot asked nonchalantly.

She eyed him coldly for a full fifteen seconds before responding. "I was bringing you a picnic supper, Little Red Riding Hood–style. Little did I expect to find the Big Bad Wolf."

"I told you I didn't like surprises," Eliot reminded her.

"Now I understand why."

He picked up one of his owls and held it, his fingers moving up and down the marble wings. "I know I must seem less than perfect to you right now."

"You always were the master of understatement." She looked at him painfully, almost afraid to ask. "Do you love her?"

"No," he replied adamantly. "It doesn't mean anything. Of course, we had some wonderful times together. . . ." His eyes glazed over as he spoke fondly. "Like the time in the reservation—all the deer were watching and . . ."

"Eliot, spare me the details, will you?" Jess said, interrupting his reminiscing.

"Sure."

She was so confused. "Why? Why did you do it?"

He looked equally confused. Was it the question that was baffling him? Was it such an illogical one? His answer was so matter-of-fact. "It was so easy. She was just there."

Let's see if she could get this straight. "So you felt *obligated* to have sex with that . . . with that . . . person?"

"You mustn't blame Pamela," Eliot said gallantly.

"I don't blame *her.*"

"She isn't the sort of young lady who just casually does this sort of thing."

Was Eliot expecting Jess to respect Pamela in the morning?

"I don't give a damn what she does in her spare time as long as it's not with my husband."

"I just don't want you to hate her, that's all."

Jess spoke patiently. "I think you're going to have to face the fact that Pamela and I will never be best friends."

"I suppose," he replied, disappointed.

"Eliot, I have just walked in on you having sex with another woman and your main concern is that I not dislike your mistress?"

"She's not my mistress."

"Well, she's not your pen pal."

"She's just a . . . close friend," Eliot argued defensively.

"Bob is your close friend. I assume you and he don't indulge in this kind of activity."

"Certainly not; what do you think I am?" he asked indignantly.

"You don't want me to answer that," Jess retorted. "Eliot, how many 'close friends' have you had?" No response. Bad sign. She didn't want to ask any more, but there was no turning back at this point. "Pamela's not the first, is she?"

"Well, she's one of the firsts," he replied lamely.

"Good God."

So much for a one-night fling.

"Jess, what you don't understand is that doctors do this sort of thing all the time."

"It's in the Hypocratic Oath?"

"Do you think I enjoy all this running around and lying and cheating? I'm exhausted. But I'm also an upwardly mobile physician, a pillar of the community. *Everyone* expects us to have a mistress. Look, Jess . . ." he continued, reaching out to touch her hand.

She instinctively pulled her hand away from his in horror. "Have you washed your hands?"

"What?"

"Since you were with her, have you washed your hands?"

He looked at his palms quizzically. "No."

"Then don't touch me," she said pointedly.

Eliot turned patronizing. It was a routine he had mastered. "You're getting hysterical. You know I can't stand loud voices. I think we should go home and try a cool-down period. We need time to process all that has happened and come to mature conclusions."

She looked long and hard at him. "Stick it in your ear."

"Now that's precisely what I mean," he commented condescendingly, confident he had proven his point. "That was an immature response. Now try to get control of yourself and we can discuss this further at home. Now, did you come by car?" He was in control now.

"Yes," she responded, totally frustrated.

"Then I'll meet you at home in an hour."

"An hour?" She was losing her cool again.

"I have a few things to finish up."

"What *kinds* of things?"

"Medical things," he responded in his that-question-had-no-right-being-asked tone. "And then I have to drop Pamela off. Her car's in the shop."

Drop Pamela off? What kind of a knucklehead do you think I am? *"I'll* drop her off."

"Jess, nothing's going to happen," he assured her. "Trust me."

"Your timing's a little off, Eliot," she responded sarcastically.

"Let's not make this more uncomfortable than it already is," he said as he bent over and kissed the top of Jessica's head. "I'll be home soon."

7

One step after another. Left, then right, then left. Jess repeated this over and over to herself so she could reach her car and not fall down an elevator shaft. On the way home she forced herself to note each corner she passed and each car she successfully avoided hitting. Horns honked in the background, but she heard no crashes. Bastards. Couldn't they see she was a respectable lady who had just found her no-good, rotten husband fucking another woman? Did they have no compassion? She honked back.

She vowed that if she ever married again, she'd force her fiancé to sign a prenuptial agreement that if she caught him screwing another woman, he'd hire a chauffeur so Jess wouldn't have to make this life-threatening journey alone.

Turn the corner, three blocks down, into the driveway on the right, step on the brakes, put into park, turn off the ignition. *Turn off the ignition*—he's not getting off that easily. Good girl. You did it.

Thus Jess miraculously reached home in one physical, if not emotional, piece.

It never failed to amaze Jess how angelic a sleeping child could look. Especially hers. There were many nights Jess would sit at the foot of Susan's canopied bed gazing at the wonderment of her perfect little dimpled hands, her little matching feet, both of which had a big toe curled under the others—undoubtedly inherited from someone on Eliot's side of the family. Susan's blond hair was turning brownish, but it was luxuriously wavy—something Jess with pin-straight hair had always wished for—and it framed her heart-shaped face beautifully. It was still too early to tell if this child was going to need braces or weekly trips to a dermatologist, but for now she had the perfect porcelain features of youth. Jess was overwhelmed with love.

But on that night, as she looked at her little daughter, she ached. Susan slept in the Royal Position, which, according to the experts, was the trait of a totally secure person.

Jess wondered how secure her daughter would be after her parents got through with each other that night. She knew that Susan was not particularly close to Eliot, but he was her father. There had to be a special bond there. No child willingly gives up one of her parents.

Jess looked carefully around the room. Pink and white, just like a little girl's room was supposed to be, with a touch of lime green. The shelves overflowed with stuffed animals. But the favorite one, a well-used brown fleeced little lamb named Lambchops, who was flattened from constant attention, rested comfortably in Susan's arms as it had every night since she had gotten him when she was sixteen months old.

On the wall directly across from Susan's bed were alphabet and number posters, both of which Jess had carefully picked out and framed while she was pregnant. She wanted this child to learn as quickly as possible and Susan often fell asleep while looking at the posters, playing alphabet and number games in her own idyllic little world.

Nothing would be denied this child. That was evident in this room filled with games and toys and love. It looked like a fun room to live in. It was the kind of room Jess had dreamed about when she was a little girl, surrounded by muted beiges and drab greens. Sometimes she thought it gave her more pleasure than it did Susan.

Susan turned over sleepily and squinted at her mother, a troubled look on her face.

"What is it, sweetheart?" Jess asked gently.

She rubbed her eyes and yawned. "I got scared."

"You probably just had a bad dream, baby. Everything's all right." Temporarily, anyway.

"Were you crying, Mommy?"

"Crying?"

"I thought I heard you crying."

Had she been? She didn't even remember.

"I was watching a sad movie on TV."

"Did it have kids in it?" Susan asked eagerly.

"No, pumpkin."

"Oh," Susan said, disappointed. "What was it about?"

"Shattered dreams."

"Huh?"

"It was about a woman who thought she had everything and found out that she didn't."

"So she killed herself," Susan declared dramatically.

She smiled gently at Susan. The TV generation. Violence. "No. She just went on."

"Then why were you crying?" Susan asked, confused.

"I felt her pain."

"How?"

Jess thought a moment. "You know, like when Buffy caught his tail in the door that time? You cried for him even though it didn't actually hurt you."

"But I know Buffy. Did you know that woman?"

"I thought I did."

"But you didn't?"

"I'm not sure anymore," she answered, gently stroking Susan's tiny face. "Hey, you, it's late. Get some shut-eye."

"Don't cry anymore. It scares me."

If only it were that easy. "Everyone cries sometimes, even Mommies."

"Not Daddies."

"Some Daddies do."

"I bet our daddy never would," Susan declared proudly.

Probably right, thought Jess. Not that that was an asset,

but Jess decided she'd better wait to discuss that some other night a few years down the road. She puffed Susan's pillow and then bent down to kiss her. "Love you, sweetie."

"Can I come get you if I need you?" Susan asked, her big brown eyes at their fullest.

"If you *really* need me," Jess answered, hoping that she wouldn't. This was one night Jess didn't feel strong enough for two.

Susan curled up happily snuggling Lambchops and dreamily closed her eyes. "Love you a million plus infinity."

Jess had to laugh at herself for feeling guilty about opening a new bottle of wine. After all, this was a special occasion. How many times did a woman get to confront her husband having an affair—or two or three? It was a good move, too. The wine took the edge off but left her feeling the way she thought she ought to: angry!

Eliot walked in while Jess was pouring her second glass of cabernet sauvignon, the good one from California that they were saving.

"How was that?" Eliot asked proudly. "An hour on the button."

Jess didn't bother looking at her watch. She knew it couldn't be more than a minute later than the last time she'd looked at it. "Very admirable," she responded dryly. He'd have to do a hell of a lot more than be prompt to get a gold star tonight.

"Drinking this late? That's unlike you," Eliot noted.

"The night's full of surprises. Anyway, it's only wine— enough to calm me down, but still let me think."

Eliot looked stricken. "That's the cabernet."

"Right."

"I mean the good cabernet, the one I told you we were saving for just the right moment."

Jess took another sip. "I guess this is it."

"But it can't be. The book clearly says it needs another

three years to achieve perfect ripeness. How's the bouquet? Did you save the cork?"

"Eliot, this is not a wine-tasting party. As far as I'm concerned the wine's purpose is being served."

Eliot gave a deep sigh. There was so much she had to learn about fine living, but perhaps this wasn't the time to discuss that. "Have you thought about everything then?"

"It's going to take more than an hour."

"How long?" he asked, disappointed.

"What's the rush? Do you have another date?"

"Jess, really. . . ." He sounded dismayed by her immature question.

Worse, yet, she felt the need to apologize. "Sorry. All right, I guess what I really need from you are answers."

"Sure," Eliot agreed amiably. "Fire away."

She glared coldly at him. "If you could manage to be a little less chipper about this it might help."

"I thought that would dissipate the tension."

"Well, it's not working. Face it, Eliot, we can't turn this into a half-hour episode of 'Father Knows Best.' This whole thing cannot be resolved in twenty-eight minutes counting commercials."

He gave a patronizing sigh. "Okay. What are your questions?"

What did he think they were? "The obvious ones: How do you feel about me? Us? Should we even try working this thing out?"

"I have very deep feelings for you, Jess."

Deep feelings? Deep feelings? What the hell did that mean? She could feel her whole body tighten. All right, just sit on it until he's through, she thought.

"I want to stay together for Susan and any other children we might have in the future," he continued in his most reasonable tone. "In a way, I'm glad tonight happened. I'm growing, Jess. I need a woman who can keep up with me—intellectually and sexually."

"Sexually?" Jess asked, floored.

"I have an inordinately high sex drive," he said flatly.

Was this the same man she had been trying unsuccessfully to seduce the last few years? The same person who went back and forth between headache and too tired? "That's certainly nothing I could have deduced from your performance at home."

"Maybe I'm one of those guys who finds it uncomfortable to do much sexually with my wife," he responded logically.

Jess looked at him as though he were nuts. Had he not overlooked a rather pertinent detail? "But 'wife' is the category I fall into. Where does that leave *me?*"

He obviously anticipated that question since he excitedly whipped out a book from his inside pocket. "Have you seen this book? It's called *Open Marriage.*"

Yes, she had seen it. In fact, she had read it. It was the book they had torn apart at her book club three months ago. They had all laughed at the absurdity of the book's premise. She wasn't surprised when the couple who wrote the book got a divorce a few years later. But then, she hadn't considered much to be serious in that book—except a quick buck. Not until now, anyway.

"I've read it," she replied dryly.

"Well, then you know what it's all about," he continued, animatedly. "You date other people as well as stay with your own mate. No jealousy. You don't own each other. You're free and yet committed."

Jess was having a little trouble conceptualizing all this. "You mean both of us would date other people . . . ?"

"And have sexual encounters," he added enthusiastically.

"With other people. . . ." She wanted to make sure she was getting this right.

Eliot was completely caught up in it now. She hadn't seen him this revved up in years. Certainly not in bed. "Go home and come as we want. Then when *we* make love it'll be because we want to, not because we're obligated to. It adds spice, a new dimension."

"A new dimension. . . ." The best she could do was repeat what he had said, just to verify it.

"So what do you think?" he asked, looking like a hopeful five-year-old asking for his first two-wheeler.

"I think you must be living in the Twilight Zone, that's what I think."

His balloon was burst. Sorry, little boy, you'll have to stick with the old tricycle. He started to pout. "Now that's exactly what I mean about not being receptive to new ideas."

"Adultery is not a new idea. Believe me, you did not invent the wheel. Check the Bible."

"If we both agree, it's not adultery," Eliot argued.

Good God, he actually believed that? "Even if we both agree, it's adultery. If thirty people agree to kill someone, it's still murder. Agreeing doesn't make it okay." Why was she even taking the time to explain this? He was no dummy. He knew what he was suggesting. "I think you need help, Eliot. At the very least, we should see a marriage counselor."

"Absolutely not," he replied indignantly. "It could ruin my reputation."

"Double dating with your wife enhances it?"

Eliot was pleading now. Those puppy dog eyes of his. Next to him, a basset hound looked like a Doberman pinscher. "All I'm asking is that you try it, Jess."

He was really going off the deep end this time. Well, she wasn't about to jump off with him. "Forget it."

Please, Jess."

"No, negative, absolutely not. Nyet, thumbs down, no sale. Am I being perfectly clear? It's out of the question. End of discussion." And that was that!

8

Desperation . . . and maybe a subtle mental breakdown. She didn't know what else to attribute it to when she walked into that singles' bar with Eliot a few nights later.

It was crazy. What could have possessed her?

Of course, she knew the answer well enough.

Eliot was tenacious. It was as though he was out to sell his Ph.D. thesis. He seemed to have a holy mission in life. Sort of a born again fornicator. In a perverse way, it was almost interesting to listen to this man describe the virtues of sex. Especially since before all this had happened, she seriously considered the possibility that he was impotent.

Eliot wore her down, all right. He came at her from every angle, armed with endless facts, figures, arguments, and sermons. She was beginning to question her own values. There were times he almost sounded reasonable and it worried her. In the end, she didn't have the energy to fight him anymore.

Yet it was more than that. The reasons were that obvious twosome: fear and guilt.

Every time she looked at Susan, she got weak in the knees. Could she be responsible for this perfect child being without a father at home?

Divorce. She dreaded the thought of it. Failure. Everyone would know she had failed. She'd be alone. How would she survive?

Damn it. Why didn't she have enough confidence in herself to just tell him to go screw himself—if he hadn't already tried it, that is. Her days were filled with doubts and tears and the kinds of deep sighs she thought only her mother had mastered. Everything she did took twice as long. Her will, her resolve, had vanished.

Why couldn't he love her enough? What was wrong with her? Why was she so unappealing that he had to have others? It felt as if she was called into the boss's office for the yearly evaluation: "Sorry, you aren't adequate enough at being a woman. Perhaps you should try something else. How about a eunuch? Look, maybe you just need more practice. Have you considered being a Woman-in-Training? Of course, there will be a decrease in status, but at least you won't be subjected to the humiliation of losing your job entirely."

Eliot acted like a teenage boy going out on his first date. He was exhilarated. He asked Jess what she thought he should wear. She considered dressing him in clashing plaids and stripes—hell, she didn't have to make him look good for some bimbo—but when it came down to the wire she decided against it; common decency, she supposed.

For his part, he had never been more interested in the outfit she was going to wear. Here was a man who never even bothered to learn her dress size, suddenly fascinated by the possibilities of her wardrobe. It was as if she and her college roomie were dressing for the big mixer.

She knew Eliot wanted her to do well. Christ, what if she bombed out? Was he giving out a report card at the end of the evening? Would it count against her if she didn't get propositioned at least twice?

She changed her outfit six times. Too low cut. Too prim. Last year's colors. Too big (she was losing weight quickly). What she finally decided upon was an understated camel tweed suit with a peach silk blouse and pearls. Well, at least she looked like a lady. Wouldn't Mother be proud?

Eliot, on the other hand, ended up wearing an Adolpho navy jacket, sleek Yves St. Laurent gray wool trousers, a pink four-buttons-open John Weitz shirt, and a fourteen-karat-gold chain, which she hoped he'd let her borrow some night. It blew her mind. Wasn't this the person who thought beige was too wild a color for a shirt? And that neck chain. Jess had no idea where he had gotten it. Probably he kept it in his pocket, the way other men kept condoms, whipping it out whenever he wanted to look cool while cruising a singles' bar.

Where was the Eliot she thought she knew? Maybe this was a test. Maybe Eliot had been kidnapped by secret agents from a Communist country or aliens from another planet and replaced by this clone. Maybe it was up to her to detect that this couldn't possibly be the real Eliot and she was supposed to contact the C.I.A. immediately. And maybe not.

Jess told the baby-sitter they'd be home early. Eliot told the baby-sitter they might be very late. The baby-sitter looked confused. Join the club, Jess thought.

"Which bar are we going to?" Jess asked in the car, just to keep her mind off Eliot's carefree whistling.

"It's not a bar, it's a lounge."

"What's the difference?"

"The clientele. A lounge has a higher class."

"And no bar?"

He gave her one of his patronizing looks before he turned the car onto Crater Street.

They walked into the bar around nine. Eliot told her that was the proper time to make an appearance. It was one point of etiquette Jess was willing to leave up to him.

As far as Jess could tell, it was a decent enough looking place. The decor was done in mellow colors. The furniture was in one piece. There were beige and gray carpets that weren't worn through. Everyone was dressed fairly well. It was as much as she could tell because it was very smoky in there. Hadn't anyone read the surgeon general's report?

The music, even the slow numbers, was playing at decibel

levels that were inhuman. She assumed she'd eventually either get used to it or go deaf—she wasn't sure which one to hope for. As her teary eyes acclimated to the smoke, she took in the scene. Couples danced together glassy-eyed, looking as if they knew they should be having a good time but hadn't quite reached that point—except for the ones who were dead drunk: they were having the time of their lives. But it was early, so there weren't too many dead drunks yet. Jess evaluated the group. The men were thirty and over. The women were forty and under. The women were better looking, the men more ballsy. They knew why they were there, and they all looked hungry.

"Is this your regular hangout?" Jess asked, hoping to embarrass Eliot.

It didn't. "I've come here a few times," Eliot confided. "The people are nice and you have complete anonymity."

"Why did I agree to come?" she asked. "I feel sick."

"Now don't get nervous," Eliot said soothingly, sounding like a father giving advice to his little girl going out on her first date. "Just circulate. Ask questions, look like you want to meet people. Above all, act interested in what the man says."

"Boy, you're a real pro at this. Have you ever considered starting an Ann Landers column for infidelity?"

"Jess, I'm just telling you what works."

"I did have a date or two before I met you, believe it or not," she reminded him dryly.

"I was only trying to be helpful."

"You want to be helpful, take me home."

His Psych 101 tone was back. "You're uptight, a very natural reaction." He gave her an encouraging wink as he started to move into the crowd. "Good luck."

"Do me a favor," she called after him, "try to avoid the ones with communicable diseases."

Where to start? Jess wandered over to the bar and sat down on a stool that had an empty stool on either side of it. The bartender approached and put down a coaster. He was a friendly looking guy in his forties who looked as if he had a ready ear. Type casting.

"What would you like?" he asked amiably.

"To be anyplace else," she responded quickly. The bartender smiled understandingly. "What do you have that relaxes you, but doesn't put you off your guard?"

"White wine. Sip it slowly. First time here, huh?" he asked as he poured from a big jug. She nodded. "It's rough in the beginning. Takes some getting used to." He looked her up and down. "You'll do fine."

Ordinarily Jess would have moved away immediately from any man who looked her up and down like that, but it was a clinical appraisal rather than a sexual one. Furthermore, she didn't feel she could afford to alienate anyone at this point.

"I'll have to ride on your confidence," she told him appreciatively.

"Is yours all gone?"

"Certainly stretched out of recognition."

He knew the signs. "Your husband walk out on you?"

"No, he took me with him," Jess replied, pointing at Eliot, who was edging up to a stacked brunette. "He's over there."

"You're kidding," the bartender said, not knowing whether she was leveling with him.

"Believe me," Jess assured him, "my imagination isn't that bizarre."

Why was it so difficult to mix with people in this place? She was still the same person, wasn't she? She could discuss the same things she always discussed: Ginott's theory on preschoolers; swapping chicken curry recipes.

This definitely was not a chicken curry recipe group. Everyone here was on the hunt. All right folks, look over the herd very carefully. Now pick your prey and *attack!*

"Hi."

"Hello," said Jess, looking at the man who had approached her. Perhaps man was overstating it. He looked to be barely in his twenties. Lucky for him they just lowered the drinking age, she thought. She looked at his face. Pimples. Not even through adolescence. Well, everyone knew how to clear up that situation.

"My name is Scott." His voice still squeaked.

"Jess." Maybe she should advise him to lay off caffeine and chocolate. Too bad she hadn't clipped that Clearasil coupon she'd seen in the paper that morning. Who knew it would come in handy?

"So . . . what are you into?" his falsetto voice asked.

Jess lowered her voice one octave when she answered. "Motherhood."

She wondered if he was going to fall onto the table with the guacamole dip as he backed away.

Which was only minimally worse than the very intense man whose lineage went clear back to the *Mayflower*—perhaps she had read about his family in this month's D.A.R. magazine? No matter. He was past being impressed with facade. He was through with labels and value judgments.

"We have to get into our feelings. People treat each other too impersonally, like objects to be used and then discarded. Too often we ignore the essence of each other's core being."

"I think you're probably right," Jess replied, impressed. Maybe she had misjudged him.

"So how about it? You want to get it on at my place or yours?"

After a while she lost count of the losers. She never had to start counting the winners.

The one saving grace was that she was popular. She danced every dance and tried to look as if she were enjoying herself, just in case Eliot should ever glance over. Although he seemed totally engrossed talking to a pair of tits belonging to a young redhead in the corner.

"I tell you," the fat man in the green plaid suit with an orange and polka dot tie said, trying to sound as if he was imparting great wisdom, "If you can't make it in law, you're an idiot. I made an easy hundred grand for my client today because that other jerk lawyer didn't prepare his client right. It's all in the preparation. Rules one, two, and three. Maybe I'm brilliant. People are always saying that to me. Say, you divorced, separated, what?"

Was this her turn for a word-in-edgewise? "Sort of separated," she answered looking into space, wondering if they made all songs longer these days or if it just felt that way.

"How long?" he asked, sweating profusely.

"About an hour and a half." Was the record stuck?

"New kid on the block, huh? Me, I been married four times. I work to pay alimony. Those broads were all dynamite in the sack. They suckered me in. Y'think I'd've learned my lesson."

"Maybe you're not brilliant at everything." Jess smiled sweetly. The fat man's hands were so clammy that when he turned her she was sure she would slide out of his grasp straight across the waxed parquet floor.

"Boy," he said looking admiringly at her body, "I bet you'd be somethin' else in the old sack."

"That seems to be the general consensus." This is a dream, she thought. A very bad dream.

The fat man drew her close to him. She was feeling her small breasts get even flatter. She imagined they now looked like two silver dollar pancakes. She also had the unmistakable sensation of the fat man getting hard. He panted as he talked. "How 'bout going someplace quiet? Get a bottle of Ripple. I'll show you a night you won't forget."

What made him think she would go? Didn't she look ladylike? Hadn't he noticed the cultured pearls? She was about to point all this out when she felt his hand grab the right cheek of her behind and squeeze as though he were checking to see if the cantaloupe was ripe. She felt her face flush, a sensation of rage engulfing her. She wasn't the least bit interested in fighting it.

"Listen," Jess said reasonably, "that's a big investment. Let's make sure you're getting your money's worth."

The music had gotten louder and more suggestive. Or maybe it was the song that was playing: "I Don't Get No Satisfaction." She didn't care to analyze it. She felt a show coming on. She started to lift her shoulders suggestively.

"How do you like these shoulders?" Jess asked provocatively.

"I like them. I'm crazy about them," responded the fat man, starting to salivate.

"Okay, fellows," Jess shouted loudly as she turned to the group. "It's show time. Here's the merchandise. What do you think?"

Jess jumped up on a table, kicked over some pretzels and someone's half-consumed gin and tonic, and began her rendition of a slow strip tease. Gone was the jacket. Gone was the skirt. Gone was the silk ruffled blouse. By the time she got to the pearls, she imagined "ladylike" was no longer an issue. She only regretted she hadn't worn white gloves. But then, who had that kind of foresight?

The music played bumps and she supplied the grinds. The cheers got louder. Was it her imagination or did every pair of pants now have an obvious bulge? She was hard pressed to remember when she had been this appreciated. Twirl that hair. Walk, shoulder, bump, grind. Wet those lips. Smile. Show those perfectly straightened teeth. Listen to those cheers. Maybe she had a career worth looking into here. Thank God she had worn the one frilly pair of underpants she had. This was no night for a hundred percent cotton.

It was fun. She certainly had no time to notice Eliot, who was doing a slow burn in the corner. She got down to her bra and panties and wondered where she was going to go from there. Wearing those white pearls or not, she still had some sense of decorum. Better keep strutting. The crowd didn't seem disappointed yet. Well, what could they do, ask for their money back?

"Jess, that's enough," she heard a familiar voice say. Could that be her Prince Charming?

"Eliot," she shouted, exhilarated. "I think they're interested. What d'ya' say, fellows," she gave an extra bump and grind for emphasis, "is anyone interested?"

She got the response she was looking for. A potpourri, to be sure, but they all added up to a resounding *"Yes!"* She smiled gratefully at the crowd. Was this the time for the Miss America thank-you speech? I want to thank my mother, my father, and the American flag.

"Jess!" Eliot hissed.

Time to thank the little people who helped you get to the place you are today. She pointed to Eliot as she announced, "Fellows, this is my teacher, my agent, my . . . what are you, Eliot?" she asked coyly.

"Your husband," he replied through gritted teeth.

"Last, but not least," Jess announced with a flourish.

"Let's get out of here," Eliot growled, pulling her down from the table.

"Sorry, boys," she yelled apologetically. "Guess the little woman has to go home now."

Eliot handed her her clothes and, of course, her pearls as they were leaving. She wondered if they were still cultured.

The fat man begged her to take his card just in case. In fact, she had a dozen cards by the time she reached the door Eliot was pulling her to. She turned to throw one last kiss to her fans and then turned triumphantly to her husband.

"Eliot. I was a hit."

9

All she could remember about the ride home was Eliot's silence—she assumed it denoted disapproval—and her giggling. Three miles from their house Jess started singing "I Feel Pretty." She urged Eliot to join in on the chorus. He didn't.

Eliot paid the baby-sitter while Jess broke open a new bottle of cabernet. Another special occasion, she figured.

"I'm developing a real taste for wine, Eliot," she said, merrily flopping down on the couch.

"Slow down with that stuff. It's bad for your liver."

"Certainly helps my circulation." She grinned. "Smile, Eliot, that was a joke. You ought to try smiling, just for the hell of it. It doesn't hurt, honest." No response. "You know what, Eliot? Tonight was fun."

Eliot removed his fourteen-karat-gold chain and dropped it on the bar. Must be back in his domestic mode, Jess thought.

"I assume you realize that you made a total fool of yourself tonight," he remarked disdainfully.

"Actually," she replied, considering, "I thought I made a total fool out of both of us."

"I didn't like it," Eliot stated firmly, hitting the bar for emphasis.

"Really, Eliot? Surprise, surprise. You weren't meant to." She gleefully took another gulp of wine.

Eliot shook his head. "I don't think this arrangement is going to work."

Finally, some sanity emerges. Jess gave a sigh of relief and agreed. "Neither do I."

"All right," Eliot continued reasonably, "you said if we had enough sex at home, that would satisfy you, right?"

"Right."

"Okay. Then we'll have as much sex as you want and I'll do whatever I want to do on the side. That way we'll both be satisfied."

She had to have that wax cleaned out of her ears. She couldn't have heard him correctly. Slowly. Repeat it slowly so there are no mistakes here. "Are you suggesting that you are still going to have affairs?"

"But take care of you when I get home." He looked like Sherlock Holmes after he had solved a particularly difficult mystery. Dr. Holmes, I've found the solution. Elementary and all that rot.

She tried all the tricks she could remember as she felt her blood pressure surge. Count to ten slowly. Not working. Take deep breaths. Not working. Think of Susan. Not working. Negative. All counterhysterical systems down. Malfunction in the take-this-nice-and-easy department. Alert! Alert! *Final straw time has arrived!*

"You son of a bitch! You no-good louse!"

"Jess, calm down."

"*Out.* That's it. It's over. Pack your bags and leave. I don't want someone like you near my child, you no-good bastard."

"Jess, you're going berserk."

"No! Berserk you haven't seen yet," she screamed as she rushed to their antique blue china cabinet and flung open the doors. "*This* is berserk!" She picked up the dishes and threw as many as she could at one time. What the hell, they were his mother's. Jess had always hated them anyway.

"Jess," Eliot protested, truly scared now, "those are family heirlooms. My mother will kill me."

"Not unless she gets here first." Jess was in a frenzy now. "Every thirty seconds you're still in this house costs her another five-piece place setting."

"All right," Eliot said hurriedly. Anything to stop this maniac, he thought. "We'll talk tomorrow."

"Oh, no. Talking is over. The deadline for civility was five minutes ago. You want to talk civil, call my attorney, because he is the only one from whom you will get a calm, dispassionate word."

"Does this mean you want a trial separation?"

Red. All she could see was red. "Try *divorce*. We did separation tonight. It wasn't far enough."

He looked wounded. "Jess, be reasonable. We can't get a divorce. My mother doesn't believe in it. It's not even in her vocabulary."

"Tell her it's under 'd' in the dictionary," she hissed. "It's there and we're getting it."

"But what about our unborn children?" he pleaded.

"That's exactly how they're going to have to stay," she snapped.

Eliot got some momentary resolve back. "I'll fight you tooth and nail on this."

Oh, you will, will you? Don't forget, I know that bravery threshold of yours, buddy boy. "Not unless you want everyone, including your dear mother, who treats you like some divine savior anointed from heaven, to know *exactly—details,* Eliot—what you've been doing and wanted me to do." She smiled slyly, enjoying this now. "Sort of gives a new meaning to the coming of the Messiah, don't you think?"

He was getting scared again. "You wouldn't."

"Try me."

She meant business, all right. He knew that look. "You really would."

"In one minute," she warned him in the calm way she knew he would appreciate, "if you are not out of here, your mother's Royal Worcester setting for eleven will be settings for ten."

"I'm leaving. I'm leaving. I'll pick up my things tomorrow when you're calmer."

"I won't be calmer tomorrow. Do it when I'm out."

"Can I at least get my toothbrush?" he asked in that reasonable tone of his.

Jess threw a cup against the wall. "You want to see a thousand-piece soup tureen?"

"You're mad," he screamed. "Totally mad."

"Eliot, please, you know how I detest screaming. Just leave before the tureen leaves my hands." She lifted the tureen above her head into perfect throwing position.

"I'm leaving. Watch me. I'm going out the door now."

"Fifteen seconds," she warned.

"Remember," Eliot yelled, pointing his left index finger straight at Jess, "you're responsible for this marriage breaking up. You threw me out."

"Ten seconds."

"I've got to get my jacket. It has my wallet in it."

"And your American Express. Don't leave home—especially for good—without it. Five seconds," she warned.

That crazy look in her eyes again. He rushed for his jacket and then for the door.

"Time's up!" Jess announced triumphantly.

There was nothing as sweet as the sound of that tureen smashing into little pieces of ex-valuable china as it hit the closing door.

10

Soap operas were not her style. At least that's what she always told herself. The truth was that Jess was afraid if she started watching them, she'd feel compelled to stay home every day lest she miss one abortion, one broken marriage, one affair on the sly.

In college, she was the only girl on her floor who had voted against having a television, fearing she'd end up watching reruns of "Perry Mason" or first runs of "Peyton Place" and flunk out of school. And since the vote had to be unanimous, she was able to prevent the installation of a TV on her floor.

Some of the girls in her dorm were hostile to her when they found out who the boob-tube saboteur was, but since it was one of those fancy Seven Sister schools known for academics, Wellesley to be specific, they didn't get far with their complaints. Jess had assumed it would work out that way.

She only made six exceptions to her no-TV rule. Twice during her college stay there were Barbra Streisand specials and, of course, she never missed the Academy Awards. She loved watching the beautiful people. Other than those deviations, she was all work. It certainly paid off academically.

So it came as somewhat of a surprise to her when she became addicted to every soap opera available in the weeks following Eliot's departure. Actually, watching the soaps was a turn for the better considering she spent eighteen to twenty hours a day sleeping during the first week they were separated. Jess couldn't remember when she'd been so tired. She was relieved when she finally dragged herself out of bed armed with a purpose, even if it was only to watch the latest soap installment.

She became actively involved in each character's actions and decisions. She would either condemn or applaud—there was no middle ground for her anymore.

Jess ironed a lot as she watched the shows. She never knew if she was ironing the same things over and over again. Once she thought about it. How much could she have to iron, anyway? Eliot was gone; Jess rarely wore anything but jeans and a sloppy shirt; Susan wore your basic Carters wash and wear. So where could all this ironing be coming from? Maybe her next door neighbor was slipping it into her basket so she could be free from the task, sneaking in each night, taking the ironed goods and replacing them with wrinkled ones. Oh, who cared, anyway? It gave Jess something to do as her eyes stayed riveted to the tube.

HE: I must have you. I can't exist without you.

SHE: We can't. I can't. We mustn't. We shouldn't. We couldn't live with ourselves . . . could we?

HE: Can we live without each other?

SHE: I can't.

HE: Neither can I. So there's no real question.

SHE: But think of our families.

"Families," exclaimed Jess, surprised. What families? What soap opera was this, anyway? She had begun to lose track. She thought she was supposed to like this couple. Damn.

Susan came running in as Jess was trying to figure it out.

"Mommy," she whined.

"Shhh," said Jess absently, intent on not losing her place.

SHE: We must consider our families. Between my five and your seven. . . .

"Twelve?" Jess was aghast. "You have twelve between you?"

HE: We'll be discreet. Who could it hurt?

Jess pointed at the TV. "Fourteen people, schmuck. That's who it could hurt."

"I thought you don't watch soap operas," said Susan.

"I don't. Shhh."

HE: We're entitled to our own happiness. My wife is so dull. But you, you're my excitement.

SHE: Oh, darling, really?

Jessie's eyes narrowed. *"Bimbo!"*

"Mommy," Susan whined again.

Commercial, then credits. One more soap in the can until tomorrow. Turn off the TV. Reenter the real world, for what it's worth.

She switched off the television and looked at Susan's puffy eyes.

"Honey, what is it? You've been crying."

"It's Hayden Rabinowitz, that's what," sniffed Susan.

"The boy at school who you're going to have fifteen children with?" asked Jess.

"Twenty," corrected Susan.

"Doesn't he want twenty kids anymore?"

"Uh-huh. But he wants them with Heidi Klein and Tammy O'Rourk, too."

"He's going to be one busy fellow."

"I'm never gonna look at another boy again."

That's my girl. Good decision. "They can be pretty rotten sometimes." It only gets worse when they grow up. "Say, I've got an idea. What say we pig out?"

"What's that?"

"We'll get every junk food we can buy and eat until we bust."

"Daddy, too?"

"No. Just the two of us."

"Neato. I love just us two."

Lucky thing, thought Jess.

It was hard to imagine, when first looking at the remnants of the gooey, fattening food, that only one adult and one child were responsible for the mess in the living room that night. Globs of ice cream, candy wrappers, half-eaten pizzas, crumbled Fritos, chocolate milk shakes, and Snickers bars missing a few bites were scattered everywhere. Strewn on the sofa, Jess and Susan, taking turns chugging Coke syrup, were totally wiped out.

"Hayden Rabinowitz made me sick," Susan announced.

11

There was something about being in the house she grew up in that reduced her to feeling like a child again. It never failed. Whenever Jess was there she felt as if she were an apprentice grown-up.

It was a warm feeling. It was an uncomfortable feeling. She longed to return to the simplicity of her youth. She wanted to escape from the oppression of her adolescence. She felt cozy and safe. She felt claustrophobic. Most of all, this home was a constant reminder of the powerlessness she had felt as a child knowing that any of her wishes could be overruled by either of her parents.

If asked, she would have had to admit hers was a fairly average childhood. No major traumas. She got along reasonably well with her parents, squabbled the usual amount with her older sister. She was well liked in school, though far from being part of the in-crowd clique. What she was was a student.

She knew she was attractive, though nowhere near as pretty as her sister, Carol, the acknowledged beauty of the family. Jess always wondered how it was that there was only one beauty to a family. Jess would sit and watch Carol dress for dates, sometimes juggling three in one night, and wonder if she would ever master all the feminine wiles Carol had. Early on she decided there wasn't a chance. But, as Jess also discovered, life is filled with compensations. Carol was gorgeous and very popular, true, but when it came to adding

two plus two, Carol was lucky if she came as close as five.
Jess figured that was because Carol didn't have to develop in
any other areas. There was no need for her to be smart.
From the day she was born, her special feature—her beauty
—was clearly defined. In later years Jess thought that was
too bad. And when Susan was born, and everyone said she
was the most beautiful baby they'd ever seen, Jess determined she would underplay that quality around Susan.
Good looks were too risky to stake your future on.

But Carol seemed to have just what she wanted. She had
married Stan, a nice but exceedingly boring man, who
helped his father with the chain of fishing gear stores he
owned. There were plenty of fishermen around, so there was
plenty of money for Stan. Enough, in fact, so that gorgeous
Carol received a Jaguar by her twenty-third birthday. By
now, at thirty, she was working on her eighth XKE, her
fourth chinchilla, a mansion in the poshest section of Engle-
wood Cliffs, a six-karat diamond ring, and her first face lift.

When Jess married Eliot, Mrs. Simon's world was complete. What a lucky woman Estelle Simon was. All her
friends told her so. Imagine, two daughters married to two
successful men (one a doctor, yet) and both living nearby.
She had it all. After knocking wood twice, Estelle had to
agree.

Jess sat at her mother's kitchen table, drinking her fourth
cup of coffee, picking at an English muffin. She looked
around the kitchen, realizing for the first time how similar it
was to her own. Of course, Mrs. Simon's kitchen had been
done by a decorator, but still it was the same sunny-side-up
yellow with matching canisters. Even the chairs were clones.
Odd that she'd never noticed that before.

In the last two months Mrs. Simon had become a pro at
avoiding the reality of Jess's situation. She refused to see any
kind of finality in what had happened between Jess and Eliot. Rather, she chose to view it as a rest they were taking
from each other, sort of separate vacations. At first she tried

to be kind and understanding. But after weeks, then months of nothing positive happening, it began to weigh on her. Jess knew it was difficult for her mother—after all, what could she say to the other heavy sighers with whom she played bridge twice a week? Still, Jess figured this time she should rate first in line for sympathy.

"Look," Mrs. Simon stated, trying to convince herself, "these things happen. Every family has heartache. There's no reason we should be immune. That's why they call us the chosen people. Don't worry, it'll work itself out."

"What'll work itself out?" Jess asked.

"This silly divorce talk," her mother answered as she got a sponge to wipe up the three muffin crumbs that had fallen on Jess's placemat. "Try to eat over your plate, dear."

"Mother, it's not going to work itself out. Eliot and I can't live under the same roof. We're not happy together."

"Happiness doesn't just show up on your doorstep one morning. It's something that has to be created. It takes plenty of hard work. Now take Eliot, for example. Eliot is a medical genius who, perhaps, needs a bit more 'understanding' than the normal man."

"The 'understanding' is the problem," Jess said with emphasis.

Jess had tried at various times in the past few months to explain the precise nature of the problem with Eliot, but her mother refused to accept it. It was as though her mother could only deal with situations she could identify with, and this was certainly outside her frame of reference. Jess knew that her mother didn't really want to know the truth. Well, who could blame her? Neither did Jess.

"You expect too much," Mrs. Simon continued. "A woman is in charge of what happens in a marriage."

"Why should that be?" Jess demanded, her whole body getting rigid in anticipation of a confrontation.

Mrs. Simon put up her arms in protest. She wasn't going to take the rap for this one, just explain the facts. "I didn't make up the rules. I merely observe them. You're a grown-up woman. It's time you faced the facts of married life. There's no such thing as fifty-fifty. A woman has to give ninety percent to her marriage. It's been that way from time immemorial. And if she can do that, make her husband feel wanted and loved and cherished—"

"Estelle, have you seen my keys around?" Jack Simon yelled from the next room.

"For God's sake, I'm your wife, not your mother," she yelled back, annoyed. "Find them yourself." She turned back, composed, to Jess. "Now then, where was I?"

"You were talking about making your husband feel important, loved, and cherished," Jess reminded her drolly.

Mrs. Simon shook her head, remembering now. She used her index finger for emphasis. "If a wife can do that, then she's a success."

Jess shook her head negatively. "I refuse to play by those rules."

"Did you hear what you said?" asked Mrs. Simon, raising both index fingers as though she had caught Jess in the faux pas of the century. *"Play! Play* by those rules. Marriage is not play, it's hard work. You have to work day and night to keep a marriage going. Maybe you should buy a new wardrobe, read some new books on . . . um . . . different things . . ." her voice trailed off.

Ah, now I've got you. "What kinds of 'things'?" Jess asked innocently. Mrs. Simon began stirring her coffee, not looking up. Jess wasn't going to let this one go by that easily. "Mother, I'm asking you, what kinds of 'things'?" No dice. Her mother kept stirring that coffee as though she were panning for gold.

"Now take Carol, for instance. She runs herself ragged keeping in shape for Stan, trying to please him. Believe me, it pays off. The other day he came home with a gold pendant for her and it wasn't even her birthday."

"I'm not Carol, Mother. I never was and I never will be." Thank God. "Mother, you're not listening to me."

But Mrs. Simon was momentarily distracted. "What is

this dust doing here?" she asked with disbelief as she lifted one of her sunny yellow Levolor blinds with the label underneath to prove it. "I hate this. You pay good money and you don't even get a clean house," she muttered, eyes narrowing, opening the kitchen door. "Maria," she yelled, "I want you to redust the kitchen when you're through upstairs."

Jess knew she wasn't getting through. "I guess there's no point in discussing it. Eliot and I have gone our separate ways. Why don't we just leave it at that."

"Eliot's mother says Eliot doesn't want a divorce," Mrs. Simon pointed out hopefully.

Of course not. Good help is hard to find these days. "Eliot wants a home-cooked meal every now and then. He doesn't love me. He wants to date." Pay attention, Mom, because I'm only going to repeat this another two or three hundred times until you hear it. *Date other women . . .* and come home when he feels like it."

There. It's been said fully and clearly now. She can't say she didn't hear it. Let it sink in. Jess stared long and hard at her mother. Had the message finally made it through the barricades?

Forget the women at the club. Forget that you no longer have two perfect daughters. Just this once, think about *me.*

She took her mother's hand and waited for her to look up so they could talk person to person. Jess spoke gently, searching for understanding. "Mother, can you really ask me to live that way, with a person who openly has sex with other women, a person who doesn't have any respect for me?"

She saw the pain in her mother's eyes. If the word could be used in such a situation, Jess knew she had won.

"He has no respect for himself," Mrs. Simon stated flatly.

Jess wasn't through. Go for the final bone. Get her while her guard is down. "Can you really ask me to degrade myself like that? Can you?"

But Mrs. Simon was overwhelmed. She couldn't respond. She didn't have to. They both knew the answer.

Mrs. Simon got up as though she had a two-ton weight on her shoulders, went to the yellow box with *le pain* stenciled across it, and mechanically brought a loaf of bread back to the table.

"Try this honey bread. I got it at that new bakery in town," she said as lightly as she could, giving a piece to Jess. "Taste it. It's good. Overpriced, but good."

Jess took a bite. It tasted like cardboard. Everything tasted lousy lately. "It's good."

"You know, I was talking to Claire Pollack the other day. She has this wonderful niece—not much in the looks department, but wonderful. So she comes home one day, this wonderful girl, and finds her husband has up and run off with a dental hygienist. No warning. Nothing. Just like that. Everything's fine at breakfast; by dinner, there's another woman. This world now . . ." She gave her deepest, most meaningful sigh from the gut.

All right, Mother, where's the not-so-subtle message?

"Anyway," Mrs. Simon continued, "to make a long story short, she pulled herself together, lost sixty-seven pounds, and looks quite presentable, so I'm told. Met a *very* prominent lawyer and married him within a year. I'll bet there are plenty of men out there and with your looks and brains, what's to worry?"

Good God, the lions haven't even finished the carcass yet. We're forming another hunt already? "Believe me," Jess assured her mother, "I'm in no rush."

Her mother was thick into planning now. The bride should wear a cream-colored dress; the bridesmaids, maybe a sky blue. "Don't show the brains too fast," she advised, ignoring Jess's last remark, "it scares some men." But she couldn't ignore it completely. "What does that mean, you're in no rush?"

"Who wants to jump into the frying pan so fast?"

"Let's face facts, sweetheart," she stated not meanly, but realistically, "what else do you know?"

Not a question Jess was crazy about hearing. She had

been hard pressed to come up with an answer to that one herself. She shrugged her shoulders noncommittally. "I've got to figure out what to do with my life."

Mrs. Simon looked at Jess as though she had just escaped from Bellevue. "What's to figure? You sue for a lot of alimony, keep your life-style intact, find another man, and marry him." It's so simple. Her life plan in front of her.

"I've already failed at marriage."

"You didn't fail. Eliot failed," Mrs. Simon corrected. "You're a victim of his insanity."

"Maybe I'm not cut out for marriage."

She's going off the deep end. Don't even let her think these things. "Such talk. Don't be ridiculous. This is a wonderful life." What was that on the windowsill? "Dust. More dust." She rushed to the kitchen door, having picked up some of the evidence with a sunny yellow Scott double-ply paper towel. "Maria," she yelled, "I want this whole house redusted."

Jess was meeting her father for lunch. She would be exactly on time, he would be ten minutes early. It was one of his habits that she especially liked.

She knew the scenario by heart. She would come into the restaurant and he would be waiting for her at a table out of viewing distance. The maître d' would know who she was from her father's description: a beautiful young woman. He would hand her a single rose that her father had bought for her to celebrate this special event—a luncheon together. She would smile, embarrassed, and then be shown to the out of the way table her father had chosen. As she approached, a broad grin would come over his face. He had done this for as long as she could remember: with both daughters together when Jess and Carol were younger; then separately when they reached their teens.

It would always be an elegant restaurant and, somehow, the maître d' never failed to perform his role to perfection. Jess often wondered if her father had a little card printed up with precise directions and then tipped each maître d' for a job well done.

Jess knew that her father went through this little routine with Carol as well. It was his attempt to make them feel individual and special. It worked. Her father made her feel like a million bucks.

As she followed the maître d' that day, rose in hand, to her father's smiling face, she was overwhelmed with a feeling of gratitude that this man was her father. He was the kindest man she had ever known.

She also knew his failings. He was incapable of saying no to anyone in his family. Jess tried her best not to take advantage of that trait. She thought about the countless times her mother tried goading her husband into being the strong one. It never worked. Caving in was as natural to him as breathing. Each time Jess saw this happen it chipped away at her respect for him. She couldn't help it. It made her feel guilty because she knew this man's essence was so decent. She loved him deeply. He was a sweet, peaceful, giving, gentle man who appreciated her fully and loved her unabashedly. So why was it so hard to accept that he was flawed? Why was strength such an important issue to her?

"You look radiant." Mr. Simon smiled warmly after he kissed her. He was dapperly dressed in a three-piece pin-striped suit looking perfect for a very important business luncheon. He was a handsome, even elegant man who seemed unaware he possessed either characteristic. The clipped salt-and-pepper mustache added just the right touch. He stood and waited for Jess to be seated, the consummate gentleman.

"I look exhausted," she corrected.

"To me you look beautiful." He said it firmly, and there was no question that he meant it.

"God bless fathers."

Mr. Simon shook his head, worried. "Not getting much sleep, are you?" Jess shook her head no. "I could kill that no-good louse."

"We're forming a committee."

"He was never good enough for you."

Funny. Until recently, everyone seemed to think her husband was the sun and the moon. "Who *is* good enough for me?"

"Royalty," Mr. Simon responded simply.

"For your princess?"

"For my favorite daughter."

"You say that to Carol, too."

They both knew that was true.

"With you I mean it."

They both knew that was true as well. Jess had always known. In some ways, it had made her feel bad. Like the time Mr. Simon was supposed to be working late, but his appointment fell through and he surreptitiously called her at home and asked her not to mention it, but could she come and meet him downtown for an ice-cream soda? She had told her mother that she was going to a friend's house to work on a biology paper for school. She thought for sure her mother would see through her lie, which was something she was not very adept at doing, but she hadn't and so Jess, feeling like Mata Hari on her first mission, snuck downtown to meet her father, who was already at the ice-cream shop waiting for her with a rose in his hand.

"Carol means well," her father continued, "but the space between her ears. . . . What goes on in that head besides clothes and jewelry, well. . . ." He shrugged his shoulders fondly. "God knows I love her. I'd give up my life for her. But you, you've given me nothing but *nachus*. So you married a jerk. Who was to know?"

"Mother thinks I'm a failure." Mother thinks you're a failure, too, Daddy. Why can't you stand up to her, just once?

She wished she had the nerve to ask him, but she didn't feel she was in a position to challenge anyone else on their marital failures. Some day she would do it. Of course, there were a lot of risks there: Her father would probably be hurt, and her mother would probably consider her a traitor. Those possibilities had to be considered.

"Your mother," Mr. Simon said hopelessly. "Listen to me, my precious daughter, you can be a success at anything you try, anything. You've got smarts and, above all, *sachel*— good common sense. And another thing, an important thing that too few people have: You've got guts. Do you know how many people stay in a marriage, unhappy, terrified to leave? First, they don't want to hurt the children. Then they don't want to hurt their mate. Then they run out of excuses altogether, but still they stay. Oh, no. I toast you," he announced, raising his glass to her. "To you. To new beginnings. *Mazel tov!*"

12

Susan wasn't one to catch a lot of colds like some of the other children in her class, but when she did, they were whoppers. Jess hated taking Susan to the doctor's office when she was sick. She longed for the days of her youth when house calls were the common practice.

Mrs. Simon maintained that it was a death wish to take a child with a fever out of the house. Jess pooh-poohed this, dutifully repeating the arguments that had been recited to her about all that expert equipment in the doctor's office which couldn't be put into a doctor's little black bag, and that bad weather wouldn't affect a child's health, but deep down she resented and feared it just as much as her mother did. She suspected it was a plot to keep sickness going and make more money for the medical profession.

Furthermore, she was married to a doctor, so shouldn't Susan be someone he could make better? Wasn't this a major perk of having a doctor in the house? But Eliot had refused on the grounds that he wasn't a pediatrician and he certainly wouldn't want a podiatrist delivering one of his babies— whatever sense that made.

Of course, it should be noted that when Jess got pregnant Eliot refused to be her obstetrician on the grounds he would be too personally involved. Too personally involved with her. Jess had thought it so romantic at the time.

Romance was no longer an issue. Eliot had been gone for

two months now, so Jess didn't bother to tell him that his daughter was sick.

A hundred and three point five and Dr. Lowell Graham, Susan's pediatrician since birth, had still blithely said, "Bring her in, Jess. Just bundle her up. The rain won't hurt her."

Damn doctors, thought Jess as she hung up her princess phone, they all think they're gods. But she said nothing and obediently bundled Susan up and brought her to Lowell Graham's office.

It was a fun office with bright pictures on the wall and haphazard puzzles on little tables. Children's books and magazines were randomly stacked in bookshelves, and chairs were made to look like animals.

She surveyed the office as she removed Susan's layers. Forty-five minutes, minimum. It didn't fool her when the nurse ushered Jess and Susan into an empty examining room. That was only to keep this "communicable" disease from other patients, and what good was that since it had taken the nurse ten minutes to get unbusy enough to even notice them? Then again, Jess figured she wasn't exactly partial to nurses these days.

Lowell Graham was a good doctor, wonderful with children. Susan adored him. He had an easy laugh and a devilish manner. Although Jess and Eliot weren't really friends of Lowell and Grace Graham, they saw each other at neighborhood parties and were more than just nodding acquaintances. In fact, Jess had had some very interesting conversations with Grace.

"Okay, Susan, you can go get a lollipop now. You should be all better in a few days."

"Thanks, Dr. Graham," chirped Susan as she quickly headed through the door en route to the well-known lollipop drawer.

"She's a cutie," he said, writing out a prescription. "I don't think it's strep. We'll know tomorrow. Give me a call around three."

"Okay," Jess said, feeling relieved and exhausted. "You know, Lowell, I think I'm coming down with the same thing Susan has. Could you look at my throat?"

"I will if you take off all your clothes and get on the examination table," he said playfully, looking up from the prescription he was writing. "Rules are rules."

"Listen," Jess said lightly, "I already did that today for the plumber and the electrician. I'm certainly not going to do it for my daughter's pediatrician."

Dr. Graham's mood abruptly turned serious. "We can do it in a more conducive setting . . . a nice motel, for instance."

"C'mon, Lowell, I'm serious."

"So am I. You've always turned me on, Jess."

"You *are* a married man," she pointed out, though she was sure he remembered that.

"That's *my* problem."

Jess felt herself getting angry, which surprised her since she thought her strength had been sapped. What the hell, she was up to a fight. "Not when it concerns me, it isn't. You're utterly despicable."

"I'm a normal, red-blooded American male."

"Is this what you think proves it?"

"Hey, I hear the rumor mill. You and Eliot split. You're available."

She could feel her corpuscles bursting.

"Well, you can tell your trusty rumor mill that I'm not available, and if I were it certainly wouldn't be to some forty-five-year-old married adolescent. Good God!" Jess moved her lips as her teeth remained stationary. "Send me Susan's records. We're switching doctors."

Beads of sweat appeared on Lowell Graham's reddened forehead. He attempted to speak nonchalantly. "Hey, it's no big deal. I tried, I struck out."

"You bet your bippie you struck out."

"What are you getting so hot . . . so angry about?" he asked, trying to calm her down.

"You think it's open season just because I'm separated from Eliot. *You men!* I'm not a piece of meat."

"Of course you're not. Who ever said you were? Let's just forget the whole thing." No lay was worth this aggravation. "Now, let's have a look at that throat of yours."

"I wouldn't let you near my throat. My throat is going to a woman doctor."

Susan thought her mommy looked awfully angry when she came out of Dr. Lowell's office and bundled her up with all those sharp moves. But she really didn't care because she was so sleepy and she knew she was on her way home to see "Tom and Jerry." She hoped her mommy wouldn't take too long making the phone call when she swerved off the road, stopped at a phone booth, and mumbled something about being right back.

Son of a bitch, thought Jess. No-good bastard creep. Who the hell does he think he is? Grace should be told how her husband is propositioning women left and right. Jess had no delusions that she was the first.

Jess finally found two nickels and deposited them, only then realizing that she didn't need to put in any money to call Information. She asked for Grace Graham's phone number. She knew it would be listed under Grace's name since no doctor would dare list his own name and chance being reached by a desperate patient—heaven forbid.

Well, he'd get his. Grace was no pushover. She'd tell him where to go—hopefully to divorce court where he belonged, the rotten schmuck.

"Hello," Grace answered in her clipped New England, everything's-right-with-my-world intonation.

Jess looked at the receiver in her hand.

"Hello," Grace repeated, this time with a little edge to her voice.

"So solly, wlong number," Jess said in her most convincing Chinese fortune cookie accent.

She hung up the phone and took Susan home.

13

It was funny about women friends. The one subject they avoided was evaluating each other's husbands. But once the hint of divorce was mentioned, the vultures descended. They picked apart the cadaver with great gusto, and when they were through it was difficult to fathom how the wife had endured that no-good bastard all those years.

"Eliot was a pill," Carmen declared as she bit into another hors d'oeuvre.

"I never wanted to mention it," Barbara concurred. "After all, you were married to him . . . but what a stiff. I mean, Christ, Jess, the guy was an authority on everything. You deserve a medal, there's no question."

"Herb and I didn't know what to say when we saw him out at Nino's one night with some redheaded floozie," Miriam claimed.

"You actually saw him and didn't say anything to me?"

"Well, what was I going to say? Anyway, it might have been business, Herb said. Monkey business, I said."

So they hadn't told her. She was sure the others had known. They didn't seem surprised. Some great friends they were. Then again, maybe they were right not to tell her. She thought of Grace Graham.

Then it occurred to her that a lot of people in town probably knew. There goes the one whose husband screws around. She thinks she's happily married, poor girl.

"What are all these wonderful looking treats?" Miriam cooed over the hors d'oeuvres.

"Indian food," Jess responded absently.

"American?"

"Far East. For seven years all we could have were dishes Eliot's mother used to make. Anything that didn't remind my dear departed husband of his youth gave him heartburn. So now I'm branching out. This week I'm cooking nothing but Indian."

"What is it?" Barbara asked, tentatively tasting one.

"Gohbie Musallam and Aloo Dham. Eliot detested it."

Barbara tried hard to swallow the whole piece. "I just discovered Eliot's one redeeming quality."

"It's really over between you two?" Miriam asked sadly. "Such a pity."

"A pity?" Barbara looked disbelievingly at Miriam. "You just got through telling us you saw the creep at a restaurant with another woman."

"I know . . ." Miriam said reluctantly. She seemed to be taking it harder than anyone else.

"Look," Jess said, patting Miriam's chubby little hand, trying to make her feel better, "we've just spent an hour attacking Eliot and we've only scratched the surface." Then her eye was caught by the picture of the family still prominently displayed on the mantel. Half of her wanted to smash it, the other half wanted it permanently laminated. "God, I feel so disloyal."

"You'll get over that," Barbara assured her.

Was that the good news or the bad?

"But a marriage is a marriage," Miriam reminded everyone. She had the look of a minister who had finally reached the point of his sermon.

Jess was one of the parishioners who wasn't buying. "You know you're beginning to sound like my mother; she was the one who got me into this mess in the first place."

Carmen, who was thoroughly enjoying both her and Barbara's portion of Indian whatever-it-was, stopped long enough to look confused. "How so?" she asked.

Jess was getting herself into a twit now, barely able to concentrate on the question. She hated when that happened. She felt so out of control.

"Mother," she growled, contorting her face. "Boy," she declared, making the promise she knew millions had made before her but never kept, "am I ever going to be different than she was!"

Barbara gave Jess one of her perfect condescending looks. "We always repeat our parents' mistakes. It's inevitable."

Jess knew she was right. "Sometimes I hear myself saying things to Susan I vowed I'd never say. Little things, but it scares me."

Barbara gave a nod of camaraderie. "I'm the Threat and Bribery Queen of the Northeast."

Jess laughed at the irony. "I guess I'm going to have to drop the line 'Wait until your father gets home.' "

"Was your mother so terrible?" Carmen asked. She had met Jess's mother and liked her a lot.

Terrible? No, she wasn't what you could call terrible. After all, she never beat Jess. She certainly loved Jess—maybe too much: She wanted to live Jess's life for her. She wanted to make Jess's decisions. She wanted to be her girlfriend. Jess hadn't wanted that, sharing everything with her mother, but when she didn't her mother made Jess feel as though she'd rejected her. When it came down to the nitty-gritty, it was all that psychological crap her mother dished out and she accepted.

"A regulation fifties mother." Jess shrugged. "The same conditioning every girl got. Marry well, live through your husband's accomplishments."

Miriam and Barbara chimed in. They knew all the stock phrases.

"Make him rich," Barbara said.

"Or make sure he has the potential to make money," Miriam added.

"A good family," Jess mimicked.

"Someone I shouldn't be ashamed to tell my bridge club about," Barbara repeated in her best Yiddish accent.

"He should definitely be intelligent."

"A good school wouldn't hurt."

The three of them looked at each other and laughed, knowing the absolute requisite they had left out and repeated in unison, *"Jewish!"*

Somehow, Carmen was having trouble finding fault with all this. Her idea of a good day had been when she could come home and not find her mother sprawled out dead drunk in the living room and her father out of work. Psychological was a luxury she had never had time to think about. Getting through the days was what mattered. Still, she wasn't angry at her parents. She was happy she had survived it. What was the problem with these women? Too much time. Too much of everything. They didn't know what misery could be.

Maybe it was the Jewish bit. "What if the *only* person who proposed was dumb, poor, ugly, from a rotten family, had a bad temper . . . but was Jewish?" Carmen asked.

The three women theatrically mimicked the responses their parents would have given.

Miriam shrugged her shoulders. "So what's the problem? Marry him anyway."

"He'll change," Barbara said optimistically.

"You'll change," Miriam said, inevitably.

"Your children will make up for everything," Jess added philosophically.

"And so the cycle goes," declared Barbara, finally.

"Do you remember Carrie Kaplus?" Jess asked Miriam and Barbara.

"Sure," answered Miriam.

"When I was thirteen, I was in this car with Carrie and Sidney Givertz. Carrie had told Sidney, who was seventeen, that she and I were fifteen, so he fixed me up with his friend, Seymour Appleshome who, defying all odds, was even uglier than his name. I mean, his acne had warts. Anyway, we went out in Seymour's 1952 blue-and-white Buick. Carrie and I tried to look real sophisticated. You know: nylons, heels, makeup—the works. One look at Seymour and my vamp lessons went out the window. I think he felt the same way about me. We exchanged maybe five words the whole evening. We divided our time watching the drive-in movie, looking at our watches, and listening to Carrie and Sidney making out in the backseat. I didn't look, but they were petting real heavily back there."

"How did you know?" Miriam asked.

"At that age, you can *hear* buttons on blouses being opened. And I knew we hadn't brought a dog, so the panting had to be hers. Anyway, the point is I told my mother about it when I got home. She said that was the type of girl who may have plenty of dates, but definitely not the type of girl a boy would ever bring home to his family."

Barbara melodramatically grabbed her heart. "The ultimate curse: spinsterhood."

Miriam scrunched her lips and then blurted out, "I saw Carrie just the other day."

"Don't tell me. . . ."

Miriam shook her head.

"Maybe she's never met his family," Barbara interjected helpfully.

Miriam shook her head apologetically. "We had a nice talk. She's a clinical psychologist."

"Probably at a home for unwed mothers," Barbara surmised.

"At any rate," Miriam continued, ignoring Barbara, "she's happily married with four children."

Barbara had her now. "No one's happily married. It's a contradiction in terms."

Miriam looked as though she had been personally assaulted. "I am," she stated firmly.

Ah, good, time to take on Miriam. "Well, you, sweetie. . . . You still look at serving your husband a pot

roast dinner with all the fixings as a prime orgasmic experience," Barbara retorted sarcastically. Sharpen those claws.

Miriam gave her hurt-but-not-giving-up look, somewhat
akin to a cocker spaniel in heat. "Oh, you're so sophisticated," she said. "I can tell you that nothing gives me more
pleasure than seeing my Herbie looking satisfied after eating
my pot roast, potatoes, and baby peas."

"When you have to count on pot roast to satisfy a man it
means he's your husband," Barbara countered dryly.

Jess was deep in thought now. It wasn't that she hadn't
really expected Carrie to get married; she hadn't believed all
that garbage her mother had fed her. Still, somewhere in the
recesses of her mind, she had expected Carrie, who in her
high school years had gone on to become a permanent member of the football team (though not on the field), to burn
out and die by her twenties. Where had all the rules gone?
Didn't it count against you anymore that you were the
school tramp? Didn't something like that catch up with
you? Carrie had practically given out Green Stamps to any
boy in an athletic uniform. And now happily married?
Where was the justice?

"What a gyp," Jess hissed. "Carrie got to have all the fun
before she got married."

"You were a virgin?" Carmen asked, amazed.

She looked at Carmen's astonished face. Maybe she was
the odd duck after all. "It was a family tradition," Jess explained. "The day after I got married the sexual revolution
started. I guess you didn't miss it, huh?"

"In my neighborhood you weren't even born a virgin."

"I got my second proposition yesterday," Jess told Carmen, trying to win back some respect.

"It's a start," replied Carmen approvingly.

"Jewish?" asked Miriam.

Barbara gave Miriam a fish eye. "Miriam, they don't have
to be Jewish for a quickie."

"They could have a communicable disease or the big C."

Barbara heaved a deep sigh Miriam's way. "From the

dark ages, this one. You think Jewish men put on some disinfectant instead of Old Spice before they do it?"

"I'm only telling you what I read." It was a fact, no matter what Barbara said. She was almost positive she had read it somewhere.

"Did you accept, Jess?" Carmen wanted to know, thinking about what it would be like to be dating again. Maybe this time she'd marry a WASP.

"Of course not. The last one had a Ph.D. in Marxism." She decided to leave out the part about his Brillo Pad hair and pot belly.

"Pedantic and useless. That one has to be Jewish," Miriam reasoned.

"Stop with the Jewish bit already. She's only been separated for forty-two minutes and you want her married off again."

"Barbara's right. Let her have some fun, then let her get married. Why should she be any happier than the rest of us?"

The room became silent. Unhappiness and marriage—the inevitable pairing was too close to the truth.

"Believe me," said Jess, "the furthest thing from my mind is marriage. The mere thought depresses me."

"Who doesn't it?" questioned Barbara rhetorically.

"I've got to figure out what to do with my life."

The issue she had been trying to avoid for months. Sooner or later she'd have to tackle it. How long could she go on with her present life-style? Every time she thought of the future, she became physically nauseous. The Alka-Seltzer didn't help. Avoidance did.

"You could do plenty of things. You were smart in school. You got into a top college."

"Right. That way I could get a better catch. Go for my M.R.S." Jess began batting her eyes, making a fan out of her paper cocktail napkin, and talking in a coquettish manner as she fanned herself. "You're majoring in what? English? Oh, you must know so many big words. Wow."

Barbara easily picked up the tone. "And you even know what some of those big three syllable words mean? What a great lawyer or doctor you'll make."

The two women fell down on the sofa, laughing at the absurd memories.

"Remember rehashing the dates each night in the dorm?"

Barbara shook her head. "And being so glad they were over?"

"And the senior rush?" asked Jess, completely caught up in this now.

Barbara remembered only too well. "Marrying whoever you were dating when you were about to graduate."

Jess continued, "Praying he was halfway decent and you'd make the social page of the *New York Times*. And if he were really good, they'd put in your picture."

"Which was not too easy for a Jew in those days," Barbara pointed out.

"Why not?" asked Carmen.

"The *Times* thrived on lineage. Most of us were only second or third generation. The shtetel never counted for much among the *Mayflower* folk," Jess answered.

Miriam joined in. She had some memories of her own. "And don't forget the intimate wedding for two hundred of your parents' nearest and dearest friends." In her case, it had been 225 at the St. Regis. At least a hundred of them had been business associates whom she'd never heard of.

"And I was one of the lucky ones." Jess smiled wryly. "I got a *doctor*—the Jewish hero."

Carmen was outside looking in again. "Maybe it's where I come from, but somehow it doesn't sound so bad."

Jess knew Carmen had a point. "One thing I definitely don't need right now is a sense of balance. Believe me, the whole scene was crazy. We never should have ended up together. You know, I don't think we even liked each other. It was simply time to get married."

Barbara looked at her friend and knew how much she was hurting. Jess's eyes were a dead giveaway. Everyone else thought Jess was such a stoic, but they didn't know how to read her. Barbara did. She could feel Jess's pain. "They give all the wrong courses in school," said Barbara gently. "Who knows then?"

"I should have," said Jess. "We were always strangers." Her voice trailed off as it all rushed back through her mind.

When she first saw Eliot Kantor, Jess wasn't the least bit impressed. He looked like every other Jewish guy at Harvard. Well, maybe he was a little better looking: a little taller; a nicer face; a little more preppy. But there were plenty around like him. He didn't notably stand out from the crowd.

Not that there were exactly crowds of men clamoring for Jess's attention. Then again, she was rarely wanting for a date either. There wasn't an abundance of Jewish girls at Wellesley in the mid-sixties. It wasn't like Barnard, where they were coming out of the walls. And although the Harvard men could have had their choice, due in large measure to a phenomenal ratio of women to men in the Boston area, the really choosy ones only wanted to be seen with an undergrad from one of the Seven Sister schools.

In Massachusetts, that effectively narrowed the field to two women's colleges. Although Mount Holyoke was in the state, it was hardly close enough to Cambridge to be considered a realistic daily commute. Smith was slightly better, but was still a good two-hour trip. That left the two main contenders: Radcliffe and Wellesley.

The easiest choice would have been Radcliffe, but there were a myriad of problems with the Cliffies. Sheer numbers alone, about 1,400 undergraduate Radcliffe women, hardly enough to satisfy the large numbers at Harvard. In addition, most Harvard men seemed to find Radcliffe women less than breathtaking in the looks department. A fact that probably would have been overlooked had it not been for one unforgivable trait of Radcliffe women: They considered themselves intellectually superior to the Harvard boys.

And that left Wellesley. A twenty-two-minute commute by car and well worth it. A Wellesley woman was generally considered to be attractive, well-rounded, and at least somewhat deferential to a Harvard man.

For the first time in her life, Jess was in demand. She was as popular as she'd ever dreamed of being. Still, it had never been her style to go from date to date, man to man. She quickly settled on David Stone her freshman year, Peter Seltzer her sophomore year, and Dave Cooperman her junior year.

In fact, much to her amazement, Dave Cooperman lasted through the whole summer between her junior and senior years. Mainly this was because they spent the whole summer writing letters to each other: he from a kibbutz where he was farming; she from a YMHA camp where she was counseloring. When they entered their senior year, Jess began to think more seriously about Dave Cooperman.

Dave was a nice Jewish boy from an upper-middle-class family who lived in a suburb of Chicago. He was doing nicely, though not spectacularly, at Harvard and expected to enter law school in the fall. Jess's family had met Dave's family at the Yale–Harvard Football Game weekend and had gotten along pretty well. The mothers talked tentatively about the future, the fathers discussed football. All in all, it was a successful first meeting. Things seemed to be falling into place.

The best thing about Dave was that he was crazy about Jess. She appreciated his warmth, his sweetness, and his intelligence. The worst thing about Dave was that he was boring. Jess was the one who kept the conversations going. She didn't mind, really. She figured Dave would get more interesting as his life experiences expanded. Anyway, they were the same age and everyone knew girls matured earlier than boys. Jess was counting on it. And it was her senior year. On December 3, they decided they would get married after graduation.

Jess was pleased. Her future had been determined. She

looked forward to Christmas vacation when they would tell their families and start the elaborate plans for a June wedding.

On December 5, Dave picked Jess up and took her to a party his brother and a few of his friends were having. Dave's brother, Milt, was a third-year student at Harvard Medical School. It was a fun party. The punch was delicious, barely giving away how heavily it was laced with vodka and rum.

It only took two paper cups of that punch in rapid succession to make Jess the life of the party. She had never been so witty. Everything she said produced laughter. She had always had a wry sense of humor, but being the center of attention was a new phenomenon for her and she loved it.

One of her many admirers that evening was Eliot Kantor, a classmate of Milt's. He asked Jess to dance three times. But he was merely one of many so she hadn't made any special mental note about him other than that he seemed very persistent.

On December 6, Jess received flowers from Eliot. When he called to speak to her, she told him that she and Dave Cooperman were planning to announce their wedding within a few weeks.

"Good," he said, "then you're a free woman for the next two weeks."

"That's not how it works," she laughed.

But, indeed, that was how it worked.

Eliot was relentless. He sent her flowers, candy, singing telegrams. He showed up outside her classes. It was embarrassing and flattering. He assured her that all he wanted was one date. What could it hurt if she were really making the right choice (which he assured her she wasn't) by marrying Dave Cooperman?

Finally, she relented. After all, she owed it to Dave and herself to make sure nothing could threaten the strength of their relationship.

She had never met anyone like Eliot. He was intelligent,

caring, reassuring, and a fabulous kisser. He insisted that he was madly in love with her, wanted to spend every waking moment with her, couldn't bear the thought of living without her. Although his words were divinely romantic, Jess noticed that none of them were followed by a marriage proposal.

By December 21, Jess was convinced that a union between Dave and her would be catastrophic. She assured Dave it was lucky they had found out then rather than five years and two kids down the road, when divorce would be the only alternative.

Eliot was ecstatic. The only thing that marred their perfect relationship was that Jess refused to go all the way before marriage.

Eliot knew every argument in the book. None of them worked. A virgin was what Jess was going to be. They could mess around a little, a bared breast, lying in bed unclothed together, even a hand job when Eliot could no longer stand his buildup, but all the way was out of the question.

What Jess didn't know was how much this was weighing on Eliot. From the time he had entered Princeton until he had met Jess, no woman had ever been so determined that she would not give in to Eliot's sexual desires. True, some women were easier than others, some held out until the fourth date even, but none were as adamant as Jess. It was frustrating, it was maddening, it was driving him crazy. What the hell could she have in that lobster pot of hers that was so damn precious?

Eliot became obsessed. He had to have her. The more he pushed, the more distant she became. At one point she suggested that if sex was such an overriding issue to him and he couldn't respect her wishes, perhaps they should cool things down for a while. That really threw him. This bitch was going to give him up. Him, Dr.-to-be Eliot Kantor.

It was beginning to interfere with his studies. He thought of nothing but taking Jess. At one point he considered raping her, assuring himself that Jess probably unconsciously wanted him to do just that. It would be good therapy for her, just what the doctor ordered. After much consideration, he discarded the idea on the grounds it might turn out to be counterproductive.

He didn't know what to do. There was no way around it. The problem had no solution. Well, it did, of course, but he wasn't too happy about finding it. Slowly, finally, he came to the only possible answer: marry the girl.

Well, why not, he reasoned. It was time. It would make his family happy. He could raise a family and live in a beautiful home and be a nice Jewish doctor. And be with Jess, of course.

He looked at her in a different way now. She was pretty (not gorgeous, but pretty), intelligent (did better at Wellesley than he had at Princeton), good figure (no tits, though), witty (which was great at parties), and probably terrific wife material. Now her virginity took on new meaning. No one would ever have entered that honey-pot except him. It would be his exclusive possession. It gave him a surge of power.

And he guessed he loved Jess. He had certainly told her enough times. He must have meant it, even though he had said the same things to dozens of girls before her. Yeah, he loved her.

When she didn't give herself to him even after he gave her the pear-shaped, flawless, two-karat diamond engagement ring, he almost passed out. But it also reinforced his feelings. She was a woman of principles. She would be worth the wait. He had made the right decision.

They were married in June. The wedding was perfect. The announcement had made the *Times,* picture and all (Eliot's father knew a friend of a friend who had pull). Jess looked beautiful walking down the aisle.

It even surprised Eliot. He hadn't thought she was that pretty. Maybe her peanut breasts would grow, too. He could hope, anyway. They laughed, they danced, they had a wonderful time. Yeah, he definitely had made the right decision.

Eliot had to admire his own self-control that night. They arrived very late at the motel at Kennedy Airport. Their flight to Mexico was five hours away and they were both exhausted. Still, it was their wedding night and Eliot knew Jess was not about to deny him full entrance this time.

Jess went into the bathroom, emerging fifteen minutes later, looking luscious in her new peach peignoir. Eliot dug his nails into his skin and calmly suggested that perhaps they should wait until the next day when they were both well rested and could spend as much time as they needed for their first real time together. Actually, Eliot felt it was a rather magnanimous gesture on his part. Jess looked disappointed. About time, he thought.

They stayed at glorious Los Brisos in Acapulco. They shared a swimming pool with three other couples, but they had a lovely three-room bungalow, with fruit and flowers in abundance, all to themselves. It looked like paradise.

On the first evening they drove their pink jeep to an out-of-the-way restaurant where Eliot told the maître d' they wanted a romantic, but not leisurely, dinner.

As guitars serenaded, Eliot looked appreciatively at his bride. She was dressed in a delicate virginal white eyelet dress. How symbolically perfect for the night's festivities, the night of deflowering. They were back at their bungalow in under an hour, both fully anticipating the moment that had arrived.

Jess had no idea how painful the experience was going to be. She was tight, he was huge, the friction was minimal, the pleasure nil. They both chalked it up to the first time.

The week didn't produce much of an improvement. Of course Eliot never had problems coming, but he certainly couldn't arouse her. She lay there like a cadaver. He gave her strict, specific instructions about how they should be doing things and in what positions. He sensed she was trying, but not hard enough.

She wanted to come, to enjoy it, but he was so rough. Each time it started to feel good down there, he lost patience. She was afraid to tell him what to do. She'd been told how sensitive men could be about this subject and she didn't want to bruise Eliot's ego. Besides which, she had no idea what she would have told him anyway. So she lay there and wished it were over.

By the end of the week they were spending a lot of time with the other couples with whom they shared the pool. Jess felt frustrated. Eliot felt as though he'd been had.

Jess was furious at her stupidity. "Why didn't I see the signs? They were so obvious. It was good for such a short time. Did I ever tell you we made friends with three other couples on our honeymoon, spent all our time with them? *That's* telling. I never wanted to see how far apart we drifted, how we filled our time, things to divert us, friends we could talk to. Sex was a chore."

Carmen smiled broadly. "Now I'm beginning to identify."

Jess was getting angrier with each memory. "Remember how disappointed Eliot was when I gave birth to a girl? He said I'd get it right next time. I think he blamed me for the next two miscarriages, as though I had willed them. He certainly never paid much attention to Susan. Why couldn't I see all wasn't right in paradise?"

"We see what we want to see," answered Carmen soberly.

"And what we have to see in order to survive," Barbara said softly.

"I'm never getting married again," resolved Jess, fists clenched. She looked at Barbara and Carmen's skeptical faces. "Okay, so don't believe me."

But Miriam was alarmed. "Don't say that. You'll find someone else."

Jess was determined. "I don't want to find someone else. I want to find me."

"Marriage is wonderful. My Herbie is a gem."

"Some people have different needs," Jess asserted.

"Some people have lower standards," added Barbara.

"If you think marriage is such a lousy deal," Miriam said angrily, "why don't you get out of it?"

Barbara shrugged her shoulders. "Then I'd have to find something else to complain about."

Jess picked up an Indian hors d'oeuvre and popped it in her mouth. Her jaw hardened.

"Well, I've got Susan and that's enough." She put up her hand as though she were making a pledge. "This time, Mom . . . this time's for me!"

14

Jess was a born volunteer. She believed volunteerism was an absolute necessity in American society. People, especially women, worked long and hard for causes that otherwise would have gone unheeded. She was convinced that volunteers were not given their due credit. Rather than society applauding them, volunteers were depicted as Lady Bountiful: overindulged, overindulgent simpletons. She knew differently.

Jess had spent countless hours working in mental outpatient clinics; aiding the Olympic Committee; organizing neighborhood collections for cancer research; leading the voter registration drive; helping out at temple functions. Most recently she was head of the P.T.A. fund-raising committee.

Women could be bitches.

She always knew it. Still, she hadn't experienced it since the time she'd been in high school and was eased out of one of the cliques and given the cold shoulder for the remainder of her junior year. Boy, that had hurt. No one even bothered to explain why she'd been rejected.

Well, she figured those days were over. After all, she was a grown-up now. She didn't have to worry about the pettiness and insecurities of adolescence.

Wrong, wrong, wrong!

Pettiness and insecurity didn't disappear. They were camouflaged by a gold ring on the third finger of the left hand

and a mix and match house in the suburbs. Take off that ring and watch anger and fear reemerge. Welcome back bitches!

Jess had taken her wedding band off when Eliot moved out. As far as the community was concerned, that was tantamount to an engraved invitation to "come and get it." If she had any delusions that Dr. Lowell Graham was an isolated incident, they were handily dismissed on the evening of the P.T.A. fund-raiser.

Jess had been gratified by the turnout. Seventy-five couples was a major triumph. Everyone was congratulating her, the women from a distance, the men face-to-face.

"You did a bang-up job," said Craig, a man she had met casually once before.

Jess was appreciative. "Thank God everything pulled together."

If she didn't know for a fact that women couldn't fly, Jess would have bet a week's worth of groceries that Ilene, Craig's wife, had swooped down from the skies at that very moment.

"Here you are, Craig. All alone with Jess, I see," she noted in that kind of offhanded tone that fools nobody.

"We were talking about what an enormous success the evening is," he said sheepishly.

"I'm sure you were, dear," she agreed, clutching his arm, steering him away with the force of a Green Bay Packer tackle and the plastered-on Pat Nixon smile. "We ought to mingle, sweetheart. Excuse us, Jess."

"What was that all about?" asked Barbara as she handed Jess a glass of punch.

Jess was still watching Ilene and Craig. She hoped he had some Ben- Gay at home for that arm. It was going to be awfully sore in the morning. To top it off, Craig looked guilty. You didn't do anything, you idiot.

"I don't think I'm paranoid. Do you think I'm paranoid?"

"What the hell are you talking about, Jess?"

"Ilene must have been the fifth woman who clutched her

husband and dragged him away from me. What, in God's name, have I got?"

"Availability, and they're afraid it's catching."

Jess shook her head. Did these women follow their husbands to work each day? Were their marriages so fragile?

"I swear, women are their own worst enemies. I wasn't coming on to any of those men. They're all crazy."

"Just a little scared and insecure. It's that kind of world out there." She looked at Jess. "That much you should know by now."

Jess shook her head hopelessly. "What can I do? I can't go on pretending I'm just a happy homemaker minus a husband."

"Then don't. Do what you feel most comfortable doing."

But what was that? Everyone had liked her when she was a goody-two-shoes doing all the right, boring things. Jess longed to belong again, but it was getting to be impossible.

Jess's neighbors, Shep and Elinor Matthews, passed by as Jess was deep in thought.

"Hi, Jess. How's it going?" asked Shep in a friendly, neighborly way.

"Okay, I guess."

"Come along, honey. I want you to taste the punch with me." Elinor turned to Jess and said ever so sweetly, "Such a lovely evening, Jess."

Jess smiled wanly as she watched Elinor grab hold of Shep's arm and steer him away. There was going to be plenty of Ben-Gay used tomorrow.

"I am definitely not paranoid."

Barbara smiled and put her arm around Jess. "Just because you're not paranoid doesn't mean people aren't out to get you."

The fund-raiser was a service auction and it went extremely well. People were buying left and right. The only item that looked as if it was going to be a clunker was the Indian dinner party that Jess had offered to cook in her home for a group of eight. No one even opened the bidding. She was considering buying her own party.

"Two hundred dollars," came a voice from the back.

Two hundred dollars was approximately one hundred dollars more than any other dinner party had gone for, even Marlo Henderson's, and she ran a gourmet cooking class at the Adult School. So everyone knew that that was both an opening and closing bid.

"Two hundred dollars going once, two hundred dollars going twice, sold to Barbara Silver for two hundred dollars."

"And well worth it!" declared Barbara.

Jess looked back at Barbara, who was happily getting the two hundred dollars out of her wallet. They looked at each other and simply smiled.

Not all women were bitches.

Over six thousand dollars! More than enough to get the new equipment for the playground. It was time for Jess to give her summation to the gathering.

She surveyed the crowd as she waited for silence in back of the podium. She knew most of these people and they knew her. She had worked with them, partied with them, shared meaningful events. Six months ago she would have looked at this same bunch and considered them family.

But they weren't family. Few of them were even friends. Most of them she hoped she'd never see again. She couldn't understand how her misfortune had struck such terror into their hearts. Were these the same people who preached friendship, compassion, love? Were these the same people she assumed she'd spend the rest of her life with? Let's hear it for the Golden Rule.

Well, this is your swan song, she told herself. Make it short and sweet. Be gracious.

When the room finally quieted down, she began her well-rehearsed speech. "I'm grateful to see all of you here tonight in support of our new playground. It's obviously a big success and I want to thank my committee, who worked long and hard. Thank you."

She turned to leave, but her feet wouldn't obey. Leave, damn it. Get off this stage. Don't say anything you'll regret. Make a gracious exit. Now.

She turned and gazed at the crowd again. Slowly, wordlessly, she looked around the room. People stopped talking, waiting for her next words. "I have another announcement. I want to tell all of you who have indicated that since I'm separated from Eliot I'm a living threat to your happy homes, in the interest of fairness, since I really can't accommodate all of them, I've decided to give none of your husbands that lucky break in the sack with me. So rest easy, ladies, you're safe from this eager little home wrecker. Leftover brownies are selling at fifty cents for eight, proceeds to the P.T.A. lunchroom supply fund. Thank you and good night."

As Jess left the podium she saw Barbara and Carmen jump to their feet and applaud. A few others joined them, but most looked simply shocked as Jess made her exit. Jaws had dropped, eyes were popping out, throats were being cleared. Jess loved the sound of their discomfort.

Notably missing from those who applauded was Miriam. She had chosen to join the jaw droppers. Jess would never forgive Miriam for that, and added her name to a rather lengthy and growing list.

15

Jess finished doodling her fifteenth cubed box on the pad of paper in front of her, got up, and walked to the window. She felt like breaking the pencil in half but decided not to. She looked at the stubs where her long, perfectly polished nails once had been. What a disgrace. She looked at her watch again. Why wasn't today over?

"Is your husband always this late?" Jack Gillman asked.

Jack Gillman was her attorney. Jess was about to have her first meeting with Eliot since she had kicked him out nearly five months before. They were going to iron out all the details. Jess was nervous.

"He has trouble with ties. He's color-blind." Christ, she was still making excuses for him. She had to stop doing that. "I would pick them out for him every morning. I used to think it was endearing." She wanted to bite one of her nails, but realized there was nothing left to bite. Maybe she'd start in on the cuticles. "God, I'm a wreck, Jack. Isn't that crazy?"

"Don't worry. I won't let him get away with anything."

"You're a little late for that," she responded wryly. Good, at least her sense of humor hadn't completely deserted her, although most of the time it was definitely on a leave of absence.

Jess jumped when she heard the buzzer. She wondered if she was nervous breakdown material.

"Should I make *them* wait half an hour?" Jack asked, going to answer his intercom.

Jess smiled wanly and shook her head no.

"Mr. Danton and Mr. Kantor are here for their meeting with you," reported the little voice in the box.

"Send them in, Sylvia," he said and then turned to Jess. "Now, we've discussed this before. I'm here to protect you. We want the best deal we can get. This room is no place to play fair. I'll be doing most of the talking. Okay?"

"Let's just see how it plays, Jack."

"I don't like the sound of that. Trust me, will you?"

"Trust me, Jack. I've gotten to know a lot of what I need in the last five months."

"This is a very vulnerable time for you, Jess."

"I'm a lot stronger than everyone thinks," she assured him, hoping she was right.

Jess looked straight ahead when Eliot walked in with his lawyer. Then she realized that that made no sense, so she got up to greet them.

Eliot looked the same, not drawn from anguish nor thin from worrying. Damn it, he looked downright healthy. He had that happy, prosperous look. Bastard. Separation agreed with him. She should only look half that good. She wished she'd had her hair done. On second thought, let him see how lousy he made her look. He had to have at least a shred of guilt in him, though God knows if he did it was slow in surfacing.

"If you don't mind, Jack, my client would like to talk alone with his wife first."

"Is that all right with you, Jess?"

Is that all right with me? What happened to "Don't worry, I'll take care of you?" First thing off the bat you want to leave me alone with this fiend, this beast? Stay here and protect me. This is a dangerous man.

Jess shook her head yes.

They both watched as their attorneys exited. Jess sat down and stared straight ahead. Eliot said nothing. She looked at him again. Maybe he wasn't so cucumber cool after all.

He cleared his throat. "You're looking well," he said uncomfortably.

"Thank you," she responded icily. Liar. I look like hell.

"New dress?"

"It was part of my trousseau."

Eliot cleared his throat again. He wanted to make an announcement. "I've decided to come home, Jess."

Actually, the first couple of years together hadn't been all that bad. They'd had plenty of good times. Even Eliot had to admit that to himself these past few months.

They'd settled into a comfortable routine. They'd gotten familiar with each other's quirks. They'd learned to live with another person. That in itself wasn't easy, but they had mastered it.

And it was hard not to appreciate Jess's appreciation. She had so much faith in Eliot. She made him feel special and he liked that part.

She was still fun to be with and a good mother and a fairly decent cook, as long as she didn't try making those horrendous dishes she learned at the Adult School.

Even the sex had gotten better. She'd been so willing to please. Of course, the only time her breasts had been a reasonable size was during pregnancy. He kept praying they'd remain that way, but they shrank as predicted. Maybe even smaller than they originally were. Eliot knew it was unfair to blame Jess for something she had no control over, but he couldn't help resenting it. He felt cheated every time he looked at those little nuggets. Christ, it wasn't his fault he wanted more. It was a natural masculine desire.

It's true Eliot wanted a son, but there was plenty of time for that if Jess was careful the next time and didn't lose another baby. In the meantime, Susan was sweet. He genuinely loved her. He appreciated her more as she got older and became a real person. He had missed her these past months. Maybe he should have tried harder to see her. There just weren't enough hours in the day.

Jess was great. Susan was great. His home was great. Everything was great.

Why wasn't it enough? He couldn't figure it out.

"Did you hear me?" Eliot asked.

"I heard you." It was hardly what she expected him to say. Just like that, he wanted to come home. Really, Eliot?

"I said I want to come home," he announced again, this time with more of his old air of authority.

"Then you're in for a major disappointment," Jess replied evenly.

Eliot frowned. This wasn't going to be as simple as he'd thought. Eliot had envisioned Jess throwing her arms around him in gratitude. He guessed she needed to hear some reassuring words.

"All right, what do you want me to say? I'm sorry you caught me with Pamela."

Clearly the wrong reassuring words. He knew it the minute they came tumbling out of his mouth. He looked for the exit doors, expecting Jess to erupt momentarily. To his amazement, she was perfectly calm.

"Not that you *did* it, just that you were caught." She stated it, pointing out the obvious contradiction.

Look, I'm willing to come back, but I don't want to work this hard to get there. Getting me back should be enough. "What do you expect from me, anyway?"

"Less and less. But how about faithfulness?"

"In my own way I'm faithful."

"I was thinking of a more universal interpretation," Jess said dryly.

"Like what?"

"Like not making love to any other woman but me?"

"Oh," said Eliot, disappointed. "I suppose I could try that."

Eliot, you are a college graduate. You're not stupid. Some

of this must have occurred to you. "What do you think the odds are?" she asked him.

"Fifty-fifty?" he stated feebly.

Jess shook her head negatively. "Not good enough."

"Why can't you accept that no one is perfect?" he asked defensively.

"You want to lose a leg, develop a lisp, forget how to play bridge—those imperfections I can live with. You want sex with other women—that imperfection I can't live with. It's that simple."

Try another angle, Eliot. "Jess, my mother is heartbroken. I don't know what to do. She doesn't deserve this."

She doesn't deserve this? Poor her. "Why don't you move in with her, Eliot?"

"I've considered that," he said seriously, "but Pamela doesn't think it's such a good idea." Uh-oh, he felt certain that he had said the wrong thing again.

"Pamela doesn't."

Eliot looked to see what Jess had near her that was throwable. She probably brought the china with her. "I know you're not crazy about her, but I think you met her under very awkward circumstances. She actually has some great assets."

"Yes," she said sarcastically, wishing she had brought the china with her, "I saw both of them."

"It's more than that," he objected sanctimoniously.

"Nimble fingers?"

"Look, she really means nothing to me." Except for those incredible jugs of hers, of course.

"Then at least we're starting off even."

"There's no need to put yourself down."

Jess gave him a hopeless look.

Clearly this discussion was going nowhere. It was time for Eliot to take hold of the situation and become assertive.

"Jess, I'm your husband," he said in his most clipped, businesslike manner. "I want to come home."

"I'm afraid we can't always have what we want, Eliot."

Time to throw his ace of trumps. "All right, just answer me this one question," he demanded confidently, "do you still love me?" Now we can wrap this whole thing up and be home in time for dinner.

All this time and energy and history invested in this one man. Did she love him? Not an easy question. She had thought about it extensively every day since he'd left. "Not anymore," she confessed sadly.

So sure had he been of her response that it took a few minutes for her answer to sink in. "Really?"

"Really," she said flatly, and she was sure it was at least seventy-five percent true.

"You can have time to think it over," he told her, sensing a feeling of desperation overtaking his body.

"I've had plenty," she assured him.

He tried to regain his composure. "Well . . . love isn't everything."

"In our case, it isn't anything."

"With that attitude, it's no wonder I was fooling around," he asserted, feeling fully justified.

"Listen, buddy, when you fell off the welcome wagon, the answer was still yes. This is a few tumbles down the road."

Now Eliot was getting into his virtuous mode. "And another thing, you're separating me from my only child."

"Credit where credit is due. You've done an admirable job of that yourself. Five months and you haven't even come to see her. It's a disgrace."

"I meant to."

"Not that it's such a radical change for her. You barely saw her when you were home. You never even took her anywhere."

"I'm a doctor."

"Yes, I know. I saw the degrees."

"I'm a very busy man."

"Lots of undercover work?" she asked sarcastically.

"Wait just one moment here. I took Susan to the zoo once," he piously reminded her.

"And promptly lost her," she reminded him.

"Only for an hour."

"Please. If it hadn't been for that nice woman who helped you find her . . ."

"You mean Carolyn?" he said, now fondly reminiscing.

"Whoever," Jess responded and then stopped dead in her tracks. Carolyn? She looked at his face and she wanted to spit. "You son of a bitch . . . even her?"

Eliot was jarred back to the present. "It was nothing big," he tried to explain and meant it. Carolyn did have a great personality and they'd had a few laughs until he discovered she wore a padded bra. Christ, she made Jess look built.

"You have no shame. And I," she continued, realizing, "have no eyes." Her calm exterior was fading fast. "And in front of my daughter, yet!"

"We didn't do anything in front of Susan. I would never do such a thing," he asserted righteously.

"I assume you're not holding out for Father of the Year." Jess looked at Eliot, disgusted. "Let's call our lawyers back in here. We have nothing to discuss."

"What's your rush?" Eliot asked sarcastically. "Are you planning a divorce party? One of the perfect things you do?"

She looked at him curiously. "What's that supposed to mean?"

Eliot shrugged his shoulders. "Just a little joke."

"You're not capable of little jokes," Jess said, trying to figure it out.

Now it was his turn. She wasn't the only one who could turn the screws with her bitchy sarcasm. "Everyone always tells me how wonderful you are: witty, charming, intelligent, pretty. Everything you do is flawless. So what do they think of you now, failing at a marriage?"

Now she understood. "You're jealous. That's it, isn't it?"

"Don't be ridiculous."

"You can't take that. God, Eliot, after the domineering mother you had . . . you really wanted a doormat for a wife."

"You leave my mother out of this," he responded angrily.

"Do I sense a raw nerve? Because this is exactly where she belongs: in between us. One way or another you let her win."

His eyes narrowed. "She was right about you."

"Oh, really? How?"

"My mother warned me you wouldn't be supportive. All this community crap, trying to overshadow me."

"Why can't you be proud of it like I was proud of all your achievements? God knows I tried to do everything to please you. But nothing worked. You were even angry when I gave a party for you."

"Which made you look like a friggin' heroine."

"I did it for you."

"Bull roar," he shouted. "You did it to make yourself look wonderful. Poor little rich girl—cooking everything yourself. Just like the house. . . ."

He was going too fast for her now. Too many bullets at one time. "What's wrong with the house?" she asked tentatively.

Now he was on a rampage, bolstered by his own sense of the obvious. "I get you the best decorator in the area, Monsieur François Louis. Do you have any idea how hard he was to get? And then you end up decorating the whole house by yourself."

She had hated Monsieur François Louis. Even though he claimed to have just gotten off the luxury liner from his beloved Paris, she was convinced when they were introduced that he was a native of the Left Bank of Brooklyn. He had wanted everything to be done in lace, muted cerise, and green paisley. She told him she didn't want to feel as if she were living in a house that reminded her of those little paramecia in her biology class. He advised her to concentrate on recipes and shopping for clothes (he thought her taste to be on the tacky side, but diplomatically didn't mention it) and he would take care of the decorating. She politely showed Monsieur Louis and his muted paisley tie to the front door as she told him she was sure there were others who would appreciate his services more.

"Because I wanted our home to reflect us—*our* taste—not some stranger's."

"So you're gone half the time at those idiot fabric houses on the Lower East Side."

"Well, guess which incredibly hard-to-get decorator was in one of those idiot fabric houses at the same time I was—except there they called him Frank Lenkowsky?"

"And what if I needed you while you were gone or wanted to bring someone important home for dinner? How would I have reached you? Answer me that."

"When did you ever need me that you couldn't reach me, Eliot?"

"There were times," he replied with less than sure footing.

"What times?" she questioned skeptically.

"And the worst part," he said, ignoring her question, "is that it looks like we can't even afford a decorator."

"To whom?"

"To everyone."

Jess looked at him long and hard. "You've got a couple of loose marbles, Eliot."

"I work my tail off. It's not easy being a surgeon."

"I know that."

Eliot banged his fist on the table. Jess hoped he broke the new Cartier tank watch his mother had given him three months ago just "because you bring me so much joy." Funny, he hadn't minded that little surprise.

"No. No, you don't know that," he yelled. "Things don't come easily for me like they do for you. You sail through things. I fight to tread water. I still don't know how I got through med school. I live in terror I'm going to blow my next operation. But you . . . you," he continued contemptuously, "you've never failed at one bloody thing in your life."

She loved to see him lose his composure like that. It had a

calming effect on her. "As you so kindly pointed out, I've failed at us, Eliot—and I wanted so badly not to."

Eliot looked so different at that moment. She thought she was seeing him as he would probably look when he was a much older man. He looked defeated.

"Let's go home, Jess. Maybe we can work it out."

How she'd been hoping. How she'd been waiting for those words. But what was the sense now? There was nothing left to repair, nothing to build on. It was time to face facts.

She spoke softly to him now. "Eliot, I don't think we can. I don't think you even really want to, do you?"

"I don't know," he answered, his voice filled with despair.

"We each want different things. I want to be more of a person than I am. I want you to love me for that, not resent me."

"I don't know what to say," he replied weakly.

He didn't either. Was this the same man she had seen as a tower of strength; the same man who knew all the questions and had all the answers? Had she deluded herself that far? Why was it so necessary to create a perfect person fantasy out of the man you love? Did all women do this or was it just her insecure need? She had certainly chosen the wrong basket to put all her eggs in. She looked at this man she had spent seven years with. He was a stranger. She had invested all her hopes and dreams and love in this human being and she'd never really known him. At that moment, she resolved that it was one mistake she would never make again.

"Then I'll say it, Eliot. We're right to get a divorce. Eliot, don't get angry, but I'm going to go back to school."

Eliot was getting angry. "You don't have to do that. I make enough to give you alimony for the rest of your life."

"I want to work."

"You, work?" he snickered. "That's the most ludicrous idea to come down the pike since socialized medicine."

Fast recovery, Eliot. And here I thought you were heart-broken for life. "I appreciate your vote of confidence."

"Let's call a spade a spade. At Wellesley you majored in

music appreciation. The best you could do is go to a concert and applaud."

"I'll tell you what, Eliot," she responded amiably, "I'll get a useful degree this time."

He eyed her warily now. "You're not thinking of going to medical school, are you?"

"I've been accepted to law school."

"You have?" he exclaimed, amazed.

Actually, she'd been pretty amazed herself. It had all happened so suddenly.

A few weeks after Eliot had departed, she and Barbara had been sitting around discussing the futility of life. Jess hadn't dressed for days. She looked like a zombie. Barbara was getting worried.

"But what would you have done if 'Mr. Wonderful' hadn't come along?" she asked Jess.

"Married Dave Cooperman, I guess."

"No, I mean if no man had asked you, what would you have done?"

"Committed suicide," she responded simply.

"Jess, really. Wouldn't you have done something else with your life? Wasn't there a profession that appealed to you?"

"I guess I would have been a lawyer. I always had a crush on Raymond Burr and I ruled out being a crippled police chief."

"C'mon, Jess. I'm trying to be serious."

"Serious, huh? Okay, serious," she said, thinking it over. "I guess I really would have been a lawyer. Poli sci was my minor. I loved that stuff."

"Well, then, that's what you'll be."

Jess regarded her friend with admiration. "You're able to grant those kinds of wishes?"

"You're not making it easy for me to save you, you know."

"If it were easy, I would've called my sister. She would've

told me to splash on some Chanel No. 5, buy two chinchilla wraps, and call her in the morning."

"You'll take the law boards and we'll get copies of your transcript from Wellesley and you'll apply," declared Barbara excitedly.

"I can't go to law school."

"Why not?"

"Well, for one thing, I can't uproot Susan."

"You won't have to. There are plenty of good law schools within commuting distance. You'll go to one of them."

"I can't," she told Barbara, her voice shaking. "Look at me, will you? I'm a mess. I mean, for me it's a big day if I'm able to get dressed and buy three items at Shoprite. Don't you understand, I'm not functioning. I can't think of tests and applications."

"That's today. It has nothing to do with tomorrow, because each day is going to be a little bit better."

Barbara walked over to Jess and sat down beside her. Jess looked away as Barbara took her hand and talked softly.

"This is rough. We both know it's a rough time. But you're going to get through it. No, you're going to do more than get through it, you're going to come out a winner. Believe it or not, Eliot leaving may be the best thing that ever happened to you. It may not feel like it now, and it won't next week either, but eventually it will. I've been your closest friend for twenty years and I'm not going to stop now. You may hate me for a while, because I'm not going to let up on you, but someday, lady, you're going to thank me. In fact, I think you'll probably want to include me in your will."

Jess looked at her friend and felt closer to her than she had ever felt to any other human being. "I appreciate what you're trying to do, but it's just too soon."

"No, it isn't. You've mourned long enough. Sleep well tonight. Tomorrow we're going to find out when the next law board test is and call your college and make out applications and. . . ."

So it went. Barbara walked her through every step.

When Jess entered the testing room to take the law boards, she thought it must be a joke. She was still so out of it. She looked around the room. Kids. So many kids. For the first time in her life, she felt old. Why was she there? She looked at the test booklet, opened it, mechanically blackened in each correlating box. She figured that the only question she had answered correctly was her name.

When she opened the envelope from the Educational Testing Service, she considered calling them and telling them they must have made a mistake: 740. That was better than she had done on her SAT's and she was paying attention when she took them. Maybe she had a career in front of her after all.

The acceptances came in abundance: Fordham, N.Y.U., Hofstra, Rutgers, Seton Hall, Columbia, and, miracle of miracles, even Harvard. She knew she wasn't going to go to Harvard, but at least she could ram the letter down Eliot's gullet.

Barbara and Jess went out to celebrate. They drank to new everythings. Jess was beginning to think the gods were coming over to her side.

"You've really been accepted to law school?" Eliot repeated, still incredulous.

I want a picture of that expression on your face, Eliot. "All I ask is that you support me through law school and then I'll support Susan and myself from then on. It's a good deal, Eliot. I'd take it if I were you."

"You never said you wanted to be a lawyer."

"Until I became Lady Bountiful with a picnic for three, I thought I had everything I wanted. Well, in the past five months I've discovered something I never knew I had: sheer determination to make it on my own. I'll never be dependent on you or any other man again."

Eliot looked at his wife condescendingly. He thought with pleasure about the inevitable day when Jess would be on her knees, begging for another chance, assuring him she'd do anything to have him back. He wondered if he'd take pity on her and take her back. Probably, he thought. After all, he was a compassionate man.

"You may be successful in this silly community crap," he patronizingly told her, "but the real world is different. You'll never make it out there. You'll be eaten alive."

Jess got a determined look on her face. "Well, love of my life, my knight in shining armor, man of my dreams, tune in about ten years from now and we'll see if you can make that same statement again."

PART TWO

Washington D.C.

1984

16

Monica Crane opened the office door and walked in with a bunch of papers she needed signed. She knew enough not to interrupt her boss, who was deep into negotiations. The tall swivel black leather chair turned around and her boss, Jessica Simon Kantor, motioned to Monica to give her the papers she was holding. This hardly surprised Monica. She was used to Jess doing at least two things at the same time, neither less than thoroughly.

"Yes, Bill, I know you think the amendment is imperative," Jess said into the phone. "We simply need more time. Remember how you needed more time when we wanted your senator's support for the emergency water supply enactment? Look, Bill, this is an election year; we can't afford snap decisions. I know you understand politics. Uh-huh, uh-huh." Jess's eyes rolled upward as she looked at Monica and mouthed the words *horse's ass*.

Monica smiled broadly. She had grown to respect this woman more than she'd ever thought possible. After all, Monica was not used to taking orders from another woman. For most of her thirty-two years as an efficient administrative secretary she had worked solely for men. She had resisted working for Jessica at first, but Senator Ford had finally prevailed on her to do so and, within a week, she was grateful she had buckled under to his arm twisting.

Jessica had proven to be the toughest and fairest person she had ever worked for. Monica was known as the best, most industrious secretary on The Hill, but she was no match for Jess. No matter what time she left at night, Jess was still there. However early she arrived in the morning, Jess was already immersed in work. Jess never complained, never demanded, she just assumed the work she assigned would be done. Monica never disappointed her. Best of all, Jess made a point of telling Monica how much she appreciated her. That was something no man had ever taken the trouble to do. Monica began to think of herself and Jess as a team.

She looked objectively at Jess for a moment. Jess was a striking woman. True, she no longer had that fresh look she had had when she came to work for Senator Ford eight years earlier, but she was still very attractive. What she possessed now was a confident bearing, carrying herself with that air of assurance of someone in charge.

Most people on The Hill thought Jess was a cold bitch, but Monica knew that went with the "successful woman territory."

Even so, Monica sometimes wished Jess could convey a softer look about her. If only she would dress a little more femininely. Her appearance was decidedly "all business." She wore tailored suits, understated blouses, and sensible pumps. If she remembered, she put on lipstick. Her nails were clipped serviceably short with an occasional coat of clear polish. Jess wore her hair pulled back off her face. A pair of reading glasses tied to a chain hung down around her neck. Her one feminine touch was a cultured pearl necklace that her parents had given her at her Sweet Sixteen and a gold pin she had received from Senator Ford after his last election campaign. The pearl stud earrings that her daughter, Susan, had given her when she'd graduated from law school eight years earlier were never removed from her ears.

"Look, Bill," Jess continued on the phone, "if it's such a shoo-in, go ahead without us. I know it would look better with a lot of co-sponsors. I'll take it up with Senator Ford. What's your absolute deadline? Okay, I'll be back to you sometime before then. In the meantime, see if you can't come to a decision about the amendment to the Crimes Control Act. I'm confident you can have an answer for me by the time I get back to you. I know these things take time. That's what I was just saying." Jess smiled into the phone. She knew she had him just where she wanted him. "Don't be silly, logrolling went out with the Kennedy administration. See what you can do. And thanks, anyway, for the luncheon invitation, but I'd better just grab a sandwich in the office. I've got a lot to go over with Senator Ford."

Jess gave a sigh of relief as she hung up the phone. She looked unhappily at Senator Ford's office door.

"That is," she said sarcastically to Monica, "if we can ever find the Honorable Senator Ford. Any word?"

Monica shook her head negatively. "Apparently he was at the hockey game last night."

Jess gave a helpless look. "Oh, God. Drinking afterwards?"

Monica reluctantly shook her head in affirmation. "Until two in the morning at McSearley's."

"And then?"

"It's anyone's guess. I spoke to the bartender," Monica noted, proud of her amateur detective work. "He said the senator told him he was going home."

"You called his apartment, I assume?"

Monica nodded her gray head of hair. "Nothing."

Jess knew the routine by now. "We'd better get Tom to go over there and check. I have the keys. And don't forget to give Tom my little discretion lecture," she instructed, reaching for the keys in her desk and handing them to Monica.

Monica took the keys. "Will do."

Jess shook her head. "What a time for him to fall off the wagon."

"What do you suppose happened? He was doing so well."

"A campaign is coming up. You know him; he can't stand the pressure."

Monica hated to tell Jess her last bit of sleuthing information, but felt she had to. "Uh, by the way, that bartender said the senator met a woman. He says that they left together."

"A woman. Jeez, we're dead in the water. All right, let's see what we can do to locate him." She started thinking out loud now. "They'll probably get unanimous consent to rescind the order for a quorum this morning. But there's a farm subsidy vote he has to make this afternoon. He'll miss the committee meeting, but that's okay. He can make the speech tomorrow. Damn it, let's hope no one jumps the gun on this one."

"Couldn't the hearing be over today?"

The question made Jess smile for the first time that morning. "Are you kidding? As long as there's network coverage these senators will stretch it two more days, minimum. Okay, we can cover the senator's appointments, except he should be here to see Curtis Randall at four. He's a hefty contributor."

Monica was taking notes as Jess talked. "What about the ladies from the League of Women Voters? They've called three times to make sure he'll be at their luncheon."

"I'll take that one. We must have ten old speeches on file. If not, I can wing it. What's on for tonight?"

Monica looked at the appointment schedule that she carefully made out each night before she left. "Embassy reception," she answered.

One more embassy reception. Boring, boring, boring. "I guess I can cover that," she said, perfunctorily looking at her appointment book. "Oops. I have to pick up Susan at seven. No good. Oh, well, these embassy affairs are massive. They'll never miss him." Monica nodded as Jess looked up. "How would you like to go to an embassy reception?"

"Me?" Monica asked like an excited schoolgirl. All these years working on The Hill and she'd never attended even one embassy function. It was one of the perks she'd always wanted but never been offered, and her sense of decorum wouldn't permit her to mention it.

"Why not?" Jess answered. Had she ever been excited like that about Washington parties? It was hard to remember. "Okay, let's get moving."

Monica finished a few notes before heading toward the door. Jess looked at the piles of work on her desk and wished they would just disappear. She'd try to catch up on the weekend. She knew she didn't have to read all this material, but she was always afraid she'd be asked a question she didn't know the answer to. Better overinformed than under, she figured. No doubt about it, she had gotten downright compulsive through the years. Selling herself short again. Not compulsive, competent. Well, compulsively competent.

Why did she have these arguments with herself all the time? She was a successful, highly respected legislative assistant in one of the toughest towns for a woman to make it. Why did she have to analyze it? Why couldn't she just be proud of who she was without affixing a negative trait to it? Work is the answer. Submerge yourself in work. Don't get sidetracked by the whys in life. Just keep working.

She was still deep in thought when the door opened and Senator Ford entered, singing with gusto, "Love Is a Many-Splendoured Thing." He smiled broadly at Monica and Jess and said in that melodious bass voice of his that was worth at least an extra ten percent of the vote each election, "Good morning, ladies. And a lovely morning at that." He strode past them, humming, into his office and closed the door.

"I believe our esteemed senator has arrived," Jess said sarcastically to Monica.

But the senator didn't feel like he sounded. He felt like hell. He caught a glimpse of himself in the mirror and objectively appraised his appearance. There was no doubt about it, he definitely looked like shit. Not quite the dapper young man he used to be, the man who was called a younger version of Tyrone Power. Well, hell, everyone got older. He looked closer at his face. Damn, not even the distinguished-man-getting-on-in-years anymore. The best he could hope for was to be described as a man who looked like he had lived life to its fullest—which was no lie. He just wished he could remember half of the women with whom he had lived it. They all came together in his mind and formed one gigantic blur.

It hadn't always been that way. He was the man who had it all. Raised by very wealthy blue-blooded parents, he possessed the best of everything. Not that a lot wasn't expected of him and his brother, but that didn't matter because neither he nor his older brother, Harriman, seemed to know how not to succeed. They were two years apart, but they could have been twins. Both graduated valedictorian from Choate; both graduated tenth in their class from Princeton; both graduated cum laude from Harvard Law; both excelled at tennis; both were outrageously handsome and both of them knew it. They dated every good-looking woman who crossed their paths, often merely flipping a coin to see who would pursue their newest conquest. Life was so simple for them, they didn't know that they should be grateful for what they had. They just assumed it would always be that way. But, of course, it wasn't.

When Harriman was thirty-four he decided he wanted to run for political office. This was the first time the brothers were not in total accord. For the life of him, Sam couldn't understand why Harriman would want to subject himself to that kind of existence. Wasn't their life a good one, Sam had argued? They had nice wives, homes, a booming law practice. They had time for tennis, for vacations, for fun on the side. They weren't cut out for politics, they were cut out for sipping margaritas on the beaches of the South of France.

But Harriman persisted. He wanted to be known for more in life than winning a summary judgment for the fat cats and a superior backhand. He wanted his two small sons to be proud of who he was. He wanted to leave a legacy in the world. He wanted to help the have-nots. Actually, this surprised Sam. Of course, they were both nominal liberals—they found pleasure in going against fashion—and they were the only two in their crowd who had ever had the audacity to declare themselves Democrats. But Sam had never taken it too seriously. After all, *they* were two of those fat cats. They were the haves. Why work against yourself?

It wasn't until Harriman had been a congressman for two terms that Sam admitted his brother was right. When Sam went campaigning with Harriman he saw poverty that he never realized existed. He began to see the injustice of a system that would spend billions on defense and a pittance on education, medical research, decaying cities, ecology, the elderly. Although he never mirrored his brother's fervor, he eventually shared his beliefs. Now, he confided to Harriman, he was relieved that one of them fought for the right things so the other didn't have to feel guilty that he still had a superior backhand.

In four years Harriman built an incredible reputation for himself in Washington. No congressman had ever worked as diligently as Harriman. He assumed he had to work hard because he was determined to right every wrong, and he knew he only had about forty more years in Congress to do it. As it turned out, he was thirty-nine years short.

When Sam learned that Harriman had terminal cancer, his first reaction was total denial. Maybe it was a virus or the tests were inaccurate or the doctor was incompetent. No one could look at the incomparable Harriman Houston Ford III and think he was anything but a perfectly healthy specimen.

By three months after the initial diagnosis, Sam was only praying that his brother would hang on at least another three. One glance at Harriman and Sam knew this was just another one of his prayers that was not going to be answered. So much for God.

Sam stayed with Harriman day and night until the end. There was nothing Sam could deny Harriman in life, and he certainly wasn't about to do so in death. Still, he was hoping Harriman wouldn't ask him to do the one thing he desperately didn't want to do. But, of course, he did. And Sam consented. Yes, if the governor asked, he would accept the appointment to finish out his brother's term in Congress. And yes, he would continue to run for public office, even the Senate if asked, and fight the fights Harriman had begun. He couldn't promise he would be anywhere near as brilliant a congressman as Harriman, but the Ford legacy would go on as Harriman had wished. Sam promised the same thing from day until night until the last minute when Harriman died, grasping Sam's hand as though he could pass his life to Sam.

Within three years Senator Samuel Grant Ford had lost his brother, his backhand, and his sobriety. He did indeed become a senator in meteoric time. And he had a good reputation, though nothing that approached his brother's. He tried, but his heart wasn't in it. He voted the way his brother would have voted on all the crucial issues. He never failed to get at least a ninety-four rating from the Americans for Democratic Action and no higher than a ten rating from the Americans for Conservative Action. He introduced some reasonably good bills, depending on how innovative his staff was at the time, but his follow-through was, at best, lacking.

The one thing Sam managed to excel at was knowing which of his constituents to be especially attentive to. This was an ability Harriman had never mastered. His blacks and whites had been clearly defined. He worked on one maxim: Do what's right. Sam, on the other hand, was more comfortable in a world of grays. He was pragmatic. He would do or say whatever was needed to get the job done. And that quality, he found, was one that got a politician loyal friends and ensured reelection.

And at least he was not a drop-down-drunk alcoholic; just a heavy drinker who could pretty much hold it—except, of course, when he couldn't. About two years before he was approaching his second reelection campaign to the Senate, it became obvious that his drinking was winning. The rest of his life had fallen apart, including his marriage, which was still intact but only legally. Since he had long ago given up any sense of hope, this final decay neither surprised nor upset him.

True, he still had plenty of people who were willing to support him, plenty of interest groups who knew he was an easy mark for their causes, so his reelection was something they wanted. On the other hand, news of his lack of sobriety was reaching the state and he anticipated an uphill battle. In truth, he wasn't eager for a battle at all; he still longed for a life of leisurely drinks on glorious beaches. If only he could shake Harriman's ghost, it would have been easy. But at this point in his life, he needed more of a reason than Harriman's ghost to keep him going.

A year and a half before his reelection, that reason arrived in his office. Her name was Jessica Kantor.

Sam looked in the mirror again. Okay, so his face had a few bags. Maybe it was puffy. The white hair saved him, he figured. Jeez, his head hurt. The pounding alone would have driven any sane man crazy. Christ, Jess would be in any second. How was he going to explain this? He felt like a little boy who was waiting in his room for the inevitable spanking. Maybe he could outsmart her. Fat chance, he thought.

Jess opened the door and entered. Without looking at her, he knew she had that disapproving look. Okay, he thought, we'll play this one as though nothing happened. We'll play this one cheery. What can she do, anyway? She was a woman twenty-two years his junior and she worked for him, didn't she? So what was the big deal? He looked at her face again. God, he hated her disapproval.

"I have a few matters to discuss with you, Senator," Jess said in a clipped tone.

Senator Ford was still looking in the mirror as he asked casually, "How do you think I'd look with a mustache?"

"Suspicious."

"You don't think it would look distinguished? Distinguished is very appealing to the public, you know."

She knew the game. The man was buying time. "Half the people vote for an incumbent because they recognize him," she answered him patiently. "This is no time to confuse them with a distinguished mustache."

"Whatever you say, Chief. You know you're in charge," he said in his sweetest, most ingratiating manner. Maybe she wasn't going to come down on him after all.

"Am I? Well, this chief had a hard time reaching you. Where were you?"

Appeal to her romantic nature. She had to have one somewhere inside her. "Jess, I met a woman. A wonderful woman. A beautiful woman—inside and out. We had a terrific evening. I feel alive. Really alive."

Trouble. "Were you seen?" Jess asked. "I mean, should we expect to see anything about this in the press?"

"We were very discreet," he assured her proudly.

"Good," Jess sighed, relieved. "A low profile would help at a time like this."

What better time for the announcement? "We're going to get married, Jess. It'll be a media event—a United States Senator getting married at the same time he's running for reelection. It sort of has a Camelot quality to it, don't you think? Like Prince Charles and Lady Di."

"Far be it from me to puncture any balloons, but you might recall that Prince Charles wasn't married with three children when he married Lady Di."

"You mean Marge and the kids?" he asked, disappointed. Actually, he saw so little of them he felt divorced. Christ, he must have had a lot more to drink than he thought.

"Perhaps only a small detail, but I think it does have some significance."

"I see your point," he agreed. "That is a bit of a problem."

"Not a minor one." Where was he going with all this? He was far from a stupid man. This had to be one of his diversionary tactics. But from what? Maybe he just needed some understanding. "Senator . . . Sam . . . you've been in love at least half a dozen times since I've known you."

"This one's different. You'd love her."

"Do I know her? Does she work on The Hill?"

"Uh . . . she used to," Sam replied, looking at his wing-tipped shoes.

"Doing what?" she asked suspiciously.

"I suppose you could call it community work," he answered in a meek, hedging tone.

"What kind of community work?" she asked, trying to figure out what he could be hiding.

You'd better get it all out on the table. "She's an ex-hooker."

"Oh, my God."

"But she's reformed," he added quickly. "She's a manicurist now. Maybe the press won't ask."

Jess shook her head. "I think I just heard all your *Mayflower* ancestors turn in their Puritan graves."

"The hell with my ancestors," he said in his best orator's voice. "I'll fight for my right to the pursuit of happiness."

"You'd better save those speeches, Senator. You're going to need them."

"This is the real thing," Sam replied defensively. "I can feel it in my gut."

"This is no time for a gut reaction. If it's the real thing, it'll last until after the election."

"Are you telling me to drop her?" he asked indignantly.

"I'm merely suggesting a temporary course of action."

"All right," he acquiesced, handing her a piece of paper. "This is her address. Send her some nice flowers and tell her I can't see her for a while."

So that was it. He wanted Jess to direct him to end the relationship. It was her fault, not his. Well, she was used to the role, though she didn't enjoy it. Men never grew up. She looked at Sam now. He was holding his head in pain, obviously paying for the night before. He looked so vulnerable, she wanted to hold him and tell him everything would be all right. But she knew coddling him was the worst thing she could do.

"Being a senator is more trouble than it's worth," he whispered, trying for sympathy. "I think I've got an itsy-bitsy hangover."

"Whatever happened to those meetings at A.A.?" Jess asked, knowing it was a lost cause.

"I was afraid I'd be recognized," Sam replied nobly. "You don't want me to jeopardize my election chances, do you?" He gave her his helpless look again. "You don't suppose I could get a Bloody Mary? Hair of the dog and all that."

"Two aspirins, Sam," Jess replied as she walked to get them from the medicine cabinet in his adjoining private bathroom. "Works wonders."

"Just a small one," he begged plaintively. "I'll get one anyway."

"Not with my help," Jess responded firmly, handing him two Tylenols and a glass of water. "Now take these."

He gulped them down obediently and said, "I thought when my mother died, I was finally free of a woman telling me what to do."

"And I thought I'd never have a little boy—so we were both wrong."

They smiled at each other fondly, knowing they had just defined a major part of their relationship.

Jess took the glass from Sam and handed him the papers she had brought in with her. Back to business. "We've got a big day in front of us. I don't suppose you read any of the material I gave you last night."

"What material?" he asked blankly.

Jess shook her head. "You're impossible. Look, we're going to win this election in spite of you."

"So you can be senator for another six years?"

It was too close to the truth and they both knew it.

At first Jess seemed like every other fresh-out-of-law-school assistant who had worked in his office, but within weeks he realized there was a discernible difference. This one worked as though what she was doing mattered. She put in long hours without any expectations of recognition. She simply had a job to do. But that wasn't enough to make her stand out to him. The crucial element was how she made him feel.

Jessica gave him a sense of worth. She did the impossible: She made him believe in himself again. He was able to give up drinking for close to a year, and in that time Jess made him become the type of senator that even he was proud to be. He gave memorable speeches; he introduced important bills; he traveled on fact-finding missions; he initiated investigations into corruption; he championed worthy causes; he became, as Jessica called him, a mensch.

For no apparent reason, toward the end of his election campaign, he began to fall apart again. He started to drink, didn't show up for meetings, forgot speeches. It lasted a month. Jess got him to therapy and spent days on end thrashing it all out. Of course, Sam knew what was wrong. His success was getting to him. Things were looking too good. He didn't deserve it.

In the end, when there was only a month left to go until the election, he shaped up. Which is not to say that he became a full-time, great senator. In the five years that followed he was still a better senator than he had been before, but not without his ups and downs. His swings were pronounced. Still, there was Jess and she managed to keep him in tow.

"Believe it or not," Jess informed him, "this is a very important day for you. You've got a confirmation hearing this morning. One in which you are extremely interested."

"Whose?" he asked, showing at least a little interest.

"James Farland. He's the president's designated nominee for attorney general."

"I know who he is. I read the paper."

"That's a good sign."

"You really think I'm a dunderhead, don't you?"

"No, I think *you* think you're a dunderhead. If I thought that, I would have left years ago. But we can discuss it some other time. Right now, I want you to look at these papers and familiarize yourself with these facts so you can be credibly outraged at the hearing."

Senator Ford scanned the page, taking it all in, shaking his head in amazement at what he was reading.

"This is incredible," he said when he was finished. "How much of this are we sure of?"

"Seventy-five percent verified, twenty-five percent bluff. Enough to nail him."

Senator Ford was getting very interested now. "Was any of this in the press?"

Jess shook her head no. "You've uncovered this scandal all by yourself."

"Good for me. How did I do it?"

Jess smiled at him. "You're brilliant . . . and you have a diligent, competent staff. So play it to the hilt as only the incomparable Senator Samuel Grant Ford can."

Sam looked at her appreciatively. "Jess, sometimes you have even me believing I can do this job."

"Stay sober and away from women and you can."

She smiled confidently at him and turned toward the door. It was at moments like these that Sam was positive Jess was the reincarnation of Harriman.

Thank God he had shown up, Jess thought as she closed the door behind her. If she could keep him believing in himself, at least through the hearing, she knew he would be terrific. The trick was getting Senator Ford to believe in himself for at least three consecutive hours. Well, maybe the momentum would keep him going.

Peter Wilkes was sitting in her office with that familiar half-worried, half-smug look on his face.

"Well? Will he be able to carry it off?" he asked, sounding more concerned than she'd heard him in a while.

"We'll see," she answered noncommittally.

"Is he at least sober?"

"As sober as a judge."

"That doesn't count for much," countered Peter, sensing he could relax.

"How did you get so cynical, Peter?"

Peter smiled wryly as he lit his eighteenth low-tar, low-nicotine filtered cigarette of the morning. "You mustn't confuse cynicism with realism. I've been in Washington for fifteen years. You've only been here eight."

Well, maybe he was entitled after all. Fifteen years on The Hill was no picnic, that was for sure. And he was one hell of a press assistant, as he so often reminded her. But she didn't have to take his word for it. He was as good as he bragged he was. She just hated feeding his ego.

Peter had been with Senator Ford for only six months when she had arrived. It was well known around The Hill that anyone who worked for Ford could consider it a vacation. The turnover in the office was legendary. If you wanted to make a name for yourself, you didn't work for Ford for very long. But Peter, who had already built quite a reputation as one of the top press assistants around, felt he needed a vacation with pay. His lover in his previous office had just dumped him for some young twit who worked in the mailroom, of all places. Peter needed time to regroup. The Ford job was perfect. He assumed he would stay a year.

But then Jessica came and the whole office turned around. All of a sudden, he was working in a highly organized, efficient office for a top senator performing an incredibly demanding job. His friends congratulated him on his foresight and gave him a big chunk of the credit, which he readily accepted, even though he knew the turnaround had little to do with him.

The real dividend was that it took his mind off his misery. In fact, his job became exciting and, for politics, almost fun. Peter attributed this to Jess, the first woman he had ever learned to love—not in the biblical sense, of course, but as a friend and colleague. He adored bantering with her and often found that the highlight of his day was giving her a hard time. The times he appreciated most—and he could count them on his right hand—were when he got the better of her.

"Do you have the press releases ready?" Jess asked him.

"I am the best press assistant on The Hill," he responded.

"That wasn't the question," Jess said, sarcastically. "We both know what you think of you."

But Peter was enthralled with the thought that had just popped into his head. "And you're the best A.A. If I weren't gay, we could have made some team. And yes, the releases are ready and they're top-notch, as usual."

Jess smiled slyly. "Good, because we're going to blow the roof off that hearing."

17

When a Senate hearing had complete media coverage, it reminded Jess of a fox hunt. The hunters were poised and ready. The dogs were let loose. What remained to be seen was who the fox turned out to be. That was at the beginning of the hearing, anyway. By now, everyone was getting bored.

Most of the people who worked on The Hill knew Jess by sight. At the very least, they knew her by reputation. She knew she was viewed as tough and cold and had done little to dispel that perception. In fact, she had grown to like it.

Observing the group in the room, she once again was taken by how young they were. She had faced the fact that most aides were in their twenties and on their way to more lucrative careers. She often thought how crazy it was that the laws of the land were determined by kids fresh from college or law school on their way to jobs that would buy them the American Dream.

Then, of course, there were the old-timers—those who were committed to their work and could make do on not being all that well off. Jessica was one of them. The pay wasn't too bad for a single woman with one child to support. The compensation she had was the one she'd grown to appreciate the most: power.

This was certainly one of those gentlemanly hearings: the senator from Mississippi had all but served mint juleps to the witness; the senator from Illinois couldn't have been gentler in his probe about a restricted club the witness had

once belonged to; the senator from Delaware wanted to
know if the witness believed in the death penalty, but appeared perfectly content with an "I'm still weighing the pros
and cons of that issue." Quite frankly, if Jess didn't know
that the witness was about to be removed from his chaise
longue and put in the hot seat, she would have left long ago.

She looked carefully at the witness: James R. Farland. He
was a smoothy, all right. From the newspapers she knew he
was fifty-four, but he could easily pass for mid-forties. Here
was a man who had taken good care of himself. Jess wondered how many times a week he worked out. At least four,
she surmised, judging by the perfectly lean, muscular body
he appeared to have under that no less than five-hundred-
dollar Brooks Brothers suit he was wearing. There was nothing flashy about him, just understated, well-heeled. The gray
at his temples added the perfect touch of distinguished. Central casting couldn't have done better.

What Jess especially liked about Farland was his voice.
The way he carried himself was wonderful, too, of course.
He had the unmistakable bearing of self-confidence. But that
voice. It had two incredible elements: the resonance and the
reassurance of Walter Cronkite. Who wouldn't want this
man as attorney general? Indeed, who wouldn't want this
man as a father? Or lover, she smiled to herself.

Once again she observed, though was not surprised by,
how easily people were taken in by facade. Even she felt a
tinge of disappointment that Farland wasn't all he seemed.
But she knew that if all went as planned, within the hour
this perfectly suntanned, gorgeous specimen of a man would
have a career that was in the toilet.

Senator Randolph of Alabama, the committee chairman,
was smiling fondly at the witness. "Mr. Farland," Senator
Randolph said in his most ingratiating Southern drawl, "I
know the committee has enjoyed hearing testimony from a
man as distinguished as yourself and I, for one, am looking
forward with great anticipation to your work as what I am

positive will be one of the most inspired attorney general-ships this great country of ours has ever witnessed."

Mr. Farland gave one of his beneficent, reassuring smiles as he took off his designer horn-rimmed glasses, which he used only for reading. "Thank you for your vote of confidence, Mr. Chairman. I assure you I shall do my utmost to ensure your trust is not mischanneled."

A feeling of well-being seemed to encircle the room. Jess half-expected little people with harps to enter and a section of the audience to rise and break into a chorus of "Hallelujah."

"Before we adjourn, are there any more questions from the committee?" Senator Randolph asked perfunctorily.

"I believe I have a few," Senator Ford noted.

All eyes were now on Senator Ford. An election year, most people in the room assumed when they heard him talk, he probably just wants some free publicity.

A number of heads turned to look at Jess. As his top adviser it would be natural for her to be sitting up there behind him. Many aides did that. They supplied the senators with added documentation or advice when they needed it. Jess always thought that looked like the senator was being fed the material without knowing it on his own. Furthermore, she was too closely aligned with her particular senator and his detractors had suggested more than once, as indeed Senator Ford had that morning, that *she* was the real senator.

Senator Ford, when he was in control, showed what Jess considered signs of greatness. She had talked with him for the last hour going over everything, making sure he knew all the facts verbatim. She walked him through every possible scenario. He had the whole thing down pat—in the office, anyway. It was a calculated risk, but she was going to remain on the sidelines for now. If he completely lost control of the confrontation, she would go through the door in back, sit down beside him, and calm him down. As long as he could see her, Sam would be okay. She positioned herself so that he could and gave a fast prayer to God that he'd get it all right.

"The chair recognizes the senior senator from Pennsylvania."

"Thank you, Mr. Chairman, and good morning, Mr. Farland. I'm afraid I have not personally been able to welcome you today," he smiled graciously.

"Senator Ford, it's an honor to meet you," responded Farland, just as graciously. There was enough charm between the two of them for a whole Miss America contest.

"A shared honor, I assure you. I have a few brief questions to ask if you don't mind."

"But, of course," Farland responded.

All right, Sam, you're doing it just right, Jess thought. You're a pro. Nice and easy.

Senator Ford smiled and talked in a friendly, yet businesslike manner. "As we've established, you are the senior partner of the law firm of Farland, McGraw, and Cummis. That's quite an illustrious, busy law firm. I'd imagine it's pretty difficult to keep on top of all the goings-on at an establishment as large as that."

"To the contrary, Senator, I make it a point to keep on top of everything that goes on in my law firm," Farland answered proudly. "You might say it's one of my idiosyncrasies."

Senator Ford looked duly impressed. "That's to be commended. I assume then that you are aware of all your major clients?"

"And, I must admit, even the minor ones."

The friendly smile vanished from Senator Ford's face as he became all business. "Mr. Farland, is it not a fact that one of your major clients is Cosco, Inc.?"

Farland's easygoing manner disappeared as he straightened himself erectly in his seat. "Yes," he answered tenuously.

"And," the senator further probed, "you are no doubt

aware that a controlling interest in Cosco, Inc., is owned by Empto Investments, Inc."

A cloud seemed to come over Farland's face as he fidgeted with his pencil, still trying to sound like the self-assured gentleman he had been not three minutes earlier. "I don't believe so, though I don't specifically remember."

Let him stop, thought Farland. I hate this son of a bitch. He's incompetent. He's a has-been. I'm on my way to the top. Damn it. Make him stop.

But Ford had no intention of stopping now. This was his chance, too, and he could smell success when it was this close. One look at Farland's face told him he was only a few questions away. The room had become silent now. Everyone was paying close attention to the exchange.

"And are you aware, Mr. Farland, that a controlling interest in Empto International, Inc., is owned by one Joseph V. Bianco?"

Farland unconsciously took out his handkerchief and wiped the sweat from his forehead. He took a large gulp of water from the glass in front of him. He had no doubt where the questioning was going, but he was going to hold on as long as he could. "No, I don't know if that is so, Senator."

"You say you don't know whether or not that is the case?" Senator Ford asked incredulously.

"No, Senator, I am not aware of that."

"A man with your professed idiosyncrasy of knowing every minute detail about your firm and you still insist you don't know who owns the controlling interest of one of your major clients? Is that what you're telling this committee, Mr. Farland?"

There was dead silence as Farland considered how to handle this bastard.

"Do you know who Joseph V. Bianco is, Mr. Farland?"

"I have heard of him," Farland answered coldly.

"But you have not met him, sir?"

"I might have met him. I meet many people. I'm somewhat of a public figure. I can hardly be expected to remember every Tom, Dick, and Harry who introduces himself to me."

"Of course. So just for some background information, I want you to know that Mr. Bianco is a known organized crime figure who has been convicted of racketeering and mail fraud and, therefore, is a convicted felon. Are you at least aware of that, Mr. Farland?"

"I believe I've seen it mentioned in the newspapers." He was not about to commit himself to more than that.

"But you are not personally acquainted with Mr. Bianco, is that correct?"

"To the best of my recollection, that is correct, Senator."

"I see," said Senator Ford. He knew he had Farland right where he wanted him. He handled his papers, but never removed his eyes from Farland's face as he prepared to continue the probe. It seemed like an endless amount of time, yet no one in the room moved a centimeter. Senator Ford began speaking in a slow, measured tone, building to a crescendo. "Is it not a fact that your relationship dates back to 1965 when you represented Mr. Bianco in several corporate transactions, and that you now have a profit-sharing interest in many of Mr. Bianco's holdings?"

Farland was extremely careful with the wording of his response. "I own no interest in any of Mr. Bianco's companies."

"But," countered the senator pointedly, "is it not a fact that the interest is now held in your wife's name and that that interest was transferred not ten months ago?"

No response.

The senator continued. "And specifically, Mr. Farland, you must be aware that Empto International, Inc., is currently under federal indictment for unlawful cream skimming practices—a case for which you in your designated position as attorney general would have direct responsibility."

Farland sat erect and answered with all the sanctimonious

dignity he could muster. "If that were the case, I would, as a matter of course, disqualify myself."

Senator Ford's eyebrows lifted as he made his next point. "But did you not, as a business counsel to Empto International, Inc., participate in and have direct financial interest in the criminal activities charged in that indictment?"

Farland's attorney, who was sitting next to him, immediately pulled his arm for a conference. They quickly exchanged words, none of which appeared to please either of them.

Farland looked up, his eyes narrowing on the supposedly harmless senator who had just smashed his chances for the new position he had coveted more than any other in his life. He hated this man who had become his adversary. Some day, he vowed, he would get back at him for this. "On advice of counsel, I decline to answer that question."

The quiet of the room a minute before transformed into pandemonium. Pictures were snapped, phones were rushed for.

"I have no further questions at present, Mr. Chairman," Senator Ford announced with decorum.

Senator Ford started to gather his papers as he snuck a look at Jess, looking for approval. Jess gave him an "I knew you could do it" smile as she made an "O" with her index finger and thumb. It was enough of a reward for him. Maybe she was right after all. He straightened his new silk tie and stood tall as the reporters encircled him.

Jess caught a glimpse of Farland trying to make a hasty retreat from the room, being hounded by reporters.

Peter, as always, appeared at exactly the right moment. "Circulate the press releases," she instructed him.

Even Peter looked awed. "Unbelievable," he said with renewed respect as he moved out to distribute the releases.

Harry Reevers, a seasoned reporter with UPI, came up to Jess. He had known her ever since she had joined Ford's staff and his admiration for her never diminished. "So you did it again, huh, Jess?"

Jess gave him a stony look. Ford had been on the wrong end of Reevers's stories one time too many for Jess to ever trust this man. She corrected him in a businesslike manner. "You mean Senator Ford did it again."

Reevers chuckled skeptically. "Yeah, right."

Reevers walked off to make his calls, leaving Jess standing in the background of the committee hearing room. History had just been made because of her backbreaking, tedious investigation. She smiled proudly to herself as she had never smiled when she was a housewife back in New Jersey.

18

Jess was giving instructions as Monica, following Jess into her office, jotted down every word she was saying. It had been a long day for both of them, but only Monica showed any signs of strain. Occasionally, when she thought no one was looking, she would rub her sleepy eyes. Since the committee hearing on Farland, they had been working an eighty-hour week, and with the senatorial primary in the not-too-distant future, she knew things weren't going to get any easier.

"And," Jess continued, "send thank-you notes to all the contributors. Anything over a hundred dollars needs a special little note written by the senator. Let's not use the robo machine," Jess instructed, referring to the electric machine every office had, which was programmed to sign its senator's signature so the constituent would think they'd gotten a personal letter. "Who in the office is our best forger of his signature?"

"I believe I hold the title," Peter answered with a Cheshire cat grin. He was sitting in Jessica's chair behind her desk.

"Put a meaningful, sincere message on all of them and don't forget to mention that you're counting on their continued support in the upcoming election," she directed Peter. "Thanks, Monica," she said, an expression of concern on her face when she realized how exhausted Monica looked.

"Why don't you go home early? You've really been working hard."

Monica appreciated being singled out like that. "We all have. You just never show it."

"The lady thrives on it," Peter noted, nodding at Jess. "The only thing that makes her tired is inactivity."

The triumvirate gave each other knowing smiles as Monica turned and exited, hoping she would be home in time to watch "Dallas."

Jess turned to look at Peter. He had become noticeably more egotistical since his handling of the Farland press coverage. He had done a great job, there was no denying that. They had hit every minor and major publication she cared about plus major network news with follow-ups and editorials. Jess knew that even though the story was undeniably newsworthy, Peter had masterfully milked it for all that was humanly possible. He was good, but boy, was he showing signs that he knew it. Jess could handle him, of course, but he could be one royal pain in the ass when he got like this.

"Sitting in my chair again?" Jess observed dryly. "Into upward mobility, are you?"

Peter got up dramatically and brushed off Jessica's seat with one of his royal flourishes. "Excuse me, your highness."

Jess nodded as she sat down in her chair. "Once a princess, always a princess."

"Catch *Time* magazine?" he asked.

She had, naturally. She hadn't missed an edition since she was thirteen and got hooked on their "People" section. However, she didn't want to swell his head any more than it already was, so she decided to play it down.

"I assume we made it?"

"Picture and all. You've got to admit, we've gotten phenomenal mileage out of that hearing."

"Just a senator doing his job," Jess responded innocently.

Peter was loving every minute of it—that was clear—and so, Jess had to confess, was she.

Peter threw his head back gleefully. "I've never seen a presidential nomination withdrawn faster."

Jess agreed. "My favorite dish: presidential face with egg on it."

"I'm sure it's just a coincidence that we've suddenly received so many contributions to the illustrious senator's upcoming campaign," he remarked wryly. He loved playing these games with Jess, especially when they were on a roll.

"Don't you just adore bandwagon jumpers?" Jess smiled, rubbing her hands together deviously.

"Why do you remind me of a cat who's just eaten a canary?"

"Peter, I have to share a secret with you: I love winning."

"And you said you'd been so content being a suburban housewife."

"Somehow this beats eliminating wax buildup."

"So, what about this weekend?" Peter asked, ready to tackle another nonstop schedule. "More work, work, work, I assume."

"Not for me. Susan and I are flying the coop."

"Out of town?" She nodded yes. "Going where?"

"My father's wedding."

Peter gave a look of mock horror. "You mean all these years you were a. . . ."

"I've been called worse."

"Wait a second. Run this by me again. I thought your father and mother were married."

"They were. Then they weren't. C'mon, Peter, I know you're not that slow. It's called divorce."

"And I thought your parents were," he said poetically, "the sure sweet cement of glue and love."

She smiled. Even she had to admit it was ironic. "It's funny, I never thought my dad would have the guts to leave. I mean, I knew he was miserable, but I thought he felt that went with the territory."

"Apparently a man of wisdom."

"So one day he came home and handed my mother this

box from Tiffany's and said, 'Estelle, for forty-three years you've told me all you needed to make you happy was a diamond and emerald ring. Here it is. The best money can buy. Now you have everything. I'm packed and leaving tonight.' And that's exactly what he did." The whole event was still unreal to Jess.

"Good grief, what did your mother do?"

It had been a rough period for everyone in the family. It was only recently that Jess could bring herself to discuss the whole situation openly. In fact, as she started talking she realized that except for a brief explanation to her present lover, Clayton, and a somewhat lengthy conversation with Barbara, Peter was the first person she had told. "The first week my mother was in shock; the second week, denial; the third week she hired a detective who discovered nothing; weeks four through nine she blamed everyone from the town librarian, who must have given my father evil books to read, to our local druggist, who must have dispensed mind-altering drugs. After that, she settled into her present state of total bitterness."

"How long has it been?"

"About two years, I guess."

"And now he's getting married?"

"To a thirty-five-year-old woman."

"Younger than you," Peter reminded her in his bitchiest voice.

"Unfortunately, Peter, lots of people fall into that category."

Peter wasn't letting up. "You don't mind what he did?"

She was still having a little trouble with that question in her own mind, but it was getting easier. "At first I was angry. I'm not all that partial to men who walk out on their wives." Understatement of the year. "It was so typically male. But he's my father, I love him, and I've never heard him so happy." Her answer sounded mechanical.

"Still, to a thirty-five-year-old woman. That's some age difference. It could be dangerous, you know."

The same thought had crossed her mind many times. "He's kept himself in shape. I'm not worried." She was damn worried.

"So did Rockefeller," Peter pointed out. "How's your poor mother taking the wedding stuff?"

"She got a dart board with my father's face on it. She couldn't get the voodoo doll in time."

"She doesn't mind your going to the wedding?"

Jessica sighed. "What do you think? I'm thirty-eight and she still has a way of saying 'How are you?' that makes me feel guilty."

Peter looked amazed. "You? Ms. Hard-as-Rocks, Nerves-of-Steel?"

"You go figure it out." She knew she couldn't and she wasn't going to pay some shrink eighty-five dollars an hour to do it for her. She had tried that for six sessions before determining that her shrink thought she was just another bored rich professional with too much time on her hands. She wasn't sure he was wrong, but why the hell should the louse take her money if he thought that? Jess had ended their last session with an undeniably hostile act. Seeing that her shrink was balancing his checkbook as she was pouring out her guts to him, she got up, took the flowers out of the Steuben vase on his perfectly neat desk (she had never trusted anyone with a neat desk, anyway), and poured the water over his head. After his head, the water spilled over to the cancelled checks, which had been written in Flair-tipped ink and thus became totally blurred. She told him he must be a genius because that was the best she'd felt in months, turned on her heels, and triumphantly left his office. She never received a bill for that last visit, which annoyed her. She had a whole letter composed in her head if he sent her one. She looked at Peter now. "Certainly you didn't escape that whole guilt syndrome."

Peter smiled at the possibility. "That's right, you've never met my family, have you? They're a dream. You'd just adore them," his voice was dripping with sarcasm. "My father's your typical beer-drinking construction worker. He was ever so pleased to find out his only son was gay instead of the football hero he'd been programming me to be. And my mother was delighted when she caught me dressing in drag. I told her she'd double her wardrobe. It turns out we're the same size—at least she was the last time they invited me over. It's been almost eight years now." He shook his head ironically. Jess thought he had never looked like such a fragile little boy to her. She could feel his pain. She started to reach out to him, but she knew he would interpret that as sympathy and so she simply shook her head understandingly.

The buzzer rang, indicating a call for Jess. They both looked relieved as she went to answer it.

"How's Susan taking all this?" Peter asked, trying to regain his composure.

"You know Susan. She's a love. She can handle anything." Jess picked up the phone and said in a businesslike manner, "Jessica Kantor." Her voice softened, but only a little. "Hello, Clayton. How nice of you to call. Yes, I saw *Time* magazine. In fact, that wunderkind of our media control is in the office with me as we speak. Clayton says you did a great job, Peter. Actually, Clayton, we're trying to cut down on positive reinforcement for Peter. It goes to his head too easily."

"Tell him thanks," Peter said.

"I think you've humbled him, Clayton. He almost seems grateful for the praise." Jess motioned Peter to leave the room, but he didn't move an inch. "I'm sorry. I'm going to miss it, too, Clayton. Give the ambassador my regrets. I'm sure you'll do just fine without me."

She listened as Clayton Amory told her for the thousandth time how invaluable she was to him as a hostess. She could just see him sitting in his huge mahogany office talking into his speaker phone. He was undoubtedly wearing one of his specially designed-for-him thousand-dollar three-piece suits, holding his most recently acquired onyx pipe, which had been filled with his newest exotic blend of tobacco. All of these he could easily afford since he was the head partner in one of Washington's most prestigious law firms and also came from a family of substantial wealth. He had been in and out of different presidential cabinet posts whenever the whim hit him.

In the past two years, Clayton had been Jessica's. She entertained for him at his home and went to the various parties he was invited to. He was bright, urbane, occasionally even witty. In his way, he was in love with Jessica. There was only one quality about her that irritated him: her unavailability. There were too many times that Jess simply refused to accompany him somewhere because she had work or had to be with Susan. Still, it never irritated him enough to sever their liaison. He knew Jessica was an asset. He enjoyed her company. Occasionally he even mentioned marriage, but he sensed it would never happen. Jess had made it clear from the start that marriage for her was out of the question. By now Clayton knew Jess was not someone who changed her mind. It both annoyed and relieved him. It was a little late in his life to be changing life-styles, anyway. He was willing to accept whatever Jessica was willing to give him.

"Thank you, Clayton, I will. You have a good weekend, too." She hung up the phone.

"Clayton's not going with you?" Peter asked, amazed.

"Certainly not."

He had to admire her. "How do you get away with it, Jess? You've dated some of the most eligible, powerful men in this city—what I'd do for your rejects—and still you call all the shots."

Jess shrugged her shoulders. "I'm not vague about my terms in a relationship. Susan and my career are my priorities. Once burnt is enough for me, thank you."

"All men are alike?"

This was one subject she was very clear about. Her jaw became more determined as she talked. "Scrape away the layers, the core is the same. I'll never expose myself to that pain again. It was a long road back for me."

For all she had sworn off men when she and Eliot split for good, Jess still had a lingering fantasy that some prince on a white steed would spot her unloading her Shoprite groceries, fall madly in love, scoop her up, and gallop back to his castle (anywhere on Park Avenue was also acceptable).

Happily-ever-after conditioning, she realized, was hard to break.

And then there was her mother. Estelle Simon was determined to find the perfect or at least sort of perfect man for her younger daughter. Mrs. Simon had a religious mission now. Nothing could divert her. Jess didn't have the strength to fight this battle. She relented.

The first man she dated was described by her mother as a sweet guy. When Jess met him she understood why he had received only one adjective. Billy Kaufman made Woody Allen look like a sex symbol: five feet two inches tall, Billy sniffed antihistamines all night and begged Jess to join him in his sexual fantasy of wearing Pampers and sleeping together in a giant crib.

"You're so particular," Mrs. Simon complained. "Not everyone can look like Cary Grant."

"Mother, I don't think it's unreasonable to want to date someone who doesn't make me gag each time I look at him."

Mrs. Simon gave a deep sigh. "I'll keep trying," she assured her daughter. "Remember, second time around you can't be too fussy."

In retrospect, Billy may have been one of the better ones Mrs. Simon came up with.

Except for Rich Seagal. Rich was a dentist ("Almost as good as an M.D.," Mrs. Simon pointed out), intelligent, reasonably good-looking, with a pleasant sense of humor.

And Jess was vulnerable.

It was the summer before she started law school. Rich

was impressed that she was doing something with her life. He admired women who were more than housewives, and he was very attracted to Jess. Grateful to feel desired, Jess eagerly gravitated to Rich. They saw each other constantly.

The sex, though hardly inspired, was at least passable.

Barbara warned Jess that it was too soon to fall into another relationship. Mrs. Simon, on the other hand, did everything but handstands to encourage the match.

As the summer was drawing to an end, Rich was becoming less and less enthusiastic about Jess going to law school.

"He thinks I won't have enough time for him," Jess explained to Barbara. "He's talking marriage."

"What do you think?"

"I'm not sure."

"I don't think you're in any position to judge your emotions right now."

"But what if he's my last chance?"

"Jess, you keep trapping yourself. What happened to 'I want to be my own person, make it on my own, never count on a man again'?"

"I lied."

"Do you love him?"

"Sort of. I don't know. Love grows . . . it'll come."

"Jessica!"

Jess decided not to tell Barbara when she wrote her letter of withdrawal from N.Y.U. Law School. She was licking the stamp when the doorbell rang.

As it turned out, Rich Seagal was indeed marriage material. Who would know better than Mrs. Rich Seagal? She wanted to meet Rich's latest fling and ask if Jess couldn't find someone who wasn't married—specifically someone other than her husband? Jess didn't know what to say, her eyes were glued to Mrs. Seagal's eight-month pregnant stomach. She finally told Mrs. Seagal not to worry about her anymore. Everything was about to become past tense.

Jess took out the envelope she had almost mailed to N.Y.U. and heaved a sigh of relief.

"Are all men schmucks or is it just that I have a talent for attracting them?" she asked Barbara.

"A little of both."

"You know what it is, Barbara? I still haven't stopped hoping I'll find a man to protect me, even though I know he'll disappoint me."

"Maybe there's one out there."

"My only chance is to learn to take care of myself, not hope some man will."

"You're starting a new life."

Barbara was just trying to be encouraging, but Jess knew it was more than talk. Two men, two strikes. All they cared about were themselves. Well, fuck them. Her life really was in front of her as long as she avoided the Cinderella trap.

"I bet you'll be different," Barbara added.

Jess's eyes were ice cold as she nodded at Barbara. "Count on it."

19

Mixed emotions. That's what Jess had everytime she left Washington. Freedom from the incessant pressure. Guilt because she wasn't working. Fear that she wasn't really indispensable.

She looked over at her daughter next to her in the front seat and felt a sense of calm. There was no doubt about it, Jess was crazy about her. The divorce had brought them even closer than they'd been before. They depended on each other. In the beginning, when the going was rough for Jess, Susan had almost become the mother: telling Jess everything would be okay; advising her what to wear; assuring her she'd be just fine on those first agonizing dates. Jess had to laugh at it, a five-year-old mother, but that was what Susan had become. As time passed, and it was clear that Jess really was going to be okay, Susan relaxed and once again became the child.

Jess looked at her precious daughter and prayed she hadn't scarred her. She knew it was a senseless wish, since no child grew up untouched by her parents' peculiar craziness. No, Susan would be neurotic—no one ever got off scott free. What she really hoped for was that Susan would be happy with herself, content with who she was.

Certainly if looks were the determinant in life, her daughter held all the aces. At fifteen, she had nearly finished the awkward period of adolescence: the orthodontist had given her perfectly straight teeth after two years of a tin grin; her complexion, which had occasional "zits," as Susan had called them everytime a minor bump appeared and she had gone into her semi-hysterical routine, had been zitless for almost half a year, her figure had maintained its lithe, slim shape unlike most of her friends, who had begun to show signs of plumpness; her natural blond hair, though not the flaxen it had once been, maintained some blond strands through the brown; her nose, it turned out, had remained perfectly straight; her face was heart-shaped; her eyes, big, blue, and sparkling. She was truly an American beauty.

The odd part was that she didn't seem to know it. As pretty as she was, Susan was convinced she was ugly. When she had first cried at age eleven because she thought she was hopelessly "disgusting looking," Jess hadn't taken it very seriously. She thought Susan was just fishing for a compliment. As the years progressed, however, it became clear that Susan truly believed she was unattractive. This upset Jess, mainly because she was afraid it was attached to Susan having a bad self-image. Upon questioning a psychologist, she was assured that everyone went through these self-doubts, and that Susan simply would have to outgrow them. Patience, he had advised. When Susan's braces came off, Jess took her to Bloomingdale's and got her an outfit of her choice, treated her to a makeover, and waited while she got her hair permed like all her friends. After the package was complete, she asked Susan how she thought she looked. The most Susan would admit to was "better."

Thinking back, Jess remembered that she had felt pretty much the same way Susan did. It wasn't until she was finishing high school that she had any sense of herself being attractive. Sixteen, maybe. Yes, she was sure it was when she was sixteen, because Billy Levin was coming to take her out to dinner to celebrate passing his driver's test on his seventeenth birthday. It was an uncommonly hot day for the first day of spring; Jess had heard that a new record high was being set. She loved to be part of historical days like that, even if it was historical only because of the weather. She had put on a pale blue sundress with spaghetti straps and a matching little jacket. She was sitting in front of Carol's mirror, the one with all the little lights around it. She had flipped the mirror to the magnified side so she could examine every detail as she put on the finishing touches of the eyeshadow Barbara had lent her. Teasing her hair to its finishing point, she picked up the hair spray and pushed down the nozzle. As she heard the whish of the spray, she looked at the reflection in the mirror. She stopped spraying and put down the can, looking somewhat disbelievingly at what she saw. The girl in the mirror was pretty. That was she. She was a pretty girl. She looked at different angles of her face and then got up to look at herself in the long mirror attached to the front of the closet door. It confirmed what she had just seen. Well, I'll be darned, she thought. From that moment on, her posture, which her mother had always told her was slouched, became perfectly erect. The recognition didn't change Jess's life, it simply made her feel better about herself.

Jess looked over at Susan again. Maybe the same thing would happen to her. One day she would simply come to the realization that she was pretty. Jess considered getting Susan the same type of magnifying mirror, but ruled it out. Knowing Susan, she would probably find five new zits no one else could see.

Susan was giggling while telling Jess a story about school. Jess tried to follow every detail, but never could. The constant couple swapping amazed her—it was like musical chairs—especially Susan. She never kept a boyfriend for very long. Jess had wondered about that, but then chalked it up to Susan's feelings about her looks. Actually, it was fine with Jess if Susan didn't date at fifteen. She didn't much care for Susan getting involved with some boy, catering to his needs.

"It was totally gross," said Susan, holding her heart for dramatic emphasis. "Boys are such duds."

Jess nodded knowingly. This was hardly news to her. "Wait until you see how they grow up."

"Why is that, why are men such creeps, I mean?" Susan asked seriously.

Jess smiled at Susan's intensity and answered lightly, "Must be in their genes." Then she smiled slyly. "They do have certain redeeming qualities."

"Speaking of duds, how's Clayton?"

"As men go, he's pretty interesting."

"Does he ever smile?" Susan asked facetiously.

"Maybe in the privacy of his own house."

"Y'know, Mom, all the men you date are like that."

"I guess I just appreciate serious men."

"Thank God you never get serious about serious men." She stretched her long legs out at the same time she noticed her mother's passive look. She hated that look. It didn't give a clue to what her mother was thinking. "You don't get serious, do you?"

"No."

Susan gave a sigh of relief. "Good. Ellen Hanning has five fathers so far." Jess laughed at that, but Susan was serious again. "Do you know that only two kids in my class don't have divorced parents?"

"That's quite a commentary on American society."

"Actually, I think we're above the national average."

"It is a progressive school."

"Well, as for me, I like us just the way we are."

She squeezed her daughter's hand. "Me, too, sweetie."

Jess looked around her mother's kitchen. It was now done in a splash of soft pink, lavender, and lime green. Mrs. Simon had redecorated her kitchen twice in the past two years, which was one less time than she had redecorated her living room. When her husband left her, she decided she would redo everything in her life—and her husband would damn well have to pay for it. Better that he spend his money on what had once been their happy home than on whatever new bimbo he might eventually find to lavish it on.

Predictably, Mr. Simon never complained about the expenses, so Estelle once again felt frustrated by her husband. Still, her home was certainly something straight out of the pages of *House Beautiful.*

Jess was sitting at her mother's table just as she had over ten years before. It was a rare occurrence these days, what with her hectic life in Washington. Jess tried to remember how they had looked back then. Had they changed? That was vanity for you, she thought. Of course they'd changed.

Her mother had taken off weight. That was the one tangible advantage of divorce: Women got thinner. But her mother looked a little too thin. Maybe she ought to mention that to her. The ultimate Jewish compliment to a woman who'd previously been on the chubby side: "Darling, you look emaciated. I hope it's nothing serious. Have you considered seeing a specialist?" On second thought, maybe she shouldn't say anything. Maybe she would just casually mention to her mother that she was wearing a little too much makeup and her skirts were a trifle short for a grandmother of three. No, she's feeling the need to look young, to seem attractive. Stay out of it. If you don't tell her what's wrong with her, maybe she won't tell you what's wrong with you. Fat chance!

Jess was looking at the album of pictures of Carol's fortieth birthday party, which her mother had just handed to her. It had been quite an event. Carol had almost killed her husband when he ran the surprise catered affair at the Club for three hundred of their nearest and dearest friends. Had she not just had a fresh manicure that day, Carol probably would have clawed her sweet hubby's eyes out. He knew how she felt about the age bit. She told everyone how much she despised parties announcing one's age. Jessica had wondered if perhaps that weren't one of Carol's husband's few hostile acts since they'd gotten married. Certainly the only one he'd ever had the nerve to act out and be able to get away with in glory. But what did it matter? Carol looked thirty. Perfectly coiffed, designer dressed, perennially tan. There was something to be said for skin treatments, not to mention the face lifts. And boy, was she slim. Jess knew Carol worked out every day (often in the bed of one of her exercise instructors), but she wondered if Carol ever ate. Besides coffee and Diet Coke, she couldn't remember ever seeing Carol actually swallow anything. Maybe she was anorexic. No, enough of this cattiness. Her beautiful older sister was still her beautiful older sister. At least she was still making it all work for her.

Time hadn't been as gentle to Jess. It wasn't that she really looked older than her thirty-eight years, but that was due to hereditary luck. She came from a line of women who didn't wrinkle or get gray young. Still, there was no denying that she had lost the softness she'd once had. The naivete, the freshness. Not only in her looks, but in her whole demeanor. Now she was all business, which was just fine with her. It felt good to be in charge of her own life. And when she needed that softness—with her daughter, with those who mattered—she could recapture the quality. Well, almost, anyway.

Mrs. Simon gave Susan one more fast hug before she scooped up half a dozen of the fresh-from-the-oven chocolate chip cookies she had just baked, put them on a dinner plate so they wouldn't stick to each other, poured a glass of milk into a lavender, pink, and lime green tumbler, and proudly handed them to Susan.

"Mmm, these smell great, Grandma."

"I baked them just for you, my sweet," she told Susan, slipping another cookie in the empty space where Susan had just removed one.

"Yumm," mumbled Susan with her mouth full of chocolate and vanilla warmth. "Thanks, they're super."

"That's why God made grandmothers, my pet. It's the least I can do. After all, I see you so infrequently. You try to convince your mommy to come more often. Your grandma will make anything your little heart desires."

"Okay," chirped Susan. "I'm gonna go watch one of the soaps."

Jess looked disapprovingly at her daughter. "Oh, Susan, do you really have to?"

"It's vacation, Mom. See ya," she said breezily as she made her exit.

"Be careful of the crumbs, my precious," Mrs. Simon yelled after her. "I'm amazed how much she's grown," remarked Mrs. Simon, inserting one of her not-too-subtle verbal knives.

"Mother, we saw you three months ago," Jess pointed out.

"Four months, two weeks, and three days," Mrs. Simon corrected her.

"Lost track of the hours, huh? We call every week," Jess rebutted.

Deep sigh. "It's not the same, dear. You'll see soon enough. Thank God Carol is around."

Don't get defensive. "Mother, I keep telling you, senators only work in Washington," Jess said defensively.

"Sweetheart, I'm happy you're a success. I tell everyone how important you are. I only wish," Mrs. Simon continued, "that you could be a success a little closer to home. It's not such a crime, especially at a time like this."

Use the Parent Effectiveness Training techniques you learned when Susan was young. It works with every age group. "You must be feeling very upset."

Understatement of the decade. *"Upset?* Why should I be upset? My devoted husband of forty-three years has become Peter Pan. Tomorrow, the Casanova of the geriatric set is marrying the next Bo Derek . . . a perfect ten: body and I.Q. The woman who showed him devotion and love for forty-three years has merely been discarded."

"I know it's not easy for you," Jess commiserated.

"God knows I tried. I gave him the best years of my life."

Mrs. Simon was revved up now, ready for her final summation. "I gave my ninety percent. He didn't give his ten." She gave a martyred sigh. "But—water over the dam. I probably won't live much longer anyway. Somehow, I'll get through tomorrow. At least Carol will be with me."

Horray for Carol: the perfect daughter. Guess you didn't notice she's anorexic and sleeps around, huh? Christ, you're thinking like a jealous sister again. You're a grown-up, remember? Stop it. Change the topic. Be more positive. "Mother, you've got to start making another life for yourself."

"What kind of a life? I'm sixty-three years old. We're not talking about some spring chicken here."

"You talk as if your life's over. It's not. Believe me, I know, life does go on."

"I'm not young like you were when you got divorced. At least that bum, Eliot, had the decency to leave you when you were still in the prime of your life."

"You're still in the prime of your life," Jess objected.

"The only prime in my life is the lamb chops the butcher gives me. What does it matter? I'll probably be dead next year. Ten more points to my blood pressure and I'm a goner. If not that, then something else."

Jess had learned not to take this seriously. Her mother had thought she was contracting one incurable disease after another since menopause. Give her a chipped fingernail, she'd turn it into undiagnosed cancer. "Mother, you're not going to die. You should keep yourself busy. It'll make you feel healthier. There are plenty of things you can do. You ought to find a new career."

Mrs. Simon started to gather together the three cookie crumbs Susan had dropped near the sink. "What would you suggest, dear? You think I should try neurosurgery, maybe? Do people mind if their surgeon has arthritis?"

Jess looked compassionately at her mother. Let's face it, it wasn't easy. She knew that firsthand. "Mother, I know you're still hurt and angry."

"Angry, I'm not angry. I want to kill the selfish son of a bitch!"

Jess looked at her mother and they both broke into laughter. She walked over and put her arms around her mother. They stood there embracing for what seemed a long time. Jess felt closer to her mother at that moment than she had in years. She wished her mother didn't have to hurt. She wished she could protect everyone she loved.

Mrs. Simon looked at her younger daughter, calm now. "You're really going to the wedding?" she asked in a last ditch effort.

"He's my father."

"That much I knew."

"I love both of you."

Mrs. Simon knew how to accept the inevitable. She nodded her head as though she understood, though she really didn't. "Then would you give him a present I made for him?"

"Of course."

"It's a cake," Mrs. Simon told her sweetly. "Make sure you hand it to him before it stops ticking."

They both looked at each other, laughed, and for the second time in two minutes hugged each other tightly. They were undeniably connected.

20

Jess had been parked in her shiny new blue Camaro outside Barbara's house for almost five minutes now. She made no effort to open the car door. She seemed glued to her seat.

When Barbara called Jess on the phone half an hour after she arrived at her mother's house, Jess was delighted. After all, besides being her closest friend when they were growing up, Barbara had stuck by Jess in that rough period over ten years ago. Had it not been for her, Jess probably wouldn't have gone to law school. In many ways, Barbara had saved her life.

Jess made numerous friends at law school and in her consciousness-raising group, women with whom she shared a common cause. The relationships had the fierce quality of those participating in a united struggle. Jess found the oneness of purpose they shared extremely seductive. They lived and breathed the same commitments and anger. For a pivotal point in her life men had been the common enemy, and release from and triumph over "the enemy's oppression" was the goal. It was, if nothing else, a totally serious period for Jess. It gave her direction and there was no room for outsiders. After all, anyone not involved in that struggle couldn't really understand.

So, for a while, she became less tied into Barbara emotionally. They began seeing each other more and more infrequently. Barbara simply chalked it up to a necessary evolution in her friend's life. She knew it was a healthy transition and so she never took it personally. Jess didn't realize what was happening to their relationship until she was halfway through her second year at law school: That was when John Rand entered her life.

John Rand was a successful stockbroker. As far as she could tell from the two hours she spent sitting next to him at Felicia Nash's dinner party, he had it all: he was uncommonly brilliant (just ask him); outrageously wealthy (he just happened to mention those little oil wells in Oklahoma his daddy drilled for a hobby); exceedingly well traveled (he'd been to every major tourist haven with the exception of Sri Lanka, which was on his itinerary for the following summer); and an expert at sports (he casually referred to the year he was an alternate on the Olympic Ski Team). The singular attribute he didn't have to state was how gorgeous he was: That fact was self-evident.

Jess wanted him.

She told her friends that John had a wonderful mind and was good company. Melody Welsch, one of Jess's more militant friends, reminded Jess what slime men were, and that if she played the game, she'd better be willing to suffer the consequences. Jess nodded her sophisticated head and told her not to worry.

Screw John's 156 I.Q., Mercedes 500 SEL, accommodating personality. What Jess really wanted was a shot at that irresistible body of his. She'd been without a good lay for long enough.

How could she be so shallow? she kept asking herself. How could principles be sidelined for physical desires? She needed to talk it out. But with whom?

Barbara was the only logical choice. She could tell Barbara anything. But, she hadn't kept up much of a relationship for the past year. How could she explain that?

As it turned out, she never had to. When Barbara heard her voice on the other end of the line, she simply asked, "Okay, what's up? The shrink's right here."

Jess heaved a sigh of relief and unloaded everything.

Barbara walked her through another crucial phase of her life, giving Jess the courage to do what she wanted: enjoy her first, though hardly her last, purely physical relationship. It wasn't that Barbara told Jess she was right all the time, far from it, but when push came to shove, when the going got rough, she knew Barbara would always be in her corner.

And when John turned out to be a wimp, completely dominated by his anti-Semitic father, Jess thanked God she had not allowed herself to fall in love with him. She was finally learning how to survive relationships. In the end, it was easier for Jess to take the breakup for two reasons: she was getting measurably stronger, more certain of who she was and what men weren't; and Barbara made herself available, waiting up for Jess's two A.M. calls, willing to listen and, when needed, advise.

As far as Jess was concerned, there could never be a friend as unique and giving as Barbara.

When Jess moved to Washington, she made a conscious effort to keep up the friendship. It was not always easy now that she was part of a man's world, where feelings and emotions were not given primary consideration. She was aware that her public persona was one tough cookie, and it was not an image she desired to alter. She just knew she had to work at not having that iciness spill over into her personal relationships.

Jess had readily accepted Barbara's invitation for lunch the next day. Had she known that Carmen and Miriam were also going to be there, she might have thought up an excuse, but Barbara hadn't told her that until the end of the conversation so there was no way she could renege.

It would be interesting to see Carmen again. They had always had a fondness for each other. They had kept in touch sporadically, mainly through Carmen's Christmas letters, which were chock-full of all that information about how beautifully the kids were doing in school, the rapid advancements hubby made at work, how nicely they were fixing up their house, and how many blue ribbons the newest pup had won at kennel shows. Actually, Jess enjoyed reading these letters, never failing to send baby gifts whenever a new addition was announced.

Miriam was another matter. In the best of times, Jess had been ambivalent about her. There were periods when Miriam was the salt of the earth, and periods she was so annoying Jess couldn't bear her. Jess had never forgiven Miriam for being so unsupportive after Eliot left. The P.T.A. fundraiser loomed large in her mind. Jess could still see Miriam sitting there, mouth open, hands in lap. Miriam had never called Jess after that incident. It was as though Jess ceased to exist.

Years later, Miriam was in Washington, D.C., with her family and stopped at Senator Ford's office demanding to see her very dearest friend, Jess. Miriam couldn't have been friendlier, hugging Jess, talking as though they had always been the closest of buddies. Eventually she got around to her true reason for visiting: the free passes and senatorial courtesies Jess could arrange. She told her family that even though she'd been told it was impossible to get into the special White House tour, she was confident Jess could arrange it. It was what they called chutzpah in the old country.

Jess felt her hand start to open the car door and she slowly got out, closed the door, automatically locking it as she had trained herself to do in Washington, and walked up the cobblestone path, mounted the five deep stairs, and tenuously rang the bell.

Barbara quickly opened the door, greeting Jess with her warm, vibrant smile. They hugged and giggled and hugged again.

"You look wonderful," Jess told her genuinely. Barbara was dressed in jeans and a sweater, her hair in a ponytail. Jess had never seen her look more content.

"Clean living," Barbara quipped.

They walked into the living room where Carmen was already sitting. Jess was surprised by how different Carmen looked. Her hair was perfectly coiffed, she was dressed in a fashionable mauve tweed suit complete with an elegant pink silk blouse and matching mauve suede shoes. Although Jess was no expert, she estimated the outfit to have cost at least six hundred dollars. Carmen wore touches of very fine gold jewelry. In appearance, anyway, this was certainly not the Carmen of years ago, but she was every bit as friendly as Jess remembered. She hugged Jess warmly and the two of them exchanged the usual pleasantries about how well the other looked.

"Strawberry daiquiri okay?" Barbara asked Jess, holding up a pitcher of the already mixed drinks.

Jess hated strawberry daiquiris. "Sounds great," she responded.

"How long has it been since the four of us have gotten together?" Carmen asked, trying to pinpoint the exact event.

"Almost eleven years. My fault," Jess admitted, more than willing to accept the blame. She sipped the drink Barbara had given her. Yuck, she hated these women's drinks.

Barbara shrugged her shoulders as the doorbell rang. "We've all gone our separate ways." She got up to answer the door and then gave Jess a sly look. "Exactly when was the last time you saw Miriam?" Jess couldn't remember anytime after that Washington experience four years ago. "You're in for a shock." Barbara said it in a way that made Jess wish she were making a speech to the Veterans of Foreign Wars about the necessity of cutting out all military aid rather than being in this room.

"I'm in for a shock from Miriam, the original Sadie Married Lady?"

"You'll see," smiled Carmen. They both looked a little too smug for Jessica's liking.

"No big surprises, please," she yelled after Barbara, who

was already out of the room on her way to the door. Jess turned to Carmen. "She is still married to Herb, isn't she?"

"They're in total harmony and the same space."

"What does that mean?"

Before she had a chance to answer, Miriam entered in a flourish. At least Jess assumed it was Miriam. It was hard to tell, she looked so different. Before Jess stood a thirty-eight-year-old flower child. She was dressed in a multicolored skirt, sandals, and a poncho. Around her neck hung a huge peace necklace, surrounded by a lei of fresh carnations. Her hair, streaked in various shades including one red and one green, seemed to have a mind of its own. Her long, dangling earrings were made of shells and her sunglasses were tinted a deep pink. Jess tried to assess what she was seeing as Miriam ran up and threw her arms around her.

"Jess, boobie, you look wonderful," Miriam enthused.

"And you, Miriam, you look . . ." Jess was desperately going through her list of acceptable adjectives, "indescribable." She breathed a sigh of relief. "How are you?" she quickly asked, trying to escape any more physical descriptions.

It didn't take much to get Miriam going. "I'm in a state of karma. Of course, I'm always growing and changing, but lately my inner self is one with the cosmos."

Miriam looked at Jess as though expecting some sort of approval. A comment, at the very least. "Miriam," was the best Jess could say. "Gee, Miriam."

"And how about you?" Miriam asked sweetly. "Still in D.C. exploiting the poor, furthering tokenism on a power trip?"

Jess looked at a perfectly serious Miriam and had to laugh. "That's not precisely my job description."

Barbara sighed as she considered emptying the pitcher of daiquiris on Miriam's head. "You agreed not to make any of those endearing value judgments of yours today," she reminded Miriam. "Doesn't Jess look great?" Barbara asked, hoping it would be considered a rhetorical question.

Carmen sipped her drink and nodded. "It's being in your thirties. The twenties are definitely overrated."

"Drink, Miriam? I've got fabulous strawberry daiquiris."

Miriam made a face at the mere suggestion. "Have you got any freshly squeezed carrot and celery juice?"

Barbara snapped her fingers as though bitterly disappointed. "Oh, shit, I'm fresh out."

Miriam looked displeased, but not surprised. "I don't get off on putting carcinogens into my body. Veggies are an A Priority. Everything has to be natural. Feed your soul, not your body. How about you, Jess?"

"Make mine a double this time," Jess instructed Barbara as she handed her her completely emptied daiquiri glass. Jess looked at Miriam, who had blossomed into a size eighteen, minimum, and decided not to pursue a body beautiful conversation. "So, Carmen, how many kids do you have now? I remember sending at least two more baby gifts."

"You know Danny."

"He's still heavy into the macho bit in our Western culture," Miriam tried to explain helpfully.

"Not anymore. After we had our seventh child, Danny lost his job so I started a small real estate agency."

"Which is now a *big* real estate agency," Barbara emphasized.

"A modest success," said Carmen.

"The only thing modest about it is her modesty," Barbara insisted. Jess appreciated that in Barbara. If she was your friend, she was your biggest booster. It was a rare quality.

Jess turned to Carmen. "Danny must be proud of your success."

"It's a mixed bag, actually. He's at home now with seven kids between the ages of four and sixteen. His cooking is great, his cleaning is getting better, his kiddy patience level could stand some improvement. He's a true house-husband. It exhausts him. Guess who has the headache at bedtime these days?"

"You're happy, though? You look radiant."

"The role reversal suits me just fine."

Miriam's eyes lit up again in confirmation. "There was always too much sex role stereotyping. There are absolutely no more absolutes anymore."

"Not true. You still absolutely give me a headache."

Miriam shook her head. "Barbara, you ought to learn to cope with this latent hostility."

"I never thought it was latent."

"I worry about you, Barbara. You're using up too much negative energy."

"Actually, Miriam, you have no idea how much restraint I exercise when we're together. You should be proud of me."

Barbara could still make Jess laugh.

"So who would have thought that almost eleven years later I'd be the only hausfrau?" Barbara asked with a smile.

It was true. After all, Barbara had always been the wife with one foot out the door. But the years hadn't been as generous to her as some. Always there for others, she was seldom there for herself. When she'd first felt the pain, she said nothing. Eventually, though, she had to face up to the reality. By then, the doctor was afraid the cancer had spread. The week Jess spent with Barbara at the hospital had been one of the most difficult ones of her life. After the removal of her right lung, Barbara seemed to accept the inevitability of her impending death, trying to soothe everyone else around her. When the prognosis appeared to be more positive than anyone had dared hope, Barbara broke down for the first time Jess could remember. Barbara pledged she would be different. The people she cared about were too precious to be taken for granted. She was especially grateful to Jess, who had given up an important week in Washington to be with her (though Jess always felt she should have stayed longer), and to her husband, Bill, who had demanded a cot be brought into Barbara's room and stayed at her side through the whole arduous ordeal.

* * *

"Well, you look like one happy, healthy hausfrau," Jess assured her.

Barbara shook her head. The truth was she didn't fully understand it herself. "Actually, these have been the best years of my life. I know it sounds odd, what with the cancer and Bill going bankrupt . . . but we've been there for each other. We're not ashamed to ask each other for support when we need it." Barbara looked almost embarrassed as she spoke. "I know it must sound corny, but we've never been closer."

"It sounds terrific," Jess responded genuinely. She was happy for her friend. Jess wondered if that kind of a relationship would have been enough to sustain her. Ten years ago, maybe. Not now. She had evolved too far. It occurred to her that perhaps Barbara had regressed, but quickly decided that different people had different needs. Odd how things worked out, she thought. Maybe her father's old expression was right: Everything presses itself out in the end.

"The best therapy," Miriam interjected, "is letting your energies interact and flow harmoniously."

Jess knew there was no way to escape it. Get it over with. Ask Miriam what she's doing with her life. "Correct me if I'm wrong, Miriam, but somehow you seem to have changed."

Barbara smiled. "Jess, you're downright intuitive."

Miriam's forty-two-inch bust swelled to capacity as she sat up ready for the challenge of explaining what had happened in her life. "I haven't changed as much as surfaced. I know everyone thought Herb and I were the perfect couple, and in many ways we were. Yet at the same time we were stagnant. We were fixated on our mutual dependency. We were tired of repression. First we attempted a trial separation from ourselves."

Jess knew it was her ingrained need for clarification, and she hated herself for asking more questions, but she found

Miriam so incomprehensible she couldn't stop herself. "A trial separation from yourself?"

"You know, from our old, traditional selves. We recycled our consciousness."

"How does that work exactly?"

"Oh, it's heavy stuff, but ultimately so rewarding. Herb and I did *est,* Marriage Encounter, Esalen, aerobics, rolfing, and got ourselves a primal therapy room. I would say Jackie Sorensen and Werner Erhard changed our lives—with the help of our swami, of course."

Barbara poured herself another daiquiri. "Miriam aspires to New York chic."

"Naturally, Herbie and I took our marriage vows again. It was spiritually gratifying. We rededicated and resolemnized ourselves. For six months we're celibate, for six months anything goes. We're up-front. No game playing. We've redefined our parameters. I've taken back my maiden name. With Herb's last name, I felt like a nonperson. In fact, I'm surprised you didn't reassume your maiden name."

Jess had considered it, but ruled it out. "I decided to keep the same last name as my daughter. Do you have more than one child now?"

"But definitely not," Miriam replied, aghast. "We're committed to a negative population growth."

"I make up for you," Carmen cheerfully pointed out.

Miriam looked at Carmen and shook her head sadly. "Very destructive. Basically, Jess, I get off on staying mellow. Mellow, it's the operative word in my life."

Jess decided it would be a lot more than ten years before she got together with the queen of psychobabble again.

21

Looking around the hall, Jess thought that her mother would have gotten some perverse pleasure had she been there that night. True, Mrs. Simon wouldn't have been crazy about the occasion—her ex-husband marrying a very much younger woman—but she would have been ten times more critical of the wedding's motif.

Jess imagined her mother looking around, shaking her head hopelessly, raising her eyes heavenward, whispering, Can you believe this place? It looks like early bordello: Purple and red for a wedding? Who do you think their decorator is? The Castro Convertible Showroom Man, maybe? Have you ever seen so much gold leafing? The *chatchkas* alone could have paid for a Cambodian family on relief. There's no accounting for taste, I can tell you that. At least the little tart had the decency not to wear white."

Jess looked around at the rows of guests and smiled to herself. No need to ask which side was with the groom or the bride. The left side was filled with men wearing yarmulkes, the right with women wearing crucifixes.

All those years that she had been instructed not to intermarry flashed through Jess's mind. Her family had been members of a Reform congregation. In fact, Jess had been the most observant Jew in her family. She had felt a special sense of warmth in the temple. She thought her rabbi was brilliant and she adored listening to his sermons and, later at the Oneg Shabbat after services, arguing with him about some of the points he had made. During her high school years, she had been active in the Temple Youth Group and had even been successful in guilting her parents into attending services with her occasionally.

But in college, she devoted most of her waking hours to studying, so her temple attendance waned. When Susan was born Jess had asked Eliot to join a temple, but he felt religion was unnecessary, so they never got around to becoming members of any congregation.

What was the reason her parents had dissuaded her from intermarrying again? Children must have been the rationalization. "A child needs to know who he or she is," her mother would often remind her. Well, if that was the reason, she imagined her father would be safe. She couldn't imagine Jack Simon fathering a child at his age. She looked at the bride. Thirty-five years old. She might still want children. What was her biological ticker telling her? Jess looked at her father and hoped he did, indeed, have a very strong heart.

Jessica sat in the front row next to Susan. She had never seen a service like this one. A rabbi and a priest stood next to each other, officiating. Interspersing English, Latin, and Hebrew, everyone had a chance to express themselves, alternating between crossing themselves and interjecting Hebrew words, followed by united "Amens."

The rabbi's turn: "Jacob ben Avram, do you take this woman to be your lawfully wedded wife, and do you vow by your religious upbringing to honor the most fundamental tenets of love, honor, and respect for her until death do you part?"

"I do."

Sure, what does a vow like that mean to a man like this, thought half the group.

The priest's turn: "Terry, christened Theresa Maria, do you embrace into your soul this man to be your lawfully wedded husband, and do you adhere to your own religious doctrines including the precious golden rule that guides you to love, honor, and obey your husband in sickness and health, for richer or poorer, until God Almighty calls you to your final resting place?"

"I do."

Her final resting place? Who is he kidding? That guy will be lucky to last through the honeymoon, thought the other half of the group.

Worriedly, the rabbi stated the next part. "If there is anyone here who can show just cause why this couple should not be united, let him speak now. . . ."

If there's anyone here who can show just cause why this couple *should* be united, let him speak out now, thought most of the group.

". . . or forever hold his peace," the priest ended the sentence quickly.

Everyone looked around, confident at least one person would object. But no one did. Terry's mother reached for a fresh sniff of smelling salts although she had little desire to have a clear head at that moment.

The clergymen showed visible signs of relief as the rabbi continued. "Then in the name of our joint religions and ecumenical spirit . . ."

"And the State of New York," the priest added.

"We pronounce you man and wife. Amen," they concluded together.

Jack Simon stepped on the traditional covered glass and broke it. Turning to his new wife, he gently lifted her veil and kissed her smiling face.

"Do I have to call her 'Grandma'?" Susan asked Jess.

Then again, the joyous feeling wasn't much better at the reception, unless you counted the musicians' enthusiasm. Horas alternated with tarantellas; pastas followed by stuffed dermas; people smiling icily at each other, whispering under their breath.

"What Estelle must be going through today. Did she deserve this?"

"Who deserves this? The Ayatollah, maybe, but not sweet

Estelle. Look at Jack dancing up a storm. Why should he be so happy?" clucked Mrs. Simon's friend Lucille.

"Look at his new wife and you'll have the answer to that question," answered Lucille's husband.

"Ah, the typical masculine voice of reason. That girl turns too quickly, her head probably rattles. What can they talk about, you tell me?"

"There are times talking's not necessary. Not a bad way to live."

"All you men ever think about is sex."

"What else is there to do *but* think about it?"

Icy stares all around.

Not that the talk at the other end of the room was any more accepting.

"Bad enough she got a divorce. Bad enough she didn't get an annulment. But marrying outside her faith to such an older man: It's a sin. I know it," Terry's aunt told the group.

"She seems happy."

"Happy? Who cares happy? She's killing her mother. Is that something should make a girl happy? Such *agita*."

But Jess was enjoying her father's joy. She sat at the end of the hall with him for a few minutes, him holding her hand, her looking into his blissful face. It was as though they were alone having one of their special lunches together. She loved this man who was her father.

"So, you think I did a rotten thing?" he asked guiltily. He still needed her blessing.

"No," she answered.

"I don't like to hurt people."

"I know."

"I'm just so happy. I wish you could be this happy."

"I am happy, Daddy."

"I mean with a man. You know what I mean."

"Maybe some day."

"I'm young again. Terry, she's bought me a new lease on life." He looked ashamed of that admission. "Your mother . . . is she very angry?"

"I wouldn't hold out for her blessing." Jess smiled tenderly as she squeezed his hand.

On this perfect day of his, her father still looked troubled. "Carol will never forgive me either. She's her mother all over. I know that. But you, I'm truly grateful you're here to share my *nachas*. It means a lot to me. I love you a lot."

"I love you, too, Daddy."

"I wish I had been a stronger man for you."

All these years she had been afraid to ask. All those moments she had almost said something but was scared she would hurt him. All this time he knew. Some day they could discuss it at length. Maybe then she could find out some answers to questions that had been plaguing her, but this wasn't the day to do it.

"You have nothing to apologize for," she said, hugging him tightly. "Your bride's looking for you," she told him as she saw Terry gazing in their direction, unsure whether or not to come over.

He got up and smiled at Terry, indicating with his right index finger that he'd be over in a minute. He looked fondly at his daughter and gently planted a kiss on her forehead.

Jess had lost count of the number of drinks she'd had when she approached the bar. That was quite unusual for her, but she had determined she would treat this as a royal celebration and she had to admit liquor was one of the few things that loosened her up. Not that she was ever really out of control, just pleasantly happy.

The bartender recognized her, a clear sign that she was too much of a regular. "More champagne?"

"Why not?" she answered blithely.

"And you, sir?" he asked the man standing to Jessica's right.

"Hmm. How's the champagne?"

Jess realized he was waiting for an answer from her. "Delicious," she answered unequivocally.

"That's a good enough endorsement for me. Make that two champagnes, please."

Jess said nothing even though she felt proud she'd been able to sell her drink to a total stranger.

"Quite a wedding, isn't it?" he said as they waited for their drinks.

"Uh-huh," Jess agreed, still not looking at him.

"Are you enjoying it?"

"Absolutely."

"Me, too. I was waiting to meet the other person in this room who was." Jess smiled. A similar thought had crossed her mind. "Are you with the groom or the bride?"

"The groom," she replied.

"Perfect. I'm with the bride. We can start the rapprochement committee." With her peripheral vision, she could see him extend his hand. "Ben Casale."

Jessica turned to face him and extended her hand. "Jess Simon Kantor."

She looked at the stranger she'd been talking to for almost a minute. She judged him to be in his late thirties, maybe about her age. He wasn't particularly tall, about five feet ten, but he was, as far as she could tell from what he was wearing, compactly, strongly built. His hair was a raven black, his eyes a dark brown, his skin olive, his nose Grecian straight. Hands were a feature she noticed right away about a man. His were large and hairy. Not too hairy, though. Perfectly placed with some on each knuckle and hand. She imagined it was a feature that continued over his whole body. He looked like a caricature of a handsome Italian stud. She looked at those strong, masculine hands again and wondered if he was a hit man. She had no doubt he'd make a good one.

"Are you related to Jack?" he asked, with only a trace of a New York accent.

"I'm his daughter—by a previous marriage."

"I'm glad you clarified that. For a second there I thought they *had* to get married." He smiled broadly. "I'm Terry's brother. So now we're related. Hmmm, what do you suppose we are?"

"Let's see," Jess answered, trying to figure it out. "You're either my uncle once removed or maybe just a distant relative."

"Hey, we just met. I neither want to be distant nor removed from you—not even once."

She looked at him and smiled. He was really adorable. A hit man with a sense of humor. At least she'd had enough champagne to enjoy this one-night flirtation. "Oh, you don't, do you?" she asked lightly, starting to have fun.

"In fact," Ben continued, putting down his champagne glass, raising his arms as though a momentous announcement was going to be made, "I'm going to do something I rarely do. I'm going to ask you to dance."

"With you?"

"No, solo. Of course with me." He took Jessica's arm and masterfully, yet gently, led her to the dance floor. She liked his style. It was certainly different from what she was used to. "Now don't get thrown if you hear me counting," he warned her. "I just learned the box step last week. If the music speeds up, we're going to casually pretend we've had enough and find ourselves two chairs."

Jess nodded as though she was in complete accord with this conspiracy. A box step, she figured, she could keep up with. "Do you want me to lead?" she asked, pretending to be helpful.

"Hey, I am an Italian, remember?"

"I lost my head."

"It's only your first strike. I have a forgiving nature."

He guided her onto the floor and she quickly realized she might have trouble keeping up with him. He was very good.

"You learned this last week, did you?" she asked skeptically.

"I'm a fast study. And I catch a lot of old Fred Astaire movies. Watch this."

As he twirled her around she began to feel like Ginger

Rogers. She was grateful she had worn the peach chiffon dress in which her mother assured her she would be over-dressed. As the band finished playing "Fly Me to the Moon," he twirled her three times and ended with a grand dip.

"That was very good," Ben said approvingly. "You've been watching the same old movies."

"You're nuts." Jess laughed, breathless.

"You would say that to an uncle? What a lack of respect."

"But funny."

"I'm overwhelming you with my charm, right?"

"I've had a lot to drink. My resistance is down."

Ben looked hopeful. "Really? Then let's go someplace more private."

"I haven't had *that* much to drink."

Ben shrugged his shoulders good-naturedly. "It was worth a shot."

When she thought about that night in later months, she couldn't pinpoint the exact moment it had happened, but she knew by the end of the evening it would be a great loss if she never saw Ben again. She tried to rationalize the feeling: it was a beautiful night; the champagne was plentiful; she was away from her business turf; he was good diversionary fun.

Jess couldn't even remember what they had talked about. She just remembered that she hadn't been that giddy or felt so carefree in a long, long while.

She took him all in as she listened to Ben talk animatedly. This man was so alive. She heard herself giggling uncontrollably. Was that really her? She was used to clever banter, but giggling? Never!

"And that," Ben concluded proudly, "is how I single-handedly won the war. It's relatively unknown. The C.I.A. wanted it that way. Security reasons."

Jess laughed and shook her head. "I bet you have a story for everything."

Ben smiled and then suddenly turned serious. He gazed intensely at Jess, his dark eyes more piercing than ever. Jess knew that look. She had seen it on other men when they were falling for her. Those times she brushed it off lightly and began talking about something in the news. This time she said nothing. She felt a flush of embarrassment come to her cheeks.

Jess turned to look up at the sky. "It's a beautiful evening, don't you think?" Was that her voice shaking?

Ben had not taken his eyes off her. He stood transfixed. "Jessie, you're gorgeous."

Gorgeous she was not. Whenever a man thought that, he was hers. Then again, she didn't know this man particularly well. It was too soon. The champagne was too good. Play it cool and light.

"It's the moonlight," Jess assured him.

Ben smiled. "No. The moonlight doesn't hurt, but it's *you.*"

They looked at each other, neither saying a word. As she was trying to figure out her next move, Ben took her in his arms and bent to kiss her. His embrace was stronger than she'd remembered from the dance floor. Firm, yet at the same time, gentle. It was an unbeatable combination. As their lips met, she hadn't the slightest desire to resist. His tongue effortlessly found its way to hers. It was the most wonderful kiss she had ever received. She felt herself respond completely as his tongue engulfed her mouth. She felt her body tingle and weaken. She was floating. She sensed she might be in big trouble.

When their kiss ended, they looked at each other and, without saying a word, kissed again. This one was even better than the last. That surprised Jess since she thought she knew what to expect. But when his tongue gently encircled hers and she felt her clitoris start to respond expectantly, she *knew* she was in very big trouble.

When they separated this time, Jess figured she'd better say something fast. "That was some incredible kiss."

He smiled, not surprised. "Do you have a lot to compare it with?"

"I was on the Olympic kissing team," she responded lightly. "Believe me, I know a great kiss when I get one."

"How much of that is the champagne talking?" he asked skeptically.

"Who knows? Who cares?" After all, it was only for one night.

Ben looked carefully at her face, trying to read it. "It's called chemistry—between two people." They both smiled. "Want to go another round?" he asked genially.

She gave one of her "why not" looks as they began their little journey one more time. Not only did she tingle, not only did her clitoris come to complete attention, but she had the most incredible sensation of complete, total enjoyment, as though she was coming to orgasm. She knew she wasn't alone in that reaction when she began to feel an object getting very hard next to her clothed clitoris.

"Don't worry. I won't take advantage of you."

She had to laugh at the absurdity of his statement. She figured that the last man who had taken advantage of her was Eliot, and maybe Rich Seagal, but that was a lifetime ago. "Advantage of *me?* I wouldn't worry about that." She was perfectly ready for the next step. "Wait a minute. What am I doing? I've got a daughter inside who probably thinks I've dropped off a cliff."

"And I've got a mother in there praying for everyone's soul. When can I see you again? I've got to see you again."

Again? Wasn't this supposed to be, at most, a meaningful one-night stand? "I have to get back to work tomorrow."

"No problem. We can meet here again next weekend. I can move to where you live. Where do you live?"

"Washington, D.C."

He raised his fist in victory. "Don't tell me there's not a prayer-answering God. That's where *I* live."

"Washington?" she asked incredulously. Ben nodded a yes. "Doing what?"

"I'm an administrative assistant to a congressman."

"Which one?"

"Richard Calvin."

She could hardly believe it. "I work for Senator Ford."

"The same state," Ben said, amazed. "It's not possible. What do you do?"

"I'm his administrative assistant."

Which meant she had more status than he. "Well, you're six months older than I am," he rationalized. Then he did a double take as he realized who she was. "Wait a second. Jessica Kantor: the 'Iron Lady'?"

She grimaced. "Is that what they're calling me this year?"

"In polite circles," he answered.

Ben quickly thought about her reputation. She was known as a ball breaker. One royal bitch. Who the hell cared? She was one exciting royal bitch, and he'd handled a lot worse. "The Iron Lady," he repeated.

"I've heard worse," she said, and meant it.

"So have I," he said, and meant it, too.

Okay, she was who she was. No goody-two-shoes image to hide behind. The cards were on the table. So much the better. "Still want to see me?" she asked him.

Ben took her in his arms and kissed her again. His erection was more noticeable than ever. Good. At least he wasn't intimidated by who she was.

"Guess," he said as they came up for air. "Look, I don't want you to feel I'm pressuring you. Let's play this nice and slow. How's dinner tomorrow night?"

She looked at him. All right, he was great looking. Okay, he was bright. Sure, he had a great sense of humor. But she really had no time to get involved with anyone now. An election was coming up. So when it came down to it, it was that incredible kiss that ultimately was going to decide this issue. Could she really be that shallow? "Why not?" she answered.

"Great," Ben responded, pleased. "Does that mean lunch is out?"

22

The minute Peter walked into Jess's office and looked at her face he knew there was only one person she could be speaking to on that telephone. He was amazed at Jess. He had never seen her so smitten with a man. And who was this man, anyway? He certainly was not in the same league as any of her previous suitors. They had positions of status. Not that this Ben Casale didn't have a good job, but really, it wasn't even as important as Jessica's. It irked Peter that he found himself liking Ben in spite of himself. But he was hardly about to let Jess in on that piece of information.

"You do, do you?" Jess said into the phone, sounding half flirty, half schoolgirl. "Where to this time? All right then, surprise me. Eight is fine. What shall I wear? Hey, behave yourself. These phones may be tapped. Our party's not in power, remember? I'll see you later."

She hung up the phone, a smile lingering on her face. She looked up at a disapproving Peter and knew she was in for some judgments about her abandonment of sanity. She quickly reached for some of the work piling up on her desk, hoping she could avoid the inevitable, knowing full well that the inevitable could never be avoided.

"Prince Charming again, I presume," Peter remarked drolly.

"Close enough," Jess responded lightly.

"You've seen him nonstop for two weeks now."

"Really?" said Jess as she thumbed through the most current *Congressional Record.* "I'm so glad someone keeps track of these things."

"Honestly, Jessica, he's a boy."

"Good, because he makes me feel like a girl."

"He's decidedly counter to your taste, you know," Peter noted as he rearranged the flowers Ben had brought Jess while she was at a hearing that morning. Really, he could have had enough class to send them through a florist. Two flowers were already nearing their final petal.

All right, he wasn't going to disappear without another go-round. "You're such an expert on my taste, are you, Peter?"

Good. She wasn't going to hide behind her work this time. "I'm aware of your patterns: older, important, boring, non-threatening."

"Then it appears I've broken my pattern, doesn't it? What do you think it means, Dr. Freud?" Half of her hated herself for asking that question; the other half was curious about the answer.

"I think it means you'd better watch yourself," Peter replied, genuinely concerned. "This one could be serious."

Jess waved her hand to assure him he didn't have anything to worry about on that score. "I'm just having a good time. We have a lot of fun together."

But that couldn't have been less reassuring to Peter. It was what he least wanted to hear. "Precisely my point. It's entirely out of character for you. The only time you have fun is when you're in power and this relationship is much too evenly matched for you."

"Baloney," she responded, dismissing his comment. *"Out. I have work to do."*

Peter picked out the two dying flowers—daisies, a flower he despised—and dropped them into the wastepaper basket on his way toward the door. He turned to look back at Jess, who gave him one of her "don't worry" looks, but he was not at all reassured.

Jess started to do some more paperwork. She was getting

behind and that wasn't like her. A great deal of what she did these days wasn't like her, and she couldn't dismiss that fact either. Ben was definitely changing her life. And Peter was certainly right about one thing: Ben was nothing like any man she had ever dated, much less known.

When Benjamin Joseph Casale entered the world in 1946, he was the fourth Casale child to be born in America to Dominick and Sophia. His brother, Alberto, was at that time seven years old; his sister, Mary Angelina, was four; his brother, George, was two. Theresa was born three years later.

Dominick Casale had uprooted himself and his new bride from their tiny village in Sicily because he believed all the stories of the fortune to be had in the magical land of America. And why shouldn't he be one of the rich for the rest of his life instead of one of the very poor, as he had been ever since he could remember? It was his right, wasn't it?

But the streets were not paved with the gold he had expected. He was willing to do good, hard work, but there was little to be found. His competition was everywhere. The first jobs went to the Americans who didn't have accents. The last jobs went to the Italians. It began to get to him.

When Sophia suggested they should move back to Sicily, where they at least had family and friends, it infuriated Dominick. That was the first time he struck his wife, but it was far from the last.

Finally, Dominick settled into a dependable job as a waiter in a Jewish delicatessen. He hated having to follow orders—especially from these people with the funny accents and customs—but a job was a job and at least the money was regular. Mr. Kaplan, the owner, was a decent man who treated Dominick and Sophia politely as he would any gentile.

Dominick knew he was going nowhere. He was tired and angry. He didn't want to think about it. He just wanted to drink his vino, play his boccie, and forget. Some land of opportunity this was.

The passing years did not mellow Dominick's disposition. He would still come home from a night out drinking his grappa and talking about the old country and pick a fight with Sophia, only to have it end with her nose bloodied. More often, though, he would start yelling at one of the children, and depending on how much rage was in him that night, he might end up beating one of them.

For as long as he could remember, Ben felt like the oldest child in the family. He was the responsible one. By the time he was five, Ben could no longer stand the beatings his father doled out.

"Where's my pasta?" Dominick had bellowed when he entered the room that day. He was in an especially foul mood and everyone knew it. Even two-year-old Terry.

"It's coming," answered Sophia in Italian. She had never bothered to learn English, though by now she understood it.

"How many times I gotta tell you? I want my supper ready when I walk through that door."

"It's coming," Sophia repeated.

Dominick eyed Mary. "How come you never help your mama?"

"I do, Papa," she answered, starting to get frightened.

"So then how come my dinner, it's not ready?"

"I don't know, Papa."

"Did you help your mama get me my meal today?" he asked.

"No, Papa."

"Then you didn't help like you say you did."

"I . . . I do . . . usually."

"But not today, huh?"

"I just got home from school and I . . ." She looked around helplessly.

He had her now. "I think it's a time for a lesson so you don't forget next time."

Mary started to run, but Dominick was too fast for her. He grabbed her arm as he took off his worn leather belt.

"I'm sorry, Papa," she started to cry. "I won't do it again."

"That's what you say now."

"No, Papa, I promise. Please don't hit me. I promise."

"So what good is a promise from you? You just lied to me. Lying to a father is bad. You're a bad little girl. You need to be taught a lesson."

He held her tightly as he administered the whipping. Mary's cries got louder and louder as everyone in the room stood frozen, waiting for it to be over. Everyone, except for five-year-old Ben. He ran to his father to try to get the belt away.

"Leave her alone. Leave my sister alone."

Dominick shoved Ben aside with one swift hit, but Ben got up and went back to help his sister.

"Leave her alone."

"You're next, Benjamin," Dominick shouted at him as he continued whipping Mary, pushing Ben aside.

"I don't care. Leave her alone."

Ben could not be controlled. Dominick could not shake him. Ben held on to his father's arms and yelled for Mary to run, which she quickly did. Dominick, filled with rage, started after Ben, but Ben darted back and forth, successfully eluding his father. In the room were shouts of "Run, Ben," "Watch out, Ben." Dominick looked at his family and then at Ben, who had his five-year-old little fists raised, ready to take his father on. Sophia was in the corner, praying. Little Terry was sobbing in horror. George and Alberto stood terror stricken. Mary hid in back of her five-year-old brother, who had leapt to her defense. Suddenly, Dominick felt sick. He picked up his jacket, walked to the door, and slammed it as he walked out. He never touched Mary Angelina again.

* * *

Ben was a leader. He organized the baseball team on his block; he led debates at the settlement house; he got groups together to earn nickles and dimes selling discarded items to local junkyards.

At school, he was considered a brain. He was the only boy in the top class. Still, no one dared call him a sissy. Because Ben was a fighter. He made that clear on the first day of school when Joey Barbone made a nasty comment about Ben's masculinity. It took four months for Joey's left arm to heal completely.

It wasn't just his own battles he fought, he also had to take care of George. Barely two years older than Ben, George had been kept back twice so they were in the same grade. George was the typical kid to be picked on. Not very bright, sniveling, and a bit of a runt, he was easy prey. Most of the time Ben was there to protect him. But when he wasn't, if George got a bloody nose, his attacker got one the next day. By third grade, everyone knew better than to mess with George.

It wasn't that Ben was such a massive kid; he simply refused to believe anyone could beat him. He had that look of invincibility that made all his opponents think, "Shit, this kid's gonna kick the crap out of me."

And he was a natural athlete. Only five feet ten, he was the best basketball player the school had ever seen. His football wasn't bad either.

When he was going into his first year of high school, he was offered a scholarship to Choate, a fine boys' school in Massachusetts. It was an honor that had never been given to anyone in his neighborhood and he knew he had to accept it.

Ben spent many restless nights wondering if he could leave his family. By that time Alberto was a mechanic and married with one kid. Mary had left high school and was a manicurist. She was engaged to be married. Terry was going into sixth grade, but Ben never worried about her. In many ways, she was a female version of him. She did well in school and she could take care of herself. His main concern was George. Could Ben safely leave him to fend for himself? They discussed it one summer evening as they lay out on the fire escape, their bedroom on those nights when it was too oppressively hot to sleep inside.

"I don't really have to go."

"Yeah, Ben ya' gotta go. Ya' can't take care of me forever. I'm gonna do just fine. Ya' gonna be proud of me."

Before he left, Ben let it be known that anyone who messed with George would have to answer to Ben when he came home on vacations.

It seemed the whole neighborhood came out to say good-bye when Ben left for Choate. As he took one last look before leaving, he knew that he would never be a real part of this neighborhood again. He would only be a visitor. It made him sad.

Ben didn't know that he had an accent until the boys at Choate started making fun of him. Three quick physical encounters stopped the mimicking, but not the embarrassment. Ben was determined to fit in. He didn't want to be thought of as "that token kid from the slums." When his English teacher, Mr. Winthrop, discreetly mentioned that he'd be available should Ben wish diction lessons, Ben jumped at the opportunity. Every day he went to Mr. Winthrop, mastering sounds he had never heard, until even Mr. Winthrop could find no trace of the Lower East Side in his speech.

Ben studied hard, proficiently played every sport he could fit into his overloaded schedule, and, eventually, made friends with the other boys. He became gregarious and popular and was even elected class president. Barely anyone would have guessed that he never felt he belonged. When he went home, he was equally uncomfortable. It was as though he belonged nowhere.

Harvard was another story altogether. There were so many different types of guys, so many misfits, Ben felt less like an outsider. Of course, he wasn't exactly the Hasty Pudding type, but then he didn't want to be anyway.

And there were so many women to be had. Not that Ben was new to that subject. He had known his way around women from a very young age. Actually, he was more comfortable around them than he was around guys. He could talk to them. He didn't have to prove himself. Except in bed, of course, and that was the easiest assignment of all. As good as he was on the soccer field, he was ten times better in the sack. After the first few times with the local hooker when he was eleven, he began to perfect his craft. To Ben, that meant satisfying the woman. He had thawed many a frigid young lady in his time.

But nothing prepared him for Jennifer Pierce.

23

Ben and Jess were laughing as they entered Ben's townhouse. He had just told one of his cornier jokes, Yiddish accent and all. Jess was an appreciative audience, mainly because of Ben's undaunted enthusiasm. He loved the telling and did it well. At those moments he looked like a little boy trying his hardest to please. He rarely failed.

Ben's townhouse was in Georgetown. Jess adored this area of Washington. As far as she was concerned, Georgetown had it all: the well-kept neighborhoods; the accessibility to shopping; the closeness to The Hill. As it turned out, they were almost neighbors. He lived on M Street, she on P. They couldn't understand how they'd never noticed each other before.

"It's not much, but I call it home," he said as they walked in.

Jess looked around, trying to take it all in. The whole aura was masculine. The color scheme was dark chocolate brown, ivory, and sky blue. The walls were a deep mahogany; the furniture, a rich cordovan leather; the curtains, brushed camel. There were bookshelves everywhere, all completely filled. Jess enjoyed looking at other people's books. She felt it told everything about the owner. She thought about Eliot, who often bought a book because he liked the color of the jacket.

"I like it," she announced her approval. "Is it all yours?"

"I didn't lease it for the night."

"I mean you don't share it?"

Sharing a house was the last thing Ben wanted to do after Jennifer. He gathered up the part of the Sunday *Times* he hadn't completed and took it with him to the kitchen. "No, I won't have to put any light in the window so my roomies don't bother us." He took out the dish he had prepared the night before. "Wait until you see what I made."

"You cook, too? Where will your talents end?"

"You've just begun to discover them," he shouted from the kitchen. "I hope you like Indian food."

Jess smiled, remembering. "Love it."

She walked slowly around the room, trying to get the sense of this man who up until three weeks ago had been a stranger and was now an integral part of her life.

Jess stopped to look at the diplomas on the wall. "Harvard Law, huh? I'm impressed."

"It wasn't a hard year to get in. They had to fill up their Lower East Side Italians quota."

"Graduating cum laude," she noted, still reading from the diploma.

"The competition wasn't all that stiff."

"And what have we here?" she continued, looking at another diploma. "London School of Economics."

"I was a professional student."

"A doctorate."

"What can I tell you? I'm overqualified for everything."

"Hmm," Jess said. "A doctor and a lawyer in one package. What my mother wouldn't give for you."

Ben came up behind Jess, carrying an assortment of Indian hors d'oeuvres on a tray. "How about her daughter?" he asked. He kissed the back of her neck. She smiled as he held out the plate to her. "Here, try one of these."

Jess took a nondescript ball on a toothpick; it tasted like lamb marinated in curry. She thought it could have used a little more cumin, maybe a pinch of ground turmeric. She decided to keep that advice to herself for the time being.

"Yum," she said enthusiastically. "What's next?"

He pulled Jess close to his body and gave her one of those kisses she adored. They never lasted long enough for her. "I meant in the way of food."

"I knew what you meant," Ben assured her. "Remember, I'm the cook so I make up the menu."

"I'm just wondering what's for dessert."

"What did you have in mind?" Ben asked, knowing the answer full well.

Jess smiled coyly. She was determined the night would produce results.

It had been an odd experience for Jess. Three weeks and she hadn't been able to seduce this guy. She couldn't understand it. She knew they were madly attracted to each other. Under ordinary circumstances, those kisses alone should have led directly to a bedroom. And she was anxious. She hadn't been this attracted to a man since John Rand. But as anxious as she was, Ben seemed determined to wait. She hoped nothing was wrong with him.

Ben was in no rush. He wanted to take his time, make sure all the other elements were firmly in place. He'd had plenty of women since Jennifer. To his great relief, he hadn't lost his touch. He'd been insatiable when he moved to Washington. He couldn't get enough sex. Then again, if one had to be an insatiable male, you couldn't find a better place than Washington. The ratio of women to men was overwhelmingly in his favor. That was one statistic of which he'd taken full advantage. After six months of one-night stands, he felt his sexual prowess had been fully proven. Ben was exhausted. He took a week off and then went at it again, this time a little slower. He began having relationships. They never amounted to much. None lasted more than a few months.

Ben knew he had cut himself off emotionally, but that was okay with him for the time being. It allowed him time to heal, room to survive. He wasn't about to let himself risk that pain again. It didn't matter, though, because in all the time since Jennifer he hadn't met anyone he really cared about.

When he was in his second year at Harvard Law School, Ben met Jennifer Wellington Pierce. She was a Cliffie. Every cliché applied: she was from old stock (of the *Mayflower* Pierces); she was smart (top of her class from Brearley); she was arrogant (which she considered an asset); and she was cold and aloof (if she liked you). One Radcliffe cliché didn't apply: Jennifer Pierce was breathtakingly beautiful. She had long blond hair that went into a natural flip. Her eyes were a steely, clear blue. Her nose was aristocratic: straight and a touch long, which made her look more regal. She was five feet ten, painfully thin, totally flat-chested, and looked stunning in virtually every outfit she wore.

When she was introduced to Ben at a mutual friend's party, her eyes and her handshake immediately communicated he'd never know her any more intimately than he did at that very moment. Ben loved a challenge.

His instincts told him that Jennifer's cold exterior probably matched a cold interior. But it didn't matter: Ben was determined to win her.

When he telephoned her the next night, she told him she had no idea who he was, nor was she anxious to find out. When she finally agreed to see him, Jennifer made it clear it was just to get him to stop calling.

After six months of dating, there was no doubt that Jennifer was steadfast in her resolve to keep her virginity until her wedding night. She hadn't the slightest interest in giving it up. Although she had warmed up to Ben in many ways, sex was not one of them. Frustrated and madly in love, Ben knew he had to have Jennifer. His marriage proposal was turned down twice, but he could differentiate between a real refusal and a perfunctory one. He wasn't at all surprised when she relented on his third try.

The big problem was trying to persuade Jackson Pierce, Jennifer's esteemed father, that this decidedly non-

Mayflower suitor was worthy of his aristocratic daughter. It took two solid weeks of intellectual references and charm by Ben at the Pierce estate in Newport. Convinced that Ben was not a mere fortune hunter, but indeed a very good prospect for success, Jackson Pierce beneficently gave his blessing, provided they married in the High Episcopalian Church whose first six pews he had donated. Ben acquiesced, though not before assuring his future father-in-law that he was and would always remain a confirmed agnostic.

Ben, on the other hand, never took Jennifer home to meet her in-laws-to-be. Even though his parents had moved to a small two-family house on Staten Island, he knew Jennifer would be appalled by their home. He thought of the living room with its green-and-gold velvet sofa and matching chair covered with plastic; the flocked wallpaper; the gold-leafed mirrors; the numerous crucifixes. He decided he was sparing everyone by waiting until the wedding. The one thing he did do in an attempt to show Jennifer his roots was take her down to Mulberry Street, where he had grown up. She was genuinely horrified. She wanted to leave the area immediately. In the back of his mind, he knew that the incident should have told him something, but instead he chose to laugh it off.

The wedding was a disaster. Sophia rocked back and forth, repeating prayers in Italian and Latin throughout the whole service and much of the reception. Dominick had chosen this day to try out his new green plaid suit, broad-striped brown shirt, and red polka dot tie. His four extra dabs of Vitalis hair cream made his hair stand straight up. Alberto, whose nails were still black from the cars he fixed, came with his wife, Rosie, who wore her hair in a one-foot-high beehive. In addition, Rosie had applied heavy black eyeliner and white pancake makeup, making her look as if she had just stepped out of the set of "The Munsters." George, who it appeared had gone to the same men's shop as his father, proudly told as many of Jennifer's relatives as he could about all the boys' faces Ben had rearranged to protect him. Mary Angelina appeared with her four children (none of whom were invited), all of whom were recovering from, but not yet over, chicken pox. Terry, who was in her last year of college at N.Y.U., came in a simple dress, clearly not expensive enough for Jennifer's crowd, but elegant nonetheless.

Ben couldn't fault the Pierces for their behavior. They were cordial and proper and obviously wished to be anywhere else. Jennifer made no secret of her displeasure during the whole event, barely able to carry on a two-minute conversation with any of Ben's relatives. Ben was annoyed with the Pierces, but more with himself, because he felt closer to who the Pierces were than to his own family.

In retrospect, the wedding may well have been the high point of their marriage. The most disastrous aspect was in bed. Jennifer was more than a challenge. She was an impossibility.

Ben tried everything he knew. Nothing aroused her. Jennifer lay as still as the mattress beneath her, waiting for the whole disgusting act to be over. Ben began to feel like the *Titanic* encountering the iceberg. He suggested they see a marriage counselor. Jennifer refused. Secretly, Ben was relieved. He had no desire to tell a total stranger that he was a failure as a lover. Reluctantly, he convinced himself that sex was not the most important element of a marriage.

The marriage lasted five years—five agonizing years.

The final straw was when Ben announced, after finishing his doctorate at the London School of Economics, that he was going to go into public service in Washington, D.C. Jennifer was outraged. Ben had been offered any number of plum jobs down on Wall Street in top law and investment firms. Why, she demanded to know, couldn't he grow up and accept his rightful place in society? He assured her he had and it was going to be in Washington, D.C. Surely Jennifer didn't need any more money; she was an heiress to millions of dollars and spent the majority of her days going over her stock portfolios with her various brokers. Both were steadfast in their positions.

In the end, they were both relieved to part. They were perfectly civil, their anger and passion both long ago having vanished. She went to join her family and friends in the luxury of Newport; he went to stay with his parents on Staten Island, sleeping on the plastic-covered couch in the living room under two crucifixes that he removed. His father, now closing in on retirement, had mellowed with time. He treated Ben like a friend; they played boccie with some other men on the block. His mother made a different pasta each night and served fresh, hot garlic bread. He couldn't get enough Italian food, having eaten nothing but French for the past five years. All his relatives came to keep him company and show their love and support. It was good to be home. After two weeks, Ben moved to Washington to work for Congressman Calvin and began to get on with his life.

And now there was Jessie. He was crazy about her. She was the first woman since Jennifer whom he desperately wanted. But part of him—a small part, to be sure, but still a part—was worried how that would translate in bed. He was praying that Jennifer was an isolated case. All right, he had to find out. It was obvious Jessie wanted him. There was just so long he could hold off. No, tonight would have to be the night.

He looked at Jessie's sensuous face. Her tongue encircled her lips in an exaggerated fashion. She smiled as she did it.

Ben pulled her toward him and patted her rump as he talked. "Look, it's my house. I get to do the propositioning."

She pushed herself against him, suggestively moving back and forth. "Can I help with the seduction part?"

They both felt his immediate hardness. Ben's heart quickened. There was no trick to her exciting him. Hell, he got a hard-on when he heard her voice on the telephone. He was just hoping for reasonable reciprocity. "You can help, but only in response to. I get to do the initiating."

"Maybe we should go to more neutral territory," she suggested, her eyes wide and eager.

"Uh-uh. We're here. I've cooked a dinner. House rules apply." Christ, they'd be lucky to get through the main course.

"Whatever you say," Jess replied amiably as she circled his ear with her finger.

Forget the main course, they'd be lucky to get through the soup. "I might as well tell you I have something romantic planned for afterward."

"Do you? Anything I'd be interested in?"

Three hors d'oeuvres, tops. "Actually, I was hoping you'd join in."

"Tell me the scenario."

"You just love surprises, don't you?"

"I gave them up eleven years ago. Tell me."

She sounded and looked like a little girl. He just wanted to hug her, to protect her. Her body was up against his now. He felt her firm breasts, the nipples at attention. His erection was still growing. She was no little girl. The hell with hors d'oeuvres.

"All right," Ben said as he stroked Jessie's hair off her face, trying his hardest not to seem uncontrollably anxious. "After this sumptuous repast we are going to have some wonderfully warm brandy in front of a fire I will build with my own strong hands. We're going to look into each other's eyes and feel each other's closeness and not be able to resist each other. And then Rhett is going to carry Scarlett upstairs and we're going to have one passionate, hell of a good time."

Jess looked dubious for a moment. "But what if you don't appeal to me?" she asked.

He kissed the tip of her nose and gently moved on to the rest of her face as he answered, "I believe you've just touched the singular item that doesn't worry me one bit." And at least ninety-five percent of him was convinced of it.

* * *

Ben chalked it up to his devotion to studying history. Who had said, "Those who do not learn from history are doomed to repeat it?" Ben had convinced himself that his loving a woman would inevitably result in the same pattern: the inability to satisfy her. He couldn't have been further off base.

Jessie was undeniably the most passionate, energetic partner Ben had ever encountered. True, she was far from the most experienced, but what she lacked in knowledge, she made up for in enthusiasm. Jessie wanted to please Ben as much as he wanted to please her. He knew that it took more time to arouse a woman than it did a man. Especially someone like Jessie, who might have had various sexual encounters but certainly hadn't known the intense pleasure he was more than capable of providing her. At an early age, Ben had discovered that the two most valuable things a man could give a woman were tenderness and time. Ben had plenty of both.

He knew he had to acquire her trust. He had to get her to relax. Once he had secured those elements, her body was his.

And what a body it was. Every part of it was erotic to him. The breasts that Jessie insisted were too small he found intensely sensuous. They were pert and beautifully shaped and the nipples reacted eagerly to Ben's feathery touch. Her hips, which she had complained had gotten larger over the years, were not even ample by his standards. To Ben, they made a simple statement: "I am a woman." He could never understand why women wanted to look like toothpicks. If he had his way, he would fatten Jessie up a bit. But the best part, aside from her gorgeous, smooth skin, was that perfectly rounded ass of hers to which his hands kept gravitating. And her face. The pleasure alone on that gorgeous face was enough to give him an orgasm at a moment's notice. Was it possible that she was getting more beautiful every day? It certainly seemed so. God, he loved her. He couldn't get enough of her.

Jess was both in heaven and confused. She had had sex.

She had had plenty of sex. But never like this. This was euphoric. She floated in ecstasy. Her world was a cloud. What had he done? Maybe all those little clichés about Italian men were true. What a hunk. Funny, when she'd first met him she thought he wasn't tall enough. She'd never dated anyone shorter than six feet. Feeling his flesh under the sheets with her, she realized how inconsequential height was. The bed was indeed a great leveler. What a body he had. Clothes did not do justice to that physique. It was firm and muscular and strong. She wondered if he worked out. After this little session, she didn't think he'd need to. She'd keep him in shape. The hell with mystery, there was nothing like raw flesh. Not that she could see much of the flesh on his barrel chest, it was so hairy. She knew he would be from the first time she had seen his hands, but she had no idea it would be so generously, yet neatly placed going down in a line from his chest to his belly button. It was a turn-on for her. It always had been.

Jess's mind wandered further down Ben's body to that enormous penis of his. She'd never seen one so big. It could have choked Linda Lovelace. She remembered hearing that John Dillinger's organ was so large he had to wear a holster under his pants to keep it from flopping around. She bet Ben's could give Dillinger's a run for his money. Could he knot it? Would he donate it to science after he died? Had he considered sending his measurements in to Guinness? God, it was huge—so huge, in fact, that when she saw it for the first time she was convinced he would tear her insides out, maybe perform an appendectomy at the same time she was having the most fantastic orgasm of her life. Not a bad idea, actually. She always loved two-for-one sales.

She realized she had never even seen a penis like his. It was uncircumcised. Instant cancer. Every good Jewish girl knew that. Every good Jewish mother had told her so. No Jewish girl gets vaginal cancer. "Show me a Jewish girl with vaginal cancer and I'll show you a girl who's been sleeping with a goy," her mother had warned her.

Of course, no Italian boy on the Lower East Side had considered circumcision a high-priority item. She had had relations with other gentiles; all of them had been circumcised. Now she would begin to look at men and wonder who was and who wasn't. Was it a class distinction? Well, whatever it was, there was that much more of it.

When she mentioned how generously endowed he was, Ben smiled and indicated she wasn't the first to notice. She imagined him walking nude around locker rooms while all the other guys grew green with envy. That's what she would have done if she were a man with those kinds of wares to display.

Then she realized he might have meant that other women had noticed his grandeur. The thought annoyed her. She knew that he hadn't exactly been a monk before he met her, but somehow she didn't cotton to the idea of his having been viewed by other women. Bad sign. Jealousy was an emotion she didn't like to have. It showed dependence. And that was one thing she didn't want to be. Especially on a man.

Her favorite movie scene was in *Fountainhead* when Dominique Francon, the heroine, threw a statue she adored out the window and watched it break into smithereens. When asked why she'd done it she'd replied that it was beginning to mean too much to her, so she had to destroy it before it became unbearable for her to part with. A little overdramatic perhaps, but the message had taken on great significance to Jess after her split with Eliot.

Ben hugged Jess and kissed her gently on the forehead. She cuddled closer to him, feeling his warm, muscular body on her smooth skin. All thoughts of Dominique Francon quickly vanished.

"Mmmmm," Ben sighed contentedly.

Jess was unsure if he had said something. "Come again?" she asked.

"It's a terrific offer," Ben replied playfully.

She smiled and then said in a semibusinesslike manner, "I was merely asking what you said."

"I said 'Mmmmmm.' "

"Is that a satisfied 'mmmmm'?" she asked.

"It's against my policy to give out tens the first time around."

"How many times have you given them out?" Jess hated competition and Ben knew it.

"Awfully nosy. I thought you weren't the jealous type."

"I'm not," she assured him, though she definitely was. "I just like to know about past events. I minored in history at college."

"Suffice to say the title's yours."

Jess relaxed, still unsure it was true. After all, it took time to get to know another person's body. It was a rare encounter that was perfect right from the start. Even so, she was willing to accept his reassurance for the moment.

Jess inadvertently reached for Ben's penis. It was still as big as she remembered, and that was at repose, though she could feel it starting to expand. Realizing what she was doing, she became embarrassed and removed her hand. Ben laughed at her reaction as he took her hand and gently put it back on the growing object.

"That's okay," he told her. "Your hand has great instincts."

Why not? It felt good to both of them. She was certain he couldn't possibly go at it again. She'd never met a man who could have sex more than twice in a night. Then again, she'd never encouraged one to try.

Jess looked at Ben, still awed by their glorious lovemaking. "You know, the whole thing . . . it was really incredible."

"It certainly was." Ben smiled.

It confused her. "I've never felt like that. I mean, *never*. Not even when I was married."

"Are you waiting for an apology?" Ben asked.

"Just an explanation, I suppose."

Ben looked at Jessie's face and patted her hair, then softly caressed her perplexed face, trying to erase the worry lines from her forehead. Could she really not know? "Jessie, you're falling in love with me."

She knew, all right. She just didn't want to face it. Then she asked the question she most wanted to avoid. She couldn't help herself. "And you? Are you falling in love with me?" she asked in as nonchalant a manner as she could muster, her heart in her throat.

He smiled, relaxed. "That's the easy part."

They lay there in silence. Jess went over the evening again and again in her mind. It excited and embarrassed her at the same time.

"I really got carried away, didn't I?" she asked. Ben smiled and hugged her again. "Was I very . . . loud?"

Ben had loved every moment of it. "You were terrific," he assured her. "I never heard someone say 'wow' so many times."

Jess shook her head, confused again. "That word's not even in my vocabulary," she insisted.

"It is now." And they both knew he was right.

"At one point I was considering applauding," She smiled. Then she looked shy again. "Can I ask you a question? Did the earth move for you, too?" She didn't care if it was trite. That's how it felt.

And the moon and the stars and the whole damn galaxy, he thought. He smiled at her and shook his head. "Umhmmmm," he replied.

"Thank goodness. I hate parties for one."

And that night Jess shared a bed with the first man in her life who was able to make love more than twice.

24

There was no denying it, Jessica was addicted. If she wasn't working or spending time with Susan, she was jumping into bed with Ben.

She couldn't get enough. Sex had never been like this. Occasionally she took time out to go to the Library of Congress to read books on sex. She explained to the rather haughty reference librarian who brought her the books that Senator Ford was looking into legislation to tighten the reign on the kind of smut she was taking notes on. The librarian looked dubious.

Jess read *The Joy of Sex, The Sensuous Woman, The Hite Report on Female Sexuality, The Hite Report on Male Sexuality, Delta of Venus, My Secret Garden, Men in Love,* and anything by Masters and Johnson.

She was overwhelmed by how much she didn't know, hadn't even imagined. She wanted to try out everything she didn't classify as objectionably kinky. She was trying her best to be open-minded.

There were plenty of things she couldn't imagine doing. She didn't want to get beaten up or inflict pain on someone else. She didn't like the idea of group sex. Orgies, other women, and rape held no appeal for her. And after reading many of the books, it was hard for her to look at a male German shepherd without wondering what he had on his mind.

Still, that left a lot of "normal" stuff she had never even

considered before. Jess was convinced she was sexually re-
pressed. She was determined to make up for lost time. She
could think of no one more exciting than Ben Casale with
whom to run the gamut.

In the two hours they had spent together in Ben's bed that
night, Jess had brought Ben to orgasm four times. Ben was
breathing hard and looked depleted. Jess loved that look.
She was delighted when she could bring him to that point.
She laughed at the joy of it. Beautiful power!

"Jeez!" Ben said. It was all he could say.

"Yes?" Jess asked, seeking approval.

"Wooh!" Ben panted, trying to catch what little of his
breath he could.

"Pretty good, huh?" Jess gave her smuggest smile.

She cuddled up in his arms, playing with the hair on his
big gorgeous chest. She adored this part. The tenderness was
great. So was watching Ben trying to recoup his energy.

At last Ben was breathing regularly again. He looked at
Jessie's self-satisfied face and shook his head, smiling. He
knew how much she was enjoying this game of hers. She was
like a little girl in a candy shop who had been told she could
have anything she wanted. And she wanted everything.

"I think you have a fallback career," he informed her.
"Have you been reading up on this stuff these past few
weeks?"

Jess's face lit up. "I am getting better, aren't I?"

"Better? Jessie, I can only say it's lucky I have a strong
ticker."

"I love when you cheer me on," Jess said enthusiastically.
She started to imitate him in a football-like cheer, "Do it
again! Do it again!"

He put up his hands in a sign of protest. "I'm stopping
that. I've got to start conserving my strength."

"I think I'll take a shower," Jess announced as she got out
from under the sheets and started walking toward the bathroom.

214   LIBERATED LADY

Jessie's naked body never ceased to thrill Ben. He felt himself getting hard again. When was his body going to start realizing he wasn't a teenager anymore? Never, he hoped. As he looked at Jessie's ass head toward the bathroom he knew he didn't stand a chance. Oh, well, there were worse ways to go.

"Care for some company?" he asked rhetorically.

"Depends. Do you have anyone in mind?"

"Why don't you let me surprise you?"

"Okay. Just don't make it one of those older types who can't get it up."

"That's quite a mouth you've got on you."

"The better to eat you with, Grandma." She gave him a bawdy smile and then turned on the water.

He was still old-fashioned. Jessie was a lady. She was refined. He didn't like her talking that way. But that was his problem. If it really got to him, maybe he'd mention it. Maybe not.

She was lathering her shoulders as he entered the shower. "Ah, the house wine," she said as she looked up and saw him. "My personal favorite."

He took the bar of soap from her hand and continued the job. He'd use any excuse to get his hands on her body. This was definitely one of the ways he liked best.

"You've got one hell of a body there, Ms. Kantor," he told her as he came from behind and carefully washed her breasts. The nipples came to an immediate attention.

"I never really knew it. I mean it. Sex with my husband . . . well, he was sort of a D.O.A."

"C'mon," Ben objected. He couldn't imagine anyone not responding to this woman.

"Honest. I never knew how incredible it could be."

Ben turned Jessie around and looked at her damp face, her hair in a ponytail, what little makeup she wore was gone. God, she was gorgeous. He kissed her gently, then passionately. As their lips parted he told her, "Chalk it up to love."

Jess shrugged her shoulders. "I loved Eliot. Until he was rotten, he was good to me. He appealed to me. I loved his physique."

Ben immediately felt his hardness deflate. His eyes narrowed. He hated when Jessie talked positively about Eliot. Especially in this setting. He wanted to give Jessie's perfect ass a good hard smack. "Do you think we could have a testimonial dinner to your ex-husband someplace else?" he asked sarcastically.

Jess knew how jealous Ben could get. It didn't take much. More power. She put her arms around him and licked around his ear, blowing softly into it. Then her tongue encircled his annoyed mouth, which began to soften and let her tongue enter. Another great kiss. She could feel his hardness return as her hands tenderly encouraged it.

"It was never like this," Jess assured him. But she wasn't willing to let him off that easily. "Well, maybe once or twice. . . ."

"Bitch."

She smiled devilishly.

What could he do? He was hooked. "I hope I'm not just a sex object," Ben said, only half kiddingly.

"I never object to having sex with you," Jess purred.

It was another glorious day together. They shopped at the huge shopping plaza in Georgetown, purchasing a new outfit for each other. Then they went to a small neighborhood gourmet market and bought Gourmandise cheese, a bottle of red burgundy, and a loaf of fresh French bread. Ben picked out two gorgeous filet mignons while Jessie chose some fresh leaf lettuce and hand-picked half a pound of fresh string beans, a dozen huge white mushrooms, and a large Bermuda onion. On their way home, they stopped at three bookstores and purchased five books they knew they probably wouldn't get around to reading for a while.

As they unloaded the groceries, Ben went to get one of the copper frying pans that hung over his stove.

"What are you going to use that for?" Jess asked as she glanced at what they had just bought.

He gave a Cheshire cat grin as he took out some of the condiments he was planning to use. "I thought I'd cook us a special dinner."

It annoyed Jess that she hadn't been consulted. "When we bought this filet mignon," Jess pointed out, "I assumed it was for the sole purpose of six minutes on each side, perfect medium-rare steak."

Ben shrugged his shoulders, undaunted. "Oh, well actually I viewed that rather mundane cut of meat as merely an ingredient in an exquisite beef Stroganoff with thinly sliced fresh mushrooms, a touch of sour cream, and some dry sherry."

At the heart of everything they did, winning was a perennial issue. The power struggle began.

"Beef Stroganoff is heavy in the cholesterol department, isn't it?" Get him where he lives.

She won't score with that one. "If my heart gives out, it won't be because of something I'm doing in the kitchen."

"I'm not crazy about beef Stroganoff."

"That's because you've never had it prepared by a master," he informed her as he started to peel the onion.

Her eyes started to tear. "Why don't you peel that under cold water?"

He knew he was getting to her. It felt great. "It takes more than an onion to make me cry," he said with a slight grin. "I'm thoroughly macho, remember?"

"And yet so handy in the kitchen," she sighed overdramatically. "Sort of Washington's answer to Phil Donahue."

Oh, he was getting to her, all right. "Look, smart ass, if you can't stand the heat. . . ."

Jess surveyed the ingredients Ben had taken out. "Is this all you're adding?"

Ben nodded.

Who was he kidding? No one in his right mind would use tomato paste for a decent beef Stroganoff. She didn't care what Craig Claiborne said. "You know, in my former life I was the queen of the gourmet kitchens."

"What happened? Did you give up eating?"

"No. I gave up having to prove my worth through my perfect briskets."

He gave her a knowing smile. "I think I can out-cook you."

She was outraged. "You what?"

He had taught himself how to cook a long time ago and he was damn good. "I bet I'm a better cook."

"That's ridiculous. You're just annoyed that I do the *Times* crossword puzzle faster than you do."

He'd never known anyone who could until he met Jess. Worst of all, she did it in ink. It really pissed him off. "No, I'm not," he objected. "Anyway, that's not what we're talking about. The issue here is who's a better chef. I'm willing to stake myself to a friendly wager."

Now it was getting interesting. "What kind of wager, big boy?" Jess asked seductively.

"You name it."

"Let's make it simple. Breakfast in bed for the winner. Anything *she*—or he—wants."

"Deal," he agreed.

"Wait a second," Jess interjected. "How will we decide who the winner is?"

"I know this is a long shot," Ben answered dryly, "but maybe we could just be honest about it."

Jess shook her head negatively. "I don't know. That approach hasn't worked in Washington for years."

Jess hadn't thought about cooking for a long time. An intricate meal at home generally consisted of a steak on the barbecue and a salad. Still, a challenge was a challenge.

They stood next to each other, hot and heavy into competition.

"Cooking that steak on a pretty high heat, don't you think?" Jess asked sweetly.

Bitch. "Hot and fast. That's how I do everything," he replied equally sweetly.

"I approach things more slowly so I can reach perfection. I guess it's an attitudinal difference."

Ben's Stroganoff was tangier, Jess's more subtle. Both were excellent.

"I cast my ballot for mine," Jess announced after two quick bites.

Ben shrugged his shoulders. "I vote for mine. This is ridiculous. We've obviously got a split decision here."

"Not necessarily," Jess responded as she reached out for Ben's hand.

He loved when she touched him. "How do you propose we break this tie?"

Her hand reached under his sleeve as she gently slid her nails up his arm. "I want a revote," Jess informed him in a sultry voice. She got up and went behind him, gently nibbling his ear, slipping her hands under his shirt, gently caressing the nipples on his chest. They responded effortlessly.

"Are you trying to influence one of the judges?" Ben asked, his head started to swim, his skin started to tingle.

"Looks that way," Jess whispered as she blew into his ear.

"Don't you think you're taking advantage of me?"

"That's what I had in mind," she assured him as her hand undid his fly and made its way to what she considered his most vital organ. "I still vote for my Stroganoff," she said as her tongue circled his ear and her fingers circled the tip of his penis. "How about you?"

It was really no contest now.

Ben sighed with pleasure. "How do you like your eggs?"

She smiled and purred, "The same way I like my men: over hard."

Their lovemaking was outstanding: on and on into the night.

"You never wear out, do you?" Ben asked her, half impressed, half amazed.

"You know, I've read that thirty-nine is a woman's sexual peak."

"How about a man's?"

"Nineteen."

"I should have guessed."

"Do you think I should try younger men?"

"Not unless you want to see them decapitated."

"But Ben, I'm almost thirty-nine. Can you imagine what I'll be like in a few months?"

"I'll make appointments to get vitamin E shots."

She snuggled close to him. Jess could see that Ben was on the verge of sleep. She couldn't blame him. It had been a full day and it was late, but she wasn't tired yet.

"Ben, do you think we're decadent?"

"Probably," he responded, half asleep.

"How about incestuous?" Jess continued.

"Incestuous?" he asked, practically unconscious.

"Well, you *are* my stepuncle."

"I'd say we're safe on that one." He yawned as he took a blurred look at the clock radio. "Jessie, it's two o'clock. Aren't you exhausted?"

"I want to hold on to tonight. Tomorrow's Sunday."

"It happens every week—right after Saturday."

"But it's our last night," she tried to explain.

So close to sleep. "For what, honey?"

"Susan comes home from her winter vacation tomorrow."

"Uh-huh."

"So we won't be able to be together like we have been."

Ben started to wake up. His mind was urging him to think. He opened his eyes and looked closely at Jessie. "You never mentioned she was coming home tomorrow."

She gave a noncommittal shrug.

"That's great," he said. "When do I get to meet the famous Susan?"

"Why would you want to meet her?" Jess asked, not happy where the conversation was heading.

Ben was fully awake now. "For one thing, I'm in love with her mother. I thought I might spread the wealth."

Jess looked uncomfortable. "What does one thing have to do with the other?"

"All right, let's have it. What's the problem?"

Jess didn't answer. She yawned and turned over as though she were going to go to sleep.

"Oh, no. You can forget that."

"I'm sleepy."

"I know the feeling. I was there three minutes ago. Now I'm fully awake and we're going to talk this thing out."

"There's nothing to talk out. I'm really dead. Let's talk about it tomorrow."

"Hey," he said, a stern businesslike look on his face, "not ten minutes from now, not tomorrow, *now*. Finish what you started."

Jess turned over and shrugged. She wished she hadn't brought it up. "It's no big deal. I was just mentioning my schedule."

"There's more to it than that." Jess didn't respond. She looked blankly up at the ceiling. Ben gently turned her face toward his. "Come on, out with it."

How could she say it? "Susan's a very lovely teenage girl . . ." Her voice trailed off.

"I think I've established I go for older women." It wasn't that. Jessie couldn't possibly think he'd make a play for her own daughter. No, that was impossible.

"Susan's never liked any of the men I've dated," Jess said flatly.

"That's because she's never met me. I'll woo her. Besides, I'm not like any of the other men you've dated."

Ben looked closely at Jessie's face, trying to determine what was going on in that head of hers. She looked troubled by his last statement. He tried to piece it all together. It suddenly made sense.

"That's it, isn't it?" he said, more a statement than a question. "You're afraid she'll like me."

"Don't be absurd," she said defiantly, though not convincingly.

He had yet to understand her. It was so simple to him. "Jessie, sweetheart, I love you. You love me."

Jess was fighting him as hard as she could. "That isn't what we're talking about."

"Well, if it isn't, it should be." Ben was determined now. "I want to meet your daughter. Wednesday sounds just fine, thank you. I'll be there at seven. I'll bring the wine."

She looked at his eyes, she looked at his jaw. Gibraltar looked more movable. She knew better than to argue about this one.

25

"Are you almost ready? Ben should be here any minute," Jess told Susan as she passed her room and noticed she hadn't even started to dress yet.

"In a minute."

"Susan . . ." Jess said with noticeable annoyance.

"What's the big fuss, anyway?" Susan asked as she continued turning a page of the latest book her mother had disapproved of her reading.

"No big fuss. I just don't think it's polite to be in a bathrobe when a guest arrives."

"But he's your guest."

"He's *our* guest. This is *our* house. So, come on—move it."

"One more page, 'kay?"

"One more and then step on it."

"You got it." Susan smiled at her mother and her mother smiled back. They were still a team.

Typical teenager, Jess thought.

Jess had prepared an all-Italian meal for Ben and was now regretting it. Surely he would be able to taste the difference between her tomato sauce from a jar with a friendly looking Italian woman on it and the sauce from scratch he had been weaned on. Why hadn't she taken that course on Sicilian Specialties at the Adult School? Bad sign, Jess. Still thinking the way to a man's heart is through his stomach.

She had added all the regulation extras: mushrooms,

sweet peppers, onions, zucchini, oregano, fresh parsley, but she knew Ben: He was a connoisseur when it came to anything Italian. She didn't stand a chance. Oh, well, she did have compensating virtues. She hoped he remembered them.

She looked in the mirror again. Her hair looked pretty. She had started to wear it down now. It was more stylish and Ben liked it. She had to admit it did look better. She looked more attractive than she had in years. Ben told her it was because she glowed from being madly in love. Jess agreed, but thought the weekly hair appointment and the Revlon makeup deserved some credit.

Maybe a little more blush, she thought. Damn, why did it matter how well she looked? She didn't want to get into that self-destructive pattern of pleasing a man again. Still, she did feel good being attractive. It did please her. Conflicting emotions again. She wished she could get it straight at least in her own head.

Jess glanced at the clock as the doorbell rang. Seven on the button. She admired that trait. She was a stickler for punctuality and Ben knew it. It was not easy for him—he was naturally late when it came to any social event. But he knew how much his tardiness irritated Jess so he made a concerted effort to be prompt. He was successful about fifty percent of the time.

Jess looked around the house as she went to open the door. She thought how differently this house was decorated from the one she had shared with Eliot. Everything was tastefully done, of course, but the frills were gone. This house was much more tailored and impersonal. Even the colors: gray and burgundy. It occurred to her that if you didn't know who lived here, you might easily assume it was a man's townhouse.

Ben was dressed in his tweediest jacket holding a bottle of wine, flowers, two wrapped packages—and he had the look of a lamb being led to slaughter.

"My God," Jess stated, looking at all the gifts, "you're not Greek, are you?"

His eyes narrowed. "Congratulations, you've got even me feeling nervous."

Jess smiled. "Come on in. Susan should be down in a minute."

"What did you tell her about me?" he asked.

"Just that you beat me and think all females are inherently inferior."

"I knew I could count on your support," Ben remarked dryly.

He was having trouble concentrating on their conversation because Jess's dog, a Boston terrier, had not stopped barking since Ben had entered. He was jumping as high as he could on Ben, growling and yapping furiously. Susan came bounding down the steps, but the dog took no notice.

"This is Butch," Jess said, introducing her dog to Ben.

The barking got louder. Okay, make friends with the mutt. "Hello, Butch. Down, Butch. Persistent little Butch. You did say Butch, didn't you?"

"It was the male version," Jess explained, turning to introduce her daughter. "Susan, this is Ben. Ben, Susan."

"Hello," Susan said.

But Ben was not about to take his eyes off Butch, who was still jumping and growling. Especially since he hadn't put his gifts down and felt defenseless. Susan started to laugh to herself. Another one of Mommy's nerds, she thought.

"Energetic little tyke, isn't he?" Ben said amiably as he began shaking the dog loose from his pants.

"Butch, behave yourself," she ordered the dog, who apparently had not learned either his name or the command yet. "Are you afraid of dogs?" Jess asked Ben sweetly.

"I'm fearless, remember?"

"You're lucky," Susan told him. "He usually bites Mother's boyfriends."

She wasn't going to be a pushover, he could tell that. "Maybe Butch is getting discriminating," Ben said, hopefully.

Susan shook her head as though she doubted it. "Sometimes he holds off for a few minutes."

"I assume he's had all his shots?" Ben asked. Butch had now moved on to his left leg, which he found no more appealing.

"Shots?" Jess asked innocently.

"Terrific. Let me get rid of these so I can defend myself." He started to distribute what he was holding. "Jessie, the wine and flowers are for you."

Jessie? That was odd. Susan had never heard anyone call her mother Jessie before. She felt as though she were hearing him say something intimate.

"Thank you," Jess said, taking the flowers and wine from Ben. "Nothing for Butch?"

"I left the Valium at home. Okay, Butch, old pal. How about if we call a truce? Do you know that you have a dangerous animal here?"

"Yes, and the dog may be a problem, too."

Jess regretted the remark as soon as she had said it. Ben gave her a disbelieving look. Susan thought they were gross.

Jess quickly moved on. "What else have you got there?"

It was the first time Ben thought it might be safe to remove his eyes from the dog. Butch had calmed down and was merely sniffing now.

Ben looked at Susan. She was a lovely young lady. He could see so much of Jessie in her. It was enough to win his instant affection. But she was a teenager. For some reason he never envisioned her that way.

Ben looked embarrassed as he tried to explain. "You know, Jessie, when you talked about your daughter. . . ." He turned to Susan. "I know you're fifteen, Susan. I just think of people's children as being . . . children." Jess had never seen Ben at a loss for words. He turned toward her and imploringly asked, "You're not going to help me?"

She was baffled. "I don't know what you're trying to say."

Ben reluctantly handed Susan the two remaining packages. "Susan, these are for you."

Hesitantly, Susan took them from his hands. "Thank you," she said, a bit confused.

As Susan opened one package, she began to understand this man's embarrassment. She took out a book and read the title aloud. *"Nancy Drew and the Hidden Staircase."*

"They were all out of Dr. Seuss," he explained sheepishly. "What are you reading in school?"

"We're just finishing Tolstoy's *War and Peace,"* she told him.

"Well, then I think we can certainly consider Nancy Drew alternative reading," he concluded.

"Absolutely," Susan agreed, hardly able to keep from laughing as she looked at her mother. Susan couldn't wait to open the next present.

"I want you to know it doesn't get any better," Ben warned her, looking even more embarrassed than before.

Susan eagerly ripped open the next gift and looked at it, biting her lip to suppress her laughter. "A Barbie Doll," she announced triumphantly.

"She does everything . . ." Ben assured her, "swims, skis, homework. It's the newest one."

Susan felt the package. There was more. She reached in and took the rest out. She was delighted. "Oh, super, three new outfits."

"The saleswoman said you could exchange them if you already had them."

"I'll have to check my collection," she said sweetly. When had she stopped playing with them? Was she seven or eight? She couldn't remember except that it was earlier than most of her friends because her mother had thought Ken and Barbie were bad role models. Those were her mother's militant feminism days.

That's wooing her, Ben. What a fiasco. He shrugged his shoulders and said to Susan, "You don't suppose Butch plays with dolls, do you?"

* * *

It was hardly a fiasco.

Much to her amazement, Susan liked Ben immediately. He was bright and witty and, she thought, fantastically good-looking for an older man. And he was all man. She could feel it in her bones. She looked at his hairy hands and then his hairy arms when he took off his jacket and rolled up his sleeves. Yuck, that was a turn-off, but she still thought he was sexy. He was in good shape as far as she could tell. He looked strong. Macho, that was the word she was looking for. Boy, she'd bet he was great in bed. Susan wondered if they did it. Oh, of course they did. Well, if you had to do it, he wasn't a bad choice to do it with. Not bad at all. Her mother was one lucky woman. Susan hoped she knew it.

They hadn't stopped laughing since they'd sat down. A lot of the time was spent listening to Ben's stories. Susan couldn't hear enough of them. Ben's enjoyment telling them was infectious. But he also listened to what she had to say. And he seemed interested. It was a novelty for Susan.

"Anyway," Susan continued animatedly talking about what her class had pulled on a substitute teacher, "when they found out, we said we had no idea what they were talking about."

"And they bought it?" Ben asked incredulously as he pulled off another piece of garlic bread.

"Hook, line, and sinker," Susan reported proudly.

Jess shook her head, smiling. "Susan, I've been telling Ben what a perfect child you are."

Ben looked at Susan and shook his head approvingly. "You would have fit in just fine where I grew up," he told her. He turned to Jess. "I don't know, Jessie. When you were that age, could you get away with all that cra . . ." he caught himself midword and corrected himself, "stuff?"

"I was the original 'goody-two-shoes,'" Jess told him.

Susan quickly sized up Ben. "I bet you weren't a goody-two-shoes," she said to him, delighted to have found a compatriot.

The mere thought amused him. "I couldn't have survived in my neighborhood. 'Three Fingers' Mahoney and Sal 'The Animal' Randazzo were my two best friends."

"Are they still?" Susan asked, dazzled by a world she'd never even caught a glimpse of.

Ben shook his head no. "It's tough to keep up a close relationship from Sing Sing."

"Are they really there?" Susan's saucer eyes grew bigger.

"Only for another ten to twenty," he told her nonchalantly as he started to move his chair away from the table. "I'm going to get another cup of coffee."

"I'll get it," Jess offered.

He put up his hand. "Sit. This way I can steal another meatball from the pot and no one'll be the wiser."

"Then you really liked the meatballs and everything?" she asked, pleased with herself. And he thinks he's such an expert.

"Sure did. It's the best sauce on the market. I use it myself when I don't have time to make the real thing."

He flashed a knowing grin. Thought she fooled him, did she? No amount of doctoring up could do that. His mother was from the old country.

Bastard. She gave him a dirty look.

"The mushrooms and peppers were a good touch, though." He winked. "And the zucchini was inspired."

She'd get him for that. What could she do to him in bed, she wondered. Her mind raced playfully.

"Great Italian cooking is something you're born with," he deadpanned. "If it's not in your genes, well. . . ."

Her eyes narrowed. "Actually, I make great lasagna from scratch."

That was news to Susan. Divorce and fast foods had entered her life at the same time.

"What a coincidence," he replied casually. I'll just bet you do, sweetheart. Let's set this trap just right, he thought playfully.

I'll have to read every Italian cookbook ever written. "Maybe we should compare recipes sometime."

She'll have to read every Italian cookbook ever written. "That would be interesting," he agreed. "Although I wouldn't count on it tasting as good as mine. I think I probably have an edge in that department."

He thinks he has me. "You wouldn't like to put it to a friendly little wager, would you?" She took off her shoe under the table and let her foot wander under Ben's pants, up his leg. Her face reflected nothing.

Ben tried to remain equally impassive. "Maybe we should get an impartial judge this time."

"Whatever you feel most comfortable with," Jess smiled sweetly.

Her foot went to the back of his knee as she made soft, flickering movements with her toe. His spine was beginning to feel gentle chills. He could feel his hardness. Would the bulge be noticeable if he got up now? He didn't dare look. He didn't want to move. He wanted to take Jessie right there. And he would have if there weren't a fifteen-year-old child present. Butch he wasn't that worried about.

"Exactly what color is that chair, Susan?" Ben asked.

Susan turned around to see what chair he was referring to as Ben abruptly got up and made a beeline for the kitchen.

"You're crazy," he mouthed with his lips as he passed Jessie's chair.

"Me?" she mouthed back innocently.

"Burgundy," Susan answered as she turned to see Ben's back disappearing into the kitchen.

"I like it," he yelled from the other room at the same time he was shaking his pants loose, splashing cold water on his face, cursing and lusting for Jessie.

"It would be nice to have someone around who likes to cook, don't you think?" Susan smiled engagingly.

Jess feigned a hurt look. "I thought between those Swanson Dinners and Burger King, we were doing just fine."

Susan and Jess could hear Ben talking to Butch in the kitchen. They both started to giggle.

"I really like him," Susan whispered excitedly to her mother. "He's so funny—not like any of the others."

"So I've been told."

"Mother, let's keep this one."

"Susan," Jess exclaimed, surprised.

But they couldn't continue their conversation because Ben returned with a fresh dish of meatballs and spaghetti.

"I gave a few meatballs to Butch," he told them. "I think I've found a place in his heart. That bowl on the floor was his, wasn't it?"

"Yes," Jess assured him drolly, "we gave up eating off the floor last week."

"Listen, I've got a great idea," Ben suggested enthusiastically. "Why don't the three of us go skiing this weekend?"

"Skiing? The three of us?" Jess repeated doubtfully.

"You think Butch'll feel left out?"

"How can we go skiing?"

"Easy. We'll fly to Vermont on Friday, be home late Sunday night."

Jess shook her head. She was letting too much work slide as it was. Her guilt and Peter's caustic comments were beginning to get to her. "Ben, I have a primary coming up."

Ben poured some more wine into both of their glasses. "Who doesn't?" he asked, reminding her they were in the same business. "But not until June. It's only February, honey."

Susan was so excited by the prospect, she practically jumped out of her seat. "Oh, Mother, please," she begged.

Jess knew her resistance level was low, but she didn't want to give in too easily. "Well, we'll see," she said.

Ben winked at Susan, who smiled broadly. The outcome of this one wasn't too hard to predict.

"It's time the *three* of us got to know each other," Ben said confidently.

* * *

It didn't take long. They spent more time together in the following weeks than most families do in five years.

By the end of their first weekend, Ben had taught Susan how to ski down the second-hardest mountain at Stowe and Jess how to get up by herself after falling. Ben found a lodge with abundant hot chocolate, a cozy fire, and friendly people who gathered around a piano and sang. He stood in the middle, one arm around Susan's shoulder, one arm around Jess's.

Ben made sure the three of them spent every available moment together. They went to the Smithsonian, the movies, bowling, restaurants. They spent quiet evenings at Jess's house reading, eating dinners, watching TV. Ben helped Susan with her homework and encouraged her to discuss her problems with him. They talked endlessly.

Within a month, they had become a family. It was warm and it was comfortable. Jess had forgotten how good it could feel. Susan had only vague recollections of those feelings. Ben had none at all. All of them thrived on their closeness.

Snow in Washington was an infrequent occurrence. When it fell, even an inch or two, the city came to a halt.

Jess loved snowball fights. It was the one outdoor sport she had mastered. She snuck up behind Ben and motioned Susan not to give him any warning. She threw the cold round fluff down Ben's shirt as he gave out a surprised shout and turned to face her. She backed up.

"You little . . ." He had to try to remember there was a minor present. "That was dirty pool."

"All's fair in snowball fights," Jess informed him.

"Oh, yeah? Are those the rules?" he asked, checking.

She didn't like that look on his face. It had too much retaliation for her liking. She didn't answer.

"I asked, 'Are those the rules?' Or are we playing boys' and girls' rules?" He knew that would get her.

"All's fair. I didn't think it needed clarification."

"Fine," he said, starting after her. Jess dodged him as well as she could. She was no athlete. He was. It was no contest, only a matter of time. He quickly tackled her and she fell on her back, unhurt, preparing for the inevitable. Ben picked up a snowball, lifting it above her face. Her struggling wasn't helping. He was so damn strong, she could barely move. She squinted her eyes shut and waited.

Ben looked at Jessie's face. It was six years old, vulnerable, and gorgeous. How he loved this woman! Jess opened one eye slowly, then the other. She saw that lovesick look on his face. God, she loved this man. She puckered her lips. Ben laughed and dropped the snowball as they kissed hard and long, blocking out the world.

In the background, Susan sighed happily. Let it last, she prayed.

Which only went to prove, Ben thought, that being cold didn't stop him from getting hot.

"I think," Ben whispered to Jess as he pushed his layered body as close to hers as he could, "that occasionally we're going to have to break this threesome up. I'm horny as hell."

Jess shook her head in agreement. Horny was putting it mildly.

26

The primary election was in full swing now. Usually during that period Jess focused on nothing else. But this was not like the other times; there had never been a Ben before. She was feeling guilty. She didn't want to do less than her typical perfectionist work. They didn't do elections over because you weren't prepared.

Peter was the only one who complained that she wasn't doing her usual job. She knew he was right. In the past two weeks she had worked harder than ever. Her efforts were paying off, but not enough. Then again, she was never satisfied that she had done enough.

Even though the days were getting longer, it was dark outside when Jess hung up the phone and announced *"Fini!"* to Peter.

"Any luck?" Peter asked.

"Let's see," Jess responded, checking the three-by-five cards she kept. "Five hundred less than last time. This primary isn't the breeze I had anticipated. Oh, well, tomorrow's another day." Jess started to straighten up her desk, which reminded her of the aftermath of a tornado.

Peter looked at Jessica's exhausted face. "My God, you look dreadful."

"Thank you, Peter. That's the kind of ego-boosting I live for."

"One minute you're ignoring your work, the next minute you're killing yourself. I'm just worried about you, love."

"No need. I've got a mother who does that."

"I thought I could save you a toll call."

"How considerate of you," Jess remarked.

"Seeing Lover Boy tonight?" he asked.

"There's a distinct possibility."

Peter shook his head. He didn't understand her. "Nonstop. Looks like the real McCoy. Even Susan says she likes him."

"It's the first healthy relationship she's had with an older man other than my father. The first decent role model."

"Thanks a heap," Peter responded, crushed. Hadn't he spent time with Susan taking her to the circus and the movies and even baby-sitting for her?

"I'm sorry, Peter. I didn't mean to hurt you. It's just different."

Peter accepted her apology with a nod. "Does marriage ever come up?" he asked.

"I sidestep it each time it does."

"So for the time being . . ."

"I'm just having one hell of a good time," Jess said, finishing Peter's sentence.

Peter gave one of his all-knowing grins as he picked up a fresh pencil from Jess's desk and pointed it at her as though he were imparting a great lesson to his disciple. "So you've finally attained the heretofore masculine role in society—using your partner as a sex object. Freud would be proud of you."

"Right," Jess said skeptically. Still, she couldn't dismiss his theory out of hand. She knew there was at least a shred of truth to it.

"But Ben's more to you than that, isn't he?"

Much more. Too much more. Too many layers. "It's been a long day, Peter. Can we dissect my psyche some other time?"

Peter shrugged, disappointed his student didn't want to delve further.

Saved by a knock, Jess thought, as she heard the rapping on the door. Ben walked in jauntily.

"Have time for a constituent?" he asked, a big grin on his face.

That was a welcome change of tone. "Hi," Jess greeted him warmly.

"Hello, Ben," Peter said in a friendly manner. He couldn't help it. As much as he wanted not to, he really did like Ben.

A look of concern crossed Ben's face when he saw Jessie. "What's with our girl, Peter? She definitely looks over-worked."

"Because she is," Peter concurred.

"You look exhausted."

"A girl's head could swell out of proportion from all this flattery."

"You need someone to take care of you," Ben determined.

"Do you have anyone in mind?" Jess asked innocently.

Ben smiled slyly. "Even the method."

They exchanged sexy glances. Jess wasn't that tired.

Had they forgotten he was still in the room? Peter cleared his throat just in case. "I'll leave you two lovebirds to your cooing," Peter remarked dryly. "Lovely seeing you, Ben." He waved good-bye as he made a graceful exit.

Ben studied Peter as he left.

"I think Peter is fond of you in spite of himself," Jess noted.

"I have a feeling if we ever break up, Peter will be the first one to call me."

"Really?" Jess asked slyly as she slipped her hand inside his pants, feeling him start to react. "I didn't know this big fella went both ways."

"This is one thing you'll never have to worry about," he assured her, his mind swimming, thinking how much he wanted to take her right there on the office carpet.

Jess could feel his excitement. Completely at attention now. Ben's right hand adroitly went to work on her left breast, then right, bringing them to a full salute. Tit for tat, she thought.

"Do you think performing these acts in a senator's office is a federal offense?" Jess asked.

"No jury in the nation would find me guilty for going after these breasts."

"What if I told you I was working undercover for the Feds?"

"Then I'd say your right hand is guilty of entrapment."

She laughed as they kissed, her hand leaving his groin area.

"As you were, soldier," he ordered.

She accommodated as they kissed again, but it was evident her kiss lacked its usual unabashed enthusiasm. He looked at her tired face.

"It's like kissing a corpse."

"I'm sorry," Jess apologized. "I'm just beat."

She also looked thinner. He knew she must be losing weight.

"What did you have to eat today?" Ben asked, sounding like a concerned parent.

Jess knew Ben hated when she skipped meals, but she couldn't help it. There was so much to do. She had been incredibly busy. Food was the last thing she ever thought about. "Five cups of coffee and three Tic Tacs," Jess admitted guiltily.

"Jessie, I've told you, you can't live like that. You're not giving your body any nourishment."

"I did put milk in the coffee," she defended herself weakly.

Ben shook his head as though he didn't know what to do with her. "You really do need someone to take care of you. Luckily, there's a volunteer in the audience. First, I'll take you to a nice restaurant and get some decent food into you; then I'll take you to my place and show you my necrophilia routine."

* * *

They ended up at Nino's, one of Ben's favorites. All roads invariably led to Italian restaurants. Ben never insisted, it just seemed to work out that way. He felt at home there. Generally, Ben tried to avoid the better-known restaurants —Candelas, or Yolanda's al Campidoglio. He loved Petitto's, even though it was an "in" place, because they served pasta and only pasta and it was extraordinarily delicious.

But they skipped Petitto's that night because Ben felt Jess needed more in her than just pasta (even though he was positive that pasta was the most underrated health food in the world).

He watched her ravenously consume every bit of her veal rollatini, linguini with white clam sauce, house salad, two pieces of hot garlic bread, and two glasses of wine. Knowing her, she probably hadn't eaten in days.

Jess didn't take care of herself. Ben was convinced of that. A typical Type-A personality. If she were a man, she'd be obvious heart attack material. She didn't even exercise. Ben ran three miles a day, played tennis, racquetball, handball, and went to a gym at least three times a week. He knew the value of a good workout. He'd have to get Jessie into some sort of regimen for her own good. She really did need looking after. That was okay with him. He'd been waiting his whole life to do that for the right person.

"That was scrumptious," Jess said as she swallowed her last bite of veal. "I feel like a new person."

Ben moved his chair a little closer to Jess's now that she was through eating. He took her hands in his and gently kissed them.

"Hey, you—I love you."

Jess smiled. "I love you, too."

"Prove it."

Jess sensed a serious subject coming up. She was too tired to think seriously tonight. "Prove it? Didn't I ask you to be my Valentine this year? That's something I do *not* take lightly."

Ben knew she was dodging the issue again. "You know we've got to talk," he said.

"Why don't we get the bill and go to your place?"

"You're doing it again," Ben said, annoyed. "Avoiding talking."

"I'm talking," Jess countered lightly. "Do you not see these lips moving? Do you not hear words coming out? I call that talking."

"About *us.*"

"My favorite subject."

"Uh-huh. Right," Ben said skeptically.

Jess knew what was bothering him. She wasn't prepared to talk commitment; he was. They both were aware of the problem. She wasn't going to give in just to please him, but she didn't want him to be angry with her either.

"Hey . . ." Jess whispered coyly, her hand going under the checkered tablecloth, starting at his knee, working its way up his leg.

He immediately started to get hard. Damn it. Why could she always do this to him? That goddamn pecker of his was more reliable than Mussolini's trains. "Don't try your feminine wiles on me." He tried to sound annoyed.

She wasn't fooled. "Why not? I'm entitled."

"It's an unfair advantage." And it was. He was alternately embarrassed and excited when she did sexual things like this in public, and Jess loved it.

"If you've got it, flaunt it," she said throatily.

End of serious discussion for now. But just for now.

27

Without going into detail about why it was so important to him, she knew Ben needed her to visit the Lower East Side with him.

Jess pieced together what she could of Ben's marriage to Jennifer even though he was fairly close-mouthed on the subject. He had told her that it hadn't worked, that it was wrong from the start, that he had tried to save it, that he had failed miserably. When Jess asked for particulars, Ben had only alluded to his feeling that they had been worlds apart. The class distinction had been too great.

There were times Ben had felt the same way about Jess. They came from such different backgrounds. Jess's upbringing was loving and secure, hardly similar to Ben's. And although her family wasn't wealthy, she had never had to worry about money. Still, she wasn't a snooty WASP like Jennifer. Jess's family didn't thrive on exclusion the way Jennifer's had.

Ben thought that Jews and Italians were similar in many ways. Warmth—that was the primary similarity—and a sense of family. Italians considered themselves one big family. So did Jews. Even during his worst moments, Ben never doubted that his father would fight for his family if he had to. It was a given. Italians loved fiercely and often died the same way. It was that sense of passion, that sense of commitment that Ben had been searching for as long as he could remember. A family of his own. He wanted Jessie to be part of that.

But first he had to take her back with him to where his roots were.

He never fully recovered from Jennifer's reaction when he'd brought her there. The whole visit had lasted no more than half an hour. First, Ben had shown Jennifer the tenement building on Mulberry Street. She looked away from it and refused to go in. She insisted on being driven to every place he mentioned, even if it was only a block away. She hated the people—they looked dirty and stupid; she hated the restaurants—they were probably cockroach infested; the smell of the area turned her stomach. She had wanted to get out of that disgusting place. She was sure they were going to be mugged or killed. When Ben realized how futile it was, he got in the car and they drove away. For the five years they stayed married, he never returned.

After the divorce, Ben visited with almost compulsive regularity. It was as though he wanted to make it up to the area he had deserted both as an adolescent and as an adult. He felt guilty. It was a place that had been good to him and he had turned his back on it. Maybe you never really could escape who you were, he thought. Maybe he no longer felt the need to.

Some high-priced analyst could probably come up with profound psychological reasons for his behavior. He didn't care. What he did care about was that Jessie come back with him. He needed to gauge her reactions.

It wasn't easy, but Jess arranged for a whole weekend off. Neither of them told their families they would be in Manhattan. They weren't prepared to deal with that aspect of their relationship yet. Terry and Jack's marriage had taken its toll. Although the newlyweds were ecstatically happy, the families still hadn't adjusted to the reality of the union.

Jess told Ben that it was his weekend. He should make all the arrangements and they could split the cost down the middle. Ben refused to split the cost. Jess had expected he would react that way. In many ways, he was still a man of the old world.

They stayed at the Plaza. It surprised Jess. She loved the Plaza, of course, but she saw no need to spend that kind of money. They weren't going to spend much time in the room anyway, and what time they did, well, Jess could happily make love to Ben on a mattress in a hostel. She finally concluded that Ben wanted her to be aware of the dichotomy that existed between uptown and downtown, and that he was a downtown boy. He had a lot to prove.

Which was exactly why he had chosen the Plaza. Riches to Rags.

None of this was articulated, of course. The two days had simply been billed as a weekend together in Manhattan. Neither of them knew precisely what to expect.

After a continental breakfast in the Palm Court, Ben suggested they go out for a ride. They ended up on Mulberry Street. Jess got out and started to look around. It was a seedy area, there was no doubt about it. But it was also an interesting one.

Jess wanted to know everything Ben had done when he was young. Where had he gone? What pranks had he pulled? Could she see his apartment? Could they watch the men play boccie? Could they see all his old haunts?

He showed her his favorite place on Allen Street. At one time it had been considered the hottest red light district in the city.

"How would you know something like that?" she asked him, pretending to be appalled.

"Everyone gets his start somewhere," he explained, grinning.

Now she was appalled. "You did it on the street?"

"No." Well, maybe a few times in an alley, but he didn't have to disclose everything. "I went back to her . . . boudoir."

"Show me where," she implored.

"C'mon," Ben objected.

She grabbed his hand eagerly. "I want to see where it all began. Besides, maybe they're accepting applications. A girl can always use a fallback career. That's why we go into teaching."

The building hadn't changed one iota. Ben was amazed.

"Do you think it's still a house of 'ill repute'?" Jess asked dramatically.

Ben shrugged his shoulders. "I doubt it. But I guess it could be."

"You act like you're not still a regular customer."

He smiled at the thought. "Pretty clever, huh?" he said and winked.

Jess began to examine the deteriorating front of the tiny tenement building.

"What are you looking for?" Ben asked.

"A plaque. I can't believe they don't have some dedication in your honor. You must have been at the top of the class."

"Actually, it was one of those pass-fail courses. There were no awards ceremonies."

The truth of it was Jess loved this area. It fascinated her. It was something she didn't know. A place she had only read about. She wanted to talk to as many people as she could. Most spoke little English or were suspicious of her, but those who were willing to talk recounted long, interesting stories. Remembrances. Days gone by. Lifetimes ago. Moments that could never be recaptured.

They touched her. She could feel the yearnings, the frustrations, the alternating despair and hope. In a way, Jess told Ben, she was jealous. He could have contact with people from the old country. It wasn't that easy for her. Only one of her grandparents had been an immigrant and he had died before she was old enough to lock him into her memory. And so many Jews had been annihilated during World War II, there was barely a relative alive in Europe for her to talk with. She had a few distant relatives in Israel, but had never met them.

Jess eagerly went from place to place, holding Ben's hand, taking it all in. They went to Kaplan's for lunch. Ben had visited Mr. Kaplan many times since he had left the Lower East Side. Mr. Kaplan was proud of what Ben had done with his life. He felt an almost paternal pride. Many were the nights Mr. Kaplan told Dominick he wanted Ben to do extra work for him at the deli and then, once Dominick's shift was over and he had gone home, Mr. Kaplan helped Ben with his studies. Ben never forgot.

It was especially embarrassing to Ben when he brought Jennifer to meet Mr. Kaplan. She had refused to have more than a Coke. After carefully examining the glass for smudges, she demanded a straw so she could drink straight from the bottle. Ben could have wrung her neck at that moment.

Jess loved Kaplan's. It was noisy, lively, amusing, rushed, informal, and the best deli she had ever eaten in. The waiters were all characters. She ordered a lean corned beef on rye and knew better than to pick out all the fat that surrounded the few lean pieces of corned beef she was served.

"So tell me, Mr. Kaplan," Jess asked as though she were a long-time confidant of his, "what was this upstanding citizen here like as a boy? Was he a holy terror?"

"Ben? Nah. He was one of the really good ones. You got yourself a nice boy there."

"You think so?"

"I know so. Listen to me, darling, this is some man. He made me proud. He made us all proud. A good boy. A really good boy. With a real *Yiddushe kopf* on him. Like a son to me."

"You know," Jess continued as though Ben weren't even there, "he speaks the same way about you. What do you make of it?"

"Ach," Mr. Kaplan objected, dismissing yet believing every word. "So tell me what else I can get you? You like kreplach? I got some kreplach soup that will give you the most delicious heartburn you ever had. Let me fix you somethin' real special. It'll be my pleasure."

When they were leaving, Jess kissed Mr. Kaplan. He openly blushed, but was genuinely pleased. He pulled Ben aside and whispered, "This time you got yourself a real lady. A real lady."

That evening they went to Grotta Azzurra for drinks, Umberto's Clam House for appetizers, Angelo's for dinner, and Ferrara's for dessert. They could barely move by the time they took their last bite of spumoni. They walked off as much as they could and then returned to their room at the Plaza and worked off the rest, contentedly falling asleep in each other's arms.

The next day they checked out of the hotel and went to Joey and Edie Manetti's for brunch. Joey, who was now in real estate in Long Island, had been a good friend of Ben's when they were growing up. When Ben left for Choate, Joey had promised to look out for George.

They had remained friends, with the exception of the five years Ben was married to that stuck-up bitch, Jennifer Holier-Than-Thou, as Joey had called her. Jennifer had made it impossible for Ben to see any of his friends from the old neighborhood. Everyone understood. They waited it out.

Jessie was down to earth. Joey thought she was wonderful, even if she was a women's libber and not even Italian. She made Ben happy, and that was enough for him. So when was the wedding? Ben dodged the question three times and finally told Joey to get off his back.

"We'll get married when we're ready, that's when. What's the goddamned rush, anyway?"

"No rush, for Christ's sake. You're just not getting any younger, buddy boy. You love her, she loves you. It's natural, that's all. Don't break your balls on my account."

There was one person Jess wanted Ben to meet. At first she hadn't suggested it—this was, after all, his weekend. But after they left the Manettis', Jess casually mentioned she'd love to introduce Ben to her closest friend. Ben proposed they try to arrange it, secretly pleased that Jess was bringing him home to meet somebody important to her.

As it turned out, Barbara was going to be in Manhattan anyway, so they planned a late afternoon meeting in the Village.

That left them two hours to kill. Jess suggested it was her turn to show Ben the Lower East Side she knew.

Shopping for bargains: the Jewish woman's mission.

"This is a talent," Jess informed Ben. "It's why God gave women fingernails: So they could claw their way up to the front of a sales table and grab the best buy."

Ben smiled broadly. "And I thought you were such a lady."

"There's some dust in the air here." Jess gave him a sly smile. "Charm school training goes out the window when you smell a mark-down within a mile radius."

Jess thought about the times she had come with her mother when she was growing up. Haggling over prices was as natural as breathing. Jess could still remember.

MRS. SIMON (outraged): Fifteen dollars! No one's going to buy it for that price. Thief! (Turns to leave.)

VENDOR: All right, twelve. But only 'cause I like you.

MRS. SIMON: Ten.

VENDOR: Sold.

MRS. SIMON: And give me two dollars change.

VENDOR (outraged): Thief! I wouldn't sell it to my own mother for that little.

MRS. SIMON: Then keep it. (Turns to leave.)

VENDOR: All right, all right. It's yours. I must be getting soft in the head.

MRS. SIMON: Maybe I'll take one for my sister. Is there a quantity discount?

And so it went.

But those were days gone by. Now the stores had standard prices—still much less than in the retail stores, but the mark-down was firm. Jess was relieved. She couldn't deny her mother got great bargains, but the process always embarrassed her.

"It's part of the game," Mrs. Simon had explained. "It's expected. You want to overpay, Saks is waiting with open arms."

The few times Jess had shopped here as a grown-up was during the week. Nothing prepared her for a Sunday. Bedlam abounded. The third time Jess was shoved aside by a customer and dismissed by a merchant as not worth waiting on, she realized her mother was right. There was still a game to be played here.

Darwin surfaces on Orchard Street. Survival of the pushiest.

"We need a suitcase," Jess told Ben.

"A suitcase?"

"We'll have too much to carry by hand," she told him. This was business, not pleasure.

Ben was amused. He'd never seen Jessie so interested in fashion before.

Fashion was the least of it.

She got a heather blue cashmere turtleneck at Forman's, a pair of Calvin Klein jeans at D&G, a classic tweed Tahari suit at Breakaway, and a London Fog raincoat at Fleischer's. She knew prices well enough to know she had saved a bundle.

Ben was next. She helped him choose a pair of Adolfo slacks at Andre, an exquisite herringbone suit at Adlers, and a Stanley Blacker sports coat at Fashion Corner that looked like it should come with a yacht.

At their last stop Ben picked out six dress shirts and three ties. Jess knew they were good buys, but she had seen two of the shirts for a little less not fifteen minutes before. She decided it was time to do some serious haggling.

"What's the best you can do for us," she said quietly to the manager she had pulled aside.

He looked aghast. "Lady, this is it."

"C'mon, the competition is going to kill you. I saw the

same shirts down the block for a song. Let's be reasonable, I've got a half dozen shirts and a number of ties here."

"Five percent more," he sighed. "And that's only because it's a slow day."

Jess looked around. The store was packed with customers. "Twenty-five," she said firmly.

"Listen, this ain't no charity organization."

Jess shrugged her shoulders and handed the shirts back to him. "Fine. Thank you anyway." She turned to leave.

"Okay," the manager said. "Ten percent, but that's final."

"Twenty."

"Fifteen."

"Eighteen. I'm talking cash in the hand within thirty seconds."

The manager looked harassed. "Okay, okay. But don't say nothing to nobody."

Jess smiled softly. "You've got it."

So much for bargaining being a thing of the past.

Ben looked admiringly at Jessie as they headed toward their car to meet Barbara, who had suggested a café that served cappuccino and Italian pastries. Jess was nervous.

In retrospect she should have realized how well they'd get along. By the end of the hour they were old buddies.

"You take good care of this lady or else I'll get my own hit man to take care of you," Barbara had warned Ben kiddingly.

"They have a department for that at Bloomingdale's?" he asked innocently.

As they kissed good-bye, Barbara whispered in Jess's ear, "If you get tired of him, send him to my house. I think I'm in love."

They went to Mulberry Street one more time before they left for Washington. They both got out of the car and stood under Ben's old fire escape, breathing in the air, taking in all the surroundings.

What impressed Jess most was that Ben had not been brought down by the squalor of this area, as so many of his friends had. He had the guts, the sheer determination to make it, to get out. And yet she knew there were still so many ghosts haunting him. Jess came up behind him, putting her arms around his waist, resting her head on his shoulder.

"Do you want to stay here a while? There's no rush to get back," Jess said gently.

Ben took one last look. "No. I'm ready to go home now."

She shook her head, understanding. Ben watched Jessie as she got into the car. He knew then, as he had known over and over during the whole weekend, that he had to marry this woman.

28

Ben was starting to get another erection. For Christ's sake, they had just finished a one-hour session that would have impressed the hell out of Harold Robbins and here he was, his prick out of control, begging for more. What a glutton.

He looked at Jessie, who was snuggled close in his arms. She hadn't noticed his erection yet. Not that it would surprise her. By now she had to realize that it didn't take much for her to get him going. Could he really have been peaking at nineteen? He sure hadn't cared if it wasn't accompanied by love in those days.

Love. Jesus, Mary, and Joseph, did he love her. He kissed the top of her head as he started caressing that sexy ass of hers. He wasn't even aware that he was doing it. It had become that natural.

"You know what I like best?" Jess said as she unconsciously massaged his rear end.

"Do it alphabetically," Ben replied, anticipating a long list.

"The aftermath," Jess stated.

"That takes care of 'A.'"

"The best part is when it's all over and we're just lying here together."

Ben looked at her oddly. That was it? "Very flattering."

"The lovemaking is dynamite, earth shattering, unbelievable. You know that."

"I never object to hearing it. Positive reinforcement is good for my ego."

"Your ego doesn't need much reinforcement," Jess pointed out.

"Everyone's ego needs reinforcement," he replied. Then, after a minute, he added, "And I love lying here with you, too."

Jess smiled that little girl smile he loved. He could feel his erection growing. Slow down, he tried to tell his prick, but there was no directing it. He started outlining her face with his fingers. It always made Jess arch her back from the chills it gave her up and down her spine.

He couldn't contain himself anymore. "Jessie, what the hell are we waiting for? Let's get married."

He knew she didn't want to deal with this subject. Why did he have to persist? "I'm not ready yet," she said quietly, hoping that would end the discussion.

But it didn't. Ben was getting progressively annoyed. He was tired of playing by her rules. "What do you need, messianic permission?"

"I need time to establish myself," she responded simply.

It didn't wash with Ben. "Come on. You're established," he objected.

"Maybe you think so, but I don't." He'd never know what it meant to be a woman in a man's world. "You're so damn sure of yourself because you've been successful your whole life. I'm new at this game."

"Eight years is not a short time. You've been a successful lawyer that long. How much more proof do you need?"

Calm down. You love this man. He's proposing to you, not firing you. Give him a reasonable alternative. "We could live together," she suggested.

Ben shook his head. "I've got my reputation to protect. Jessie, I'm serious. Living together is not enough for me."

"What do you want from me?" she asked, tired of fighting.

"What I want from *us* is a substantial commitment. I

want a family," and then he quickly added, "at least one child between us in addition to Susan."

She shook her head negatively. "I've had my family," she stated flatly.

"You said you wanted more kids."

"When I was younger."

"Just deliver them. I'll have you back in court in time for your summation."

She had wanted more children—that much was true. She loved being Susan's mother and she adored the unquestioning love you got until your child became a teenager and suddenly discovered your perfection was laced with flaws. But even as relationships between a teenager and mother go, hers and Susan's had gone pretty smoothly. More children? Part of her still yearned for that, but not a big enough part. She was almost thirty-nine. Time to get on with her life. Too much of it had been spent avoiding growing up. She didn't want to move backward.

"Ben, I'm past the formula and diapers stage. I'm too old to start over."

"No you're not," he stated firmly.

Typical male response, she thought. "Don't try to bully me. I know who I am."

"Sometimes I don't think you have the slightest idea who you are," he told her.

"I don't sound like much of a bargain," she countered. "Why do you even want me?"

"Justice and love are blind. And I am madly in love with you, Jessie." He was trying to gauge why she looked so troubled. It worried him. "You are in love with me, aren't you?" That was the one thing he had to be sure of.

She sighed, her soft voice filled with anguish. "Frighteningly so," she told him.

"Why frightening?" He needed to understand. "Honey, what's the problem?"

How much could she tell him? She wasn't even sure of all the reasons herself. She only knew that whenever they talked about marriage, her blood ran cold. Still, she knew she didn't want to give Ben up. She loved him more than she'd ever loved any man. Maybe she wasn't capable of a real commitment. There had to be an answer.

Ben drew her closer to him. "Look," he told her reassuringly, "we can negotiate terms. I don't want to lose Susan and you."

"Can't we talk about it tomorrow?"

"All right, Scarlett. But give it some serious thought. I'm getting antsy."

"Is there anyone else?" Jess asked teasingly.

"Don't I wish," he said with half a laugh. "Jessie, I'm serious."

"I know. And I do love you."

"I hope enough," he said, still worried.

Well, at least she had found the sure fire way to get rid of his hard-on.

From then on it became Ben's most intensive campaign. He wanted Jessie to marry him. He loved her. He needed her. Nothing was going to deter him.

When they watched *Casablanca* on television with Susan, Ben noticed Jessie's eyes well up during the final scene between Bogie and Bergman. He seized the moment. Giving her his rumpled handkerchief, he motioned toward the twosome parting on the screen and whispered, "See what can happen? Marry me, for God's sake, before you wind up on a one-way plane to Algiers." Jess managed a smile through her tears.

He left flowers on her desk with proposal notes attached; he sent telegrams; he planted messages in her pocketbook; he got her a subscription to *Bride's Magazine*; he sent her a jar filled with what he said were her tears. He considered hiring the Goodyear Blimp, but decided it was too expensive. He thought about withholding his body, but concluded he had no desire to punish himself.

Jessie always seemed pleased by his gestures, but not

enough to change her mind. Everyone liked the chase, but this was getting ridiculous. And annoying. And aggravating. Ben's patience was running thin.

A normal Sunday. Spring was finally breaking through. Cherry blossom time in Washington. All the greenery was returning. The time of year for lovers. Ben pulled the car over and pointed at the church across the street. The newlyweds emerged, too blissful to be ruffled by the rice that was being pelted at them by their wedding party. Ben looked at Jessie, sitting by his side.

"I want you to marry me. When will you decide?"

Jess felt torn once again. "Soon. Maybe not tomorrow, but soon. Believe me, I'm trying."

His patience was running *very* thin. "Try harder."

The restaurant was perfectly charming. And French food, yet—that was a change. From the moment she entered, she felt as though she were in Marseilles. What Jess liked best was the intimacy. She estimated there couldn't be seating for more than forty patrons. And although every table was taken, there was not a sense of being crowded together. It was evident that this was a very popular, if relatively unknown, restaurant. Every dish she ordered was exquisite, right down to the chocolate torte. She figured the restaurant must have opened recently, yet even so, it probably took pulling a few strings to get a reservation.

Ben had been especially attentive and loving. She was relieved. She knew she wasn't pleasing him with her indecision. She looked at him lovingly as he took her hand.

"How was the dessert?"

"Divine," Jess told him, kissing her fingers with her lips for emphasis.

"Hey," he objected, "you only do that in Italian restaurants. In French restaurants you say '*magnifique.*'"

"Ah-hah." She nodded.

"I'm only asking," Ben continued, "because I was dying for a taste."

"You were?"

"You didn't see me salivating?"

"I thought that was because I left an extra button open on my blouse."

"Only partially."

"Anyway, since when did you get shy? You usually just take without asking." As she pointed this out she put her hand to his face. It was rough. His beard grew quickly and he could have used a shave twice a day, but it reeked of masculinity and she enjoyed touching his face then.

Ben put his hand on top of hers and moved it to his lips. "I've been reading all those Emily Post columns. This is a chic establishment. I wanted to fit in."

"I see." Jess nodded. "Trying to improve your social standing again. Where on earth did you find this place? It's phenomenal."

"I have my sources. I wanted everything to be perfect tonight. I have a little something extra for dessert."

"What?"

Ben took out an oversized ring box and carefully put it on the table in front of Jess. She looked at the box, almost afraid to lift the lid.

"There's something in there, if you'd care to open it."

Jess shook her head, unable to speak. Well, it had to be opened. She couldn't just look at it until the check came. Slowly, she reached for the black box and opened it, hoping there was a little paper jack in the box that would jump out and they could both have a good laugh. But, of course, it wasn't a gag. It was a delicate marquis diamond ring surrounded by emeralds. Her heart jumped, her stomach got upset.

"It's beautiful," she said haltingly.

"It's not a friendship ring," Ben informed her.

"No?" she said, feigning surprise.

"Should I be down on one knee?" he asked. Jess smiled. "All right, if that's what it takes . . ." He got out of his seat and took her hand as he got down on his left knee. "Jessica Simon Kantor, will you marry me?"

By now, most of the guests had noticed what was going on.

"Ben, people are staring," Jess told him, embarrassed.

"Who cares? I want you to marry me." He turned to the group of people in the restaurant and addressed them. "I want this woman to marry me," he announced. He got up and took the ring out of the box to show the group. "Look at this ring. Isn't it a knockout?"

The group was caught up in the excitement of the moment, some volunteering "Beautiful," some "Gorgeous." Their sense of decorum vanished. Ben had made them part of an event and they were enjoying it.

Ben turned to Jess, elated. "They like the ring." He turned back to all his newly found friends. "We're madly in love. Don't you think we should get married?"

By now the group was unanimous in their agreement, yelling "Yes!", "Absolutely!", and "Go for it!"

He turned back to Jess. "That's an overwhelming consensus, Jessie. Especially in a town that sends everything to committee."

She had to laugh. "You're definitely deranged."

"That much we knew. The issue at hand is whether you'll marry me."

He was adorable. How could she refuse? "Yes, yes, I'll marry you. Now sit down."

He turned excitedly to the group. "The lady said *yes!*"

He grabbed Jessie and kissed her passionately as the group cheered in the background. He looked at her, asking with his eyes if she really meant it. She nodded a gentle yes and he felt safe.

He turned to the group and made his final announcement. "I want you all to give your names to the maître d'. You'll be receiving your wedding invitations shortly."

* * *

He couldn't believe it. She really said yes. Well, why not? He was going to make her happy. He was going to love her. He was going to take care of her. They were going to be the happiest couple in D.C.—no, in the world. He was madly in love with her and it wasn't just because of his perennial erection whenever they were together.

Ben sang all the way home. Jess was very quiet. She smiled whenever Ben looked at her. It was a forced smile. She wondered if he could tell.

"Let's wake Susan and tell her," Ben said as they walked up the path to her townhouse.

"It's a school day tomorrow," Jess objected.

"So what? You're getting married. This is twice-in-a-life-time news." He felt so euphoric, he could barely contain himself. "Why don't we all take off tomorrow and go somewhere?"

"I can't," she said weakly. "I have appointments. I can't break them."

For the first time since the restaurant Ben noticed there was a cloud still hanging over her. "Is it my imagination or are you not being carried away by the excitement of the moment?"

"I'm excited," she answered unconvincingly.

"So who do you think we're going to make happier: your mother or mine?"

"I'd say it's a toss-up."

The cloud was still there. He lifted her face with his hand. "Jessie, sweetheart, I'm not Eliot. This marriage is going to work. Believe it."

Believe it. The words kept ringing in her ears. But how could she believe that any marriage was going to work? She hadn't seen a really decent one in all the years since she'd been divorced.

Believe it, huh? That's all she had done while she was married. She believed that if you were a good wife you would have a faithful husband. Wrong. She believed that a marriage was a fifty-fifty proposition that you both worked at equally. Wrong. She believed that a wife had as much power in the relationship as her husband did. Wrong. She believed that love conquered all. Wrong, wrong, wrong!

And it wasn't just Eliot. Over the years—in law school, in encounter groups, in Washington—she had found her story was mundane. Everyone had a husband who was emotionally absent. Even those who stayed with their mates. And they were the worst. First, because they remained anchored by the fear that they were no one without their husbands, both economically and socially. Second, because they were right. Third, because Jess had almost been one of them.

Fear—that was the worst enemy. There wasn't even a close second. When Jess realized how immobilized fear made women, she became determined to overcome it. And she had. She became a survivor. No, more than that. She became a winner. She learned how to outfox men at their own game. She got the rules down cold, she learned the ropes, she mastered the techniques. She became a lady with balls and she loved it. She loved the power. Men didn't know how to handle her. They only knew they had to watch out for her.

It was hard to believe what a naive babe in the woods she had been when she and Eliot had first separated. She still thought that there was a prince out there waiting for her. Each encounter with a man toughened her up a little more.

Rich Seagal was only a beginning. Every time she hovered around commitment in a relationship, something went wrong. Push came to shove, the man didn't come through. The healing process was always rough, but gradually it became easier.

Barbara was hardly surprised. She knew the score. When her own husband came through for her emotionally, she was certain that it was only transient. Eventually the other shoe would drop. Men were insensitive to women's needs. Oh, they could play the game for a while, but sooner or later they'd disappoint you. It wasn't that they meant to, Barbara assured her, it was simply their conditioning. But, responsible or not, it all came down to that clearer-than-a-bell message: Men are shits.

By the time Jess was in her third year at law school, she had pretty much sworn off men. She decided that Susan and studying were all she needed. Her only diversion was the time spent on Professor Irwin Black.

Professor Black was Jessica's torts professor. He was intelligent and dynamic—one of the best teachers Jess had ever had. His reputation was renowned.

All of torts fascinated her, but she was especially interested in *New York Times* v. *Sullivan,* a case dealing with the slandering of a public official. What confused her was the exact application of "reckless disregard." She was sure that Professor Black could clarify it for her.

In fact, Professor Black couldn't have been more generous with his time. Since another class was about to begin where they were talking, it seemed only natural when he invited Jess to finish their discussion over a cup of coffee. Indeed, Jess found the whole conversation enlightening and beneficial. After an hour, she thanked Professor Black for his time and was on her way.

It couldn't have surprised her more when Professor Black asked her to join him for another cup of coffee after their next class. Relieved that she had a *Law Review* meeting, Jess politely declined.

The third time Jess politely declined Professor Black's invitation, he became noticeably irritated.

"You know, Ms. Kantor, your grade in my class is rather important as to whether you stay on *Law Review,*" he informed Jess very matter-of-factly. "You should be more, shall we say, friendly. I think we should spend more time together."

Antennae up. "What do you mean, Professor Black?" Jess asked innocently.

"You know what I mean," he answered with emphasis. "I think we should spend more time together."

Within twenty-four hours Jess had filed an administrative complaint with the Ethics Committee of the law school asking for a hearing and requesting that Professor Black be censored for his chauvinist behavior.

The letter from the five-member, all-male committee enclosed a copy of the response from Professor Black addressing Jess's allegations. In it he delineated the time and place Ms. Kantor had approached him to discuss some aspect of defamation law. Trying to be as responsive as he could, he noted that he had offered to finish the conversation over coffee. That was the one and only time they had gone somewhere—a rather public place, at that—together. Perhaps, he suggested, she had misunderstood the nature of his assistance. That being the case, it was unfortunate and, indeed, a rather sad commentary on the state to which student-professor relationships had deteriorated as a result of the Women's Movement. This was something he profoundly regretted.

The committee determined that they could see no reason to go any further in their investigation.

"Son of a bitch," Jess complained bitterly.

"At least you got an 'A—.' "

"I deserved an 'A' and he knew it. No-good bastard."

"It's the system," Barbara told her simply. "The old-boy network."

"There must be a way to get around it," Jess insisted.

"Have you considered a sex change?"

"Seriously."

"Believe me, this is the best it gets."

Jess shook her head, refusing the resignation. "I'm going to beat them at their own game."

Barbara gave her an all-knowing look. "I hope you have a fallback wish."

Oh, she would succeed all right. She loved that challenge. Working twice as hard for half as much was the answer. If that's what it took, that's what she'd do. Well, Barbara was right about one thing at least: Men were definitely shits. Some just took a little longer than others to surface.

Washington, it turned out, was the Men-Are-Gods capital of the world. Deferential treatment was de rigueur. The one person who accepted her on the quality of her work, however, was Senator Ford, and for that she was profoundly grateful.

But, she quickly learned, it was only the first round. Mostly she was resented because she had acquired power without sleeping around to get it. Yet as much as she was resented for not playing by those rules, it also made her highly desirable.

Odd how everyone wanted what they couldn't have. Well, that suited her just fine. Now she was the one who called the shots. Peter was on target about that. If she wanted a man, she could generally have him. Her most attractive quality was her unavailability. Now that she was no longer warm and giving, men craved her. All types of men. She had her choice. She had relationships with the ones she wanted, slept with them when she desired, but never got emotionally involved.

In the years that followed, she settled in with the men who were powerful in their own right but had less to prove. Generally they were older, bland in personality, mildly interesting, willing to give Jess whatever she asked for. When Jess got tired of the relationship, she'd simply call it a day and move on. The terms of a relationship with Jessica Kantor, though never specifically articulated, were clearly understood: when she was with you, she was caring and wonderful; when she wanted out, it was over—no questions asked.

Jess walked away from all her relationships and never looked back. She had built a protective shield around her feelings and it served her well. She was completely in charge. She made sure she never got hurt again.

But she hadn't counted on someone like Ben coming into her life. Damn him. Why was he doing this to her? She had been fine until he came along. Now, for the first time in such a long time, she was allowing herself to feel, allowing herself to love and be loved. She was becoming dependent on a man again. And she knew he'd inevitably hurt her.

She knew the whole M.O. She had seen it often enough. Eventually reality would set in. The one absolute pattern she had discovered in the traditional male/female courting was that the man loved the chase. Once that was over, true colors hit the fan. A woman expected marriage to be the beginning of a long and wonderful happily ever after. A man considered it the beginning of "that's great until something better comes along." Maybe a man didn't think that consciously, but it always worked out that way. Time after time, Jess saw the scenario replayed.

So why set herself up for the inevitable fall? She had planned never to remarry. Who needed it? Happily ever after was for schoolgirls.

And then she thought about Ben again. Could he really be as good as he seemed? He sure was in bed. Then again, Eliot had talked a good game before they got married. No, Ben was definitely better than Eliot had ever been. For one thing he made sure Jess enjoyed the sex, too.

Ben. He had his flaws, but who didn't? And he was the first man she had ever been so honest with. She told him her feelings. Of course, she hadn't trusted him with everything she felt, but she confided more than she ever had to any other male and he still hung around. Perhaps his best asset was that although he was strong, he didn't want her to be weak. In fact, he seemed to admire her strength and show pride in her achievements.

Ben. They had so much fun together, shared so many of the same interests, were devoted to most of the same principles.

And then there was Susan. She was mad about Ben. Jess couldn't dismiss that. They had become devoted to each other.

Damn that bastard. She was in love with him. There was

no way to escape it. She ached at the thought of what she could no longer avoid. She couldn't walk away from this one.

She didn't sleep the whole night. It was 6 A.M. when she went to the bathroom to take her makeup off from the night before. She looked in the mirror and saw her rumpled, tired face. She had grown to respect that face through the years.

"I hope you know what you're doing, pal," she said to her reflection.

Then she looked at the ring on her finger. It wasn't a spectacular, drop dead ring, but it wasn't one her mother could call unimportant either. It was simply a ring bought with love. And that made it gorgeous.

She lifted her hand and addressed the ring as though it were Ben. "Okay. But this time, damn it, make it right."

29

Let's see, how should Jess break the news to Peter? Not that he'd be surprised. Disappointed, maybe. He still had lingering hopes that she'd meet some foreign dignitary who'd whisk her away in his private Lear jet. Peter refused to accept the whole Jessica-Ben affair as anything more than that. An affair. A passing phase. Jess found herself looking forward to Peter's disdain.

Walking jauntily into her office, she was totally unprepared for the chaos that greeted her. The whole staff was shouting and scurrying, looking as though major disaster had befallen them. The minute they saw her they stopped dead in their tracks. It was as though they were waiting for the director to shout "Action!"

Jess looked quizzically at Monica, who simply shook her head sorrowfully, then at Peter.

"I assume you've seen this morning's *Post,*" he stated superciliously.

In fact, she hadn't. Normally, she glanced at the *Washington Post* while she dressed, when she drank her quick cup of coffee, and even while stopping for the red lights as she drove to work. It was the newspaper to read in Washington and, as far as she was concerned, it surpassed the *New York Times* in reporting and coverage. This was something one did not announce too readily, however, since it was tantamount to intellectual heresy among the snobs who worked on The Hill.

But this morning, although she had it with her, she hadn't even looked at the headline. Too many other things on her mind. "Why? What's happened?"

"Come with me," Peter instructed her as he headed for her office.

Sensing she'd better do as she was told, she followed him to her desk, making sure to close the door behind her. "Well?" she asked, once they were at her desk.

Peter threw the newspaper down in front of her. "See for yourself," he told her, and then proceeded to report what was in the article. "Congressman Calvin announced at the Newspaper Editors' Dinner last night that he's opposing Senator Ford in the June primary."

"You're kidding."

She looked at the story on page eight. The article was hardly big news for this town, but it sure would be front page material in every newspaper in Pennsylvania.

Peter wasn't going to let this one pass without getting all the mileage he could out of it. He glared at Jessica. "Didn't your buddy, Ben, tell you? He is Calvin's administrative assistant."

"He never mentioned a word of it," Jess answered, shocked.

"Weren't you going to go to that dinner with the senator?"

"It didn't seem necessary. I changed my plans at the last minute," she told Peter defensively. Jess looked at Peter, realizing what he must be thinking, knowing that this was not exactly the right time to tell him her engagement news. It looked as if Peter was right after all.

She could hear the phones ringing throughout the office. "Damn it," she muttered. Time to get back to where she belonged. She glanced at the newspaper article again. "It says here Calvin is having a noon press conference. He's bound to want a debate. We've got our work cut out for us. I want a full staff meeting in one hour. Tell Monica to come in. Send someone to pick Senator Ford up at his apartment and make sure he doesn't make any premature statements before I talk to him." She started writing notes to herself on her pad and then realized Peter hadn't moved. If he thought he was going to start lecturing her now, he had another think coming. "What's the problem?" Jess asked in a cold, forbidding voice.

"Nothing."

"Then let's get moving. We've got an election to win."

Peter shook his head crisply, relieved to see the old Jessica at last. "By the way, Ben called three times this morning. What should I say the next time he calls?"

"That I'm unavailable. Tell him I'm in the middle of a campaign."

Peter smiled to himself as he exited. They were a team again.

Bastard. Damn fucking son of a bitch. He double-crossed me. They're all alike. Jess took off the ring and put it back in the black box where it belonged.

Ben hadn't sat down since he walked in the door. But then that wasn't as much of a surprise to him as it had been to Jess. He hadn't missed the article in the *Post.*

Having had the most peaceful night's sleep he could remember, Ben got up leisurely, put up some coffee, sang while he showered, hummed while he shaved. He whistled as he put some whole wheat bread in the toaster and walked to his front door to get the paper.

Usually a fast reader, his mind wandered to what his future was going to be like: married forever to the woman he loved; a warm home life; maybe a few more kids; raking autumn leaves; playing football with his kids; having intimate dinner parties with friends; spending night after night in bed with the most exciting woman he'd ever known. Sharing. He was a happy man. He felt an overwhelming sense of tranquillity.

He almost skipped the article on page eight, but then the name drew his attention: "Congressman Calvin"—good, he liked publicity—"to Challenge Senator Ford." He had to refocus his eyes. He read the article twice. He didn't believe it either time. The third time it sunk in. He stopped whistling.

Goddamn that Richard Calvin. I'm going to kill him. Why the hell does he do something like this without telling me? I'm his goddamn administrative assistant and that schmuck doesn't give me the courtesy of advance notice. If this doesn't stop, I'm going to wring his neck. I'd better call him and find out what the hell happened.

And then he remembered Jessie.

He ran to the phone. Dead. No wonder he hadn't gotten any calls. Goddamn phone company. He was going to deduct this from his bill. Someone had to pay.

Ben left his half-eaten toast, chugged down his coffee, rushed into his bedroom to finish dressing, and ran to his car, screeching out of his driveway. He pulled over to the first phone booth he saw and called Jessie's phone number. Seven rings. Eight rings. No answer. Gone. He called her office, but she wasn't there. At least that was what Peter told him in his most icy tone. Damn Peter. He'd call again when he got to the office.

That was easier said than done. Apparently, Congressman Calvin had been trying to get in touch with Ben all night, but kept getting a busy signal.

Calvin was like a little boy on Christmas. He told Ben how he had decided at the dinner the night before that he *had* to announce he was going to run against Senator Ford. It felt right. He was convinced he could be a better senator. Ben agreed. During the years he had worked for Dick Calvin, he had grown to respect the man for his dedication, his integrity, and his voting record. Ben was sure that Calvin would be infinitely better than Ford, who Ben considered a political hack.

The problem, of course, was Jessie.

Ben knew just how much her work meant to her. But she could get another job, probably better than the one she had now. And, damn it, Calvin was the better man. No contest there. It was politics. Jessie would understand. She had to.

Ben tried to call her three more times. Unavailable. He would get to her as soon as the press conference was over. They'd talk it out. Everything would be all right.

No-good bastard. She could have killed him. Shooting was too good for him. Maybe hanging. Something slow and painful.

So he screwed you. Big deal. It had to happen eventually. Better now than after you were married until death do you part. Son of a bitch.

And to think she'd accepted his proposal. He undoubtedly knew what he was doing all along. Divert her while he made Calvin's plans. He'd explain it somehow. Well, he could damn well take that explanation and shove it. Did he really think she wouldn't care, that his job was more important than hers? Was he naive enough to think she was going back to just being somebody's little wife? No way, José. Those days were history.

She looked at her face in the mirror in Senator Ford's private bathroom. She couldn't tell if her eyes looked puffy from the tears. She splashed cold water on her face and made a decision. Those were the last tears she was going to shed for this failed relationship. In an hour, Ben's only identity in her life would be that he was running the opponent's campaign. No more, no less. Her personal feelings for him were severed. The queen of repression was back in town, this time to stay.

Okay, she looked fine. Eyes dry, mouth determined. She had one last bit of business to attend to. She checked her pocketbook to make certain the ring was still there and then opened the bathroom door and went to the intercom on the desk. She buzzed Monica to tell her she was stepping out of the office for twenty minutes.

*   *   *

As she rode the subway between the Senate Office Building and the Rayburn Building, Jess estimated she had said hello to fifteen different people she knew. Clearly her life was here.

Jess checked her watch as she approached Congressman Calvin's office. Twenty to twelve. Perfect.

As she opened the door, she noticed that it looked like a miniature of Senator Ford's office. The workers were obviously in a mad rush to meet a deadline. And Jess knew precisely what that deadline was. She stared across the room at Ben, who was busily jotting notes down as he talked into the telephone.

The people in the room stood motionless, silently watching as Jess briskly walked to Ben's desk.

"Right," he said into the phone. "You'll have all the details in the news release we're handing out at the press conference." He hung up the phone and continued writing.

"Mr. Casale," Jess said coldly.

Ben looked up. "Jessie," he said, relieved to see her. "I've been trying to reach you all morning."

"So I've heard."

"I've got to talk to you. When can we get together?"

"Right now would be fine." The ice on her words was not melting.

Ben looked at the clock on the wall. "Ummm, I have a press conference scheduled in fifteen minutes."

"So I read. What I have to say won't take long."

Ben looked at the rigidity on her face. The coldness of her tone had not failed to register. "All right. Calvin's office is free. Let's go in there," he told her as he took her arm to usher her in. "No interruptions," he instructed everyone as he closed the door.

Jess stared at Ben. Her eyes narrowed. There was no doubt in Ben's mind that he'd better be prepared for the worst, but he was ready to fight it.

"A funny thing happened this morning," she said sarcastically. "I was reading the *Post* and came across this article that sort of caught my immediate attention. I bet you can guess what article it was."

"I had absolutely no idea he was going to make that announcement last night," Ben asserted firmly.

I'll just bet you didn't. "Are you telling me that Calvin never mentioned he wanted to run for the Senate?"

"He mentioned it, yes. But only as something he was considering."

Jess gave him a knowing glare. "Politics really does make strange bedfellows, doesn't it."

"Our relationship had nothing to do with politics and you know it," he said, getting angry.

Jess liked it when her opponent lost his cool. She was winning. She could respond calmly. "Exactly how much of what I've told you about Senator Ford have you told Calvin?"

"You've never told me anything that wasn't common knowledge. Let's face it, Ford isn't exactly a choir boy."

"Who is?"

"Some are closer than others."

"And you didn't know that Calvin was going to announce his candidacy last night?" She questioned him again as though she could break him down.

"I'd have been there if I had known," Ben responded reasonably.

Jess gave a haughty laugh. "You expect me to believe that?"

"Of course," he responded sharply.

"Why?"

"Because I've never lied to you about anything." He was trying to understand how she felt. "Look, I know this is going to put a strain on our relationship."

If looks could kill. "It's going to do a lot more than that."

"What the hell does that mean?" he asked angrily.

A secretary opened the office door meekly. "Ben, ten more minutes until the press conference."

He turned to her and growled, "I'll be there. I said no interruptions."

The secretary quickly closed the door. Damn it, don't take it out on her. Calm down.

He turned to Jess and tried to be coolheaded and reassuring. "We can weather this, Jessie. We'll talk it out later."

Jess shook her head in a firm no. "I don't want to talk it out later."

Ben was losing his patience. He felt himself racing the clock and it put him on edge. "What *do* you want, Jessica?"

Calling her "Jessica." A sure sign he was upset. He had never called her that before. Good, because upset is just what she wanted him to be.

"I want you to convince Calvin to pull out," she announced evenly.

It was an untenable demand. "You know I'd never do that," Ben responded.

Final test. "How important am I to you?"

"Before I sleep with you, I have to be able to sleep with myself."

Ben's assistant opened the door, looking worried, speaking anxiously. "Ben, it's getting closer."

"Goddamn it, two minutes," Ben exploded. His fists tightened as he turned to Jess. "You couldn't have timed this any better, could you?"

"Don't worry," Jess responded nonchalantly, "I won't be intruding in your life anymore."

"Perhaps you've forgotten we're engaged to be married," he reminded her.

Jess reached into her pocketbook and took out the ring box, handing it to Ben. "I believe all the jewels are still intact."

He felt like the bull looking straight at the red cape. "Here's what I think of that." Ben grabbed the box furiously and walked to the toilet in the adjoining bathroom, angrily throwing it into the bowl and flushing it down. "A fitting symbolic gesture for our relationship," he shouted, wanting to wring her neck.

"I'm sure you've made some poor alligator very happy," she said coldly.

He wanted to shake her until there was some sense in her head. Instead, he looked at her, trying to understand why she was doing all this. And then he did. "Boy, this is what you wanted all the time, isn't it: the easy way out."

"I looked at that ring all night," she replied sadly. "I finally decided I really wanted to marry you."

"And now you've done the noble thing," Ben retorted. "After all, before you're a woman, you're a professional. I've become the enemy, haven't I? Once again confirming all you've believed about men. Well, guess what, sweetheart, you're your own worst enemy."

"Oh, am I?" Jess came back sarcastically.

"You're damn right you are. You're plain scared."

"Of what?"

"Of being married."

"Don't be an ass. I was married for seven years."

"And the first time the going got rough, you bailed out."

"I tried hard at that marriage," Jess protested.

"Bullshit. When things were going smoothly, you were fine. I don't condone what your ex-husband did, but did you ever work to get it back together—seek counseling, anything? He failed you, like every other man including your beloved father."

"Well, if that's true," Jess retorted, "you certainly haven't ruined my track record."

"Oh yes I have, and that's what's killing you. I'm mature enough to ride this out. I love you enough for that. You're spoiled, self-centered, and self-indulgent, but as far as I'm concerned you're mine and when all this is over I'm coming for you."

"I wouldn't hold my breath if I were you," she countered defiantly.

He smiled confidently. "If you think you can never under-estimate a woman scorned, try a Sicilian."

"What are you going to do, put out a contract on my life?" she asked, not the least bit scared.

"You won't get off that easy."

The meek secretary entered again, stark fear in her eyes. "Ben, I'm sorry, but Congressman Calvin says he needs you."

"Okay, Harriet, tell him I'll be right there," he answered her gently, trying to make up for his previous outburst.

He turned to Jess. Okay, he had lost this skirmish, but the war was a whole other matter. For the time being he'd better take care of something he could do right. "We're going to give you some run for your money. And we're going to win."

Jess smiled. She was ready to do battle. "Not without the fight of your life. I may not have grown up on the streets like you, but I've learned to fight just as dirty. All's fair. . . ."

"So you've always told me," Ben assured her.

"Well," Jess said as she turned toward the door, "I believe you have a very important press conference waiting. I wouldn't want to keep you. See you at the polls."

Ben watched her walk toward the door. The woman he loved. The woman he wanted to grow old with. The woman he felt like murdering.

"Lady," he stated emphatically, "you're one fourteen-karat bitch!"

30

Jess's car had been out of commission for the last three days. It was the best news she'd had. Sure, it meant a new transmission, which meant another six hundred dollars if they didn't find anything else wrong, which they usually did, and the car was only two years old and she should have been furious that the transmission had given out prematurely. But instead she felt relieved because Peter had offered to chauffeur her around and that netted her one less detail to worry about.

Jess hated driving. It was the one thing she detested about being single and in charge. She was responsible for driving and maintaining the car. Eliot had loved to do all that. It wasn't enough reason for her to stay in a disastrous marriage, but she sure missed it.

And besides, Jess thought, she was probably too exhausted to drive a vehicle competently. She envisioned herself falling asleep against the steering wheel while she was tooling up Independence Avenue. And if she did it would be more rest than she'd had in days. Such was her work schedule of late.

"How much sleep did you get last night?" Peter asked of the corpselike companion sitting next to him in his car.

Jess inadvertently yawned. "During a primary I don't sleep. We're only six points ahead in the polls. That's not a comfortable margin with seven weeks to go."

"Calvin's running some campaign," Peter pointed out. "Someone on his staff must be very competent."

"Certainly determined," she noted.

It was true. Calvin was coming on like gangbusters. He was everywhere, doing everything: There wasn't a baby left in the state he hadn't kissed, a news item he didn't have a comment on, a problem he didn't have a solution for. Worst of all, people were learning his name quickly. He was catching up to Ford's recognition factor. And his "competent staff" had begun to convince the voters Calvin was another John Kennedy.

For Jess, the worst point had come during the debate. Jess had avoided setting it up for as long as she could, but the newspapers were starting to make Ford's refusal an issue; so, reluctantly, she acquiesced.

It wasn't that Ford was bad—far from it. Jess had done everything but sleep in his apartment to make sure her senator was in tip-top shape—definitely off the sauce—and so he was lucid and well-spoken. Calvin's answers, however, were crisp, fresh, and brilliant. If she weren't committed, she undoubtedly would have voted for him. The debate easily cost them four points and plenty of psychological advantage.

Ben and Jess sat out of camera range on different ends of the stage. Jess thought Ben was trying for eye contact with her a few times, but when she finally looked over at him, she realized she must have been mistaken. He was obviously in his "this is war and we're going to kill them" mode. Fine, so be it. It was an attitude she could identify with, so she wasn't bothered until the end of the debate, when Calvin zeroed in on Ford in a rather peculiar way.

"Senator Ford," Calvin said pointedly, "I noticed that when you answered the last question, you weren't responsive to either the exactness or the spirit of that question. Rather, you reiterated your qualifications and the bills you've introduced. Interesting as that may be, it's not pertinent to what we were asked. Personally, I think we candidates have an obligation to the electorate to give all the relevant information available. That's the kind of public servant I'm going to be. No tap dancing around the issues."

Jess found herself not concentrating on the rest of his response as she began analyzing what he had just said. In fairness, the observation was hardly novel. Many politicians used the last few minutes of their time to reinforce their appeal to the audience by restating their qualifications. It was certainly a tactic Ford used. It had always been effective. But it had generally been so proficiently woven into the context of the answer that no one realized, as Calvin had noted, it was not responsive to the last question.

What bothered her was twofold: Calvin seemed ready to make that point—it was clearly not something that had just occurred to him; and she had told Ben about this little strategy of Ford's one night when they were discussing ways to win an election.

When she went over that discussion in her mind, she realized that Ben hadn't divulged anything about Calvin, rather he talked in very general, Poli Sci 101 terms. It was she who had given concrete examples, mostly those used by her senator.

What really worried her was that she had confided a great deal more about Senator Ford than she was comfortable with now. At the time, she had thought nothing of it. Now she was concerned. Just how much had she divulged? She could have kicked herself. Politics really did make strange bedfellows.

Ben offered an outstretched hand at the end of the debate. "Good job," he said, flashing his dazzling smile.

She reluctantly shook his hand. "Interesting observation about how Senator Ford handled that last question. I wonder where Calvin got that little tidbit?"

Ben shrugged his shoulders as though he had no idea what she was talking about. "I guess he's a pretty observant person."

"What a useful quality," Jess noted, "especially when you have scouts who are taking such precise notes."

When Ben said nothing, Jess knew she was right. She shook her head and turned on her heels, rejoining Sam to tell him how wonderful he had been.

Strange bedfellows, indeed.

"Heard from him?" Peter asked casually.

"Peter, I've told you, that subject is off-limits." Jess certainly had not discussed her confidentiality breach with Peter.

"Awfully touchy about someone you don't care about anymore," Peter noted bitchily. Jess was too tired to give him the dirty look she felt he richly deserved. "How's Susan taking the split?"

Jess shrugged. "She knows what life is about by now."

"That's odd. She was so crazy about him."

It certainly seemed like she was. Jess had been extremely nervous about telling Susan that she and Ben had broken up. It was almost eerie how evenly Susan had taken the news. She was so dispassionate, as though she had expected it. Maybe Jess had misjudged Susan's feelings after all.

"You know, I think she really did want a father in the house," Peter continued. "Didn't Ben even try to get in touch with her?"

"I think he called her a few times."

"What did he say?"

"I didn't ask. It was their conversation."

"You weren't even curious?" Peter asked incredulously.

"No."

Peter had to laugh. "You have the highest repression level known to mankind."

"So you've told me innumerable times."

Jess was grateful she possessed that trait. It served her well all those times in her life when she didn't want to face her problems. She quickly convinced herself everything was for the best. Besides, she was working so hard in this campaign, she didn't have time to think about anything else.

They pulled up in front of Jessica's house. Jess hoped Susan would settle for a light dinner. She didn't feel like going to Burger King again, and cooking was definitely out of the question. Then he noticed a red 280 Z parked in her driveway.

"I wonder whose car that is?" she said aloud.

A home-cooked meal, Jess thought as she entered the house and was greeted by the delicious odors of fresh food cooking. Bless Susan.

"Hello. I'm home."

She smiled as a delighted Susan ran to Jess and hugged her.

"Well, well, what's this? Is it my birthday?" Jess asked as she hugged her daughter back.

Susan's face was filled with that excited look reserved for youth. "Mother, guess who's here."

"Oh, the car in the driveway. I forgot to ask . . ."

"Close your eyes." Jess gave Susan a questioning look. "C'mon, Mother, please."

Jess obediently closed her eyes as Susan took her hand and led her into the living room.

"Susan, you know how I hate surprises." Jess was getting an uneasy feeling.

"Okay," Susan announced, "you can open them now."

And there he sat. Eliot. Good old Eliot whom she hadn't seen for years. She said nothing as she looked at him. Well, he looked good. Obviously still trying to keep in shape, still trying to look younger.

"Hello, Jess," Eliot said warmly.

Jess shook her head. "Honestly, Eliot, you do turn up at the oddest times."

Susan was the grand hostess. "I've made you drinks, hors d'oeuvres, and dinner."

Jess looked at her daughter. "I'm impressed," Jess told her.

"This is a special occasion," Susan remarked, pleased with herself, as she went into the kitchen to get the water chestnuts and bacon she was broiling in the oven.

Jess turned back to Eliot, who was looking intently at her, no doubt mentally undressing her as he had half the female population. It made her feel uneasy, as though her privacy were being invaded. He wasn't entitled to those looks anymore. "You look wonderful, Jess."

"You always were a sucker for me, Eliot," Jess remarked dryly.

"How long has it been, Jess—a year or two?"

"Try five, Eliot."

"It can't be that long."

"Trust me. It was Susan's tenth birthday. I only remember because you had to leave before the party even began. Susan cried for a week after you left. What was her name— Margo?"

Eliot looked genuinely upset. "I had no idea."

"Yes, well, I picked up the pieces."

As she had done many times throughout those years. True, Susan had relied less and less on Eliot to keep his word, but the hurt was nevertheless there. Jess couldn't understand why Susan wanted to see this man at all. He had disappointed her so many times. But even Jess had to admit that when Eliot came through, he did it with style. Like the time two years before when he took Susan on a fairytale weekend to the St. Regis Hotel in New York. They'd huddled up under a blanket in one of those horse-drawn carriage rides through Central Park that dazzle girls and women alike. Susan had come home in seventh heaven. Jess was annoyed. How could Susan be so easily taken in?

When she mentally calculated it, Jess estimated that Eliot disappointed three times out of four, but that fourth time was such an upper, it wiped out the down times. The year before, Eliot had taken Susan to Europe. True, he had to be there on business anyway, but still he did make time for Susan and, as always, managed to make her feel special.

Jess had to remember that Eliot was Susan's father. She couldn't fault Susan for wanting to believe he loved her. There were plenty of qualities in her own father that she had overlooked.

Still, it didn't seem fair. Here was a man who, as far as Jess was concerned, left his family for one more zipless fuck and, despite the facts, was still forgiven and adored by his daughter. Where was the justice in it all? Then again, Jess had read in every psychology book that if a daughter believed her father loved her, she stood a better chance of becoming a well-adjusted grown-up. For that reason, Jess tried never to speak against him. It wasn't easy.

After the divorce, Miss Goody-Two-Shoes vented her anger in her consciousness-raising group. Jess reached depths she never knew she was capable of. She really hated Eliot in those days. With the passing years, she tried to bury those feelings. As she looked at him now, she realized that the intensity of her feelings had diminished. At least she didn't feel like putting a bomb under his seat.

It was a good dinner. Susan cooked the one dish she had mastered in cooking class, beef teriyaki. She had even baked a cake. She was animated and lively and Jess was glad to see her daughter happy.

"Well," said Susan, clearing the last of the dishes from the living room table, where she insisted on serving dessert, "I've got some homework to do. Anyway, I bet you two want to be alone," she added devilishly as she exited.

Jess looked after her. "Children are such romantics."

"You've done a wonderful job with Susan," Eliot said as he raised his coffee cup to Jess.

Jess was grateful for the recognition. "She's one terrific kid."

"Thank goodness I was with her most of her formative years." He caught Jessica's sharp look and was quick to add, "But most of the credit belongs to you."

You bet your sweet petunia it does. "Thank you," she said.

"In fact, you've done a lot with your life—much more than I ever imagined you would."

That wasn't saying much. "And you, Eliot? Are things going well?"

"I'm successful . . ." he answered in a forlorn tone.

"But . . . ?" Why did she ask? She didn't want to hear any of his problems.

"I don't know. I don't seem to be going anywhere. I can't . . . capture the joy anymore. I should be happy. My mother's always telling me that. I'm successful, respected, well off. . . ."

"But . . . ?"

"I'm burnt out, Jess. Three marriages can really take their toll."

"Plus God knows what else on the side," Jess added helpfully.

Eliot nodded his head in agreement. "It's exhausting—physically and emotionally."

"Poor Eliot," she said, holding her heart.

"Turning the big four-oh really got to me. No one even did anything for me. When I was thirty you threw a great party for me, remember?"

"Vividly," she replied. So he had liked it. So much for that eleven-year-old burning question. On the other hand, maybe it was like childbirth—you just forgot the bad parts.

"My priorities are so haywire," he sighed deeply. He did that after a lot of his sentences. It was music to her ears. "I've got to figure out what's important. I've taken a sabbatical. I'm going to teach medicine for a while."

"Really? Where?"

"I've gotten a post right here in Washington. I thought it was perfect. I could get to know Susan better. After all, she is my only child."

"Well, I'm sure Susan would like that." She wondered if he'd already told her.

"Maybe we could even reacquaint ourselves," he added quietly.

Jess shook her head no. "I gave up masochism when we got divorced."

"They say love is lovelier the second time around."

"It would have to be."

He looked genuinely hurt. "C'mon, Jess. We had something good once."

Jess didn't feel like rehashing it all over again. "That was a long time ago."

"You know, I go over it endlessly in my mind. Sometimes I think you were the best thing that ever happened to me. I can't believe what a jerk I was to let you go."

She couldn't fight him on that one.

"Look," he continued gently, "maybe we can get to know each other this time. We never really did before."

"Even so, Eliot . . ."

"I'm convinced there was a good reason we got married. I just think we got divorced too fast. I know how angry you must have been."

"You can say that again."

"And you had every right to be."

"I don't think you know how furious I was," she told him.

He smiled. "Listen, I still have nightmares about china flying at me. It was the night I became a jogger."

They both laughed. She had forgotten the Royal Worcester dishes.

"Look, I'm serious about wanting to get to know you. I know you're busy now, but will you at least think it over?"

He looked so down-in-the-dumps helpless. "I'll think it over," she told him.

"Anyway, I'll be so local."

"Where are you living?"

"Well . . . I thought," he said, smiling unassumingly as he looked around the living room, "you have such a nice big house. . . ."

So that was it. Forget all this "I done you wrong" crap. "Here? You think I'd let you move in here? Eliot, you've developed a sense of humor," she said, not laughing one bit.

"But it's a natural."

"There's nothing natural about it. You must be crazy. You are the walking definition of chutzpah."

He had to be out of his head. What could have made him think he even had the right to ask?

Susan came bounding in, still glowing from dinner. "Hi, how's everything going? Did Daddy tell you yet about moving into the guest room?"

Jess sensed a conspiracy. "You knew about your father's plans?"

Susan nodded proudly. "It was my idea. This way you won't have to worry about me while you're busy campaigning and when you're home, we'll be like a real family again."

Did Susan really think it was that simple? Jess looked at Susan's sweet, determined face and realized this wasn't going to be as easy as she'd thought.

31

Life had been crap since they broke up.

Unlike Jess, Ben had been unable to repress. He thought of her day and night. It wasn't that it affected his work negatively. Far from it. Knowing she would be aware of every strategic move he made, he outdid himself to be efficient and innovative, and his efforts paid off. He was running one hell of a campaign.

But that didn't help him when he ate dinner alone, or at night when his body ached for hers.

When he saw her at the debate he melted. He wanted to grab her and hold her. He wanted her to tell him what a jerk she'd been and that everything was going to be all right. But, of course, that didn't happen. Not that he'd really expected it to.

Bitch. He could have strangled her.

Actually, he thought about doing a lot of terrible things to Jessie since she gave back the ring. The recurring fantasy was yelling what a spoiled brat she was, taking her over his knee, and spanking her senseless. That was probably something the little princess had never had done to her, and as far as Ben was concerned she was long overdue.

It wasn't that he would ever do it. But in his fantasy it sure felt good to whack the crap out of her, like he felt she had emotionally done to him.

He also missed Susan. He really loved the kid. Jessie had robbed all three of them.

He called Susan a lot at the beginning. He wanted her to know he still cared. But the conversations seemed to get more strained with time and he finally decided it would be better for both of them if he stopped calling. He discussed it with Susan and she agreed—a little too willingly, he thought.

After two weeks; he decided that he'd had it with feeling sorry for himself. After all, she wasn't the only woman in the world. In fact there were plenty. Especially in the nation's capital.

It had never been difficult for Ben to meet women, very willing ones at that. The singles' bar route definitely wasn't for him. But he'd always been invited to party after party, generally declining the offers. That was going to change. He was going to take people up on their invitations.

The first woman he met took only five minutes before she asked him back to her apartment. She worked for HUD and seemed reasonably interesting. More important, she was built like a ton of bricks. Her dress, which was snugger than the Isotoner gloves Jessie wore, left little to the imagination. Her face was okay, not great. She still had bad skin from her teens, which she tried to hide with a heavy layer of makeup. She had a pleasant smile and bouncy red hair. When he noticed he was talking to her boobs, he realized how incredibly horny he was. Her place sounded just fine.

Her apartment was a mess. She cleaned up as she talked. Within ten minutes they were going at it between the sheets of her unmade bed. Neither of them made any attempt at foreplay. The whole act was over in record time. He had no desire to please his partner. She didn't seem to care.

She asked if he minded if they watched the "Tonight Show" since Joan Rivers was the guest host and she hated to miss her. As soon as Joan finished announcing who her guests would be the next night, the redhead switched off the TV and they had their ten-minute dose of sex again. Then the redhead fell asleep, and Ben got dressed and left.

The whole incident depressed him.

The next day at the office Ben received a call from the redhead. She told him their encounter was the best time she'd had since she arrived in Washington, and if he ever wanted to repeat it to please call her. He did so five more times. He knew her telephone number and her first name—Rita. He never bothered to learn her last name. All in all the arrangement suited both of them.

There were others, of course. Rita was only called when he needed to unwind without talking.

For three weeks it seemed as though he slept with a different woman each night. He wondered if Jessie was doing the same thing. He thought he'd murder her if he found out she was. He cursed Gloria Steinem.

Some of the women he had sex with were pretty, engaging, intelligent, warm, sweet, eager to please.

He missed Jessie.

He was exhausted. It reminded him of the period following his divorce. He decided to stop sleeping around so indiscriminately. Whatever it was he had to prove to himself, it wasn't working itself out in bed. He vowed to concentrate on the campaign; if he met someone else, fine. In the meantime, if he needed relief there was always Rita.

Her name was Margaret O'Hanigan Steel, but everyone called her Mag. Ben preferred calling her Steel because that's what her personality reminded him of. He had hired her a month after he'd come to work for Richard Calvin and he had never regretted it. She was tireless, loyal, and smart —all the assets he was looking for in an assistant. The fact that she was also in love with Ben had its good points and bad.

Ben had been very clear that he felt business and pleasure were a lousy mix. Mag assured him she wholeheartedly agreed, even though she didn't.

To be perfectly honest, Mag didn't appeal to him. It wasn't that she was an absolute dog, but she reminded him of every Marymount undergrad he had ever dated and they were a turnoff. Her skin was freckled, her hair a glossy brown. She was just under five feet tall and shaped like a miniature pear. But she was a dynamo. And she cursed like a football player after losing the Super Bowl.

"Fuck that schmuck," she complained as she tossed a copy of the *Pittsburgh Press* article on Ben's desk.

"Ford Appears Unbeatable" read the headline.

"Shit," was all Ben could say.

"And I spent time with that asshole," Mag continued. "I could cut off his balls."

"How about if we hold our revenge until *after* the election, okay? First let's concentrate on making this article incorrect."

"Yeah, well, when you're running a campaign like a goddamn tea party, it's a little hard, if you get my drift."

"I'm lucky if I get fifty percent of your drift. What the hell are you talking about?"

"Cut the crap. You know," she said accusingly.

"What, for Christ's sake?"

"You're playing nice because of that broad you almost married."

"Don't call Jessie a broad."

"Excuse me," she said sarcastically, holding her heart as though she were guilty of an unpardonable sin. "I wouldn't want to slander the queen."

"I just don't want you calling her a broad," he said defensively.

"Well, I'll give her ladyship high grades on strategy, buddy, because she sure has figured out how to win an election."

"What are you implying?"

"I never imply anything. I'm stating this loud and clear: I think you're throwing this election away because you don't want to hurt your lady friend: Jessica Simon Kantor. Clear enough?"

"You don't know what you're talking about," he yelled angrily.

"Oh, yeah? Since when did you become Mr. Nice Guy when it came to winning an election?"

"Never."

"Really? Is that a fact?" she yelled back, knowing she was right on target.

"Haven't we gone up twelve points in the polls?" he pointed out.

"Yeah, sure, and you know what that'll make us: respectable losers—and for my money that sucks."

"And you don't think I'm working to win this?" His face was turning beet red.

"I happen to know you got two leads on Ford that could do him in." She had heard part of one conversation and all of the other.

"They were unverified crap," he said, brushing it off.

"Oh, yeah? You followed up on them, did you?"

"For Christ's sake, Steel, they were dirt. The *Enquirer* wouldn't have printed that garbage."

"Yeah, well we're not the *Enquirer*. We're going down for the count here and you're wearing white linen gloves."

"What do you expect me to do?"

"Leak the stuff, Casale. Any other election and it would have been on every editor's desk before your unidentified source hung up the phone."

He knew she was right. "Not true."

"My ass it isn't. The hard fact is you're out to impress someone with your nobility factor. Well, while you're playing Cyrano, Calvin could get the lead role in the *Titanic*," she shouted.

"You have a problem, why don't you talk it out with him?"

"Who are you kidding? He leaves his dirty work up to his staff and you know it. He's Mr. Clean."

"Not a bad way to be," Ben said.

"Yeah, clean and unemployed."

Ben looked at Steel's half-hostile, half-defeated face.

"Look, you find me something juicy I can verify, I'll go with it."

Mag looked at him, trying to understand what he was going through, and she immediately regretted it. She was always a sucker for him. "Ben, why are you hanging on?"

"I'm not."

Mag knew different. She tried to talk reasonably. "Yes you are. She's in your head and you can't get her out."

"Maybe sometimes."

"More than sometimes. And that would be your business if it weren't affecting the campaign. Think about it, Bozo. You're not being fair."

Maybe Steel was right.

"And she's not worth it," Mag added.

Steel wasn't right about that.

"She's ruining who you were. You aren't the same man. No one's worth that," she concluded.

Maybe she was right about all of it.

He nodded his head. "Bring me something I can use, we'll talk."

It didn't take her long.

Mag threw the photostatic copies on Ben's desk. "I can get you backup verification if you really need it. It may cost us, but I can get it."

He looked at the material carefully. According to the information, Senator Ford had paid practically no income tax for the years 1975 and 1976.

"So he got off easy with the IRS. That makes him lucky, not illegal."

"Yeah, except the way he got so lucky was by investing in various questionable tax shelters."

"How questionable?"

"Real questionable. Like cattle raising and overseas motion pictures that never got made and a nice hefty chunk of Florida land that has yet to be found."

"Maybe he was an innocent investor."

"Yeah, and maybe Charlie Manson was a goddamn cub scout leader."

"What are our sources?"

"I've been contacted by some very close friends of James Farland—the guy who was almost the A.G. until Ford deep-sixed him at that hearing. They'd be delighted to return the favor."

"Even if this stuff is true, he's past the statute of limitations. It's all academic."

"You know damn well it won't smell academic to the voters. And I'll give you odds there's current stuff. The IRS will jump on it."

"Give me overnight to look it over."

"What's to look over?" Mag asked, exasperated.

"Just overnight," he hissed. She was a goddamn pain in the ass.

"Jesus Christ, either shit or get off the pot." She screamed as she turned on her heels, slamming the door as she left.

Damn her. It wasn't that easy.

This would be the clincher. If there was ever a remote possibility that he and Jessie would get back together, he knew this would kill it. He tossed and turned the whole night trying to figure out what to do.

The tough part wasn't that he didn't like ruining a man's career; it wasn't even that he was going to do Jessie's candidate in. Hell, he could live with both of those. The tough part was that Jessie had told Ben about Ford's tax evasions while they were sharing a vintage bottle of Chablis one night after some exhaustingly glorious sex. Undoubtedly she had thought she was telling him in confidence, though, of course, she had never said so. She had laughed about it at the time.

" 'When I found out what Sam was doing I almost killed him. 'Sam,' I said, 'these investment deductions are debatable at best. What the hell are you doing?' "

"What did he say?" Ben had asked.

"He was mortified. Obviously he was being taken for a ride, just an innocent investor. He withdrew immediately. I mean, he certainly didn't need the money—lord knows he can't spend what he has. Just the carelessness of the very wealthy, I suppose. Can you imagine being that rich?"

He had looked at her radiant face and assured her, "I already am."

Ben replayed the conversation over and over in his mind. How could he expose Ford after that? This one was a bitch. It wasn't comparable to any other conflict he had had so far.

Of course, Jessie had been right when she accused Ben of knowing Calvin was planning to run for Ford's seat. He and Calvin had discussed it for months before he'd even met Jessie. But Ben had been careful not to lie by using very precise words when he told Jessie, "I didn't know he was going to announce last night. If I had I would have been there." After all, the game plan had Calvin announcing his candidacy the following week. But he had gotten carried away by the momentum of the event he was attending and announced prematurely.

Damn Calvin. Besides putting an incredible strain on the staff, it screwed up all of Ben's carefully conceived plans to prepare Jessie for what was going to happen and map out a survival course between the two of them. So much for good intentions.

He had no qualms about not confiding in Jessie about Calvin's plans. After all, he considered it confidential information that he was obligated to keep to himself.

He had been surprised by Jessie's accusation at the debate. He hadn't even realized that his strategy was based on something she'd told him. When he thought about it, he realized she probably was right, but that was an unconscious mistake, so he didn't feel guilty.

But now there was this income tax evasion issue to deal with. There was no way he could persuade Jessie that he hadn't used her. He was beginning to feel like a heel.

By the same token, he had an obligation to do whatever he could to win the election for Calvin.

No matter what angle he looked at it, it was a no-win proposition.

What he finally concluded was that he had to proceed whatever way he would have absent a Jessie/Ben relationship. It was the only way he could stay in his job and respect himself.

After all, he wasn't the one who disclosed the material. It was given to him. There were too many sources for the details not to leak out one way or another. In any other election, under any other circumstances, he wouldn't have hesitated for a minute. Steel was right about that one.

Jessie would simply have to understand. If she didn't, she didn't. That was life.

"Steel," Mag answered her phone in a clipped manner the next morning.

"Steel, this is Casale. Take what you've got and run with it."

Steel smiled, relieved. "Welcome back."

32

Well, at least Jess didn't have to worry about what Susan could do when she grew up. Politics was a natural. Never had she seen such an efficiently run campaign. The candidate was Eliot; the electorate, Jess. The blitz was on.

Ever since Eliot had moved back in, Susan was full of little surprises in her attempt to get her parents back together: cozy suppers; lazy picnics; candlelit after-dinner drinks all provided by Susan. It was touching and heart rending.

At first, Jess had resisted Susan's repeated requests to let Eliot move back in with them. But Susan was relentless.

"Look, Susan, we're divorced. It's been ten years. You've got to face it." It had been the fourth time they'd discussed the subject in the last two days. It was getting tiresome.

"I have faced it."

"Then what's the problem?"

"You always told me Daddy divorced you, not me. I mean, you said it had nothing to do with me. I wasn't the issue."

"That still stands."

"Then why can't he move back in? Why should I suffer?" Susan asked reasonably.

"Because divorced people don't live together. That's the way it works."

"It's just another one of society's stupid rules." Susan pouted. "You're just following the crowd."

"Honey, if I wanted to continue living with your father, I wouldn't have divorced him. That's the statement divorce makes: 'I don't want to live with you anymore.' "

"Suppose I want to live with him?" Susan asked.

That hurt. "Do you?" Jess asked tenuously.

"Maybe," Susan answered defiantly.

She can't mean it. Call her bluff. "If you really feel that way, maybe your father and I can work something out—joint custodywise—as soon as he finds his own place."

"But that's not fair," Susan objected.

"I don't know how I can be any fairer."

"You can let him move in here," Susan insisted.

"Susan, honey, we've covered this territory more than once. My decision hasn't changed."

"But this is my home, too." Susan was on the verge of tears.

"And we both have an equal vote in who lives here. We *both* have to agree."

"You would have let Ben move in," Susan pointed out.

Jess shook her head. "Not if you didn't want me to."

"Yes, you would have. And you'd have married him even if I didn't want you to. I know you. You would have said I was a child," Susan said accusatorily.

She was probably right. "But you are a child, honey."

"Well, a child needs her father."

"Susan, I'm not trying to separate you from your father. Go live with him, if you want to." Don't. I don't mean that.

"Is that what you want?" Susan asked, hurt.

"It sounds like that's what you want." This is going very badly. Where are you when I need you, Dr. Ginott? I want time out to call my Parent Effectiveness Training instructor.

"I don't want to leave my house."

"I'm not throwing you out, sweetie."

"It sure feels like it." Susan's lips were quivering.

Jess hadn't seen Susan this agitated in years. She put her arms around her daughter. "Honey, I have separation anxiety when you go to summer camp. How could you possibly think I don't want you here?"

"Let me ask you something, Mommy."

Mommy. She hadn't called Jess "Mommy" since she was eight. "Fire away."

"If Grandpa came to you and asked you to take him in, would you refuse him?"

The answer was obvious. "No," she admitted.

"Well, that's what I'm doing: refusing him entry into my house."

"No, Susan, that's what I'm doing."

"And what you're forcing me to do and I think it's unfair."

She looked at Susan's face, which had tears rolling down. Whoever invented guilt did a masterful job on me, she thought.

"It'd only make things worse if he moved in here. You're setting yourself up for disappointment."

Susan knew the signs. Her mother was weakening. Pull out all the stops. "It would only be for a little while," she promised.

"How little?" Jess asked, knowing it was showing that she was relenting.

"Until the end of the campaign."

"The end of the campaign?" Jess gasped, totally frustrated. "Assuming we win the primary, we're talking seven months."

Go for the big one. "Do you realize how it feels when you're full force into a campaign? I'm so lonely . . . and scared. At least there'll be a grown-up in the house to protect me. My own father. Please, Mommy, I really need him here."

She looked at Susan's saucer eyes. Guilt enveloped her. A masterful job, indeed.

* * *

She explained it all to Eliot—with an emphasis on the temporary aspect of the situation. He couldn't have been more grateful.

"You know, Jess, this is something I've dreamed about for years: a chance to really get to know my daughter. You'll never know how much I appreciate what you're doing."

Maybe Eliot had changed after all. Or maybe she'd never really known him. The last possibility plagued her.

To be sure, he was nothing like she remembered. Perhaps she had built him up into such an ogre in her mind that there was no way he could have been anything else.

Then again, Eliot was full swing into a campaign of his own. Besides Susan, he wanted Jess back. He was willing to do anything to get her. She began to remember how good he was at the chase.

The timing couldn't have been worse. Jess simply didn't have the energy to work on a revived relationship with Eliot. She tried to be friendly. Once she even tried to respond to his incessant overtures. It didn't work. It wasn't that there wasn't a level on which he still appealed to her. It wasn't even the residual anger, which she had to admit was still with her. What it boiled down to was her basic distrust of him. It was an emotion that hadn't dissipated.

"You don't have any romantic feelings for me?" Eliot asked, a basset hound look in his eyes.

"Anything I feel is purely academic, Eliot. We're history."

"My past behavior was lousy," he admitted.

"To put it mildly," she concurred.

"I was young. I was stupid. I didn't know what I wanted. But being here with you has grounded my emotions. I know what I need now. In a nutshell, you're it."

"Eliot, I wouldn't build this up into more than it is."

God, he loved a challenge. "I want you, Jess. I look at that body and I think, 'How could I have been such an idiot to throw it all away?'"

The kiss wasn't all that bad. His tongue wandered gently

through her mouth. When he came up for air, his tongue encircled her ear and then did little flicks with it inside her right ear, then her left. An Eliot patent she'd forgotten. Her clitoris was at attention. She realized how horny she was.

"I want you so desperately," he whispered.

Her resolve was weakening, but it hadn't collapsed. "I can't," she told him, wondering how it'd feel to have him come down on her.

His hardness was against her. His breathing slowed down, he patted her hair gently. "I'm in no rush," he assured her. "I know when something's worth waiting for."

Maybe just a quickie. After all, he was your husband once. No, for God's sake, take hold of yourself.

He fondled her breasts. They hadn't grown. Shit.

"I can't handle this," Jess told him.

"Then let me." Eliot smiled.

Wrong. It's all wrong. Whatever happened to that indomitable will of steel? "I'm going to bed," she said.

"Want company?" He grinned slyly. I'm getting closer to that driver's seat, babe.

He thinks he's in control again. Forget it. "No, no, a thousand times no. *Capiche?*"

Damn her. Still a bitch. "Whatever you say," he calmly reassured her.

For his part, Eliot was admirably patient. He asserted he had finally matured. He was a new man who had come to terms with priorities in life, and those priorities rested with her and Susan. He guaranteed Jess he understood how she felt, but that with time he would prove his integrity. She was the only woman he had ever really loved and he wished she'd let him prove it to her in bed. No matter how much time he had to wait for her to trust him again, he was willing. He wanted his family back together and, more than anything else, he wanted Jess. The thought of any other woman revolted him.

It was flattering, she had to give him that.

Of course, the biggest impediment was memories of Ben.

She felt guilty when she kissed Eliot, when her clitoris started throbbing, when she considered getting it on with him. But why should she feel guilty? She'd bet a week's salary Ben was screwing his head off.

Still, she couldn't get Ben out of her mind. Her famous repression was failing her. It confused her.

Above all else, however, the one thing that kept her on the straight and narrow was her overriding conviction about men: No matter how terrific and loving they are today, you can be damned sure that sooner or later they'll disappoint the hell out of you.

33

When the news of Ford's tax irregularities hit the press, it neither surprised nor upset Jess. She expected it as soon as it became evident at the debate that their bedroom talk was fair game.

In a perverse way it pleased her.

So while Ben was agonizing over what he should do, Jess was preparing for the inevitable. With only a six-point spread, anticipation had to be her trump.

First she contacted Michael Lieb, the accountant she had engaged after she had Senator Ford fire Albert Kent. She suspected Kent had known precisely what he was doing when he directed Sam to buy into all those "you can't lose" business deals. She hadn't openly confronted Kent at the time, but she indirectly let him know she was wise to him. It was enough to get him exceedingly nervous.

Michael Lieb had been meticulous and discreet, straightening out every detail. By the time he was done, Sam's tax portfolio was cleaner than clean. And Michael had all the specific paperwork to prove it. She made sure Michael had copies of everything, ready for when the news broke.

Then she called on Jeffrey Walker, her friend at the IRS. At her request he agreed to initiate an independent audit covering the years since Senator Ford's return had displayed some irregularities.

What Jess had failed to disclose to Ben when she had told him about the incident was that she had made sure that

Michael Lieb and an IRS agent had spent many hours together figuring out exactly how much money plus interest Sam owed the government. As far as Jess was concerned, the sum was staggering, but Sam had simply shrugged his shoulders and made out a check to cover it.

Never being able to predict how people react to income tax audits, Jess had kept the whole episode quiet. Now that it was out in the open, she planned to make hay with the publicity.

"Actually, I'm surprised it never surfaced before," she told Peter, who was pale from hearing the news.

"Well, lovey, I'm delighted you can be so lah-de-dah about all this."

"We've been in tighter situations than this, Peter. Trust me."

"Trust you? Trust you?" Peter yelled hysterically. His anxiety level was surging.

Jess had to be coolheaded for both of them. "Sit down, Peter," she told him calmly. "Now listen very carefully to what I'm saying, because I think you're about to have a life-threatening coronary."

Peter was perspiring now. "I am," he whined.

"Okay," she told him reassuringly, "so listen to Mama Jess and you'll be just fine. What we're about to make out of this news, which, I'll grant you, sounds very grim at the moment, is the story of a man who could easily be the hero of a Frank Capra movie."

Peter was beginning to show some interest now. "What do you mean?" he asked.

"What we've got to do is focus on the elements of this situation that make Senator Ford representative of John Doe, American."

"How do we do that?"

"Well," she continued patiently, "I think it's safe to assume that most people hate to pay income taxes. And they always think they're paying more than the next guy, who they're sure is probably getting off scot-free. When this story breaks, that 'guy who got off scot-free' will appear to be Senator Ford to most people."

"Including me."

"Right. So our job will be to make Senator Ford look like one of them and to do that all we have to do is state the facts. If we present them right, they speak for themselves."

Peter was still confused. "How?"

"Make the average citizen see himself in the senator. Look, everyone wants a way out of taxes. Even a senator. Who can't identify with a guy who tries an honest way around taxes? Hell, it's the American way. What puts our integrity-ridden senator into the starring role of a Capra movie is that when he finds out he's been taken, he's man enough to bite the bullet, confess to the IRS, and make restitution."

"They'll think he's nuts to turn himself in."

"Yeah, they wouldn't do it themselves, but they sure as hell would want their senator to."

Peter had stopped perspiring. "But they'll say Ford did that to look good."

Jess smiled. "But to whom? It happened over seven years ago and he never went public with it. It only came out now because his 'vicious opponent' chose to slander him. Think of it, here's a man who went through a private hell, came out smelling like a rose, and never mentioned it. That's not only a role James Stewart would die to play, it might be a person suitable for canonization."

"You know, Jessica, you might be right. In fact, you may be brilliant."

She grinned triumphantly. "Actually, I think you're understating it."

In all fairness, it wasn't Priscilla Crawford's fault. Politics wasn't her thing. Parties were and she gave terrific ones.

It was the middle of the week and Ford's tax irregularities were still big news. Opinions changed by the hour. It was draining Jess. One of Priscilla's parties was just what she needed. She eagerly accepted the invitation. She was relieved that Eliot had a business dinner so she didn't have to ask him to join her.

Ben was equally exhausted. The plan that had seemed so foolproof was beginning to backfire. Two of Steel's "unshakable" witnesses had conveniently disappeared. Ben needed an evening out to take his mind off everything. One of Priscilla's parties would be a welcome change.

"You invited Ben and Jess?" her husband asked. "They're in a primary campaign. They're mortal enemies. They'll probably shoot each other."

Priscilla shrugged her shoulders. "Don't be absurd. We're all civilized."

When Ben saw Jessie across the room, his heart stopped. He wondered how he should handle the situation.

When Jess saw Ben, her eyes shot daggers as she turned and made her way toward the bar to get a double Scotch, no rocks.

Ben figured he didn't have to worry about how to handle it. She clearly wasn't talking to him anyway.

When they found themselves inadvertently reaching for the same Indian hors d'oeuvres, they knew they'd have to speak to each other.

"Go ahead," Ben said, "you have it."

Jess's voice dripped with sarcasm. "Always the perfect gentleman."

Two could play at that game. "That's how I was brought up: Miss Manners was my aunt."

"Actually, Mr. Casale, I'm surprised you aren't at the sushi table. Are they out of raw shark?"

"I only enjoy it when it's alive."

"I'm sure," she concurred. "It's so much more fun to inflict pain when you can actually see them suffer, isn't it? Not too different from your social life, I suppose."

"Boy, you really had those claws sharpened for tonight, didn't you, Jessica?"

"Actually, I'm just warming up."

"That would be a refreshing change."

"Oh, you see how silly Henry was," announced Priscilla as she put her arms around both of them. "He thought you two weren't getting along."

Jess gave a surprised look. "Whatever could have given him that silly idea?"

"Oh, who knows?" remarked Priscilla, dismissing the absurd idea. "You know men."

Jess shrugged her shoulders. "Some better than others."

"Henry tells me that you two are in some sort of contest?"

"It's a primary, Priss," Ben told her.

"Oh, right. Well, did anything exciting happen lately?"

"Just your usual double-dealing and back-stabbing this week," answered Jess. "Nothing out of the ordinary for Mr. Casale."

"Yes," agreed Ben. "Business as usual. Exposing graft and incompetency."

"Graft?" asked Jess amiably. "Should I expect something new? I'll have to get a list of the women you're sleeping with these days."

"I can give you one. Would you like it alphabetized?" Ben asked amibly.

I'd like to cut you into little pieces is what I'd like. "How do you do it these days? I mean, do you take notes while you're screwing or do you just bring a tape recorder?"

You're not going to get me angry. "Actually, I try to get two adjoining rooms. Then I put a person in the next room who presses a glass against the wall and jots down whatever's said."

I wouldn't put it past you. "You're getting more efficient."

Priscilla was delighted. "You see, I told Henry you'd all be ever so civilized. After all, you are both adults."

"Fifty percent of us, anyway," Ben agreed.

"Didn't you feel nice when you saw Ben tonight?"

Jess considered. Nice? "Actually, that wasn't precisely my reaction."

Priscilla couldn't have been more helpful. "Then what was your reaction, dear?"

"To tell you the truth," Jess answered as sweetly as she could, "my first thought was that I'd like to cut off his balls."

Ben played it just as straight. "And I was thinking how I'd like to slap her silly and then fuck the hell out of her."

Priscilla's back straightened and her mouth puckered as if she had just swallowed a lemon. "Yes, well, good for both of you. I think it's healthy to get those things out in the open. Well, you darlings will excuse me, won't you?"

As Priscilla floated away into the crowd she thought that maybe she would listen more carefully to Henry's advice in the future.

As it turned out, things did not go as smooth as Jess had anticipated. Instead of the two-day diversion she had hoped for, the turmoil didn't die down for a week. Frenzied interviews were given. Editorials were written and retracted. Voters changed their minds a dozen times.

Despite all her efforts, by week's end Senator Ford was down another point. She held Ben personally responsible.

When it came down to it, the primary appeared to hinge on only one thing: which candidate got the union endorsement.

34

Jess looked at her black lizard watch as she got off the elevator on the third floor and headed for the labor union office. She was running seven minutes early. That was fine with her. She had a fetish about being on time, and this was one meeting she had to play just right. There would be a smoke-filled room of labor leaders who wanted to know that they could depend on her senator. She wouldn't disappoint them. In return, she would expect their endorsement. She would more than expect it: At this point, their endorsement was essential.

Jean Murdock had been the union secretary for close to thirty years. She was one female who didn't approve of women being in charge. She liked power in the hands of men like her boss, Jim Farley: gruff, precise, dictatorial, gentlemanly, a man's man. After all, this was still a man's world and Jean had no desire to see that changed. She didn't appreciate women like Jessica who wanted to rearrange the apple cart. Still, she was always cordial to Jessica because that was her job.

"Please have a seat, Miss Kantor. Mr. Farley will be with you momentarily."

"Thanks, Jean." Jess smiled as she sat on the sturdy mud brown couch and rested her heavy leather attaché case on the seat next to her.

"Can I get you some coffee or tea?"

Jess eyed the coffee and got up. "That's okay, I'll get it."

Jess didn't like secretaries waiting on her. It made her uncomfortable. At the same time, she knew that Jean felt this was part of her job and resented Jess's not allowing her to do it. As Jess saw it, the problem was unresolvable.

"How are your boys? They must be teenagers by now."

"They're eighteen and fifteen and they're fine, thank you," Jean answered perfunctorily.

Actually, that had been the most information Jess had been able to extract from Jean in the six years she'd known her. Jess smiled wanly and looked through her notes.

Jean knew that the correct thing to do was to buzz her boss and tell him that Jessica Kantor had arrived. Then he would know to take his guest out another door. But Jean wanted Jessica to know that she'd have to work hard for her boss's endorsement. The competition was in there right now. And as far as Jean was concerned, Ben Casale was far worthier than Jessica.

Jim Farley opened the door, laughing as he entered the reception room with his arm around Ben Casale. It was a deep laugh. Jess had always loved hearing it. Except this time.

Jess looked at Ben and was momentarily shaken. She had forgotten how attractive he was. That night at Priscilla's, she had only concentrated on verbal warfare. Now she was taken by surprise, and so in those five unguarded seconds she looked at him objectively. He was still the same man she had fallen madly in love with. His body looked just as strong, his smile just as warm. Damn it, don't even think about him. You're here on business, lady.

Farley was looking at Ben and did not notice Jessica. "A pleasure meeting with you, my boy. I think we have a great deal to offer each other. I'll have the committee's decision today." One more slap on the back as he turned and saw Jess. It jarred him. Jean was delighted. "Uh, Jess, honey bun."

"Hello, Jim," Jess said warmly.

Farley kissed Jess on the cheek and became his old jovial

self. "You look like a million." He gave another hearty laugh, though this time a little more forced, as he motioned to Ben. "This is Ben Casale. I guess you two know each other."

"We've had the pleasure," Jess answered, nodding perfunctorily.

"Washington's a small town," Ben said evenly.

Farley shook Ben's hand good-bye. "Well, Ben, thanks again for coming."

"Thank you, Jim."

"C'mon in, Jess. We've been waiting for you."

Ben nodded to Jess as she followed Farley into the next office. "Good luck in there, Miss."

Jess smiled and narrowed her eyes playfully. "Now, why do I get this feeling you're less than sincere?"

"Probably because you're such a lousy judge of character," he answered her as pleasantly as he could.

Jess's eyes scanned the room when she entered. This is how clichés are born, she thought to herself.

Six men sat around the large mahogany table. With one exception, all of them were smoking cigars. Five of them were overweight by at least twenty pounds. They were friendly, tough, streetwise men who had made it in their world. She was comfortable with them and she knew that they respected her as a powerful force in Washington. She had made it clear to them many times that she was their friend. She could be relied on. They responded in kind.

"You know most everybody here," Farley said.

Jess nodded enthusiastically and went around the table with her eyes. "Frank, Sal, Joe, Harry, Vito, Pete. The gang's all here."

"I guess this is more than a friendly chat day," Farley said. He was getting down to business quicker than usual. Bad sign.

Jess looked around the room and got an uneasy feeling looking at their body language. The "gang" was holding back, not quite as chummy as usual. So be it. More of a challenge.

Jess smiled amicably. "I'm willing to be friendly. Senator Ford always has been where unions are concerned." She looked directly at the men. Vito and Sal looked down. How much had they given away? "Friends who came through for each other," Jess added, undaunted.

Farley opened the top button of his olive polyester suit. He looked more serious than she'd ever seen him. "Jess, let's lay our cards on the table. This is an important endorsement for you."

Jess shook her head in total agreement. She unbuttoned the last button on her Liz Claiborne beige corduroy suit jacket. "I can't dance around it, Jim. We're neck and neck with Calvin in the polls. That's hardly news. And this endorsement is essential. That's hardly news either. We need you. I'm not ashamed to say it. But to tell you the truth, I hadn't contemplated much of a problem after all these years."

Farley smiled at her. Damn it, he liked her style. No pussyfooting around there. Still, business was business. "Well, little lady, we've got to face facts here. Your opponent is like the new Kennedy. And as far as labor is concerned, well, I don't have to tell you where he stands. Hell, Jess, he's much more forward thinking on minimum wage and social security benefits. He's a goddamn crusader. Ben Casale put up one hell of a good case for Calvin."

Jess shook her head in agreement. "Mr. Casale can certainly be convincing."

"Calvin has been very vocal in Congress," Frank piped in defensively.

Jess shook her head as though she were on Calvin's side. "No question about it. He's a good man. I wouldn't be foolish enough to sit here and argue that Calvin isn't good for labor. The question is: Is Calvin the best candidate for membership *and* management?" She let the question sink in and then added emphatically, "I think not."

"What d'ya mean?" asked Vito, suddenly looking up.

She smiled slyly. She had their attention now. They wanted to talk nuts and bolts? She was ready. "Look, those things you're talking about aren't real issues for union management. Minimum wage puts lower-price workers out of work and diminishes the number of union members working —and your dues income. Social security is for people who aren't active union members."

"But they're important issues to our membership," Farley pointed out guardedly. He wasn't about to be on the record as having said something wrong when it came to social security.

Jess spoke reasonably. "I don't disagree with that. I recognize those are symbolic issues for your membership, but let me outline a program for you men in this room—one I'm confident you can persuade your membership is good for them *and* is good for you as well. You're all aware of the Henderson-Debolt Act, which prevents elected union officials from serving as trustees of union pension funds and also prevents union pension monies from being invested in enterprises in which union officials have a financial interest."

"Of course," said Farley, loosening his paisley tie.

"I propose to you," Jess continued, "that my senator will introduce the Ford Labor Reform Act, legislation that would eliminate those restrictions and thus give you gentlemen a great deal more, shall we say, 'flexibility' over the enormous financial power of union pension fund investments."

She stopped there, waiting for them to digest what she had said. None of it was illegal, all of it was plausible, even constructive, Jess had convinced herself.

The interest was instantaneous. The men were whispering excitedly around the table. Greed and power. Those two elements were more seductive than ten naked Bo Dereks. Jess gave them a minute and then continued.

"I propose that for public consumption this legislation can quite effectively be sold as a reform that will give the working man and his union representatives greater control over their own monetary resources. I also suggest that the interests of the men in this room will be much better served by this concrete effort to enhance the power of union leadership—much more than the rhetorical genuflection of our opponent to minimum wage and social security benefits."

"That certainly is an interesting approach," Farley reflected.

Jess smiled lightly. She knew it was more than an interesting approach. It was a clincher.

"Ford *is* a long-standing member of the Labor Subcommittee," Vito noted.

"And come January, Senator Ford will have not only the seniority, but also the promise to be chairman of the Labor Subcommittee."

"But Calvin's been a champion of workers' rights," Pete McCleary objected.

Jess knew McCleary would be her toughest opponent. He had been a vocal Calvin supporter from the day Calvin had entered Congress. It was well known that McCleary had raised Calvin's labor consciousness.

"Look, Pete, are we talking union rights, or the ability of management to control its own destiny?" McCleary would always be a lost cause. Jess turned toward the rest of the group. She had to win them over and to do that she had to get them where they lived. "Let's not lose sight of the fact that any renegade can overthrow incumbent union management. That could create the chaos and instability in the leadership of the movement I'm confident you gentlemen want to avoid."

"How do we know Senator Ford will follow through on what you say?" Pete asked belligerently.

"I have Senator Ford's endorsement and pledge for anything I say to you today."

"Hey, c'mon, what's with you?" Vito asked McCleary, raising his right hand for emphasis. "We know who gets Ford's work done on The Hill by now."

This was hardly the time to correct that statement. She continued, "The union is ultimately stronger with stable union leadership. That is, gentlemen, *your* leadership. And Senator Ford will fight for your right to maintain that stability."

"But what about Calvin?" McCleary objected.

Jess shrugged her shoulders. "I can't sell Kennedy charisma or youth. What I can sell is commitment to the stability of your leadership and maintenance of control over your pension fund investments. In my book, that's worth a hell of a lot more."

She looked around the room. Okay, forget McCleary. The rest of them were hooked.

Ben couldn't understand how he could be so goddamned emotionally involved with one person. But he was. It was driven home to him one more time when he saw Jessie that afternoon.

Actually, he thought he'd played it pretty cool. He hoped she hadn't noticed his hard-on.

He knew she'd be disappointed when she was told the union was going to back Calvin, but that was politics.

He wondered if Jessie was really as gorgeous as she looked to him in that split second he had seen her. Still in love. There was no escaping it.

Ben and Jess both arrived at Farley's office promptly at five. They greeted each other with a cordial, yet distant, hello. Farley was his old jovial self as he ushered the twosome into his inner office and offered them drinks. They both declined, obviously intent on learning the final decision.

"We appreciated both of your presentations," Farley began as he gulped down some of his bourbon and water. "I only wish we could support both of your men. This is the toughest decision we've ever had to make."

Farley smiled, hoping a party mood would develop, but

Jess and Ben merely nodded. He knew it was time to alienate one of them.

Farley cleared his voice, trying to give himself courage. "After careful consideration, the committee has decided to back Senator Ford."

Jess nodded and smiled, unsurprised. Ben was stunned.

"How can that be?" Ben asked.

"Miss Kantor was very persuasive that Senator Ford would best serve our . . . that is, the union's interest. Please thank Congressman Calvin for us. I wish we could support them both. And you can be sure that if he does win the primary, we'll be behind him a hundred percent in the general election." He looked at his Concord watch and then chugged down the rest of his drink. "Gotta run. Thanks again. I'll be in touch tomorrow to talk over the specifics, Jess."

He ushered them out as smoothly as he had ushered them in.

They walked down the hall together. Jess knew enough to be quiet. Ben was smoldering. She couldn't blame him.

"What the hell did you promise them in there, condominiums for their unemployed?"

"Let's just say I tailored my presentation to my audience," Jess answered cryptically.

"Oh, I'll just bet you did," he said sarcastically. Okay, it was politics, but he was still pissed.

Jess looked at Ben. She knew she still felt something for this man. And she knew how he must be feeling about losing this endorsement. This was, after all, the whole ball game. "You know, for the first time I'm almost sorry that I won. I wasn't in there to beat *you*."

"Oh, weren't you?" he asked doubtfully.

"Well, maybe a little."

"Then don't accept the endorsement," Ben said logically.

"I'm not that sorry," Jess smiled.

They continued on toward the elevator, avoiding looking

at each other. Still, he could smell her and it activated every gland he had.

"How have you been?" Ben asked casually.

"Okay. Working long hours. I've had a difficult opponent." She looked at Ben as they reached the elevator. "You know, you're harder to get over than I thought." The statement surprised her even as she said it. After all, it was something she hadn't allowed herself to think about. Talk about subconscious.

"Is that my consolation prize?" he asked.

She looked at Ben and felt kinder than she had in months. She had beaten him at his own game. She could afford to be gracious. "Are you very upset with me about today?" she asked.

"I'm just adding it to my list," he replied. "Look, I'm a big boy. I can handle disappointment. I'm not crazy about it, but I can handle it." Not true. It's killing me, damn it.

"I'm trying to sort things out." Was she? She thought she already had. Why was she saying all this?

"Are you, Jessie?" Give me some hope. Something to hang on to.

This is ridiculous. Don't string him along. Be mature. "Look, I really think you should see other women."

Don't say that, goddamn it. That's the last thing I want to hear. "I didn't think I needed a note from home, thank you," he assured her. "So, can I drop you off somewhere? Your house . . . your office . . . the Potomac?"

35

Jess couldn't wait to tell Sam the news. With union's endorsement she felt confident the primary was a shoo-in. It was the first time she could recall breathing easy in the last few weeks.

As she entered her office, Peter was the first to greet her. "Hail to the conquering heroine." He looked pleased, as did Monica standing next to him.

"Thank you, thank you, thank you." Jess shook her head. "It was only ten minutes ago and you know already?"

"Washington is a very small town," he reminded her.

"Right." She motioned toward the senator's office. "Is he here?"

"He's waiting," Monica replied.

She knocked on the oversized mahogany door and entered without waiting for a reply.

"Hi," she greeted Senator Ford. She plopped down in one of his grand red leather chairs. "Want to know what I've been up to?"

The senator didn't turn around. He remained stationary, gazing out the window behind his desk. It looked out on the small courtyard between the offices. It was his favorite tranquil setting. Jess had found him staring out that window more and more in recent months.

"We did it!" Jess announced excitedly. "You've got Labor's endorsement. Calvin can't beat us now."

"I never thought you'd do it," he said listlessly.

"Shame on you for doubting me, Sam," she chided him.

He smiled wanly at her. "I forgot your track record." He turned back toward the window. "Look at those birds in the courtyard. I don't think I stop to look at things like that very often. Look at them, Jess. They're so free and . . ." His voice trailed off as he looked down at his scuffed brown wing-tipped shoes. It was so unlike him to have scuffs on his shoes. There was a time he'd been a perfectionist about his appearance. He looked sheepishly at Jess. "I can't do it."

"Do what?"

Senator Ford sighed heavily. "I don't want to be a senator anymore."

"What are you saying?"

How could he explain it to her? "My heart isn't in it. I wasn't going to run last time, but you were so enthusiastic, so eager . . . I couldn't disappoint you." He looked down at his shoes again. So scuffed. "I can't do it again—not another six years. I'll be dead."

Jess knew it was true, she had had to convince him to run before. She had given him pep talks to keep him going. But she had never heard the sense of hopelessness he had in his voice at this moment.

She had to convince him. "No, you're wrong. This job will keep you going. You'll see, it'll keep you alive."

He slumped into his chair, a man defeated. "It doesn't work for me anymore. I've been in Washington for twenty-four years. I'm plain tired."

"But you're a great senator," Jess argued.

He shook his head in disagreement. *"You're* a great senator. If I could give you the title, I would." He started to fidget as he spoke. "I spent the weekend with Marge. You know, it's funny, I remembered why I married her. We're going to give it another try."

Jess nodded, but couldn't respond. All she could feel was her carefully constructed world tumbling down around her.

"Jess, for God's sake, say something."

"What do you want me to say?"

"I want you to forgive me."

She looked at Sam's face. When had he gotten so old? She hadn't noticed it. But he did look old and, more than that, drained. All the vitality she remembered was gone.

He wasn't a strong man, but then he'd never advertised himself as one. It was his world crumbling, too. He had a right to try to put it back together. And as much as he had been capable of, he had been there for her until now.

She saw the tears well in his eyes and the maternal instinct she always had for him came out. She walked over to her senator and hugged him.

"I hope you'll be happy, Sam. God knows you've paid your dues."

He was grateful. "Thanks to you I can walk away with my head held high."

They stood in an embrace for a minute, trying to give each other the strength neither of them seemed to possess anymore.

"Let's set up a press conference so I can throw my support to Calvin. And call Farley so he can gracefully change his mind. Don't worry, Calvin's going to be a good senator."

"I know," she responded listlessly.

"I've talked with the president about appointing you to an independent regulatory agency. When you're ready, there's a job waiting." He looked at Jess and felt for the first time in their eight-year relationship that she needed soothing more than he did. "Jess, there are other things in life besides politics."

She had to laugh at the irony of it all. "Yes, it's beginning to dawn on me."

36

Jess loved media coverage. It gave her a thrill when major newspapers and television networks took notice of something she was involved in. But on this day, the coverage held little appeal for her. At this news conference her senator was throwing in the towel. She thought of W. C. Fields: All things considered, she'd rather be in Philadelphia, too.

Jess made herself available to the press for questions when the news of Senator Ford's decision got out. She told them the unvarnished truth: Senator Ford was simply too exhausted to face another campaign. Few believed her. Most assumed there was juicier news to follow. The IRS was called by reporters demanding to know about cover-ups. A few contacted the Justice Department to see if there were any impending indictments or, at the very least, investigations being conducted concerning Senator Ford. They found nothing. It frustrated them. It was hard to believe anyone would simply toss all that power to the wind. They were going to look until they found something. The truth wasn't interesting enough.

Senator Ford delivered his withdrawal remarks with a mixture of fire and sincerity. He was Senator Ford at his best and that was saying plenty. It was a good speech, all right. There was no reason for it not to be since Jess had written it —except for the part he put in about Jessica Kantor's invaluable guidance, expertise, and loyalty. Jess was grateful for that.

Jess looked at Congressman Calvin. If nothing else, he looked the part: chiseled features; tall in stature; great bearing; hands in pockets; a full head of hair that he kept pushing off his forehead. Vintage Kennedy.

"And so," said Senator Ford, "it is with great pleasure that I enthusiastically endorse Congressman Richard Calvin to be our party's candidate in November for United States Senator from our great state of Pennsylvania."

Thunderous applause. Handshaking. Joint victory signs.

Across the room Ben was watching Jess applaud. It wasn't hard to guess her feelings. He knew a forced smile when he saw one. All things considered, he couldn't blame her.

Within an hour there was only a skeleton of people remaining in the room. After finishing up with the reporter from *Newsweek,* Jess started to gather her papers together.

"Excuse me, Ms. Kantor. May I speak to you for a moment?"

She didn't have to turn around to know the voice. She had heard it fielding questions for the last half hour. She faced the handsome man and smiled. "Of course, Congressman. Congratulations."

He looked at her and grinned. It made her feel uneasy. She wondered how much of her personal life he knew. "Thank you." He cleared his throat and continued. "I imagine this must be a difficult time for you."

She nodded in agreement. He came across as a very sensitive person. She hadn't fully assessed him yet. "But I sincerely believe you'll make an excellent senator."

He looked relieved. She had given him a perfect lead-in. "Good, because I'd like you to help me do just that. You see, I'll sorely need some of that expertise and guidance Senator Ford praised you so highly for. I'd like you to consider joining my staff."

She looked surprised. "In what capacity?"

"A.A., of course."

"I believe you already have an overly competent A.A.," Jess pointed out.

Calvin nodded. "I couldn't agree with you more. Unfortunately that overly competent administrative assistant of mine plans to join a rather prestigious law firm come January. Personally I feel private practice is highly overrated, but Ben is a rather determined man. So you see, I really will need someone top-notch."

He looked earnest enough, but then he was a politician. "May I ask whose idea this was?"

"I'll let you in on a little secret," he answered with a twinkle in his eye as he adjusted his navy-and-red club tie, "not all my brilliant brainstorms are exclusively mine."

"I see."

"Excuse me, Congressman, I have just a few more questions." It was the aggressive reporter from *USA Today.*

"I'll be right with you," Calvin answered. He took Jess's hand and shook it warmly. "Let me know when you've reached a decision. We can iron out the particulars."

"Thank you for the offer. I'll get back to you."

And then the man she had no doubt would be Pennsylvania's next senator turned to the reporter and gave him the same undivided attention he had given her not a moment before. The reporter eagerly took notes as he walked out of the room with Calvin.

Jess started considering the ramifications of Calvin's offer as she put her material in her briefcase. Somehow it didn't sit right with her. Then she realized that Ben was standing behind her. She could feel his presence.

"Come here often?" he asked lightly.

Jess continued gathering up her papers. "I simply can't resist a good concession speech," she answered sarcastically.

"Ford didn't make a concession speech," Ben corrected.

"I've written his victory speeches. They don't sound like that."

"He decided not to run," Ben said, as though he were teaching a rather obtuse student.

The tone annoyed Jess. "I know. I was paying attention."

Ben shook his head. "You really can't deal with disappointment, can you, Jessie?"

"I'm getting better. I didn't slit my wrist." She didn't owe him any apologies. "What can I say? I don't wear defeat well."

Ben nodded, understanding. Jess looked around the large room wistfully, feeling like a child who had just lost her favorite doll.

Ben gazed at Jessie, dressed in her favorite all-business pin-striped gray suit. For a moment he wanted to ask if her tailor would make one for him. Did she really want to look that much like a man? Well, it wouldn't help. Just standing near her, smelling her presence, made him remember exactly how much of a woman she was. He was flooded with memories.

"Did Calvin mention his offer to you?"

"Was that *my* consolation prize?" she asked bitterly. Ben gave her a hopeless look and she immediately regretted the question. "Sorry," she said softly.

"Rough day, huh?" Ben asked gently.

Jessie shrugged her shoulders. She looked so helpless. The little girl he had fallen in love with. He wanted to hold her and then some. He tried to position the navy jacket he was holding over his arm in front of his pants so she wouldn't notice his immediate biological reaction to her. Maybe it was finally time for that negotiated truce he had been fantasizing about. Jessie looked more vulnerable than he had seen her look in a long time.

"Say, how about if you let me take you to dinner?" Ben asked in as offhanded a manner as he could muster. "You can even pick the place as long as it has linguini. Fair enough?"

"I'm sorry, I can't," she said tenuously.

"C'mon, you can do it."

"I have to go back to the office," Jess said, looking down at her black-and-white spectator shoes.

Don't push her. Giver her space. "I'll pick you up when you're finished. They don't call me Mr. Flexibility for nothing."

"I have to go home after that." She swallowed hard. Don't tell him about Eliot. Whatever you do, don't tell him about Eliot. He'll get so angry. You don't want a scene. "You see, Eliot is back."

Eliot? "You mean your ex-husband Eliot?" Jess shook her head yes. "What do you mean 'back'?" Ben asked, confused.

"He turned up one evening . . ." She was clearly hedging.

"So you took him in?" She wasn't making this very clear. The only thing he was sure of was that he didn't need to keep his jacket in front of his trousers anymore.

"You should have seen him," Jess continued defensively. "He looked like a homeless puppy."

"That's what the S.P.C.A. is for."

Jess knew she was heading for trouble. It had been hard enough justifying Eliot's presence to herself, but trying to rationalize it to Ben was a totally hopeless cause. She talked quickly now, trying to get it all in before Ben torpedoed her. "Susan seemed so anxious. She really wanted a man in the house and Eliot is her father and I felt guilty that I'd kept them apart. Even you said I hadn't tried hard enough."

"That was about when you separated, for Christ's sake. Not eleven years down the pike."

"But he seemed so desperate. If you could have seen him, Ben. He wants another stab at making us a family."

Ben looked at her face closely, trying to digest what she was telling him, gauging the way she was saying it. No use beating around the bush. "Do you love him, Jessie?"

Give her an intellectual issue, she could analyze it in two seconds flat; give her an emotional question, she was out to lunch. She didn't know what she felt anymore. Her whole life was topsy-turvy. Did she love Eliot? She considered the question carefully. She had loved him once. But, now? "No," she answered flatly.

Ben looked at the tension lines on Jessie's face. Clearly this was not easy for her. Still, he could feel his jet black hair turning gray. It didn't make sense. He had to straighten it out in his own head. "And still you let him move back into your house?"

"Yes."

His eyes narrowed icily. "Into your bed?"

"It's very aboveboard. I haven't let him do anything big yet."

The minute she said it, she knew it was a mistake.

"Anything big *yet?*" Ben repeated. He could feel the rage inside him. He wanted to strangle her. He took a few breaths and told himself to calm down. He gritted his teeth as he talked. "Do you see how controlled I am?" As he continued, he tried to convince himself that what he was saying was true. "Who would believe that an Italian—a Sicilian, yet— could keep so on top of his emotions under such stressful conditions?"

Jess looked at this man and all she could see was a volcano ready to erupt. "I admire you for it," she responded, hoping that positive reinforcement would halt the eruption.

But it didn't. Ben's face got red with anger. The top button on his Oxford shirt popped. Jess knew enough not to laugh. Instead her eyes were riveted on Ben's two clenched fists. How well did she really know this man, anyway? She decided that the best tack was not to fight anything he said.

Ben started to yell. "You are the biggest ass that ever walked this earth. What the hell do you have in that head of yours: Jell-O? For a seemingly intelligent woman. . . . Don't you realize that Susan is dying for a family because that's what *we* were?"

"You're just angry that Eliot's back."

"I don't give a crap that Eliot's back." He knew that wasn't true, but he wasn't about to correct himself. "What drives me crazy is your totally ludicrous reasoning. You know, I wouldn't be at all surprised if you've completely screwed up Susan's total perception of men."

That was ridiculous. "If I have, maybe I can rectify it now."

"With Eliot?" Surely she couldn't believe that. "What's the matter with you? Eliot's a zero. He's a negative role model. Positive role models—that I can give you. But you have to prove your thesis one more time, don't you? Men are no damned good. You alone can provide happiness for yourself and Susan."

"That's absurd," Jess protested, turning to leave the room.

But Ben cut her off and held her shoulders tightly, forcing her to listen as he talked. "Why don't you be honest with yourself for once? For almost eleven years your life has been directed toward your achieving. Proving all you had to prove to yourself. Depending on nobody. Making sure any relationship you had was a dead-end street. You've convinced yourself you have to give up who you are in order to make a positive commitment to a man. It must have blown your bloody mind to fall in love with me."

"Thereby proving love conquers all?" she asked sarcastically.

One tough cookie. "It helps," he replied, "but it sure as hell isn't enough. It takes commitment by *both* partners, honest communication, hard work, and acceptance that some disappointments are inevitable."

Her words were pure ice. "I believe you had a previous marriage that didn't work."

"I'm not proud of it, but at least I learned from it." Shit, why did he love her so much? In a way, he felt sorry for her. But he loved her more than he felt sorry for her. It was a goddamned curse. "Damn it, Jessie, you're no more grown up than you were eleven years ago. Your Hollywoodized version of happiness was always the one-dimensional married lady shtick. Now it's the one-dimensional liberated lady shtick. There has to be a balance in life. It's the one thing you won't allow yourself. Life is riddled with grays."

"Do you think I don't know that?" she asked incredulously, thinking of all she had been through in the last twenty-four hours.

He took her hands in his, trying to get through to her. "Jessie, in three years Susan will be in college. Then where will you be?"

She tore her hands out of his angrily. Susan going away to college was a subject she didn't allow herself to think about. "I'll be just fine, thank you. I don't need your lecturing. I've told you: You're out of my life."

He knew he'd hit a raw nerve. He touched her face. Her skin felt soft and sensuous. He wanted her. "Jessie, I love you. You love me."

"That's not the issue," Jess said sharply. She didn't want him to touch her. It felt too good. She jerked her face away and walked across the room to get her pocketbook.

"If it isn't the issue, it should be. You're just too terrified to deal with it."

"Not true," she replied curtly. Bastard. She turned angrily toward him. "You men think you know it all. If you can't cower a woman into thinking you have all the answers, you think your prick will force her into submission."

Ben was getting angry again. "Is that really what you think a relationship is all about?" he yelled.

"No," she answered sharply, "I think that's what *this* relationship is all about."

"That's insane."

"Oh, is it? You seem to think we have some great paragon of a relationship going here. Well, I think it's worth diddly. Because in my book the perfect man doesn't trade on personal confidences between him and the woman he loves just to further his own ends like you did."

"I never said I was perfect."

"Thank you, Mr. Humility," she said coldly.

She was right. He couldn't just avoid it and hope it would go away. "Do you want to discuss it? We need to talk it out."

"There's nothing to talk out. It's over between us. We're yesterday's news."

Ben looked sadly at Jessie. He loved her. There was no denying it. He could mentally undress her and have a hard-on in less than two seconds. He could also think of the outrageous things she did and lose it in three. That was a one-second advantage in her favor. But there were a hundred other things he loved about her and they far outweighed the few he couldn't stand. Still, at this moment, he felt confident she was going to make his greatest fear a reality: She was going to let her fears get in the way of their being together. Try as he might, there was no way he could make it happen.

With that realization, a total feeling of sadness engulfed his body.

Ben threw his jacket over his right shoulder and turned to Jessie, shaking his head, resigned. "Eventually, you're going to take that chance and commit yourself to someone. And when you do, lady, I hope for your sake I'm still interested."

Jess watched as Ben turned toward the door and left. She slowly looked around the large empty room and realized just how alone she really was.

37

A bar. What was a nice Jewish girl like her doing in a bar? Getting a drink, obviously. Maybe she'd get a lot of drinks. Maybe she'd fall down dead drunk. Screw ladylike. Her nerves were beginning to fray.

Ben was no help. He was only out for his own interest, like every other man she had ever met. Fuck him! Then she realized that that was probably something she'd never do again. Well, so be it. There were plenty more fish in that pond. Okay, maybe not as sexy, but there was more to life than sex. Plenty more. She wished she could remember what.

She motioned to the bartender.

Where was she ever going to find sex like that again? She had never enjoyed making love like she had with him. Damn Ben.

"What'll it be, Ma'am?" asked the bartender as he placed a paper coaster down on the bar in front of her.

"When did it go from 'miss' to 'ma'am'?" Jess asked, half to herself.

The bartender looked confused. "Beg your pardon?"

"Nothing. Just thinking out loud. I'll have a double Scotch, no rocks."

He nodded his head approvingly and went to get her drink. Bartenders were always impressed when Jess ordered a double Scotch, as though she had cleverly grown her own balls.

Jess watched the bartender pour her drink. So young. He looked as if he wasn't even old enough to drink, much less work. Then again, everyone looked young to her these days. Especially policemen. She thought that they must go straight from their bar mitzvahs to directing traffic.

She took a quick gulp and immediately sensed her pain floating away. She settled into that dreamy state she experienced every time she drank on an empty stomach. It felt good.

She looked around the bar. Jess knew that her mother would have taken exception to that word. "Ladies do not go to bars," her mother had often reminded her. "They go to cocktail lounges where they daintily sip a cocktail or two before dinner."

Sorry, Mom, this is definitely a bar. Your little girl is downing a full-scale drink in a bar. Make that two full-scale drinks. Guess things just didn't work out like you planned. Don't worry, there's a lot of that going around.

Maybe she ought to call home and tell Susan she was running late. There was no telling what little surprise Susan had planned for her and Eliot tonight. Poor Susan. Poor Eliot. Poor Jess. Such a sad family. Maybe she should try to be friendlier to Eliot. He was so helpless, so remorseful. Caught off guard by a midlife crisis. She really did feel sorry for him.

She motioned to the bartender to hit her again. Now he was really impressed. Somewhere along the way in Washington she had developed a hollow leg. No one could hold their liquor better than she. She could drink this much and feel nothing. It was all in your mind, she was sure of it. Right now she had nothing better to do than give in to the eighty-proof alcohol, so she simply let herself float.

She was bemused as she took in the clientele. Men in pin-striped suits, almost as nice as hers. Ladies in understated matching outfits. Except for Eliot and the girl he was with. But the others looked just perfect.

Eliot!

How much had she had to drink? She focused her eyes as precisely as she could. That was Eliot all right. Eliot and some blond, preppy-looking wide-eyed girl who appeared to be only slightly older than the bartender.

Jess picked up her glass and, mesmerized, walked over to where Eliot and the girl were sitting and slid into the booth behind them.

"God, you're divine," enthused Eliot as he kissed the girl's fingers one by one. "I'm alive when I'm with you. I've never felt like this before. Those itsy-bitsy fingers of yours are magic."

The girl giggled. "Oh, Professor Kantor . . . Eliot."

"It's as though I have a new lease on life, you little vixen."

She giggled again. "Oh, Eliot."

Eliot grabbed her sensuous body close to his. The circle pin she wore meant nothing to him. Her tits said it all. "You were wonderful last night. I've never known such sublime ecstasy . . . such total fulfillment. It's what life is all about, my sweet. We can find new meaning together. Ride the heavens and the stars."

"But what about your family?" the wide-eyed girl asked.

Not a bad question, thought Jess.

Eliot stroked the girl's silken blond hair tenderly. He loved touching it and he knew from his experience with her the night before that it was all natural. God bless those furry little honey pots. So much for "only your hairdresser knows for sure." He smiled reassuringly. "My daughter's only six. She won't be a problem. My wife, on the other hand, could be a little more troublesome. You see, she's deeply in love with me so she may fight a divorce at first. But don't you worry that pretty little head of yours. We'll work something out. It'll just take a little more time and patience and above all we'll have to be discreet."

Jess took the girl's next giggle as a cue for her appearance. Finishing the last sip of her drink, she stood up and faced Eliot, smiling sweetly. The rosy color in Eliot's face immediately drained, becoming a chalk white. Now this was the kind of surprise Jess liked.

"Eliot, my pet, consider this problem solved."

Jess had to give Eliot credit. He got his composure back faster than any caught-red-handed person she had ever known. By now he looked not only happy to see her but hopeful that she might make it a threesome.

"Jess," he said congenially, "hi there. Um, may I present Miss Sally Fenderholtz, a student in one of my seminars. She's a most talented young lady."

"So I've just been hearing," Jess replied icily as she turned to get a better look at Sally. Déjà vu. Sally was definitely a collegiate version of Nurse Pamela. Same besooms, that was for sure. "I hope you've gotten that 'A' he promised in writing."

Sally looked amazed. "Why no. I never thought to."

Jess gave a Cheshire cat smile and turned back to Eliot. "Well, Eliot, it looks like those old spots haven't changed after all."

How long did she expect him to wait for her, anyway? It was getting tiresome. All right, maybe he'd give it one last-ditch effort. Eliot gave her one of his dismissing gestures. "Oh, this? I can explain this. Jess, you know how much you mean to me."

"If I wasn't sure before, I certainly am now."

"You're jumping to conclusions again."

"You mean because you don't have your pants down this time?"

"Jess," he replied indignantly, "that remark was beneath you."

"So are you, Eliot." She shook her head and spoke in her most controlled voice. No way was this bastard going to get the best of her again. "I want you out of my house within twenty-four hours or else I will have you forcibly ejected. Clear?"

But there was Susan to consider. He really cared about

that kid. "This won't look good for you at election time," he reminded her, not above blackmail.

"Nice try, buddy, but I'm out of the election business and you're out of free room and board."

"Wait," he said, an air of desperation in his voice, "doesn't Susan have anything to say about this?"

She looked meaningfully at the blond preppy and asked, "What does a six-year-old know anyway?"

With that, Jess turned on her heels and started to walk out.

Well, what could he do? He tried. It just didn't work out. He'd explain it all to Susan later.

But was this how Jess wanted to play her final scene with Eliot? Had she said what she felt? Exactly what did she feel? The anger, the humiliation. There were still loose ends to tie up. Once again she was walking out without slamming the door.

She turned around and stormed back to her ex-husband's table. Had she really loved this man once? It was hard to believe.

"Eliot, I have two things left to say to you." She kissed him hard on the lips. "That's for freeing me. For years I thought our failed marriage might have been my fault. Well, maybe I get partial credit, but the bulk has to be attributed to your total lack of maturity. You are the *oldest* adolescent I've ever met." Get him where he lives. "And this," she concluded as she picked up the half-full carafe of red wine on his table and emptied it over his head, "is for being a total schmuck!"

It felt good enough. Loose ends tied up, she handed the empty carafe to the collegiate-looking Sally Fenderholtz, whose mouth was now wide open, turned, and made a bee-line for the door.

Eliot, dripping in the house wine, sat motionless, uncertain exactly what he could do while still making sure he retained access to Sally's huge, flawless tits.

"You were right," Sally said, more wide-eyed than ever. "Your wife really doesn't understand you."

Eliot nodded as he gave his best sinned-against sigh. Sally's tits were still his.

38

One thing about Butch, he was always there to greet her when she got home. It was more than simply greeting Jess, though. The dog acted as though her coming in the front door was the most exciting thing that had ever happened to him in his life. Jess patted him gratefully and wondered why people couldn't be as unconditionally loving as dogs.

She went into the kitchen and gave Butch the other half of a corned beef sandwich she had been saving. Hell, any living object who could make her feel even remotely happy today was entitled to some sort of reward. She didn't even make him sit up and beg. He didn't deserve to be humiliated like that.

Jess poured some milk into Butch's bowl, which he sniffed and then turned away from. Jess shook her head knowingly. So now even Butch had rejected her. Christ, she was beginning to think like her mother. Dangerous sign.

She scratched Butch behind his ears and told him it was fine with her if he didn't want the milk. She restrained herself from telling him about all the starving dogs in India and about the dogs who were banned in Peking, but she did think about it. Jess decided that she'd better stay on his good side since he was one of the few friends she had left.

She dragged herself up the stairs and walked into her bedroom. It looked completely uninviting. She stared at the bed as though it were her enemy and wondered if she'd ever use it again for anything other than reading and sleeping.

She felt sorry for herself and she didn't care that she was wallowing in a feeling she despised: self-pity.

She sat down at her dressing table and looked into the mirror. God, did she look like hell. She easily could have passed for a middle-aged matron. Oh, sure, the features were all still good, but the rings under her eyes made her look as if it was put-her-out-to-pasture time.

Her hair was pulled back too severely. Her eyes were cold, almost dead. Her skin looked as if it hadn't seen sunlight in years. No wonder she had been rejected by two men within the last couple of hours. She looked like mortician material.

What had happened to that fresh, vibrant Jessica of old? She must have run away without leaving a forwarding address.

She was fully savoring this rush of self-pity, and was annoyed to be distracted by giggles from the other room. Except that she knew it was Susan with a friend and, maternal to the end, she was happy that at least Susan was having a good time.

Jess walked toward Susan's room as she knotted the belt on her Joan Crawford pink terry cloth bathrobe.

Susan was with Betsy Manheim, a sweet, plump girl who had been Susan's best friend ever since they'd moved to Washington. Jess adored her.

Susan's room was still as pink and frilly as it had been when she was five years old. It was one of the few things Jess had retained from that era. The door was half closed. Jess lifted her fist to knock for permission to come in and then stopped herself, unsure of what she should say to Susan. She stood, unseen in the hallway, trying to sort things out, half listening to the girls' chatter.

Susan was draped over her bed as she watched Betsy take different items out of her closet.

"I think you should wear this," declared Betsy excitedly as she held up a red-and-white crepe dress for Susan's approval. "You'll look like Cyndi Lauper."

Susan turned up her nose. "Oh, Betsy," she objected theatrically, "I'll look ancient in that."

"You look totally sexy in it," Betsy maintained.

"C'mon," Susan said.

"I mean it. Totally sexy," Betsy repeated. "And I defy you not to want to look sexy—even you, the number-one boy hater of the entire Western Hemisphere."

"I don't hate boys."

"Hey, this is Betsy you're talking to. I know you. Everyone knows you hate boys. You go through them like I go through frozen Milky Ways."

Susan shrugged her shoulders as she started brushing her hair, the first of the one hundred strokes she had promised herself she would do each day. "I like them for what they are: useful tools."

After all these years, Betsy still couldn't understand her friend. If she looked like Susan and had half the opportunities Susan had to date boys . . . well, she sure wouldn't have wasted them. "I might marry Devon McNaughton," Betsy announced.

"Maybe you ought to try dating him first," Susan suggested. Twenty-two, twenty-three . . .

"Isn't he dynamite-looking, though?" He was perfect as far as Betsy was concerned. And he'd never even worn braces.

Forty-five, forty-six . . . "He's okay," responded Susan, noncommittally.

"What do you think of David Carson?" Betsy asked cagily, confident she had Susan this time.

"Well . . ." said Susan, considering, "he's not superobnoxious."

Betsy sighed, totally frustrated. "Susan, what makes your Richter Scale register, anyway?"

Betsy was sweet, but sometimes she was such a child. "I just think it's pointless to depend on a male to do anything more than disappoint you," Susan explained patiently.

"They're not all unreliable," Betsy objected, pouting.

So naive. "My experience has shown them to be."

"Pretty limited, isn't it?"

This discussion was going nowhere. Sixty-three, sixty-four
. . . "I observe the world. Look at our school. How many
kids have divorced parents?"

Betsy shrugged her shoulders. "A third?" she guessed.

"Try fifty percent."

"Then fifty percent have parents who aren't divorced,"
Betsy deduced happily.

The eternal optimist. It was an endearing quality that Susan wished she shared. But she didn't. "That's the difference
between us, Betsy. You look at marriage as a goblet of champagne," she said dramatically. "I see it as a Dixie cup with
evaporating water."

"That's sad."

"Just realistic." Susan put down her brush for a minute
and looked long and hard at her friend. "Tell the truth, are
your parents really happy with each other?"

Betsy giggled at the thought. "Who knows? They never
talk to each other."

Point won. "That's what I mean." Susan picked up her
brush again and resumed counting as she brushed. "I'm
never going to get married. Marriage is dumb."

"But your father's back. I thought you were happy about
that."

"It won't last," Susan maintained. Should she tell Betsy?
No. She didn't feel like going through the whole thing now.
"He'll pull out sooner or later. Men are like that. They take
what they want and when they're done, *poof:* gone! You
can't count on them."

"You didn't think that about Ben."

Right. Exactly. Don't join the debating team, Bets. "So
where did that get me? Do you see him around? No. You'll
learn soon enough. I'll never depend on a male. Look at my
mother. She's a strong, independent woman. I'm going to be
just like her."

Susan frightened Betsy when she got like this. She was so

worldly. And also like a chunk of ice. Betsy felt so inferior. She never understood what Susan saw in her. "Does this mean you won't go to Jayme Schweitzer's Sweet Sixteen party?"

"Don't be silly. I'll use a boy when I have to."

Betsy look admiringly at her very best friend in the world. "God, Susan, you know so much about life."

Ninety-nine, one hundred. Susan nodded. She guessed Betsy was right about that one. She wondered if that was the good news or the bad.

In the hall, still unseen, Jess stood, trying to assess this female Mr. Hyde she had created. She wished she had a mother to escape to who could hold her and comfort her and tell her everything would be okay. But she knew she had only herself. Today it didn't feel like much.

Jess was lying on the pretty flower-patterned chaise longue she had found on sale at Bloomingdale's. It was very unlike her tailored taste, but she hadn't been able to resist it. She told herself she had purchased it because it was so comfortable, but deep down she knew it was the feminine boudoir look that had won her over.

She was in a fetal position, which she knew any analyst could run forty yards with for a touchdown. She didn't care. She had some heavy thinking to do.

There was a perfunctory knock at her door as Susan entered. Jess pulled herself up straight and smiled at her daughter.

"Hi," she said with a false chipper tone. "Did Betsy leave?"

"Uh-huh."

"She's nice."

"Yeah," Susan agreed. "Young, but nice."

Jess looked painfully at Susan. So beautiful. A young lady, true, but to Jess this porcelain doll was still the little five-year-old she had reassured and hugged and cuddled so long ago. Jessica's heart ached for her child. She knew she had to talk to her, but it was not going to be easy.

"Susan, I have something to tell you," she said calmly and then took a deep breath as she started. "Your father and I have decided that this—'arrangement' won't work. It was wrong from the beginning."

Susan showed no signs of surprise. "Daddy says you're throwing him out," Susan said flatly.

"You spoke to him?" Jess asked, surprised. She could detect no evidence of emotion on her daughter's poker face.

"He called a little while ago."

Probably just after she left the restaurant. Dripping in wine. Eager to get the first word in so he wouldn't look like the heavy. Bastard. She should have known. Who cared? He was the heavy and no twenty-five-cent call was going to cancel that. "I am throwing him out. God knows what possessed me to let him back in in the first place."

Susan seemed more dispassionate than when she got a run in an old pair of nylons. Jess realized her eyes looked like a chip off the old iceberg. She didn't like what she saw.

"It doesn't matter," Susan asserted. "I knew it would happen. After all, he's a *man,* right?"

"No," Jess quickly corrected, "he's *that* man."

Susan threw her long hair back and shrugged her shoulders. "Six of one . . ."

"No, that's not true. Ben wasn't like that."

"He stopped coming around," Susan said pointedly.

"It was me, my decision."

"Because he screwed you in the campaign, right?"

"He did screw me, but I think it was also a convenient excuse I used to end it."

"But why?" Susan asked, showing a little anger for the first time.

Why? It was time to tell her that her hard-as-rocks mother wasn't completely all she seemed. "The truth is I was scared of being hurt so I beat him to the punch."

Susan looked long and hard at her mother. She understood the reasoning all too well. "Mom . . . I'm like that, too. I mean, every time I start to like a boy, I . . . I don't know, I guess I just pull back."

"Do you?"

"Mom," her lips were beginning to quiver, "I don't want to be like that."

Jess got up and came over to Susan and hugged her as tightly as she could ever remember doing. She smoothed Susan's hair and kissed her forehead. "I know, sweetie. I know."

They held each other for a long time as the tears ran down their faces.

39

Action was her trump suit. It had been ever since her divorce. She made a decision and immediately implemented it.

So why had Jess been driving around Ben's townhouse for the last thirty minutes? She was half hoping she would be picked up by a cop on suspicion of loitering.

This is craziness, she told herself. You're a big girl. Either make up your mind or get the hell out of here.

Jess pulled into a space half a block away from Ben's house. She looked in the car mirror. She had reapplied the mascara and any other makeup she could remember, but she still thought she looked lousy. She was wearing a gray angora dress with pearls. She remembered Ben saying she looked terrific in it, sexy and ladylike—just before he removed it.

Christ, she hadn't remembered to put on perfume. Damn it. Why couldn't she consciously remember to do what other women did automatically? Oh, well, if this relationship hung on Chanel at the proper pulse points, it wasn't worth saving anyway.

Jess sighed once more for good measure and then opened the car door, determined. She didn't know who she was fooling with this sudden burst of confidence, but it certainly wasn't herself.

* * *

Ben had spent the major part of the night since he had talked to Jess cursing. He cursed the drivers in front of him; he cursed the traffic lights that took too long to change; he cursed his front door, which took too long to open; he cursed his record collection for not being in alphabetical order; he cursed his coffee, which tasted like shit.

When he finally finished kicking different pieces of furniture, he slumped down into his favorite chair and reassessed the real problem. Jessie. In a nutshell. Well, he had dealt with disappointment before. He could deal with it again. Things weren't going to work out. He had to face it.

Bitch. Then he laughed because he felt like punching himself for insulting the woman he loved.

The woman he loved. Damn it. It had been so long since he had felt love. He didn't want to end up like some tragic, pulp-novel hero. And he wasn't going to.

He put on the most Ivy League outfit he had and sat down to write a speech Dick Calvin was going to need the next night. Maybe he ought to remain with Calvin. He could use being needed by someone. He got out his yellow legal-size pad and started to write an earnest I'm-going-to-save-the-world speech. When he reread what he had scribbled half an hour later, he realized he had written "bitch" or "Jessie" seventeen times. If he deleted those words, it was a pretty decent speech.

The sound of the doorbell jarred Ben's concentration. He was in the middle of rewriting the closing paragraph. It was giving him trouble.

He walked to the door still deep in thought and automatically opened it. He looked at Jess, shivering in a thin jacket. She was wearing the dress he loved. He hoped it was a good sign. Play it cool, Casale. Don't let on how excited you are to see her.

"Washington has a very high crime rate. You're not supposed to open your door without asking who it is. You told me so yourself, remember?"

He remembered. "That's only for people who were brought up in sheltered suburbs. It doesn't apply to those of us who grew up in the streets."

She nodded. There was an uncomfortable silence. It was clear she was going to have to start. "May I come in?" she asked.

Don't lose your equilibrium. "Let me see if the coast is clear." He turned and called out to no one in particular, "Bambi, Mitzi, Cookie—any of you still here?"

Jess smiled. "Sounds like you're dating the seven dwarfs."

"I see you've met the family. Well, they appear to have left. Come in. Let me take your jacket."

She handed it to him. Ben took it and shook his head. A thin cotton jacket. It was cold out. The woman simply didn't take proper care of herself. He became a Jewish mother every time he was with her. He wanted to rub his hands over hers and warm them up, but he restrained himself.

Jess walked toward the fireplace, which had a fire roaring in it. She loved the crackling sounds. "Oh, good, I was counting on one of your renowned fires."

He walked over to where she was standing. "It's an incalculable asset to my masculine mystique." Ben studied Jess's face, trying to make out what was going on in her head. "You're looking well. Don't seem to have aged much."

"In four hours?" she asked and then thought, He should only know.

"How about some wine? I have some breathing in the other room."

She nodded her head. "That would be great."

Ben figured they both could use some. He poured them each a hearty glass of cabernet. She looked more uncomfortable than he felt. And so vulnerable. What it must have taken for her to come here. He gave her the glass of wine, which she gratefully accepted.

"What shall we toast to?" he asked, raising his glass.

"Why don't we just clink glasses now and fill in a toast later?"

Ben shook his head in agreement as they clinked glasses and took a sip of the wine. It went down their throats warmly.

Play it nice and slow, Casale. Don't rush her. Talk about the weather, the Redskins, anything but why she came here. "So, what brings you here?"

Where to begin? "You were right about one thing. I deserted my marriage entirely too quickly."

Forget it. I don't want to hear this. "Are you here to tell me the hundred and one reasons why you're going back to Eliot?" he asked, an edge to his voice.

"Just hear me out, okay?"

If only he could gauge where she was going. "Okay," he reluctantly agreed.

"I spent eleven years filled with anger and repression because I didn't want to deal with what happened. I only wanted to ascribe guilt and stop hurting. I was pretty successful at both. Well, I don't know if we can work this out, if this relationship is even worth working on, but I do know that I'll be damned if I'm going to walk away from us without at least learning something." She cleared her throat. "Which is my way of saying I'm taking you up on your offer: Let's talk this out."

Sounded reasonable so far. "Okay. Where do you want to start?"

Maybe if she could rush through it, it would be easier. "I've been doing a lot of thinking . . . trying to figure out my behavior. You've got to admit, I did act somewhat self-destructive at times," she declared as though she were trying to convince him of something he'd never believe.

"Who said no? All right, given that premise, what did you conclude?"

That was the hard part. "Basically, that I can't figure it out."

He smiled at her assessment. "It certainly was worth the time invested."

She knew she made no sense. It annoyed her. She went to the fire and poked it with one of the irons. She watched the smoke escaping. Everything was starting to look symbolic to her. The fire was her life going up in smoke. "When I left you this afternoon, I went to a bar. You'll never guess who was there."

"Please, God, let it be Eliot with another woman," he replied without hesitation.

Jess was floored. "How did you know that?"

"Who do you think hired her? All right, Eliot," he cheered, "I knew I could count on you."

They both laughed. It was the first good laugh either of them had had in a long time and it felt wonderful.

"He really screwed me up all these years."

"You were a pretty willing accomplice," Ben reminded her.

Jess knew he was right. "I was so damn angry eleven years ago. So shattered. I had so much to prove. I guess I did view Eliot as the paradigm for all men I met. It was a survival technique I taught myself: Assume a man will disappoint you and you won't be disappointed—the Gardol Protective Shield against emotions. It never failed me."

"Until you met me," Ben interjected helpfully.

"Not quite, Sherlock. You were right up there on the 'men who have failed me' chart."

"Because you expected me to be."

"Partially, but you sure fulfilled that expectation."

"Okay, I screwed up. I'm sorry," he said, hoping that would be enough.

But it wasn't for Jess. "Uh-uh. Clean slates aren't given out that easily."

"What do you want me to do?"

"I want you to explain it to me," Jess answered softly.

Part of him really didn't understand. "Jessie, you always said everything was fair in politics."

She shook her head. "And I believe it. But between two people in love, everything isn't. You used our relationship—consciously or unconsciously—and it's a hard thing for me to justify."

Still a tough cookie. "Are you telling me you wouldn't have used that information if you were me?"

"I had no problem with that. What bothered me is your source: me."

"But you were only my initial source. I wouldn't have given it to the press if I hadn't been approached with a lot of corroboration. I want you to believe that."

Jess looked closely at Ben's face. "I do," she assured him. She knew he was telling the truth.

"Besides, you never specifically told me not to use anything you said," he asserted logically.

You should have stopped when you were ahead, Casale. "There are some things that should be understood between couples involved in carnal activity. After all, I hardly knew Calvin was about to be a contender for Ford's job."

"Did you expect me to tell you?"

"No."

"Then what did you expect?" he asked, frustrated.

"I expected some concern for the position you were putting me in."

"Even though I never used what you said until it was given to me by other sources?" he asked.

"Even then. I respect you for not leaking that information straight from the bedroom, but the point is you're no apprentice in this field. You knew what was happening," she accused him matter-of-factly.

"What?" he asked.

"You were privy to more information than I was. And as much as I wanted to win that primary—and I wanted it badly—I don't think I would have done what you did."

"How could I have avoided it without exposing my hand?"

"That was your job to figure out. At the very least you

should have side-stepped discussing issues that you knew could ultimately help you and screw me. That way you could have run a cleaner campaign." She paused to analyze her thoughts. "I don't know. Maybe I'm still too much of a woman. I can't compartmentalize the way men do: work here, love there. My emotions overlap. I guess I tried to sever them so I could make it in a man's world on a man's terms. I can do that, but I can't do it when it forces me to choose between the person I love and the work I believe in. The principles are too contradictory for me."

Ben tried to digest what Jessie had said. It was true. He hadn't tried to stop her disclosures. He should have seen the tightrope he was walking. "You're right," he admitted. "I could have stopped you. It never occurred to me. I guess I have some rough edges to work out, too."

"You?" she asked with exaggerated surprise.

"Hard to believe from an ex-perfect ten, huh?"

"You won't have a tough time convincing me." She smiled.

He looked at her. One hot number. And then he remembered. "Before we continue this discussion, just tell me one thing: Is Eliot out of your house?"

"Uh-huh." Ben looked relieved. "Actually, I think I had some left-over feelings for him. The time I spent with him wasn't a complete throwaway."

Ben could feel his blood pressure rising. "Look, just because I'm Catholic doesn't mean I want to hear true confessions."

"Nothing happened," Jess assured him. And then she remembered how great it felt to make Ben jealous. "Nothing much, anyway," she added coyly.

His blood pressure surged again, his eyes narrowed. He knew it was part of the game, but he still hated it. "Don't start with me," he warned her.

"Are you telling me you were into celibacy all these months?"

He looked down. "In my way," he answered.

"What's your way?" she asked.

"I did it, I just didn't enjoy it."

"I see. Then you wouldn't mind if I did that?"

"I think I might get overly hostile. For instance, I might shoot you," he stated good-naturedly.

"How is that fair?"

"It isn't. It's called a double standard. Give me a break, will you? I'm working them out one at a time." He gave her his Dustin Hoffman smile.

He really was adorable. She couldn't deny it.

"Without going into detail, what about you and Eliot? Have you worked it out in your head?" Ben asked tenuously.

She was sure of this one, anyway. "Funny thing about Eliot. He turned out to fit perfectly into the equation 'the more often you see him, the less desirable he gets.' "

"Must be the new math," Ben quipped.

"You were right about me being afraid to commit to any other relationship," she continued as she played with her pearls. "God, how I hate to be proven wrong," she added as they both smiled. "I've got to tell you, it still terrifies me. But I'm willing to take that chance now."

"Tell me why," he asked gently.

"You want to know the whys?" Jess asked, wondering if she could articulate them. Ben shook his head yes. Jess started thinking about it as the words came pouring out. "I'm afraid I've cloned Susan into a male hater just like you said. I want to show her that a good relationship is possible. I'm also afraid of what I've done to myself. I'm ready to put my love on the line again because . . . because . . ."

"Yes," he said, trying to pull the words out of her, "because . . ."

"You're fishing," she accused him playfully.

"After the hell you've put me through? You're damn right. I want to hear it all."

"Because I love you, damn it. I can't escape it. I really love you and," she added quietly, "I can't bear to lose you."

He took her hands and kissed them and then put them next to his face. "It must have been hard to admit that."

"No," she replied, realizing, "it felt good—almost cleansing."

"How I love these religious experiences."

He drew her close to him and they kissed, gently at first, then much more passionately. As good as they remembered it, neither of them remembered it as good as this.

Jess was so grateful for Ben. "I haven't given you an easy time of it, have I?"

He kissed her face as he responded, "Believe me, if I didn't think we were worth it. . . ."

"I've missed you so much these past few months," she told him as she held him tight.

"Good thing. After all, I've got one hell of an investment in you."

"Emotional?" she asked.

He looked at her like she was crazy. "Forget emotional: economic. Have you any idea how much hard cash I've spent on you?"

She laughed again and then suddenly looked serious. "I want to spend my forever with you."

"I'm going to disappoint you sometimes, Jessie."

"I'll roll with it," she assured him.

"Good girl."

She looked apprehensive. "Are you going to disappoint me a lot?"

He didn't want her walking into another fairy tale. "There may be times we won't like each other too much, but I promise I'll never stop loving you." It was a promise he felt confident making.

"But are you going to disappoint me a lot?" Jess wanted to know.

Ben smiled as he looked at her forehead wrinkling with worry lines. "I guess you'll have to hang in there for the final chapter."

"I want you to tie everything up with a bow."

"That's not how life works," he told her simply.

Okay. Maybe not. "Which reminds me, is my ring gone forever?"

The ring, huh? Not exactly a popular subject with him. "The next one is on you, sweetheart."

Damn. She liked that ring. It was small, as her mother would have said, but sincere. "That was a dumb thing, flushing it down the toilet."

"Dramatic," Ben corrected her.

"Dramatic, but dumb," Jess added.

"That big box stopped up the toilet and flooded the whole office."

That had been some day. A major announcement by Calvin and he had to worry about the water seeping from the bathroom into the congressman's office. Try and explain that to everyone. Ben had spent two hours with a plumber trying to retrieve that damn thing. Everyone in the office knew better than to make any wisecracks about it. Even Calvin steered clear of the subject as though water coming into his office were the most natural thing in the world.

Tenacity had paid off. Ben walked over to his rolltop desk and opened the top drawer, pulling out a badly worn black velvet box.

"You lucked out," he told her with an edge on his voice. He brought the box over to her but looked unsure if he wanted to give it to her. Jess smiled broadly as he appeared to be giving in. "Oh, all right, will you marry me? But I'm warning you, this is absolutely the last time I'm going to ask."

"Really?"

"Well, unless you turn me down again," he conceded. "I told you that after all this political crap was over I was coming to get you. Take my word for it, honey, I make a lousy loser."

Jess took the box and opened it. "I'll have to have it appraised first," Jess said lightly. Then she took out the ring and put it on. A perfect fit. "It is beautiful," she claimed approvingly. "You really are wonderful."

"Haven't I been telling you that all along?"

"Let's call Susan and tell her," she urged Ben excitedly.

"Uh-uh," Ben replied. "I want to tell my daughter in person. Let's just get married as soon as possible."

"Don't you trust me?" she asked, coyly. The ball was back in her court.

And Ben knew it. "Almost. Let's tie the knot next week."

Next week was awfully soon. "I don't know. I'm still working. I have appointments."

"Reschedule them, Jessie."

"I can't."

"Damn it. Reschedule them, Jessie," he repeated, this time firmly.

Jess realized how important it was to Ben. "Okay."

He felt relieved. "I didn't know it was that easy."

"It won't always be," she assured him.

"I'll take them as they come." He meant it. His confidence was back.

Now it was her turn. "I mean it, too, Ben. I'm not that sweet, adoring wife type I was eleven years ago. I'm independent and assertive now. I'm my own person."

"It's one of the things that attracted me."

"Attracted, yes, but can you live with it?"

"You want to advise me of your liabilities?"

"I want you to know what you're getting into."

"Thank you, that's very decent of you. Look, I don't expect everything to go my way. I'd prefer it, but I don't expect it. Neither should you." He was trying to be reasonable. "We'll disagree, we'll talk it out, we'll compromise."

"Do you think we'll be fighting all the time?"

He shook his head no. "I can think of other constructive activities we can engage in." He smiled broadly, but he could see she was still troubled. "Jessie, sweetheart, all we have to promise is to try to work out our disagreements, not run from them. I can make that promise. Can you?"

"I guess," she answered, unsure.

"What's the alternative?" She still looked unsure. "Ah, you're right, it's not worth risking your ego. What the hell, we had some good times. Let's call it a day." He reached out his hand to shake hers and smiled slyly. "It was real nice knowing you."

Jess looked at his outstretched hand and then his shit-eating grin. She knew she wasn't going anywhere. So did he. "Screw you," she said.

"Finally you're on my wavelength."

They laughed as they embraced and kissed. They couldn't get enough of each other.

"Ben, as long as we're putting all our history on the table, I have one more question to ask."

"Okay," he mumbled, not concentrating on anything but her lips and her gorgeous ass, which he was joyously fondling.

"What was the real reason you got divorced?"

He stopped dead in his tracks and looked at her. "What do you mean 'the real reason'? I told you, we were worlds apart."

"There's something else. Something you've left out. I know you by now. What is it?"

He looked at her long and hard. He hadn't admitted it to anyone. He sure didn't want to admit it to Jessie.

"If you really can't tell me . . ." she said, making it impossible for him not to answer.

Ben took a deep breath and blurted it out. "I couldn't satisfy her sexually," he said, gritting his teeth.

Jess burst into laughter. "That's impossible. You shouldn't have given her a divorce, you should have had her committed."

He laughed as he pulled her to him and kissed her long and hard, feeling the warmth and firmness of her body.

"Ben, are you really going to join a law firm?"

"Uh-huh. It's *my* stab at growing up, honey."

It was not an idle question. "What would you think of starting our own law firm?" she asked him.

"I never thought about it," Ben answered, considering. "It might work . . . 'Casale and Casale.' "

"You mean 'Kantor and Casale,' " Jess corrected. "You can't expect me to give up my professional name."

He eyed her closely. "Then it should be 'Casale and Kantor.' "

Jess edged her way close up against Ben's body and purred, "I think 'Kantor and Casale' sounds better." Her tongue circled his ear and then she blew in it as she slipped her hand inside his pants. "It's a wonderful symbolic gesture."

She was one pain in the ass and he was dead in the water. Fully erect, ready for action. He didn't stand a chance and they both knew it. "Why don't we discuss it later?" His eyes looked up toward his bedroom. "I'd like to perform a symbolic gesture of my own."

"Before we're properly married?" she asked with mock surprise. But his hands were caressing her breasts and her whole body was reacting, begging for more.

"There's nothing worse than being rusty on your wedding night."

And then Ben swept her into his arms Rhett Butler–style as he began to mount the steps.

"Who should we contact—possible clients, I mean?"

What a dirty trick. He was going to be the more romantic of the two. "Shh," he told her. "This is the pleasure part, not the business. In a movie it's the romantic fade-out scene. We're supposed to be whispering sweet nothings to each other."

" 'Kantor and Casale.' *Fantissimo!*" Jess started kissing Ben wildly all over his face. "I love you. I love you. I love you."

Ben held her as tight as he could and continued up toward his bedroom, loving every delicious minute of the anticipation. "Much better. I think you're finally getting the hang of it."

And at that moment Jessica Simon Kantor knew exactly what a nice Jewish girl was doing in a place like that.